FIERY PASSION

She was furious at him — that ugly, gigantic, arrogant, overbearing hunk of man-meat, that bull. He belonged with a herd!

Suddenly she saw his eyes change and she grew wary, tense, ready for anything. He saw her go tight and hotness jumped into his loins. He grabbed her by the shoulders and she yanked free. With all the strength and fury in her, she slapped his face.

That did it! He caught her punishing hand, and carried her kicking and screaming into the bedroom. Before she could do more than twist, he had her face down across his knees; and, with a rage he could not contain, was spanking her bare white bottom and watching as it turned red and hot — as fiery as the fury and desire burning inside him . . .

First Fire

FRANCESCA GREER

SPHERE BOOKS LIMITED
32-32 Gray's Inn Road, London WC1X 8JL

First published in Great Britain by
Sphere Books Ltd 1980

TRADE
MARK

Printed in Canada

For Gloria, Judy and Jeane

Contents

Part I

THE ULTIMATUM

1

Rae-Ellen had never been so angry in her life.
She ran abruptly out of Pana's library, leaving him
rigid and white-faced, and fled across the specially
woven Persian rug, which gleamed like a ruby
on the pale marble floor. At the wide doorway she
paused to fling open the heavy oak door, then
slammed it angrily behind her.

Across the tall, pillared gallery she sped, past
the first of the huge columns of magnolia trees which,
only a few months ago, had been laden with the
great, cream-white blossoms she loved. Her soft, pas-
tel kid shoes were quick and sharp on the driveway,
beating against it as if she were ten, not twenty.
She got behind the wheel of the sleek white Lincoln
as though she'd had it for years, not just a week.

He'd given it to her for her birthday, the fif-

11

teenth of August—him, back there. Papa. It had been Mama's gift, too, of course. They did everything together, decided everything, like twins. Rae-Ellen was deceived by no part of it now. It was Papa, mostly. With his millions and his generosity. Oh, yes, his stifling generosity. For which he expected to be repaid.

Blind to the beauty of Magnolia Hall with the curving, tree-lined driveway, Rae-Ellen trod gas, making for the street and the open road. The soft gray trunks of the seventy-foot-tall magnolias were a blur; their big, green-topped, rusty-bottomed leaves were a smudge as the car leapt ahead. To her left shimmered the swimming pool where she'd spent so many carefree hours, but she hardly saw it now. Nor did she notice the outbuildings or stables beyond the pool.

It was simply more of Papa's bait. All the luxuries, the fabulous gifts, the indulgences, were bait. He was a fisherman with a clever hook, hidden and padded and made enticing with all the things she loved. And now she'd found the bare hook; he'd actually used it, tried to snag and pull her, protesting, into his strong, manicured hands to use her for the only purpose he'd ever had in life.

Driving past harvested tobacco fields and along the outskirts of Durham, Rae-Ellen inhaled the pervasive smell of tobacco. North Carolina is nothing but tobacco, she thought furiously, tobacco, tobacco, the word on every tongue, the odor assailing every nostril.

She hit a straightaway. There was traffic, but it was thin and she could drive as she pleased, which was fast and sure. With the first burn of rage now smoldering, she could think now, could remember.

Papa smiled kindly and asked her, at breakfast, to come to the library before she went out. Even at fifty-two, his intensely blue eyes held the devil in them, reminding her that he'd been quite a rake in his youth, so Mama said, and that a good portion of the roguishness remained yet in his nature.

His eyes danced over her just once, the way Rae-Ellen sometimes took a lone dance step when she was happy over something, and then they became intense. "I have something to discuss, darling," he said seriously. "If you'll indulge me."

"You know you've got me in a good mood!" she laughed. "Anyone who gives me a gorgeous car may have one short moment!"

"And speak as he pleases?"

"That, too, and maybe I'll listen and maybe I won't!"

"Fair enough." He rose from the table. "Shall we?"

She pranced out of the room, leaving Mama with Adah, who was nineteen and as quiet as she herself was volatile. She knew what they'd talk about —clothes. They planned a shopping tour this morning.

Papa quietly closed the library door. As Rae-Ellen was about to throw herself onto one of the leather sofas, he gestured. "Wait. Let me look at you. My beautiful, grown-up daughter."

She laughed and stood before him. As he looked her over, she examined him as she'd never done, and found him incredibly handsome and youthful. Against the background of mahogany and richly bound books, her father was elegance itself.

Wearing white slacks and jacket, he was an inch under six feet and perfectly built. There was a look

13

of smooth suppleness to him. His hair, which had once been blond, was snowy now and crested from his clear-cut brow in one big wave, but the brows above the blue eyes were still blond, and his lips were firm and red. She'd never seen a more handsome man, and she was proud of him, indeed.

"I'm a lucky man to have such a daughter."

"Oh, Papa! I'm too tall, you know it, five feet six! And I need to watch my diet or I'd get so fat you'd disown me!"

They laughed together.

She knew how she looked, and wasn't displeased. Her hair was brown with natural streaks of sunny auburn, and it hung past her shoulders in a gleaming cape. Her eyes were blue like Papa's. Though she was tall, her figure was slim and shapely enough to get its share of whistles.

Her features were chiseled, like Mama's. She didn't have to touch her eyebrows; they arched the way she wanted them to. Her lips were red like Papa's—too red. Their natural color limited the shades of lipstick she could use, so she usually let them flame as they were.

She was fond of the dress she was wearing, too. It was almost as blue as her eyes. It was made of the latest, softest, most clinging fabric, fashioned on loose, flowing lines, the waist tucked, the hem mid-calf, a swirling blue mist when she moved.

Now Papa's smile dropped away. Rae-Ellen's smile faded and wariness enveloped her. What was he up to? Indulge her he did, but he had his ruthless side, and it looked as if she was about to see it.

"You're woman-grown, now, Rae-Ellen and you don't have a career. You don't run with the jet set, either."

14

"That's a waste of time! And I do have an interest!"

"Horses!"

"What's wrong with horses?"

"Nothing. You've kept horses for years; we've all belonged to The Fox Hunt Club. I've maintained the stable, provided good mounts. I've even had the stable enlarged, and in a few days the first of your racing horses will be delivered."

"Is this all you wanted to talk about? The horses?"

"You can't deny that I give you every advantage, cater to any whim," he pressed on.

"You wouldn't take me to Louisville to pick out the race horses!" What was he leading up to, she wondered.

"I preferred to do it my own way. You'll not be disappointed. I'm certain I've made the proper choices for you."

"And for Adah!"

"Your sister is included, naturally. Also, she's appreciative."

"My adopted sister!"

He shrugged.

"She might not be so appreciative if you expected of her whatever it is you're going to demand of me!" Rae-Ellen cried. She could feel sparks of rage lighting her face as sudden knowledge flooded her.

"I've never demanded anything of you, Rae-Ellen. I've hoped. Expected. I'm surprised you think—"

"*Think!*" she cut in. Let him believe that she'd known, that she'd read his mind. Never let him know how much it hurt, this discovery!

"*Know* is the word!" she plunged on. "I've always known that you're the great man in the Piedmont, in the foothills! Raymond Pettigrew, son of the founder of the Pettigrew Tobacco Company, who built it bigger, who is now a multibillionaire!"

"Not quite that much, my dear. Though there is money."

"And I'm the eldest, but I'm not a son to take over and build your dynasty to even greater heights!"

"No. I have no son."

"So you want me to produce a grandson! As if I were an eldest son, passing our heritage down through generations!"

"You are the eldest daughter, Rae-Ellen."

"I'm not a filly to be bred!"

"You speak as though I'd want you to marry just any man!" Papa exclaimed, the anger sparking from him, matching hers.

"No, not that, never that! You'd be most particular about the man! I'd not be traded for a fortune to match yours, but traded for Pettigrew's! To a man who'd take over until his son reached his majority! The man, further, would come from a fine southern bloodline!"

"If you must argue, Rae-Ellen, do it sensibly. There's a great deal at stake. You will marry one day, and I see no reason why that marriage shouldn't benfit Pettigrew's."

"Also," she fumed, not hearing him, just caught in her own rage, "the lucky man has to be as obsessed by tobacco as you are! And he's got to be well enough off that he has no need to marry for Pettigrew money!"

Papa's jaw was set firmly, eyes shooting blue fire. "I'd advise you to think clearly in this matter."

"Very well," she said coldly. "Who would please you? Fawn Morehead? He works like a demon running your factories; he worked his way to the top. Of course, he has no private fortune, but he's saved money and comes form a fine Beaufort family. And *he's* really got a passion for tobacco!" She glared at him contemptuously.

"What's wrong with that? Have you turned him down, you little fool?"

"He's been too proper to ask! So has Pete Battle. Would you accept Pete, Papa? He's worked his way up like Fawn, got himself put in charge of growing your special tobacco, curing it and aging it! He's also without a fortune, but with fine New Bern blood! And a *thing* for tobacco and for work!"

"Hush," Papa whispered, "control that temper. Count you advantages. I don't know what more to do for you, what would please you, what would lead you to see my side of this problem."

"Fairness! You expect repayment from me, none from Adah. Bribes! Bribe after bribe! And you don't even have the nerve to come out and name the man you want me to couple with!"

"You make it sound cold-blooded."

"It *is* cold-blooded! It's like the eighteenth century!"

"I'm concerned with your happiness, Rae-Ellen. Be reasonable. Look around. Take your pick. You can, you know. Just a—suitable man. Which I'd ask in any event."

"Only what you really want is a grandson! The truth now!"

That angry sparkle took him again. "By damn —yes!"

"What real man do you think will change his

name to Pettigrew? That *is* what you want! Why can't I run the company? Women do run great business complexes now."

"I prefer a male Pettigrew. I'm counting on being active another twenty or more years. That gives time. You mentioned Fawn Morehead. I have no idea he'd change his name. Nor Pete Battle. But, should you marry one of them, my grandson might hyphenate the names. The company would still be known as Pettigrew's. Would, in actuality, be Pettigrew. By blood."

"I won't do it!" Rae-Ellen cried wildly. "I'll not be a brood mare! I'll marry the worst bum I can find! I'll—"

"One year!" hissed Papa, patience gone. "One year for you to choose!"

"And when I don't?"

"Then I—I've given this thought, understand— I'll adopt Fawn or Pete. I'll leave your sister a modest trust fund. The fortune goes with the man."

"You'd punish Adah for my refusal?"

"No. I spoke in haste. Adah will get her millions."

"Then let her produce your grandson!"

He turned pale suddenly. She wondered, disturbed even in rage, if he might have a heart attack. But then a hint of color returned to his lips, and she saw that he was all right.

He was, however, speechless for a moment, too angry to speak. He knew, as well as she—better— that what she'd said about Adah producing a grandson was out of the question.

She turned to go.

"Wait!" he commanded, and she waited.

He was her father; she'd possibly brought him

to the verge of a heart attack. Though at this moment she hated him, deep under the hate were twenty years of love, and there was the hurt that he wanted to use her. Her heart seemed to rip its moorings.

If she were a different girl, if she were like Adah, she'd try to do what he wanted. But she wasn't Adah. She was her own person. She was Rae-Ellen Pettigrew, eldest daughter of Raymond Pettigrew, and as determined and driving as he, as set on doing what she thought was best.

But at this command, she did wait. She gave him that respect.

"Where are you going in such a snit?" he demanded.

"To drive the car you gave me!"

"No destination?"

"A definite one. I'm going to see Lance. About the fox hunt."

She took one step, and he caught her arm. She stood, fuming, fighting back the instinct to jerk free, to get out of his sight. She didn't want to see him for days. But she would—he'd be civil and she'd be civil. For a year.

His hand was warm, not the least hurtful. "Why don't you visit your own stable?" he asked in a reasonable tone. "The trainer I hired is at the cottage."

"You told me that yesterday."

"You might at least give him the courtesy of—"

"Let him come to me!" she retorted. "I run to no man!"

And here she was, doing what she'd told him she'd never do. She was running to a man, driving like the wind to Lance, whom she'd loved for years, for whom she'd kept herself a virgin. She was heading for Twelve Oaks, his cotton plantation on the opposite side of Durham from Magnolia Hall and its home acres.

The breeze lifted the hair from her face, streamed it behind her like a shimmering dark copper banner. The misfortune of her nature, she thought angrily, was to feel that love was everything. And Papa had given her an ultimatum! One year to wed. He didn't care about love!

Without love for a man, life would be a void. No riches, no possessions, no costly toys such as this car, the hunting mounts, the stables, the race horses, could make up for the absence of love.

She was ready and eager to give up all possessions for her one absorbing passion. She needed to love and be loved as surely as she needed the air she breathed. And the only man she wanted, had ever wanted, was Lawrence Lee Buford—Lance, darling Lance, of whom she dared not hint to Papa.

Much as he liked and admired Lance, Papa would be dead set against him as her husband because he raised cotton. Because he had not one jot of interest in tobacco.

One year to settle a lifetime—without love, it couldn't be done.

2

She glimpsed a motorcycle cop in the rearview mirror, quickly dropped speed. The policeman passed, turning a stern face in her direction, and then he was gone. Rae-Ellen wondered if he'd look that stern if he were invited to marry the Pettigrew heiress, if he were given the privilege of siring the great man's grandson.

Everything she'd done since she became of marriageable age was an utter loss in the face of Papa's insane demand. She'd adored Lance Buford when she was a small girl and he had held her and Adah on his lap. She'd loved him as a woman since she was seventeen, had dreamed of his falling in love with her, thrilled and tingled with hope.

Lance was a man of importance, too. He owned

a great cotton plantation, had served two terms as state lobbyist in Raleigh, was Master of the Fox Hunt Club. He was respected, his opinion asked for and accepted by intelligent men older than him.

He was perfect—utterly perfect. He was the most eligible bachelor in the Piedmont, yet Papa expected her to carry through his impossible demand. He'd never accept Lance.

And here she'd kept herself a virgin for him. To make things worse, he treated her like a young sister!

Why am I really a virgin? she fumed. She began to be impatient with Lance himself, almost to blame him. Have I been lying to myself, turning down every boy when I was younger, every man, these last years, who has tried to tempt me? Have I truly been saving myself for Lance?

Or am I . . . frigid?

Yet, if she were frigid, would she go weak at the sight of him, would her heart pound and the pulse in her neck race? Would her knees tremble?

Would she be unable to sleep at night, thinking of him? Would she try to imagine what it would be like if he were in bed with her? Would she turn and toss, would she long for him to be there, touching, kissing, receiving, all she had saved for him?

Maybe she'd been wrong to keep that girlish dream of having Lance be the first and only man to make love to her. If she'd given in to even one of her dates, she might have learned womanly tricks with which to intrigue Lance.

Besides that, the thought slammed, maybe she should have tried other men. She knew with her heart that Lance was the one, but suppose her body didn't choose to go the way of her heart? If she'd lain with other men, her body would be experienced and could adjust itself to her heart.

Maybe that was the sensible way. Why, she wondered, angry at herself, have I saved myself for him? For love, oh sure. But am I a fool, a prude, or only particular?

Certain facts remained, all in Lance's favor. He had the fine southern blood, all the other qualities, quite a bit of money, a stable for hunting mounts, a pack of fine hunting dogs. People vied to be included in his hunt, as they were now clamoring to be in the first one this fall, set for the last week in September. Lance would never hunt with more than twenty horses, so the field was limited.

Even Papa was a member of the hunt. The Pettigrew family was included as a matter of course, as were the Buncombes from Raleigh, and Fawn Morehead and Pete Battle.

She glowered at the passing cotton fields. If only Lance weren't practically married to them! If only—but not even love would convert him to tobacco.

He'd made a few remarks to Rae-Ellen about Papa. Oh, very respectful, but the point was carried. Lance was aware that Papa would expect Rae-Ellen to marry tobacco, though she hadn't believed it at the time. But she now had that conviction to batter down along with everything else.

Adah, too. She was always in the way. She'd mooned after Lance even when they were children. He treated Adah as though she were the child he used to hold on his knee, which reassured Rae-Ellen. She was further comforted by the knowledge that because of the family secret, Adah could never marry Lance.

She turned into the half-mile driveway of Twelve Oaks. It was lined on both sides by tall oaks, silvery moss dangling from them like jewels. At the far end of the drive she watched the plantation house emerge.

The mansion took its name from the giant oaks which encircled it, seeming to hold its vast beauty in loving embrace. The front of the great white structure was two-storied, with a twelve-pillared gallery stretching across the front, holding up the roof. There was a newer one-story wing on each side of the original main house and, at the rear, another such wing. It was said there were thirty rooms in the house, but Lance would never admit to it, saying it was more like twenty.

As she brought the car to her usual shrieking stop, she turned the ignition off. Her hands flew to her hair. It was a wild tangle of waves and curls.

Damn! she thought, running her fingers through it. I rush to entice a man, then drive like crazy and turn up on his doorstep a mess! She peered into the rearview mirror, snatched a comb out of the glove compartment, and pulled it through her hair, which sprang into deep shimmering waves.

"Hold it!" laughed a quiet, assured voice.

She glanced up, lips apart. "Lance! I wanted . . ."

"To make certain you're beautiful," he teased.

His eyes, gray as a gentle rain, were laughing, his firm, kind lips were smiling.

You wouldn't know he's thirty years old! she marveled. You'd never guess! The sun was glinting his blond hair, warming his tanned skin, adding a golden tinge to his beige slacks and open-necked shirt.

No wonder Adah was obsessed with him! No wonder all the girls— But she was with him now. This time she was going to do something about it!

"Where's Adah?" he asked. "I rarely see just one of you."

That was damn true. Rae-Ellen never had him to herself. Either Adah tagged along or another girl would turn up before Rae-Ellen could get his full attention.

"Adah and Mama are shopping," she said. "You've got me all to yourself!" She smiled, her eyes holding his, she hoped meaningfully, but he only grinned.

"Had your breakfast?"

"With the family."

"I'm just about to eat," he told her. "Can you hold some beaten biscuit? Hattie has been beating and mumbling in the kitchen for a long time. Mumbling that I should have comp'ny if I want her to beat her knuckles off for those biscuits! She's a fierce one, my Hattie!"

She would have eaten beaten biscuit with him until her stomach burst. Even if she had already consumed two batter cakes. She'd eat if it put three pounds on her. For him, she'd get fat. Or she'd skin herself down to a rail. Whatever Lance Buford wanted of her, he'd get.

"Sure I'll eat, I'm starved for beaten biscuit!" she declared brightly, and somehow kept her hand from trembling when he took it to help her out of the car. She tucked it into his arm and put her other hand on top to still the tremor, as they walked up the steps.

He was two inches under six feet; this made him

tower over her nicely. She swallowed. Even his height was perfect!

She glanced up at him and saw that he was looking down at her, smiling. She saw again, for the ten thousandth time, how his patrician features became warm and exciting when he smiled, how that strength of character showed, even then.

Everything about him denoted strength—his confident voice, his build, which was slender yet smoothly powerful from laboring in the fields, from training his hunters and riding, and from playing racquet ball.

He was a man created for living, for loving. Her breath quavered as she walked along beside him across the gallery, down the gold and white hallway and into his pine breakfast room.

"You get lovelier every day," he said. He pulled out a chair at the round table and seated her. "You and Adah both."

"You flatter us!" she laughed, the thrill of his words dulled by his inclusion of Adah.

"Not at all!" he teased. "I've watched it happen, the two of you getting prettier and prettier, until now . . . " He shook his head in mock despair. "Have pity! Don't ever, under any circumstances, enter a beauty contest. You'd drive the judges out of their minds. They'd never be able to decide."

His banter, delivered with a solemn face, set her to laughing so hard she almost got the hiccups. She was still laughing when he tinkled the silver bell at his place.

A door slapped, and there stood Hattie, the mammoth housekeeper. She was scowling, but when she spied Rae-Ellen, she smiled, revealing broad white teeth.

"Why, Miss Rae-Ellen!" she said in her bass voice. "Now it's perfect! Mastah Lance been whining 'round 'bout beaten biscuit . . ."

"I didn't whine, you fake," Lance interrupted, grinning. "It was you, and well you know it. Last night, moaning that I don't think you make a beaten biscuit fit to eat . . ."

"That 'cause you don't nevah ask for it!" Hattie broke in, her shining black skin sparkling indignation. "A Mastah what think his cook make good things *ask*—he don' jus' take what's set in front of him, like they ain' no difference 'tween ham hock an' ice cream, even!"

"Well, I asked for beaten biscuit last night!" Lance teased. "After you hinted, deliberately, as you did just now, and I also asked for fried ham, redeye gravy and grits!"

Hattie was chuckling, the sound rising from her great body like soft thunder. "You see, Miss Rae-Ellen, this Mastah Lance, he got to *ask!* Else how I know he ain't yearnin' for fry chicken while he eatin' pork chops? He eithah got to *ask* or he got to get himself a wife to do the askin' for him!"

Rae-Ellen felt her skin go hot from face to ankle. She stole a look at Lance. She knew the outspoken Hattie was utterly serious, knew that Lance would rarely tell the black woman what to cook.

"No wife, Hattie," he placated, "could dream up menus better than yours. I assure you that I'm satisfied with the variety you serve! Besides, you know you don't want some white Missy to come in here and boss you around!"

"It depend on who the Missy is!" snorted Hattie. "The right Missy, she let me boss them lazy girls that keep this house clean, an' all she got to do is see

I knows, all the time, what you really want to eat!"

Rae-Ellen was burning still, biting the tip of her tongue to keep from crying out that here she was, that she'd do anything, even submit to Hattie's bossing, to be Mrs. Lance Buford!

Laughing, Lance told Hattie to get her big self back to the kitchen and bring in that breakfast that he asked for.

He was still chuckling after Hattie returned to the kitchen and he met Rae-Ellen's eyes. She didn't feel quite so hot now, and she hoped her awful blush was no longer visible. While his attention had been on Hattie, she must have been scarlet!

"Are you still as much in love with that new car as you were yesterday?"

"Indeed, yes," she murmured. "I'm in love!"

She stole a look at him, but the patrician face was calm. If he'd got her double meaning, his expression didn't betray it. Quiet strength emanated from him, and she felt comfortably enveloped in it. No wonder she was in love with him. No wonder Adah was besotted with him—and all the girls in the Piedmont.

Hattie served the meal, offering the plate of biscuits first to Rae-Ellen, then to Lance, with exaggerated grace. She waited until he'd sampled a biscuit and pronounced it the best ever, then she returned to her kitchen, her face set in triumph.

"I'm a fortunate man," Lance said. "Beaten biscuit, redeye gravy, and a beautiful girl to share them with. To what do I owe this fortune?"

"I wanted to see you," she blurted. Then, to hold back another flush, she held her breath for a few seconds.

"About what, Rae-Ellen?"

"Oh," she replied, "partly I wanted to drive. And to talk about the fox hunt."

"Yes. It is getting to be that time."

"You haven't picked your cotton yet. Will that be done in time for the hunt?"

"Blanchard starts the first picking crews tomorrow. At any rate, we have no need to ride out over the cotton fields. I've planned it so we start north, through that stand of timber. In fact, the picking can go on even as we hunt, if it comes to that."

"Mr. Blanchard . . . he's a good overseer."

"Best to be had. That's why I can be away from Twelve Oaks when I choose. He keeps things running."

"And so you can get ready for the hunt," she smiled.

He nodded. "Things are progressing. I took the hounds out for a run yesterday. Bugler led the pack, the way he did last year. All the dogs are in top shape."

"And Prince is always tops."

"Best hunter I ever had. All the hunters are in fine condition, both mine and the ones I stable for Buncombe."

"Papa keeps saying we're going to run out of foxes," Rae-Ellen ventured, just to have something to say, to keep from crying out, Oh, look at me, really look! Can't you see, can't you tell, I'm the one to marry, I'm the one who can get along with Hattie! I'm the one, the only one!

"Everything's shaping up for the hunt," Lance said. "I've talked two more farmers into letting us ride their harvested fields and timber. I've plenty of foxes in the thickets here at Twelve Oaks; they've bred well the past year. Now, with my land as well as these two new farms and the one we used last year, we'll have the space."

Rae-Ellen nodded, her mind on the hunt because it was of importance to Lance. In the old days, and even when she was a small girl, there'd been vast reaches of land over which the fox could run, the pack in full cry behind him, the hunters, in their pinks, urging their mounts on, taking fence, wall, and ditch, flying through the air, it seemed.

But now, with the way towns and cities had grown, with more and more farming land converted into residential sections, made into concrete horrors studded with condominiums, every year it became harder to hunt. This year, for instance, there were to be fewer hunts; Papa had said that was a result of lack of space.

Though she knew this to be a fact, Rae-Ellen asked Lance if it was true, just to keep him talking, to hold the sound of his voice in her ears. "There really are going to be fewer hunts this year?"

"I'm afraid so. We don't want to overdo it."

"And next year?"

"Hopefully as many as this, even more. Don't worry that lovely head. If nothing else, we'll confine the hunt to Twelve Oaks and the original farm I lined up. The farm is big, and the owner is glad to get the money we give him for the privilege of crossing his land. Considering the bind farmers are in today, crying hard times and not planting all their land, I think we can depend on the hunt to continue indefinitely."

As he spoke of the future his face lit up. He was crazy about fox-hunting. She kept him on the subject as long as breakfast lasted.

His face brightened even more as he talked of

the racing horse he'd bought, soon to be delivered, that he was going to take to Florida when she and Adah took their new racers.

They decided to have their last cup of coffee in Lance's study. They moved along the parquet floor of the hallway, which Hattie kept so highly polished Rae-Ellen caught the reflection of her own shoes, to the study. Hattie followed with the tray, her great feet padding along, mumbling under her breath about folks ought to set at the table for the whole meal, not traipse through the house.

The study was large, one wall lined with books, another filled with a green-veined marble fireplace, the remaining two hung with paintings of hunters Lance had owned, and their sires, which his father, long-dead, had owned. There was a new painting of Prince, Lance's favorite black hunter, over the mantel, and this Rae-Ellen paused to admire.

The room was furnished in sturdy natural pine. An enormous rolltop desk stood in the middle, a captain's chair drawn to it. A pine sofa cushioned in nubby brown stretched along one wall, under paintings, and a big table, flanked by pine armchairs, was under the second group of paintings. The floor was carpeted in green, the windows shuttered with pine louvers.

Rae-Ellen watched Hattie plunk the tray onto the table in front of the sofa. "Desk in the middle of the room!" she grumbled. "A mess!"

"Only way I can work," Lance said, laughing. The rolltop of the desk was open. It was littered with papers and ledgers; the pigeonholes were stuffed with folded documents and bulging envelopes. Some of the drawers were partly open and they, too, were crammed with papers.

Hattie rolled her eyes at it all. "No wife'd put up with that mess," she mumbled, and left the room.

Lance grinned. "You going to pour the coffee, or shall I?"

"I'll do it," Rae-Ellen said quickly. Anything, any little thing at all, might be the magic that could lead him to see her in a romantic light. In this room, where he did the paperwork on his holdings and on the hunt, to see her perform this small rite could influence him.

She poured two cups, set them close together. This necessitated Lance's having to sit fairly near her on the sofa.

Neither took cream or sugar. Rae-Ellen had given up sugar in her coffee ages ago in order to take it the way Lance did, and now she preferred it black. As they sipped, she thought how super it would be if they could have after-breakfast coffee in this room every morning of their lives.

She set her cup down carefully, her heart in her throat. But she was going to do it. She was. This was the twentieth century. A woman no longer need sit back and wait. No law said she had to raise and lower her eyelashes coyly, hide her lips behind a fan. She could speak out, no matter how scared she was, how unsure.

"Lance. There's . . . I wonder about you." She made the plunge.

He looked at her, puzzled. "Why? In what way?"

"You're thirty years old."

"Nearer to thirty-one."

"You have everything. Twelve Oaks, scads of cotton, millions—"

"Make that one million."

She gestured. "You're Master of the Fox Hunt Club, you've got every girl in the Piedmont, and her mother, drooling. You've everything except a wife. Why don't you get married, Lance?"

There! It was out! The first part, anyhow. Now it was his turn to be serious. She struggled to breathe normally, to hide from him how upsetting it was, speaking out the way she had a right to do.

He reached over and took one of her ringless hands. "I don't know what to say, Rae-Ellen," he told her gently. "You've taken me by surprise."

"So? What's wrong with your getting married?"

"Nothing. Nothing at all. I consider a good marriage one of the greatest blessings."

"Then—"

"It takes the right girl, Rae-Ellen, honey. I've had my eyes open. And no girls have met my standard except . . ."

"Except what?" she breathed.

"Except the Pettigrew sisters."

Her heart stopped, actually stopped. And then it plunged.

"Well?" she whispered.

"I recognized that years ago, when I became marrying age. Ten years ago."

"But that was . . . I was . . . !"

"Yes. I was twenty. You were ten. Adah was nine. You were little girls, and I couldn't marry a little girl, now could I?"

"I'm not a little girl anymore!" she whispered. "I'm twenty years old, and I—"

"I know how old you are. And Adah. Nineteen. And, to make it worse, you're sisters. Since I couldn't choose between you ten years ago, how can I choose between you now? The age difference alone—"

"That's nothing! You're ten years older than I am, Papa's ten years older than Mama! It's made no difference! You know it hasn't!"

"It doesn't look well for a man to choose between sisters," he said soberly.

"Adah's not my sister!"

"By law, adoption. She has Pettigrew blood; she's a cousin. You've been raised as sisters. Everybody looks on you as sisters."

Rae-Ellen bit her lower lip. It would never do to blurt out the truth. It might even turn him against her. It wouldn't be fair to Papa and Mama, or to Adah, darn her, not even if it meant Lance would propose now, on the spot.

She snuggled to him; he was forced to put his arm around her. She'd done this as long as she could remember, though not in the last few years.

She turned her face to him. Their lips were almost touching. "Kiss me," she breathed. "The way you used to do. Oh, Lance, please!"

Slowly, after hesitation, he put his lips on hers. They were warm and gentle, and felt as they'd felt when she was ten. They moved on her lips with that same light gentleness, but her lips moved firmly, clung. Even when his arms tensed to push her away, she clung to him the way her lips did, and her eyes closed, and she drank his kiss, his one kiss.

She could hardly breathe, but she held that kiss. It sank into her loins and glowed; her heart beat so violently she could feel it against his chest and knew he could feel it.

He pulled his lips from hers, firmly set her away, picked up his coffee and took a sip. She sat with whirling brain and burning loins. Her lips were trembling, out of control, and she made no effort to still them.

It was in the open now. The kiss had told him. They'd have a showdown, here and now.

Apparently Lance had no such intention. He spoke so quietly, she had to strain to catch the words.

"Rae-Ellen Pettigrew," he said, "don't ever kiss like that again. Not me, not any man."

"Why shouldn't I?" she cried.

"Because that kiss is an invitation. And you must realize it, for your own protection."

"I know it's an invitation! To you, my darling!"

He stared; his surprise was honest.

"I thought you were just being daring. But now I find you don't know what you're saying!"

"Oh, yes, I do! I'm asking you to take me, here, now, on this sofa! I'm asking you to teach me man-woman love!" She tried again to get into his arms, but he held her off.

"You're joking, you've got to be!" he exclaimed, but his tone betrayed that he knew better, that he was trying, like the gentleman he was, to get her out of the situation gracefully. "Come, now! Be my good girl; stop the act!"

"It's no act! I want you to make love to me! It's my first time, I swear it! I know—people say I'm wild, but I'm not wild when it comes to sex!"

"For what you want, man-woman love is needed," he argued, holding her, for she'd fought her way into his arms again. "The kind of love that leads to marriage."

"That's what I'm talking about!" she wailed. "I love you, Lance Buford, have loved you and wanted to be your wife since I was sixteen! If you don't feel that kind of love for me right this minute, why I don't mind! Truly I don't! Because you'll come to love me! Just give me the chance!"

"It's not that easy, Rae-Ellen." He took hold of her arms and set her away from him, putting her onto a far cushion. "Going to bed doesn't create love."

"How do you know?"

"Experience. There have been a few women in my life."

"But not me! It's not fair to refuse me the chance!"

He shook his head.

"I'll make a bargain!"

Seizing on this to regain the teasing adult mood, he smiled. "What bargain, you little girl?"

"If you'll make love to me, I'll marry you if you find out that I'm right, that you'll want marriage. If I'm wrong, I'll be your secret love for however long you want, for always! Then you'll never need to marry anybody!"

"Rae-Ellen, Rae-Ellen. No, no and, again, no. I don't want to hurt you, not for a moment, but it's out of the question, and in your heart you know it. Please, be yourself."

"I am being myself! At last! I've hidden this, waited for you to—and you never did! I want to marry you, want it more than anything in the world! But I'll settle for the other!"

"It's impossible, dear little girl."

"It's Papa, isn't it? He's been at you, tried to get you into tobacco! Well, you don't have to promise that—"

"I don't know what you're talking about."

"Papa, wanting me to marry a tobacco man and give him a grandson for Pettigrew's! He'll rave when we marry, but he'll come round when our son is born! Because he wants him for the tobacco!"

"This is crazy. But just for the record, I'd never let a son of mine—"

"You don't have to! I promise! I'll disinherit myself! I'll give up my share of the money! I'll do anything!"

They were standing now, eyes locked.

He took her shoulders, shook her a trifle. "I'm going to level with you," he said. "And when I've done it, all that's taken place here is to be wiped out as if it had never happened."

"Nothing can do that! You do love me, you've always said it!"

"Rae-Ellen, Rae-Ellen, of course I do."

"Then why—?"

"I love you, but not the way you want. It's Adah for me, has been Adah since she was nine and I was twenty. She bewitched me. I've only waited for her to grow up. Today has brought things to a head. I'm going to start courting her, gently. As soon as I win her woman's love, and I hope I can, I want to marry her."

Rae-Ellen's breath stuck in her throat. He shook her again, a bit harder, and her breath came free.

"So you did choose between us, after all!"

"My heart chose, Rae-Ellen."

"It's impossible!" she whispered. "Papa will never—he'd not do that to the Buford blood!"

"What do you mean? Her being adopted will do nothing to the Buford blood."

"Skip it!" she evaded, aching to reveal the whole shameful truth.

37

"There's something—out with it!"

"It's the—connection—Adah comes from. It put common blood into her."

"That makes no difference. None whatsoever."

Rae-Ellen whirled away from him. She fled, sick and trembling, wounded and rejected. She ran, willing that Lance would never find out what a terrible difference knowing about Adah could make.

3

She gunned her motor, sent the car roaring down the driveway, sped away from Twelve Oaks. Sobbing, tears ran down her cheeks, and she let them.

She'd never been like this, had never dreamed that anything could make her feel so torn, bereft, devastated, mortally wounded. And utterly humiliated.

But Lance hadn't meant to humiliate her.

No matter what he said, she couldn't believe that he truly loved Adah, that he'd actually marry her. He didn't want to marry anyone. Not Lance, darling Lance, who was content with life as it was.

Her breath quivered. She wiped away her tears, first with one hand, then with the other. As she drove, her resolve grew. She'd not give up. If it were true, if Adah did present a real threat to Rae-

Ellen's winning Lance, she'd just work harder to get him. She loved Adah, but not enough to let her marry Lance.

The wind was blowing her face dry. There'd be no more tears. She had to plan her course, had to carry it out. And that was going to take some doing.

Houses passed in a blur. Trees, roadside restaurants, cars. She glanced at the speedometer. She was going faster than the law allowed, but if she kept it just a trifle above the limit, chances were she wouldn't be stopped. She ached to press the pedal to the floorboard, to fly along; going like that her mind would move swiftly and she'd know what to do first about Lance.

One thing was certain. She was going to become like other girls, like Mary-Lou Buncombe. Mary-Lou wore a charm bracelet; from it dangled glittering little figures, each a trophy representing a man with whom she'd slept. There were so many charms that when she moved her arm, they tinkled.

She recalled the last one her friend had added.

Mary-Lou had driven over from Raleigh especially to show it off. She'd got to Magnolia Hall in time to have midmorning coffee with the Pettigrew sisters.

They used the sitting room of Rae-Ellen's suite. It was furnished in pale walnut, decorated in tones of burnt orange and gold, with touches of green. The bedroom matched, the rooms opening into each other through double French doors.

Mary-Lou was only five feet three, weighed a hundred pounds, and was a bundle of curves. She had fiery hair, hazel eyes, and laughing lips. Her features were delicate and beautiful, sparkling with the joy of life.

"You'll never guess what, you two!" she cried in her soft, delightful drawl as Norma, the uniformed maid, closed the door to the hallway.

She waited, on tiptoe, everything about her laughing, even the ends of her long, curling hair seeming to laugh. Her eyes danced from Rae-Ellen to Adah.

Adah, who had risen from the settee, ran to the redhead and embraced her. "Mary-Lou, you darling," she said, her rich voice lower than usual. "How sweet of you to surprise us! It is a surprise?" she asked, her golden eyes flying to Rae-Ellen. "You didn't know, did you, sister?"

"Not a hint! And we didn't have a thing planned!"

"Not even to go to the stable?" Mary-Lou teased. "To kiss the horses again, you two lovely . . . virgins?" She whispered the last word, gave a gurgle of laughter, then lifted her arm and jingled her bracelet.

"Mary-Lou!" gasped Adah. "You didn't . . . again!"

"New man in Raleigh!" declared Mary-Lou. "Engaged to some filly in Virginia. Wasn't going to have any part of me!" She laughed, jingled her bracelet again.

Rae-Ellen watched Adah gaze numbly at their friend. Her features, clear-cut as Papa's, except for the dimple in the chin, were rigid.

Mary-Lou tapped a tiny golden horse with the tip of a finger, giggled. "This man is pretty upset! Thinks he's betrayed his fiancée, the whole works!"

"And you," Adah whispered, olive skin going pale, "think it's funny?" She waited, standing so still that not even the gently upturned ends of the

41

almost straight, tawny-gold hair on her shoulders stirred.

"Of course it's funny, you goose!" Mary-Lou laughed. "It's nothing, hardly more than heavy kissing . . . well, it's more than kissing, actually. But you know what I mean! It's not important! This man is all mixed up, thinks he's in love with me. I explained until he understood, though. And because he understands, we have another date tonight!" She whirled, dancing on the rust and gold carpet.

Rae-Ellen, who felt some of the shock that Adah showed, smiled at the exultant Mary-Lou, and shot Adah a warning look. Adah, whose lips were trembling, managed a brief smile, too.

Rae-Ellen felt a bit disappointed in Mary-Lou. But she was their dearest friend, and she'd always been the most daring. They hadn't been with her much the last two years, because Mary-Lou had got in with the jet set and she'd flown over the world to madcap parties and gatherings.

It was then she'd started her charm bracelet.

Now Mary-Lou, quieted as much as her volatile nature allowed, went to Adah and put her arms around her. "Adah darlin', I know I shock you! I know you're a . . . well, a really old-fashioned girl, and I love you for it! You and Rae-Ellen both! But you don't know what you're missin', and you don't know what you may miss altogether if you stay old-fashioned!"

"You mean, if we stay virgins," Rae-Ellen said.

"Yes, I do mean that! Men have always taken their fun without botherin' to marry every girl they sported with! Now women have come to their senses, most of them, 'ceptin' for a handful like you two!"

"This last charm," Rae-Ellen said. "He felt something about what he'd done. And he's a man."

"He was a prude! I had to work on him, and that made it more fun! He's still goin' to marry his Virginia girl, but in the meantime he's lived extra!"

"Mary-Lou!" Adah exclaimed. "You're not like that."

"Oh, yes, I am! Why put up with a man you're tired of? The world is full of them, and they're all willin'!"

All but Lance, Rae-Ellen thought now, speeding along the highway. She could still see Adah's stunned face, still feel how it hurt Adah for Mary-Lou to be so terribly liberated.

Lance, if he wasn't a gentleman, would say that Mary-Lou was promiscuous. She did play the field, but she wasn't promiscuous. Far from that. She was selective, being intimate with men of breeding only.

Mary-Lou had every intention of finding the right man and settling down. Meanwhile, her father, who was in textiles and had a great fortune, encouraged her to have her fun now, unencumbered.

"My Daddy knows I go to bed when I choose!" she'd declared. "He knows that's the best way to find out which man it's safe to marry! So you won't get tired of him! And then have to go through one of those borin' divorces!"

Mary-Lou could have worked in textile design. She'd studied at the best school, but she didn't want a job.

"My children will be my job when I marry!" she was heard to say occasionally. And she never ceased to urge Rae-Ellen and Adah to follow her example. "Have fun!" she exhorted. "Keep yourselves clean,

43

choose your men with finesse. You'll find the perfect one. It's the only way, believe me!"

Again Rae-Ellen bore down on the gas pedal. The car shot ahead. She was startled by a wailing siren, but even as she lifted her foot from the pedal, a motorcycle cop motioned her to pull over.

He was red-faced from sun and wind. His hair was sandy, and his complexion went with it. His eyes looked the color of wind—if wind had a color.

She wondered if some girl went to bed with him. Or if he was married. She glanced at his left hand. No wedding ring. Which proved nothing. Maybe she should try a Mary-Lou trick on him, at least lead him to believe she'd do more than flirt.

"I clocked you at seventy," he said in a gravelly voice. "Limit's fifty-five."

"My mistake, officer," she said, her voice coming out Rae-Ellen and natural, with no enticement in it. No hint of recent tears, either.

"You know what the limit is, don't you?"

"I know."

"Let me see your driver's license."

She dug into her purse, handed the license to him.

"No excuses?" he asked, beginning to write the ticket.

"Not really. I had a problem. Speed . . . helps. And I forgot the limit."

The windy eyes came up and over her. His fingers hesitated at their writing and he studied her. She hoped he couldn't see she'd been crying. No part of what had happened to her this morning was any affair of his.

"If I let you off with a warning," he asked,

"think you can keep the speed limit in mind? Permanent-like?"

She stared. Nodded.

He handed back the license, stuffed the citation book into his pocket. "I'll count on that," he said, got onto his motorcycle and roared off, himself building to a speed which was certainly over fifty-five.

She tooled the Lincoln back into traffic and kept it at a toddle. It wasn't necessary to go seventy in order to think—just to be behind the wheel was sufficient. Moving steadily with the now endless stream of traffic, she came to certain decisions.

She would be like Mary-Lou, at least to a degree. She would give up her virginity. She wouldn't wear a charm bracelet, but she'd be like other girls. It had gotten her nowhere to save herself for one particular man, one she'd never really dated, at that.

She'd had lots of dates. Beginning at age fifteen, she'd gone to movies and dances and on picnics and swimming parties with boys she knew. All of them kissed her, and this she permitted. Most of them tried to get fresh, tried to feel her breasts and lower, and this she had not permitted.

Dates over the last two years had been harder to handle. The boys were men now, had developed style. Their earlier fumblings and successes with other girls had taught them various approaches, and she'd had every one of them tried on her. But, aside from passionate kisses, and letting a hand cup her breast on occasion, she'd drawn the line because of Lance.

She'd rebuffed a far greater number of males than the charms on Mary-Lou's bracelet. Her friend, she thought, had seldom rebuffed a male because she was selective and dated with care.

Well, Rae-Ellen Pettigrew wasn't going to rebuff another man! She was going to sleep with the first one she could get. No! she thought instinctively. Not the first one, but the first she decided to date. She'd choose him with care; he must be the absolute best.

She'd learn what sex was about. Then she'd turn it to her own benefit with Lance. She'd no longer be innocent, but experienced, and even if it took sex with several men to learn the tricks, she'd be equipped to tempt Lance.

She was nearing Magnolia Hall. She decided she might as well look over the addition to the stables again. And meet the new trainer.

She was going the full fifty-five when she stepped on the brake and screeched to a stop in front of the cottage. She'd just cut the motor and was waving her hand in front of her face to thin the veil of gravel dust, when she saw a giant of a man long-legging it out of the stable.

His every step was one of fury.

He made straight for her, six feet one or maybe six feet two, big-boned and fleshed just right to make him tremendously large.

Papa had said the trainer was twenty-six, but he hadn't said he was the homeliest man on the face of the earth. He was the ugliest human she'd ever seen, with oversized, rough features, sun-faded brownish hair which would later grizzle, she'd bet on it, and a mad, bullheaded mouth. Furious at his rage, at his ugliness, she saw, with added irritation, that he had beautiful brown eyes. The more she looked at them the madder she got, especially at those bold eyebrows above them.

Ugly and bold. Unbearable.

"Hey!" he called in a deep, assured, maddening tone, "what do you mean, screeching those tires? We've got some high-strung hunters in the corral! What do you think you're doing?"

"They're used to me! This is my stable, partly mine! I'll stop my own car at my own stable as I please!"

"There's also some high-strung race horses going to be delivered here," he boomed, those eyebrows jumping down onto his nose.

Now she was even madder than she'd been at Papa. This upstart, telling her how to behave on her own property! And he nothing but a hired hand!

She drew in her breath, held it, mind racing, seeking words to put him in his place.

"Who do you think you are?" she demanded imperiously.

"Burr Travis. Hired by Raymond Pettigrew to run this stable and see to the welfare of the horses! And it ain't to their benefit for you, or anybody like you, to keep them jumpy and scared!"

"I've been around horses all my life!"

"I pity the horses!"

Burr glowered at the spoiled beauty in the fine car—a high-handed girl whose hair wasn't exactly brown because it had red streaks, and he never had liked red hair. Not that it was really red, but the red showed. And those blue eyes, piercing and arrogant, used to mowing down the opposition. Hell-bent to have her own way.

He sure had her number. Spoiled beauty or no spoiled beauty, she'd found her match. He recalled, with satisfaction, the interview he'd had with Raymond Pettigrew when they met in Louisville to talk business.

47

They sat together in a restaurant. Burr liked this youthful, snowy-haired man who knew a lot about horses and wanted to know about Texas cattle. "Since I've let my daughters talk me into buying racers," Pettigrew said, with a smile, "I may, in the future, look into the possibility of a cattle ranch. Think it's sensible?"

"Any rancher thinks that," Burr said. "That includes me. I just happen to be horse-crazy. Racing is what I want, and breeding racers."

"A man should do what he wants," said Pettigrew.

Burr nodded, half-grinned. The more he talked to this North Carolina fellow, the better he liked him. He was a man with a mind of his own, but consideration for other men.

"You say these racing horses are for your two daughters, sir?" Burr asked.

"That's right. They've ridden since they were children. Now they want horses to race—Kentucky Derby, Churchill Downs, Florida, all over. And I want a good trainer."

"Looks like you'd want a top trainer."

"Not at first, with only two racers. And you know horses."

"Been raised with them, on a ranch. I've worked under some trainers here in Kentucky. I can do the job."

"The money's satisfactory?"

"Entirely. I want experience, mainly."

"Then it's settled."

"Not definite yet, sir. You say the stable and the horses are for your daughters?"

"That's right."

48

"Who'll I be working under? I think you should know I won't take orders from a woman."

The older man smiled. "You'll not have to. You'll give any orders around the stable, as to management of the horses, their care, all that. You're accountable only to me."

It was settled then and they'd bought the horses together. One was a sweet little filly, Starstruck, a beautiful dapple gray. The other was a stallion, Thunder Boy, big, powerful and also dapple gray. They bought twin yearlings of the same color.

"Sorry to be so insistent on gray," Pettigrew said. "But I do spoil my daughters, and they want all the Pettigrew racers to be what they call silver."

"Women take notions," Burr agreed. "These are all beauties, best of any we've looked at, according to me."

"And, according to me," agreed Pettigrew.

The buying done, Raymond Pettigrew flew home and Burr went back to Texas. "To pick up my gear. I've got some books and other truck," he explained. "I'll be at your place on schedule."

And now here he was, with authority, accountable only to Raymond Pettigrew.

Looking at this girl's defiant chin, he thought she might very well try to make him accountable to her. She wasn't a bit like Adah, who was soft and friendly, and to whom he'd been drawn by her gentleness.

He found himself glaring at this one. She was glaring right back. Whatever the trouble was—oh yes, the way she'd shrieked her tires—the anger was mutual.

"You're one of the Misses Pettigrew?" he growled.

"I'm Rae-Ellen Pettigrew. I'm the elder."

"Burr Travis here. I met your sister yesterday."

Rae-Ellen remembered Adah had mentioned coming to the stable, but she hadn't said much about the new trainer, except that he was a big man . . . that he had an air of capability.

"You have a right to know," Burr Travis said, "when your father hired me, we came to an understanding."

"I couldn't care less."

"It may be you will care. I told him I take orders from no woman. My orders come from him."

"That's the silliest thing I ever heard of! Suppose I want a horse saddled? Do I have to wait until Papa comes to the stable and orders you to saddle it?"

"Talks about silly!" he snorted. "*Ridiculous* is more like it. I'm sure you know that orders apply to policy."

"Such as *you* giving *me* orders how to drive my car?"

"Inasmuch as it affects the horses, yes."

"I won't stand for it! I'll—"

"I'll not have horses I'm making friends with, gaining the confidence of, kept jumpy by sudden noises. Such policy orders as that are in my territory, and I'm going to enforce them."

He had a twang to his speech she couldn't abide.

"You're from Oklahoma!" she accused. "I can tell from the way you talk!"

"Texas."

"A cowpoke, no doubt! Papa said you worked with horses."

"What else did he say?"

"I wouldn't know. He talked to Adah about you. I didn't listen. But if you were on a ranch, you were a cowpoke."

"You-all might call me that."

"How did you get here?" she demanded. She glanced around the parking area, looking for some kind of car. "Did you drive?"

"Nope."

"Hitched then, I suppose?"

He hesitated. Then he said, "You can call it that."

"What does a cowpoke know about race horses?"

"Considerable."

"You conned Papa into hiring you! Into helping pick our racers!"

"He knows this is my first full-time job as trainer. He knows I worked under some trainers in Kentucky. He knows I can recognize a good horse when I see it."

"You don't have to keep repeating yourself!"

"With some I do, and with some I don't!"

"Implying that you're headstrong and high-handed!"

Rage crackled in the air.

Rae-Ellen opened the door of the Lincoln and flounced out. It enraged her that tall as she was, he was at least a good seven inches taller. She had to look up, way up, to meet his glare.

As they stood inches apart, sparks flying, Burr Travis gritted his teeth. He'd never met a female so irritating, so maddening! How two sisters could be raised together in the same house, by the same parents, and one turn out as gentle and appealing and . . . well, just plain nice as Adah, and the other make him so furious he felt the hair on his neck stir, he couldn't understand.

Except for the solid business agreement he'd made with Raymond Pettigrew and the cordial reception he'd had from Adah, Travis knew he would grind his boot heel in the gravel and walk out on this filly right now.

He tore his gaze away from her and turned abruptly back toward the cottage. When he turned, the sound of his heel against the gravel seemed to rouse her.

"You're even dressed like a cowpoke!" Rae-Ellen cried. "Boots and all!"

He turned back. "It's odd you didn't mention my clothes before," he said evenly.

"I . . . didn't notice!" She'd been too stunned by his size, his homeliness, his stubborn mouth, those damnable brown eyes, to see that those muscular shoulders were covered by a denim work shirt, sleeves rolled high to reveal smooth, sun-darkened arms as powerful-looking as the muscular thighs, revealed through tight-fitting, faded jeans. She just hadn't seen that he was dressed like a television cowpoke.

"Your father has no objections to my rig," he said. "Or your sister. However, much as I hate to give in to arrogance, you've got a point. I've got regular boots, regular training clothes. I've been meaning to wear them, just ain't unpacked them yet."

Ain't! He actually had said the word! No tell-

52

ing what damage he'd wreaked inside the cottage with his high heels.

"I want to see inside the cottage!" she demanded.

He bristled, eyebrows on nose again. "What for?"

"To be perfectly frank, to see if you've scratched up the floors with those boots. My sister redecorated the cottage while the stable was being enlarged. We made the kitchen curtains and we polished the floors on our hands and knees!"

"You *work?*" he blurted, surprise making his mouth look meaner than before.

"Of course I work! When I want to! I curry the horses, work out with them, practice—I—"

"Seems to me you said you want to see inside, Miss Pettigrew. Come on. Let's go in."

Sparks crackling between them, they walked to the cottage side by side, Travis towering over Rae-Ellen in an infuriating way. She wouldn't be surprised if he'd broken down every chair, he was so big, so heavy. But not fat, curse him. She couldn't call him anything but gigantic—perfectly and gigantically proportioned.

He held the door open.

"You first, *Miss,*" he drawled with a mocking bow.

4

Rae-Ellen stormed into the cottage, head high, blazing eyes everywhere at once. Burr Travis lumbered noiselessly behind her, which was most exasperating. *Lumber* wasn't exactly the word—he was too light and sure on his feet—but he was so overwhelmingly massive she couldn't think of any other way to describe his loathsome movements.

She strode purposefully across the sitting room. Furnished with mahogany, which had originally come from the big house, the sofa and broad-armed chairs were covered in wine-red leather. Between colorful Mexican throw rugs, the hand-rubbed floor gleamed as brightly as she and Adah had left it. The rugs repeated the same wine-red and like the heavy, leaf-designed drapes, had bold splashes of brown and burnt orange.

Adah had wanted to decorate in shades of yellow. Rae-Ellen had been surprised that Adah would entertain such a fanciful idea, but the younger girl had turned her golden eyes on her sister, her hair moving on her shoulders like a golden halo. "Why not?" Adah had looked closely around the then shabby rooms. "You can't say the cottage doesn't need brightening up! We should have done it for old Bill Jewett before—"

"He wouldn't let us, remember? He told us his last days on the job were his own, and that when he retired to California we could paint the cottage pink, for all of him!" Rae-Ellen reminded her sister, laughing. "And yellow is nearly as bad as pink! Papa's hiring a *young* man to be the horse trainer, Adah. We can presume he'll be masculine, and should prepare the cottage for that sort of man!"

Which they had done.

"See any scratches on the floor?" Burr Travis demanded. His voice was so deep it was maddening! Worse than his lumbering! The nerve of this—this brute!

"No!" she snapped, and went into the bedroom. Here the drapes and throw rugs were brown and red and deep gold. There was a king-sized bed with an oak headboard, and the roomy dresser and chest were also oak. This floor, too, gleamed. Furious, Rae-Ellen knew that even if she searched on her hands and knees and crept from wall to wall, she'd not find one scratch. "This pass inspection, too?" Burr demanded.

Her chin went hard. She nodded, one motion only.

"Now for the kitchen and dining nook," he

said, determined to go along with this insulting tour and not stoop to her level.

"Bathroom first!"

Maddeningly, it was in perfect order. He'd even pulled the brown shower curtain closed so it could dry on the inside, and his big bath towel was spread neatly on its rod.

The kitchen looked model perfect. The doors of the shining walnut cabinets closed, the rust-colored refrigerator gleaming, the matching stove store-new, with only the teakettle on one of the burners. His breakfast dishes had been washed and were stacked in the drainer, covered with a spotless dish towel.

She whirled on him, eyes snapping.

His brown eyes were sneering, actually sneering. Rae-Ellen thought that in Lance, their look would have been one of friendliness and warmth; in this great hulk the only thing possible was a sneer!

"Your sister complimented me on my housekeeping," he drawled. "Ain't you got a word of . . . er . . . recognition?

"You've been here one night!" she flared.

"Three nights."

She gestured impatiently. "Ask me that same question in three months! It takes constant work to keep a house looking like this. In three months dirt will gather, you'll live on top of it, it'll get dirtier, and you'll live on top of that! So!"

"Don't count on it," he said tightly.

"Then you'll neglect the stable!" she shot back, "because you're cleaning house!"

Rae-Ellen stood there, hands on hips, knowing she was being unreasonable, but she couldn't stop herself. Travis had now hooked his thumbs into the slit-pockets at the front of his pants, and was sort of rocking back and forth on his heels—and not in a teasing manner. That bullheaded mouth was set, and those maddening brown eyes were narrowed, mocking her and shooting sparks.

So he was mad, was he? Good! Rae-Ellen ached to fire him on the spot, but knew intuitively Papa wouldn't back her up. He'd say that she had no basis for her instant dislike of this lout. He'd say that Adah had gotten along with him fine. That Rae-Ellen was unreasonable. Unreasonable!

She had to get rid of him. She *would* get rid of him. Give him rope, she thought, using the very words she'd heard Papa speak, and he'd hang himself. All she had to do was wait—but could she wait? To have him gone, once and for all, out of her sight, was all she could think of!

She glared at Burr. Her fingers trembled as she had to hold herself back from flying at him, from scratching those eyes right out of their sockets. She longed to slap him, too, across that mouth, to see some other expression on it. How she'd love to slap the arrogance off that mocking cowpoke face!

She flipped into the dining area, and of course that was orderly, too. When she strode back into the sitting room again she spotted a book on the reading table, with a pipe stand beside it and a box, presumably holding tobacco. There were books stacked neatly on the shelves beneath the windows.

She was dumbfounded that he'd have books.

She said so.

"Why wouldn't I?" he countered, "I've got a good library on horses. When I hire another stableboy and groom, I'm going to get them interested in some of the more elementary books."

"Why, for goodness sake? They only—"

"Work around the stable, yes. But the more they learn about horses, the better the horses will be. Any horse, even one that does nothing but pull a plough, works better if his driver thinks like a horse."

There! He'd said it himself! He thought like a horse, was proud of it! That was the trouble with him. He wasn't a gentleman!

She had a fleeting thought of the mythical centaurs, bold and strong and lusty—half man, half horse—all power. She wondered, briefly, why, when she loved horses so much, she should hate him because he was half horse, and then swept it out of her mind. Centaurs, indeed!

Burr stood rooted in the middle of the sitting room, feet apart, thumbs hooked into his pockets, meeting the unexplained fighting rage piercing and stabbing him from those startling blue eyes. He met them squarely, giving her spark for spark, glare for glare.

At the same time, he got a full look at her, and he'd seen few who could match her for beauty. Regardless of the fact that he didn't like a woman with any stubborn-red in her hair, Rae-Ellen's waving wealth of brown curls, streaked with highlights of red, looked arresting. The fiery hair framed her face and she looked like an angel on fire. Damn it, hate it though he did, he was stilled with admiration.

She was tall too, almost as tall as some of the Texas girls, and that was a plus factor. Her shape, in that soft, pale clinging blue, set his imagination astir. Like a filly, she had long, supple legs, petite, beautifully turned ankles. Her prideful stance made her breasts stand firm and proud, pushing haughtily out at him. Burr caught his breath sharply.

He felt a sudden warmth in his loins, set his mouth harder, fought, and overcame the warmth. This thoroughbred was sex on the hoof. She was a menace; she didn't have a scrap of human kindness in her—nothing but defiance and arrogance and every other attribute of a spoiled brat.

Disregarding the return of the warmth to his loins, one thought only filled his head: He'd like to spank this high-handed, unreasonable, beautiful girl. He'd like to give her a good walloping right on her flaunting, provocative behind. Way she acted, she'd never had so much as a finger laid on her, even when she was a bratty little kid.

He told her so.

"Know what, *Miss* Rae-Ellen Pettigrew?" he heard himself demand. "You're the first girl I've ever wanted to spank."

"You touch me," she whispered, those curved red lips thinning, "you dare to, and I'll . . ."

"You'll do what? I can handle two of you. Three."

"You're fired!" she whispered, louder now, a rasping sound. "Pack up your horse books and put them on your back and gallop back to Texas! Right now!"

"Only one person can fire me. That's your father."

"So? All I have to do is tell him—"

"Tell him what? That I didn't scratch the floors? That you've taken a dislike to me? That you

59

don't care how good I am with horses, you're going to get rid of me because you don't like the way I hold my mouth?"

"You can pack now," she commanded coldly. "I'll watch you."

He swept a slow look over her deliberately, taking in every enticing, exasperating detail. Then, speaking slowly, aware that his drawl was enraging her, he told her about her sister's visit the day before.

"She came to see if I was comfortable in my quarters. That's a *real* lady, your sister. As great a one as we have in all Texas. Not a bit like you, is she?" he taunted.

"All Carolina girls are ladies!"

Rae-Ellen was beside herself. That this cowpoke had the temerity to compare her with Adah! While those damnable eyes mocked at her, he told of Adah's visit.

It was midafternoon, and Burr was on his way from the stable to warm up the coffee pot. A pale yellow Buick, gleaming with polish, was breaking to a smooth stop near the cottage. Then this girl —couldn't be over five foot four or weigh more than a hundred and ten—got out and stood waiting.

She was smiling. Her eyes were a deep gold, like they'd trapped the sunshine and darkened it. Her hair was straight and almost the same gold of her eyes. Her skin was olive, yet with a gold tinge, and she was wearing a deep gold dress.

"You're Burr Travis," she said, as he came up. "I'm Adah Pettigrew."

He shook her firm little hand, taking note of how gently rounded her figure was, and that she resembled her father, except that she had a dimple in her chin. He felt a sudden warmth at his neck. He'd never cared for small girls, because he was so damned tall himself, but this one had instant appeal and didn't make him feel that he was too huge.

And he let her see it, smiling broadly at her. She smiled again, and sort of purred in her throat. "I'd say Papa did a good job hiring us a trainer. You look as if you can handle horses or anything!" she said with admiration.

He wondered if he could handle this attraction he felt for her. But, hell, of course he could. She was the boss's daughter, he was the trainer. The two definitely don't mix. He had a long way to go and had to do it fast. If he meant to have his own breeding farm by the time he was thirty, he had no time for women—and especially not the boss's daughter!

He invited her in for coffee and she accepted. They sat at the table in the dining area. He loaded his coffee with cream and sugar; she took hers black.

"We learned, Rae-Ellen and I—"

"Rae-Ellen being your sister?"

"Yes. We learned to drink coffee black from Lance Buford. You'll meet him. He's one of our best friends. I saw him earlier, and he sent you greetings, says he'll be over to see you."

"That's considerate of him," Burr said. Something about the way she spoke of this Buford guy, the way her voice softened on his name, warned him. She might not know it, but Adah was hung up on Lance Buford. It was just as well.

"We're having a fox hunt the last Saturday in September," Adah told him. "Lance is the Hunt

Master. He asked me to invite you to join us. He'll invite you himself, when he comes over. Papa wants you to come, so people will know our trainer."

"Fox hunt means a red coat, don't it?"

"Pinks, yes. If you don't have one—"

"I sure don't. We don't wear pinks on the range."

"Lance can find an outfit for you." She eyed him. "You're such a grand size, there may be difficulties. But Lance can manage anything. And we have an extra hunter in our stable, so there'll be no trouble about a mount for you."

"I see."

She laughed suddenly, laid her small hand on his impulsively. "Listen to me! Ordering you around! Maybe you don't want to go on the hunt!"

"Think I'd like it, change of pace," he said with what gallantry he could muster. He didn't take to the idea of dressing up in a red coat, but it was hard to say no to this charming, friendly girl. It wouldn't kill him to go on just one hunt. As long as horses were involved, he might even like the fast, hard ride, the jumping of fences, walls, ditches, hounds in full cry. It'd be an invigorating ride.

It wasn't until Rae-Ellen broke in on his thoughts now that he realized he had stopped talking. "You said you'd go—just like that?" she cried, eyes electric.

"Sure. I was invited and I accepted."

"Why, that's what I want to know? You're hired to—"

"I said yes because your sister is a lady. She invited me like a lady, invited me on the say-so of the Hunt Master himself. Also, your father has

62

told me to get acquainted with all the horse people in the Piedmont, and I aim to do it."

"And you always do what you want to do?" she flared.

"Nearly always."

"This is the end, the absolute end! That *scum* can walk in here and—the hunt! Because you want to! What'll you want next, tell me that!"

He'd never met a girl he'd taken such a dislike to. He'd never laid eyes on one so stubborn, sassy, unreasonable, exasperating, so infuriating and generally unbearable. He was so riled he itched to grab her and shake her until her pretty white teeth dropped out.

As for Rae-Ellen, she could almost read his mind. She didn't understand her illogical fury at him, but it was in her, alive and throbbing. No, her fury wasn't illogical, not at all.

He was an ugly, gigantic, arrogant, overbearing hunk of man-meat. He was a bull. He belonged with the herd, should be head of the herd.

Then she saw his eyes change and didn't know whether to be mad or wary. She tensed, ready for anything.

He saw her go tight.

Hotness jumped into his loins. He stared down into her flashing eyes, shot his brown venom into their blue, and grabbed her by the shoulders.

"What I want is to put some sense into that empty head of yours!" he yelled.

She yanked free, swung back her arm, then brought it forward, slapping him across the face with all the strength of the fury she felt for this—bull! Without warning, he caught her hand and swooped her up, one arm under her knees, the other around her shoulders, and strode furiously into the bedroom, with her kicking and clawing.

"Put me down!"

He didn't. Instead, he sat down on the bed, still holding her. Before she could do more than twist, he had her face down, across his knees. With his left forearm pushing her shoulders down so she couldn't use her hands, he flipped her dress up with his free hand. She kicked wildly, and he whacked the soft back of her legs, half-numbing them.

"You stop that!" she screamed. "You stop—!"

"You can't tell *me* anything!" he yelled back at her, holding her down more tightly. She struggled furiously. And then he stripped her blue lace bikini panties off, flung them away, and spanked her bare white bottom. He spanked so hard that it stung his palm, but he kept on spanking. She was shrieking curses at him, but he didn't pay attention to them. He watched, mesmerized, as the luscious bottom turned pink.

Her wriggling on his lap, over the hotness in him, added to his rage, was more than he could stand.

Suddenly, with one fierce motion he stood, flinging Rae-Ellen back onto the bed. She was sprawled on her back. Her rumpled dress was up, and he saw that the red streaks in her hair were natural.

Before she could straighten up, he dropped to the edge of the bed, grabbed her in his arms, and slammed his mouth fiercely over hers. He'd never tasted a sweeter mouth; he pressed the lips open and it was sweeter still. He pushed the top of his tongue just past her lips and she bit down hard, quick as lightning.

Anger such as he'd never felt toward a female took him, and with it, uncontrollable desire. She began pummeling him with her fists, but he grabbed them easily. Holding her, he stripped off her dress, her bra, and she was naked in his arms. He threw her back onto the bed, suddenly realizing what he had done. Their eyes locked.

"Well," she wanted to know defiantly, "what are you going to do to me next?" Her fiery hair was wild and her lips were like trembling rubies, but she just lay, staring at him in fury yet looking suddenly like she had some plan of her own.

"Guess you'll just have to wait and see, won't you?"

He swept his eyes over her, saw the rounded breasts with pink, uptilted nipples set in circles of darker rose. He touched one with the tip of his finger, and it budded and grew hard. Rae-Ellen didn't move, but watched him, lips parted. He stroked first around one breast, then the other, and she lay tense under his hand, quivering, but still not fighting him off.

He stroked the insweep of waist, the curve of thigh, ran his palm under one cheek of her buttocks, which must still be burning from the walloping he'd given them. He stroked his eyes down along her perfect legs, her slender ankles.

His own rage and that near bursting in his middle, put him in such a hurry that he ripped and yanked at his clothes to get them off. The boots were the hardest, but he managed, then stripped off pants and jockey briefs and came at her, the fiercest look she'd ever seen on his face.

"You wouldn't!" she breathed, disbelief widening her eyes.

"You wouldn't want me not to!" he snarled.

He was bigger naked than dressed, if that was possible. His body was as beautiful as his face was homely. It fitted together, mammoth and smooth. He was an Atlas of a man without the hideous, bulging muscles.

His maleness was enormous and as it came closer to her, she caught her breath. There might still be time. This wasn't what she wanted— Maybe if she could roll fast, run out of the cottage naked—

Before she could act, Burr was on her, his huge body covering her completely. Then he was entering her and she suddenly cried out in pain. He withdrew, and Rae-Ellen glimpsed his surprise, but then he thrust at her a second time and again there was resistance. The third time, he crashed through her virginity, and she cried out again—in pain, and then surprisingly, in pleasure.

He began to move, violently at first, then slowly, feeling his way, it seemed. When he did that, it seemed natural to Rae-Ellen for her to move, to meet him at the juncture of their combined thrust. His breath was hitting her face, and it held a sweetness to it, and only the faintest trace of tobacco, but even that was sweet.

Her breath was hitting his face, too, and bouncing back. His movements became faster, fiercer, and instinctively her own movements caught his rhythm until she was gasping at the perfection, was reaching, reaching, for she knew not what. She was aware that her arms were around him, holding him, enjoying the smoothness of his broad back. She couldn't remember how they'd gotten there, but that was where they belonged, where they must be— holding him.

66

She tightened her hold and now it was she who went faster, and he who matched her pace. And on the next stroke he was the leader, and she was moving fast and more fiercely to meet his great fierceness. And all the while, the reaching was greater, harder, sweeter, and now, now . . . The tingles started at the base of her brain, ran down her back, through her body and centered there, where she was joined to him.

As the soft, tremendous explosion took place in her depths, she clung to him, sobbing, tears rushing down her cheeks. "Burr . . . Burr . . . Burr . . . !" she moaned, and she thought he was saying "darling," but she couldn't be certain, because that inner explosion lasted and lasted, then, very slowly, was gone.

She realized what he'd done the instant it was over. She pushed him off her and sat up, furious. He'd rendered her helpless. He'd done the unforgivable thing, he'd robbed her of her mind.

She put one arm up to hide her breasts, the other hand to cover the part he'd outraged. "You raped me!" she whispered hoarsely. "You . . . animal!"

She glared at him, panting, accusing and self-righteous.

He was breathing hard. He nodded.

"Reckon I did, Rae-Ellen. In a manner of speaking. I sure-hell never dreamt you was a virgin!"

"You attacked me! You took me by force!"

"I'm sorry about the virgin part," he said, eyes sober. Then his mouth set and after that he went on talking. Whether she wanted to hear or not. "But I didn't attack you. And I sure-hell didn't take you by force. You could have stopped me at any time."

"Not the way you were! An Amazon couldn't have stopped you!"

"I take exception to that!"

Suddenly she wanted to cry. He'd raped her, and she'd let him do it to find out about sex, she really had, and now she wanted to cry. Tears jumped into her eyes, but she was suddenly so mad again that the heat of anger killed the tears. She wanted to rage at him, to make him understand and realize what a despicable animal—no, worm—he was, but the rage choked the words in her throat, and she could only moan.

"I ain't sorry about what happened, except for your virginity," he said. "You asked for it, you know it."

"I . . . did . . . not ask!" she choked out. "You grabbed me and you raped me!"

"You liked it." She remained silent, fuming. "You did like it! A man can tell. It was your first time, and you loved every bit of it except for the first part. You ain't a liar . . . admit you liked it!"

"I don't have to admit anything!" She looked imperiously at him.

He smiled. It made him look more bullheaded. "Lay still," he ordered mischievously. "Or I'll rape you again. This time, I want to show you a thing or two we didn't have time for. You've got a lot to learn."

She began to quiver with rage! She wanted to get off the bed and grab her clothes and run. But there was an inner force to the awful anger his words roused. She had to get revenge! And she knew exactly how. Who exactly did this bully cowpoke think he was!

She sat up abruptly, and he let her. Her objective, sparked by the way he'd treated her, became the only thing in the world.

"Lie down!" she ordered abruptly. "On your back! The way you had me!"

Amazement uglied his face, but he shrugged, then sprawled, spread-eagled, on his back, hands clasped casually behind his head.

"What are you up to now?"

"What you did to me, I've a right to do to you!" she blazed.

"You can't." He was amused.

"Wait and see!"

"You can't because I—Hell, there've been girls. I ain't a monk. What them girls and I done together keeps you from raping me. On top of which, a woman can't rape a man."

"You just shut up! We'll see!"

He just grinned and lay motionless.

Rae-Ellen sat beside him on the bed, the way he'd done with her. Then, drawing a deep breath, she put her lips on his and kissed them. This wasn't as revolting as she'd expected. He kissed back, which she hadn't done, and she almost bit him for it. Then she remembered, and thrust the tip of her tongue between his lips.

He caught it with his teeth and pressed.

She'd bitten him, hard. It infuriated her that he merely pressed. She wasn't going to let him throw her off stride, no matter what he did.

Now, copying his actions, she touched his right nipple with the tip of her finger. There was a scattering of light, curling brown hair between his breasts, and a light strip below his flat stomach.

His nipple was already hard, so she couldn't

tell whether her touch had caused that or not. She steeled herself and stroked her palm around the first nipple. She moved her hand through the fuzz of hair to the other one. Then, holding her breath, she moved her hand down his side to the waist, along the flat, hard thigh, pushing her fingers under his buttocks.

He lifted to her touch. Her face burned when she saw that he had sprung up again. But she wouldn't let that stop her. She realized, in fact, she needed it like that. He was going to submit to everything to which she'd been subjected. She looked slowly down his strong legs, saw there was a light fuzz from the knee down, looked at the big ankles and feet.

Some man-animal, she thought, even in the midst of revenge. How he must be hating it, to be treated as a woman, the way he'd treated her. How it must hurt his male ego!

Finally, she was astride him.

If she could get that—that— If he could do what he'd done, surely there was a way she could do it to him from the top.

He laughed, wrapped his arms around her and rolled. He was inside her before she could catch her breath. It was she who began pounding this time, so mad she couldn't wait to assault him.

And then all the fierceness returned, and his lips on hers held a momentary sweetness which was gone into fierceness, and there was that bursting within, that flooding hotness and surprise and wonder and delight that filled every pore. It took her while she was in the grip of rage, held her for the seconds, hours, years, it lasted. And while it held, she was pounding at him, seeking revenge.

Through it all, in the heart of rage, in the very soul of sensation, some far thing in her was taking note of everything they did, the two of them, man and woman.

And that far thing was learning and it would remember.

I'm a woman now, she thought with a sigh. I'm a full, real woman!

Part II
THE BETRAYAL

5

Not uttering a word, they went into a flurry of action, dressing as fast as they could retrieve garments and struggle into them. Rae-Ellen was determined to be the first one clad, the one to walk out on him, not the other way around.

Her thoughts that now she was woman, had vanished. Instead, she felt ravished, used, stunned. Yet beneath these emotions there lay a mixture of triumph, fury, and hatred.

She pulled at her lacy blue bra. The fastenings slipped out of her fingers as she snatched at them and hooked them clumsily into place. One thing was certain. She knew exactly what sparked every single thing she was feeling.

The triumph was that she'd rendered that lumbering, mouthy Texas cowpoke a quivering mass in bed. Once inside her, she'd held all the power. He'd been helpless to do anything but move, seek, give his manhood into her body, but claiming it for a moment only, and then it was hers again and there wasn't a thing he could do to change it.

The fury was that he had raped her, hadn't waited for any sign that she was willing to receive him. She would never forgive him for that, even if she knew him the rest of her life, which she certainly would not. The quicker she got him fired, the happier she'd be.

And the hatred she felt for him . . . ah, that! It had been instinctive, the instant she saw him. Hatred for his size had sprung full-blown; intense dislike for his homely face had flowered immediately. Furious aversion to his eyes, which had no right to be beautiful and brown and . . . almost able to speak, they were so expressive and alive . . . had struck her like a blow. His every action, from boasting how he'd not scratched the floors, through his describing Adah's visit and bragging about what a fine lady she was, ending with his spanking her—Rae-Ellen Pettigrew—then tearing off her clothes and raping her, had fed her initial dislike until it had grown into unbearable hatred.

She snatched up her bikinis, got into them, found her dress and put it on. Well, maybe he hadn't actually torn anything, but it was a miracle he hadn't. She fastened the belt, and leaving him helling and damning at his boots as he yanked and tugged at them, dashed out of the house to her car.

Burr Travis, whispering curses at his boots as she fled, was amazed, astounded, and amused. Rae-Ellen Pettigrew was the wildest woman in bed he'd ever known. The first one, to give her just due, who'd been able to match his tremendous passion. She'd given as good as she'd got. Not that he'd slept around all that much, but he was in a position to judge. Certainly, she wasn't!

Listen to her gun that motor. She was in a real snit. He chuckled. She'd even tried to rape him! He chuckled again. He should have waited, should have found out what crazy, wild thing she'd have tried. He'd bet a race horse that she didn't know enough to take the dominant position and, in a way, come near to rape. Wild as she was, and strong, she'd been absolutely ignorant.

He sobered. Hell, the encounter had been the best he'd ever had, sure. But he'd never have touched her if he'd had even a suspicion that she was a virgin. That is, he wouldn't have unless she'd come right out and consented, which she surely had not.

She'd just lain there on the bed, made no move to leave. Even so, he could have discovered before he did—when it was too late to stop—that she'd never been with a man. Considering it again, he decided they'd both been wrong. He should have been more gentle with her, that way he would have found out. But, damn her, she should have let him know —not just lay there, then cry rape.

He was tightening his belt when he heard her take off in a shower of gravel. His dander flared. He had a damn good notion to jump into the pickup, run her down, yell some sense into her.

He gave that up. The next impulse, to go to Raymond Pettigrew hit him, and just as quickly died. No man, not even a Texan, could go to a father and say, "I've just raped your daughter. Don't blame me. She sat up and begged for it."

If a Texan was fool enough to do that, he'd be

fool enough to go the whole hog. "I'll marry her," he'd say. "I'll see that no harm comes to her."

He snorted, walked outside, and meandered toward the stable. He had gut-knowledge that Rae-Ellen wouldn't go to her father about this. The knowledge told him that she wasn't even sorry it had happened, not yet. She was too raging, raving mad. She'd tell nobody, not even Adah, her own sister. Anger now, pride later, would keep her mouth shut.

But he'd have to be on the watch for some move. She wouldn't let this simply fade into the past, not her. The least she'd try to do would be to get him fired, and as long as he did his job, Raymond Pettigrew wouldn't give him the sack. The worst she could do was woman-things. She could heckle him; how, he couldn't think, but she was capable of dreaming up retaliation. She could do that until she made him mad enough to quit.

"The hell I'll quit!" he muttered, kicking a small rock out of his path, kicking it again so it wouldn't wedge into the tread of a car tire. "No matter what she does, what she pulls, I'm staying here to get my training experience!"

He was, however, going to keep his distance from her. When she came to the stable, he'd stay far away. He'd be all cool, polite business, his talk only of horses. Wild as she was, and reckless, she might lead him on, trick him into wanting to repeat what had just happened.

Adah, now, that was a different matter. He half-smiled, thinking of her visit, of her gentle beauty and quiet ways. He almost felt a warmth in his loins, might have, except that Rae-Ellen had drained him —for the moment. He went on, smiling, enjoying

the feeling of being drawn to Adah. The quiet, innocent pull she exerted was the exact opposite of
the angry aversion he felt for Rae-Ellen.

Rae-Ellen, at this moment, was racing the highway at seventy. If she got a ticket, she got a ticket.
She had to work off the pure fury which had built
in her. She couldn't go home in this state. Mama
would notice and there'd be questions to which she
couldn't give the true answers, dare not give them.

Undoubtedly that roustabout had, until now,
taken only waitresses to bed. As she drove, Rae-
Ellen could just picture how it was.

He'd be tooling his beat-up jalopy along a Texas
road, and he'd hunger for a hamburger and for a
girl. He'd wheel into a roadside place, a clean one,
give him that much credit, and he'd clomp inside,
spurs jangling, and straddle a stool at the counter.

The gum-chewing waitress, probably a dyed
redhead, would sweep her eyes at him, and she'd
know. Working in such a spot, she'd always know
when a guy was on the make. That was the language
she'd use, the terms in which Rae-Ellen was thinking, which she'd learned from movies.

He'd sweep those ungodly beautiful eyes right
back at her and wink. That's what he'd do! And the
dyed redhead would wink back, and her painted
lips would quirk, and Burr Travis, *animal*, would
grin.

After that, the mechanics of which she wouldn't
lower herself to imagine, they'd be together in one
of the tourist cottages at the rear. They'd practically
break the bed, maybe even actually break it, so Burr
would have to pay for it.

They'd kiss. They'd run their tongues into each

79

other's mouth, clear down the throat. A he-animal and a she-animal. They'd have their hands all over each other, and he'd—hell and damn, Burr Travis would make that waitress feel the very same way he'd made Rae-Ellen feel! And not give a damn!

He was making her swear. Mama hated it. Adah never said anything stronger than "darn," but any girl would swear about this! That Burr Travis should dare to treat a southern girl, one who'd been to the finest private schools, and an heiress of a huge tobacco company, like a waitress!

Her fury almost cooled as she thought of Lance. To be fair, Lance was the underlying cause. She'd thrown herself at him; she'd pleaded for marriage or for loving outside marriage, and he'd turned her down. Had gone so far as to say he'd marry Adah if she'd have him!

Well, she'd certainly proved that Lance wasn't the only man on earth! She'd also learned what it means to be a woman, learned how wonderful love-making with Lance could be, in the future.

She thought back on how it had been with Burr Travis. He'd been rough, but gentle too, he really had. He'd been extremely fierce. But he had been, at times, almost sweet. If he could forget about dyed redheads, he might change. If he changed, and if he loved a girl—

But that was preposterous! Burr Travis was incapable of love. The only thing he could feel was lust —lust or rape. That was his speed.

No, she thought, newly angered, there was more! He knew how to teach sex. She had the proof of that in her loins, which were beginning to throb again. She jammed her foot on the gas. She'd have no more encounters with him, no matter how much magnetism he had. Not magnetism—he was only male—and a despised one at that. Still, at least she'd learned enough to handle the next man *she* would carefully select.

Not ready to face her family at lunch, she drove into the parking lot of a roadside place, as she'd imagined Burr doing. It was new, all chrome and glass. There were no waitresses. Boys in white were behind the counter; boys instead of waitresses.

Rae-Ellen ate slowly, not tasting her meal, seething. She'd wanted to study some of those waitresses, to examine their features, their movements, to appreciate their attributes, if they had any. And there were no waitresses! She wished she could blame Burr for that.

The waiters she gave scarcely a glance. They were all slim and so young. Not one approached Burr in age or in size.

She sipped her coffee. The food tasted like cardboard. And she was hungry; her stomach cried out for beaten biscuit. Her body cried out for Lance, for the explosion of delight she had this morning experienced, for the joy of that explosion cradled in Lance's arms, his lips on hers.

She recalled how she'd bitten Burr's tongue. She hoped she'd made it bleed, even a little. She hadn't tasted blood, but he'd had her in such a state she couldn't have tasted anything.

She left money on the table and returned to her car. She raced home. She was now outwardly calm; being with Mama and Adah should calm her entirely. She wasn't going to let what Burr Travis had done ruin anything; life was going on in spite of him. In fact, because of him her life was going to march forward, right into the arms of Lance Buford!

Papa wasn't at home. Norma said he'd left right after lunch. The mistress and Miss Adah were up in Miss Adah's rooms.

Rae-Ellen ran up the stairs. She could hear Mama and Adah murmuring and laughing. Their voices, as always, were controlled, gentle and happy. Rae-Ellen felt a wisp of peacefulness come into herself, just listening to the soothing sound of them.

Smiling for their benefit, for she was far from a smiling mood, she knocked at the door of Adah's bedroom. "It's me!" she sang out. "Wow—what's going on?"

Adah's room was golden, a golden room for a golden girl. The carpet was pale yellow, the spread and drapes were gold and yellow, the furniture was white with graceful turned legs, the chairs covered with dark gold brocade.

Garments were strewn over every available space—the bed, chairs, sofa, doorknobs, open closet door, which filled one wall and all of it, from a warm woolen coat to the frothiest bikini panties, was some shade of gold.

Mama—Marguerite, the girls called her when they wanted to tease—stood in the middle of the room, watching Adah model a shimmering, glittering evening gown made of golden sequins.

Marguerite, at the age of forty-two, was an inch taller than Rae-Ellen, thus her auburn hair was an inch above Rae-Ellen's auburn-touched hair when she embraced her. Her powder blue eyes were filled with love as she glanced from one daughter to the other.

She was wearing a powder blue dress which showed her figure to be as slim and firm as that of either girl.

"You really look like our sister today!" Rae-Ellen told her. "Papa'd better watch or some other tycoon will spot you!"

Mama laughed. "Don't be silly! You goose!" she protested, and Rae-Ellen noted how cultured her tone was compared to that of Burr Travis. That . . . creep! To think of him in Mama's presence was beyond betrayal.

Her face went hot. Here, with Mama and Adah she burned with shame over what had happened. She burned even hotter when she remembered the way she'd responded to him. And the way she'd tried to rape him! Here, in this golden room, seeing through into the matching boudoir, she felt dirtied. And was filled anew with rage at Burr, with resentment toward Lance—then still hotter anger at Burr for causing this mess!

"I've finally done it, sister dear!" Adah exclaimed. "How do you like this gown? I thought it was a little daring . . . the sequins . . ."

"The style is modest enough," Mama soothed. "And the sequins just daring enough." She smiled at Rae-Ellen. "You still have no comment, darling, about the gold? That she's actually done it?"

"That's what it is!" Rae-Ellen said, suddenly coming back to the present. "Adah, you've decided to wear only shades of gold!"

"It's my favorite color, you should know, sister dear."

"Don't I know, haven't I heard, all these years?"

"And Lance says it's my color," Adah murmured happily.

Rae-Ellen winced inwardly.

"What are you doing with your old things?"

Adah had a large wardrobe, both girls did, and strewn about were enough new things to fill all the hanging space and all the drawers.

"Norma," Adah said. "She's to have first choice. Six outfits. The rest she'll take to the Thrift Shop, and the money goes to the orphanage."

"What did Papa say to this? Or does he know?"

"He knows," Mama said, smiling. "Adah dragged him up here before lunch. He took one glance and backed out, muttering about two spoiled brats, and said he'd see the things as she wears them."

"But he agreed, at the table," Adah declared, "that gold and yellow are my colors! I told him he brought it on himself, calling me his golden girl!"

"Adah said something, too," Mama offered. She turned her face, the patrician features as delicate as they'd always been, to Rae-Ellen.

Rae-Ellen waited. A shiver went down her spine. Burr! It might be something about Burr! But how could it be? Mama and Adah had been shopping all morning. They couldn't know that she'd even met that Texas bum!

"Darling, where is your curiosity?" Mama chided.

"I'm waiting to hear," Rae-Ellen said. She had to be careful with these two. They sensed things; it was as if they had antennae which picked facts out of the air.

"Adah suggested to your father that, since she's now the golden girl, you should buy a new wardrobe also. Everything you want."

"I have everything I want, Mama! I don't wear half—"

"But not all blue!" Adah interrupted. "Don't

you see? With those eyes and that hair, you should wear shades and shades of blue, nothing but blue! I'll be the golden girl, and you'll be the blue girl!"

Blue, in another sense, Rae-Ellen thought. Then she shrugged. They had no suspicions, thank goodness.

"I decline," she said, making her tone light. "I like to wear the colors of the rainbow. If you've got to have a title for me, Adah, call me Rainbow Girl! I refuse the other, absolutely! For you, the gold is right; for me, I'll stick to my usual helter-skelter ways!"

Mama laughed, drew both girls to her, gave them a hug. "I'm going to look through my own wardrobe," she announced. "I have some things for Norma to take. Have fun, you two."

She was gone, closing the door.

"I suppose you want help," Rae-Ellen said.

"Well, the closet has to be emptied, the things folded, and the new put away."

"Where's Norma?"

"She's taken the station wagon with the first load."

"You've got more than one load of old clothes?"

"No. She loaded on some chairs Mama sent, and just one box of dresses. It'll take another trip."

"Where's Charles . . . why isn't he driving?"

"He's gone to the dentist."

They began to take clothes from hangers, to fold them and lay them in neat piles on the carpet. Rae-Ellen watched Adah. Adah, who had called on the trainer at his cottage. Adah, who frequently visited Lance at Twelve Oaks.

She looked so innocent, her golden eyes so limpid and devoid of worldly knowledge, her lips so gentle, that Rae-Ellen often wondered if her sister were as naive as she appeared.

She wondered if Lance had ever kissed her, if he'd held her in his arms. If he'd—if they'd verged on doing what she and Burr Travis did this morning. If *that* was the reason Lance planned to marry Adah, out of honor.

Suddenly a deep disturbance over the whole day—Papa's ultimatum, Lance's rejection, sex with the Texan, the absolute rape and all the feelings she'd had about it—overwhelmed her.

Surely, when her own world was in such dark turmoil, there couldn't truly exist a golden world, like the one in these rooms. It was a sham, it had to be!

Rae-Ellen stood clutching a shortie nightgown of pale yellow cobweb gauze, crushing it in her hands. She wheeled on Adah, who was placidly folding a dress.

"Don't you do it!" she cried. "Don't do it, hear?"

Adah almost dropped the dress. Her lips fell apart, and her eyes stared. It was as if Rae-Ellen had struck her.

"Don't do what?" she asked, bewildered. "What is it, sister darling? You don't want me to be called the golden girl, you object to that? If I'd known, I'd never have—without discussing it!"

Rae-Ellen resisted the impulse to take Adah into her arms. To cover the impulse which, under the circumstances, would be madness, she gestured sharply, then wadded the gown into a ball and hurled it on top of the frothy things on the bed.

"It's not that, you golden fool! It's Lance!"

"Lance?" Adah's eyes grew wide.

"Don't you dare marry him, hear?"

"He hasn't asked me to," Adah breathed. Tears shimmered in her eyes. "And I don't think he w-will."

"If he does ask, and you say yes, I'll tell him, and he'll never take you, understand? He'll reject you with every cell of his body! Oh, he'd be gentle, but he'd turn you down, and you'd only be humiliated by the gentleness of his refusal!"

Adah, stricken, seemed as innocent as before. Only she wasn't that innocent, couldn't be. And Rae-Ellen knew it beyond question.

She heard herself cry, "I'm warning you! I know what his rejection is like, what it was with me!"

"With you, sister darling?"

"He turned me down! This morning! I threw myself at him; I offered everything! Without marriage, even, and still he said no!"

"Rae-Ellen!"

"And don't you dare say anything!"

"I won't! I promise!"

Adah tried to put her arms around Rae-Ellen, who whirled away. No, indeed, Adah wasn't the complete innocent! She'd known that for years. Adah was devious, and now she was covering up all the secrets she held in her seemingly sweet, gentle mind. She was hiding facts she'd hidden for years.

"Don't!" she cried as Adah tried again to hold her. "The truth holds us apart!"

"I don't know what you mean, sister dear."

"I mean that night when Mama and Papa told you the secret!" Adah just stood, appalled. "They didn't tell *me!* I was born Pettigrew, and you were only adopted! Yet I wasn't entrusted with the family skeleton!"

"It was because they didn't want to hurt you!"

"I heard! I eavesdropped! I know it all, and I haven't told anyone, until this moment!"

"Sister dear, you wouldn't—"

"But I did! I listened then, when I was seventeen and wild about Lance, and I hoped— Anyway, I found out! You don't believe me? Well, this is what I heard. . . ."

6

Raymond Pettigrew, on his twenty-ninth birthday, was a handsome, woman-crazy rake. He quieted considerably at the age of thirty, when he married Marguerite Devine, the most beautiful debutante in the state.

Wild as he was over beautiful women, he was equally wild over his inherited tobacco realm, all phases of it, from planting and growing, through curing, aging and the final step, the manufacture of cigarettes. He'd gradually eased off girl-chasing even before marriage and put his time and attention on tobacco.

His hair was blond, and it crested in one big wave that drove the girls crazy. His sideburns, too, which he wore long, halfway to his jawline, they loved. He never so much as cuddled a girl but she'd have a finger stroking up and down those sideburns, telling him by that action, and others more overt, that she was available.

All but Marguerite. When he tried to get her slim beauty into his arms, she resisted. Once, when he tried, she let him put one arm around her in the roadster he was then driving and slip a hand in the vicinity of her breast, then slapped him.

He was enthralled. The slap, added to her exquisite beauty, her gleaming auburn hair, her clear blue eyes, her pearly skin, her gentle nature, was the final challenge. She was every inch a lady. He not only determined that he would marry her, but fell so deeply in love that he didn't stray from their marriage bed once in the first two years, not even when she was first swollen with Rae-Ellen.

He saw beauties at parties, saw them around his office and moving along the streets of Durham. He saw them working as maids in his mansion, Magnolia Hall. But he resisted, contained the impulse to smile back when one of the girls gave him an intimate look, an inviting, slow gaze. He resisted because he loved Marguerite to his depths and she loved him. With her, he had everything, including variety, for she'd learned fast and become as adept as he at lovemaking.

The last six weeks of her pregnancy he was in torture. Doctor Cline, whom she saw every two weeks, banned lovemaking for three months; six weeks before the birth and the six weeks to follow.

The first night of abstinence, they lay in bed, not touching. Though he'd made love to her the previous night, long and tenderly, and with tremendous satisfaction, he now yearned for her as he hadn't since their wedding night.

Only, on the wedding night, she'd been waiting. Their love had been fed. They'd made love, off and on, all night.

This was different; it was damn different. There she was, not six inches from him, and he dared not so much as touch her hand, because if he did, he'd go out of control.

As if she'd been right inside his mind, she turned to him. His arms opened, and she was pressed to him as closely as her big stomach would permit. He'd been ready before she touched him, and with a groan he entered and was immediately floating on the waves of delight that she, and only she, could provide. He was moving deep in and far out, deep in again, lingering, floating, that rage of joy filling him as only love with her had ever done, and she was moving with him, was gasping softly as he moaned.

Afterward they lay very still.

"I'm a beast," he murmured.

"No! You're my husband, you give me joy! Oh, Ray, it didn't hurt me, I'm the same! It didn't hurt the baby! If we're careful—"

He placed a finger over her sweet, urgent lips.

"From this moment," he said, "we follow doctor's orders. We'll make up for it later. After we have our son."

He prevented repetition of this night by moving into one of the guest rooms. Marguerite wept, but he was adamant.

"You've never gone without!" she sobbed.

"How do you know that?"

"Your—reputation. All the g-girls said you had a d-different woman every week!"

This hit so near the mark that he almost flinched.

"And you believed them?" he demanded. Anything to keep her from following him to bed.

"Y-yes."

"And married me, not knowing whether I'd give up my wild life!"

"I t-thought our love would be enough!"

He'd almost taken her then. Because her love was enough. But he'd resisted, no matter how she lured and appealed. The safety of his unborn son was more important than his wants.

The nights and weeks dragged past. This was the first time he'd practiced celibacy since he was fifteen. He'd kept celibate while he dated Marguerite, but there'd been first the belief and then the surety that they'd marry. That whole period had lasted less than a month; he'd made it a whirlwind courtship because he couldn't wait.

This, now, was already infinitely longer. And indescribably worse because he was deprived of the greatest joy in love he'd ever known. He set his jaw, remembered the son to be born, admonished himself that he could wait.

His eye roved. Wherever he looked, it seemed, he found enticement. Logic told him this was from deprivation, but his aching manhood assured him that it was a need.

He began to notice the pretty quadroon downstairs maid. She was more than pretty. She was a tan-colored, graceful beauty in black uniform with a neat white apron and headpiece.

Her eyes were big and brown, with dark,

winged brows. Her hair was brown, cut short and covered her head with soft ringlets. She was deliciously curved and, though she walked sedately, her perfect little behind had a seductive swing.

The more he thought about her, the more he wanted her. She didn't belong in this job. With her beauty and grace she should be on the stage, in the movies.

Or in a love nest, under the protection of a reliable man.

He was deliberately late starting for the office one morning. He came into the library to get his briefcase, and she was bent over from the waist, rubbing the leather books on the bottom shelf.

He stared at her perfect legs in black silk stockings, the seams faultlessly straight. He fidgeted, cleared his throat.

She came erect, turned. Her big eyes widened, bemused. Her rounded features were soft and dimpled. Her deeply red lips quivered into a smile.

"I beg your pardon, sir," she said. "I thought you'd left, and came in to tidy up."

"That's all right, Delphine. That is your name?"

"Yes, sir. Delphine Dupree. I've been here less than six weeks, sir. I'm to dust the books ev'ry two weeks, Mr. Andrews, the butler said. I did them last week, sir. This week I rub the spines so they'll shine. Next week—"

He gestured, smiling, hoping the bulge in his trousers wouldn't grow. Being face to face with her like this was similar to his first meeting with Marguerite.

"I'm sure you'll keep my books spotless," he said, and smiled. "How old are you, Delphine?"

"Eighteen, sir. Closer to nineteen. But I've

worked in other houses. I know how to clean, and answer the door when Mr. Andrews isn't—"

"Have you a beau, Delphine?"

"No, sir. My daddy, he said I shouldn't have a beau until I'm nineteen."

"Your daddy . . . what's his work?"

"He was one of your extra gardeners, sir. Before he died. That was a year ago."

And she was still obeying her daddy's wishes. She still didn't have a beau. And it had been six weeks—Marguerite was overdue—since he'd moved into that damned, lonely bedroom, six weeks of the torture of sitting across the table from Marguerite, wanting her, longing for her.

"Do you serve the mistress, Delphine?"

"Oh, no, sir! Marie won't let anybody do for the mistress but herself! She just barely let me inside to be introduced, after Mr. Andrews hired me!"

Raymond grinned. Marie, white and competent, ordered the black servants to call her by her given name but became warlike if they tried to do anything for Marguerite. She regarded the mistress as her holy charge, especially now that she was pregnant.

"And the mistress, she stays upstairs," Delphine added. "I hardy see her, sir."

Marguerite stayed upstairs because he begged her to. Gently as the stairway curved, as big as Marguerite had grown, the least misstep could result in a fall. To humor him, she spent days in her rooms, coming down in the evenings only, and then on his arm.

"I'll see you again, Delphine," he said. "That is, if—" He broke off, then plunged. "If you'd care to see me again. As a man, not an employer."

There was admiration lurking in her eyes, yes, there was. Now they grew surprised and very wide. She lifted her rounded chin, met his gaze and, in the softest, most musical tone replied, "Yes, sir. I'd like to see you again. As a man."

He wasted no time. His damnable, hurting need drove him. That morning he rented a cottage on the outskirts of Durham. It was nicely furnished, and he'd give her money to get whatever she thought would make it more attractive.

It took maneuvering, and it took a fib to Marguerite—that he had a business meeting—but he got Delphine into his car and sped for the cottage.

He unlocked the front door, flipped on the light and stood back, permitting her to enter first. The tiny sitting room was furnished in oak, and she moved across it, looking at everything.

"Will it do?" he asked.

She turned, eyes shining. Her lips trembled. "It's beautiful. Whose is it, sir?"

"It's yours, Delphine."

She was wearing a thin white dress. She looked like a bride. Her eyes were shining. She also looked like a dusky angel. His heart began to throb, along with his loins.

"You're not . . . frightened?" he asked.

"Some, sir. My daddy—"

"He was a good man, and he was right. But he's not here to protect you now, and I am, Delphine."

"P-protect, sir?"

"Surely you know how, in the old days, back in New Orleans—"

"Yes, sir. It was in my family. One of my ancestors was chosen by a white gentleman at a quadroon ball. He got her a house on the Ramparts, and he freed all four of their children. He took care of her for life."

"That's what I'll do, Delphine. Take care of you for life."

And he would. When this awful time of waiting for Marguerite ended, he'd settle enough money on Delphine that she'd never have to work again. She'd benefit from it. Marguerite would never know, consequently would not be hurt. But he'd be rid of this hunger which he could no longer endure.

Delphine gazed at him. "I'm . . . my mother, it was her ancestor lived on the Ramparts. Those children married black, and so did their children, and on, until you couldn't tell there was a drop of white in my mother. My daddy . . . he was mostly white."

"You're beautiful," Raymond said. "They must have been proud of you."

"My mother died when I was born. Daddy, he raised me. He taught me to be proud of my blood, and of that long-ago quadroon lady on the Ramparts."

He could hardly stand still. He wanted to take her into his arms, to kiss her, to—

"Sir," she half-whispered, a pulse beating in her throat. It was like seeing velvet throb. "Sir, this is all so . . . may I speak?"

He nodded, his fingers curled into fists to keep from grabbing her.

"I . . . it's come down in my family that I'm like that quadroon lady, because my mother was like her except for color, and I'm like my mother. She . . . that first quadroon . . . loved her protector and he loved her. And I . . ." The pulse in her throat leapt.

"I saw you the first day I came to work in your house, sir. And . . . it was the same with me." Her chin firmed. "Otherwise, I wouldn't be here with you now."

He didn't wait. He swept her off her feet and into his arms, put his lips on hers, took her kisses. She tasted like honey. Her lips clung softly, giving him back kiss for kiss, and all the while he was stumbling as fast as he could to a bedroom.

He stood her down and swiftly undressed her. The dress fastened down the front, and he had it off in no time. She wore a slip, bra, panties, and these he stripped away, with her help.

When he saw her nude, he sucked in his breath. She wasn't tall, and didn't weigh much over a hundred pounds. Her breasts were high and firm; the nipples stood erect. They were tan, and the area around them was tan, melting into the velvet tan of her body.

Her waist was tiny; he spanned it with his two hands. Her shapely bottom was dimpled. Her upper legs curved maddeningly, cradling the brown, soft place of her womanhood, then flowed, exquisitely from knees to perfect ankles and narrow feet.

He couldn't take time to kiss her again. He tore off his clothes, ripping seams, but he didn't give a damn. By the time he was naked, she was on the bed, arms open.

She was a virgin. It took two hard thrusts to enter. She gasped as he plunged into her hot, moist, tight depths, and then she murmured in her throat, and her hands came to his hair, and after that her arms held him.

He wasn't the least considerate of her, couldn't be. His yearning was such that he had to assuage it, and it made no difference whether she moved or whether she lay quiet. But she stirred; she moved. She met him, seeking thrust for seeking thrust. And all the while she gasped, made a purring sound in her throat, and at the end, when he flooded her with his passion, she called out his name.

"Ray" she moaned. "Ray . . . oh, my love!"

It was so natural, he wasn't the least surprised. "My little love, my beautiful love," he whispered, his body still in hers. And like that, in that moment, he fell in love with Delphine Dupree.

Later, when he was in his office, when he thought of her, he couldn't reconcile the feeling. His feeling for Marguerite hadn't changed. She was his wife, his partner, his dearly beloved. She was the mother of his child-to-be, and for this he worshiped her.

His love for Delphine was consuming and he was ever on the edge of starvation for her. Because Marguerite was forbidden, was now protected, he took his fill of Delphine. She had quit her job, and at his request awaited him in her little cottage, as her ancestress had awaited her protector. And every time he made love to Delphine, his love for her grew, and he was in quite a dilemma, loving two women.

He couldn't measure the loves against each other, couldn't compare them. They were different and equal. He'd never give up Marguerite for Delphine, even if the girl were white. Nor would he, in truth he could not, give up Delphine because of Marguerite.

With one heartbeat he knew he was betraying his wife. With the next, he knew when Marguerite recovered, he would betray Delphine with her.

This was worse than when he'd been free. Then,

he could play the field. Now, he was, in effect, married to two women, caught for life.

At last Marguerite was rushed to the hospital. Raymond, pacing the corridor, face sheet-white, knew that she was having a difficult labor.

"I won't hide the truth, Ray," Doctor Cline said to him at one point. "She's . . . we may have to operate to save either your wife or the baby."

"Operate, then!" he said. "Don't waste time!"

They waited two more agonizing hours, and then they wheeled Marguerite into the operating room. When they wheeled her out, they'd taken from her a perfect baby girl.

They let him see Marguerite for five minutes. Five useless minutes. She was still asleep from the ether; she looked like she was dead. Even her lips were white.

The doctor urged him out of the room, down the corridor to chairs, sat with him. "She's going to be all right, Ray," he said. "But when the surgeons got inside—the baby was fine—but everything else was messed up. It was one of those freak tricks of nature. We had to perform a hysterectomy. She'll never have another child. She'll never be able to conceive."

"I don't care about that," Raymond said.

He did care, of course. He told Delphine he cared. Delphine tried to comfort him with her love and, while he was in her arms, she succeeded.

When she was well again, Marguerite named the baby. "I'd like to call her Rae for you, darling," she said. "And Ellen for my mother, in honor of her memory. How does Rae-Ellen sound to you?"

He considered. "I like it," he said.

"If she'd been a boy, she would have been

Raymond, Junior. Darling, I know you're devastated. I know you wanted an heir, and now—"

"You're alive, the baby's alive. Nothing else matters."

"No, darling. You can't fool me. You expected a son. You need a son to carry on Pettigrew's. And there is a way."

"Adoption's out."

"See, you do feel strongly about it! Divorce is what I have in mind. It's the only answer. If you divorce me, you can marry a healthy girl and—"

His reply was to make love to her, greedy love, for the first time in over three months. He groaned, at the end, felt the strong clasp of her legs, and knew he'd never marry any other woman.

She tried again to discuss his nonexistent heir.

"Hush, darling," he murmured against her lips. "Everything will be fine. Rae-Ellen will grow up, and she's bound to give us a grandson. I'm satisfied and happy. All the trouble is behind us!"

Only it wasn't behind them. Loving both women, he delighted in his wife nightly and continued with Delphine by day. Both loves, when he let himself dwell on the subject, grew deeper as the months went by.

And then the afternoon came when Delphine greeted him with her news. "I'm pregnant," she said simply. "If you like, you can send me away. New Orleans, maybe."

He stared at her. At first he couldn't speak. Then he croaked, "To have the baby, and— You don't mean to put it up for adoption?"

"Ray, darling! I'm going to keep my baby! If you don't . . . I can get work! I can support myself and one little baby!"

"You sweet, lovely fool!" he grated, sweeping her to him, trailing kisses along her cheek. It was salty now, and he held her as she wept, murmuring comfort and assurance. "You'll stay in this house. I'll come to both you and the baby. We're a family, Delphine! How could you think it could be any other way?"

But it was another way. Delphine died giving birth to her child, a small, lovely girl with tawny-gold hair and yellow eyes.

Dazed, bereft, Raymond made private funeral arrangements. Then, taking Doctor Cline into his confidence, he got possession of the baby and went straight to Magnolia Hall.

Marguerite was in the living room when he entered. He'd walked past the butler, into the room and closed the door. Marguerite, who had come running to him, stopped in the center of the room when she saw the bundle in his arms.

She gazed at it, then up at him.

"This is my child, Marguerite," he said bluntly. "Delphine Dupree—do you remember her, the downstairs maid?"

"Yes, I remember. She was a good girl. Sweet."

"Delphine was the mother. She . . . died. Our baby daughter, hers and mine, has no place to go."

"So you brought her here. To me."

As in a dream, Marguerite held out her arms. He put the baby on them. She folded back the blanket, looked at the blonde hair, the faintly olive skin, the tiny hands.

Raymond waited.

"What is it you want me to do with her, Raymond?"

"It'll be your decision. Maybe you want to divorce me. Be rid of us both."

She sank onto a sofa, holding the child. Even her voice had a dreamlike quality. "Not that, Ray. Never that. Tell me how it happened."

He sat on the edge of the sofa beside her. Gazing at her white face, he told her how he'd first been attracted to Delphine, how he'd established her in the cottage, even how he'd grown to love her.

"But you love me, Ray."

"More than ever."

"And you loved her, too."

"I can't understand it. Or explain. To love two women equally but differently is a contradiction. But it happened."

"You want to keep this baby."

"I—God help me, yes!"

"Delphine was quadroon."

"Yes."

"Then this baby is octoroon. She's blonde enough. She has straight hair. She . . . looks something like you. Her features are yours. We could say she's the orphan of a distant Pettigrew cousin. We could make it work."

"You'd do that? After what I've done to you?"

"I married you knowing your past," she said with quiet courage. "I knew that someday, in our marriage, there'd be another woman or even women. I married you accepting that, knowing it could be a problem, hoping I could hold you in spite of anything!"

He was trembling with hope. She saw the tremble.

"It's not that I'm a forgiving angel," she went on. "You've only done what I realized you might

102

do. But the thing I didn't expect was that you'd
. . . fall in love."

"But not out of love with you, Marguerite."

She put her finger on his lips, glanced at the
sleeping infant. "I'll make a bargain with you. You
honor business bargains. I'd expect you to honor
this."

"Name your terms, my dearest."

"I'm willing for us to adopt this baby. We can
truthfully say she's a Pettigrew orphan. We can raise
her with Rae-Ellen, even follow southern custom
and use part of the elder daughter's name in the
younger daughter's name. Adah. That's a name I
considered for Rae-Ellen. It's a pretty name, and
she's a pretty baby. Adah-Ellen Pettigrew, she can
be."

"Anything, I'll do anything!"

"It's very simple and shouldn't be impossible.
I've thought many times about a bargain in the event
you . . . weren't faithful. I'll agree to the adoption,
even come to love the child, if you agree never to
take another regular mistress. Notice I say regular.
I know you can't be held to a hard-and-fast rule.
Except this one, that you never consort with another
woman more than once or twice, that you never
again put yourself in danger of falling in love."

In the moment, years later, when Raymond Pettigrew finished telling Adah of her blood and of
the bargain, which he had kept, silence closed over
the room. Adah turned to the woman she called
Mama, and the woman held out her arms. The girl
went into them, sobbing.

"You ran a terrible risk! I m-might have turned
b-black, or had kinky hair!"

"It was most unlikely," her father said. "You

have less than an eighth of the blood. You're as white as any girl. You must never tell anyone. We've told you because we think it's your right to know."

"I can never marry! My children—"

"Will be less than one-sixteenth mixed, and their children less than one thirty-second."

Adah faced Papa. "But you wouldn't want my son to be your heir?"

"No, sweetheart. Your sons will have position and wealth and power. But the line of inheritance must be undiluted."

Now, today, this moment, standing in the midst of Adah's new, golden garments, Rae-Ellen flung out her hands violently. "So you see! I know all of it, the whole scandal! Why didn't they tell me? Do they love you more than they love me?"

"It's that you're impulsive, sister darling! They thought they were right!"

"You're in love with Lance!" Rae-Ellen accused.

Adah blushed, a dull red showing under her olive skin. "I've loved him forever," she said simply. "If he asks me to marry him . . . I . . . oh, Rae-Ellen!"

Rae-Ellen fled to her own rooms. There she locked the doors, paced. Papa's drive boiled in her, making her mad with impulse to rush to Lance and tell him all. But the drive was tempered—and for that she blamed Mama—by a sense of fairness. It was, after all, Adah's secret. She threw herself onto her bed and wept stormily, feeling that there were two people inside her. She felt that she was at war with herself, in a battle she could never win.

7

She stayed in her rooms the rest of the day and all evening, not even going down to dinner. Mama came to her door, worried, and Rae-Ellen cracked it open and assured her that she merely had a headache, wanted no food, had taken aspirin, would be fine in the morning. She'd sleep late, skip breakfast, have brunch later. Mama, after promising to make sure no one disturbed Rae-Ellen, departed.

Safe from disturbance, she wandered from bedroom to sitting room. She threw herself into an armchair. Sometimes she wept; other times she stared out the window, forbidding herself even to think.

When it was late enough, she went to bed. Here the floodgates broke and she wept convulsively. Occasionally as the night wore on, she fell into an exhausted doze. Then she started awake and cried some more.

In this manner, time did pass.

Daylight came, filled itself with sun.

Unexpectedly, as she lay still weeping, shame enveloped her. She gulped, crushed back a sob. She hiccuped, sobbed again, cut it off.

She jumped up, driven by a new resolve, ran to her bathroom, turned on the ice water spigot and bathed her eyes and face. Slowly and carefully and long she bathed them. When she'd finished, only a trace of the weeping showed, and this she dealt with at her dressing table.

Now. The face that looked back at her from the mirror appeared normal. She tried to smile, couldn't quite make it. A sob quivered through her, but she held it back and worked on the anger she had begun to feel at herself.

She'd acted the fool. She'd been a perfect ninny. Well, it was going to stop. She went to her bedside telephone and dialed Mary-Lou's home in nearby Raleigh, managed to keep even a hint of quaver out of her voice as they spoke.

"Can you meet me at Wolverton's for lunch?" she asked when Mary-Lou took the call. Wolverton's was a rustic diner halfway between Durham and Raleigh; she and Mary-Lou had met there before when they had reason for privacy.

The little redhead at the other end of the line didn't hesitate. "Sure thing! Half an hour! Something big?"

"Very big," Rae-Ellen replied, whispering lest Adah, coming for reconciliation as was her nature, accidentally hear.

"See you!" Mary-Lou whispered, and hung up.

Rae-Ellen lingered an instant, frowning into the mirror. She adjusted her black skirt and short-sleeved white T-shirt. As an afterthought she added a black-and-white paisley scarf.

As she started downstairs, Marie, carrying a tray, began to climb. The tray would be for Adah; she'd probably been upset after their set-to yesterday and didn't want to face anyone at the table.

Marie started to speak as they neared each other, but Rae-Ellen put a finger to her lips.

"Now what you up to?" hissed the housekeeper as sternly as she had when Rae-Ellen was a small, mischievous girl. "Why are you sneaking out in the middle of the day?"

"I'm just meeting Mary-Lou for lunch," Rae-Ellen whispered. "We want to be alone, so I'm not advertising it, and I'd appreciate it if you'd—"

"I won't tell Adah!" Marie snapped. She stopped in the middle of a step so that Rae-Ellen couldn't get past her. "You be careful," she warned. "You're up to something! Every time you get that blaze in those eyes—and that Buncombe girl's a wild one!"

"She's just full of spirit!"

"And mischief! Well, you going to let me past before Adah's lunch gets cold?"

Rae-Ellen sighed. There was no beating Marie. Especially if you had reason for secrecy. She let Marie go up the stairs. She herself ran the rest of the way down.

This time she kept to the speed limit. The quickest way to Mary-Lou was to avoid getting a ticket. She drove right at fifty-five, impatiently watched familiar buildings, trees, farmhouses, flow past. At last, ahead, was Wolverton's.

The restaurant was a long building of dressed

logs. It was set back from the highway in a grove of live oak; the parking area was large and so laid out that almost everyone could park under a tree.

She stopped in an open space, got out and hurried for the entrance. She couldn't see Mary-Lou's Mercedes; either she'd parked in the rear or hadn't arrived yet.

Inside, the walls were of vertical split logs, highly polished. The booths had looped brown drapes, which could be pulled together, making each booth into a tiny chamber. The tables and benches were also of split logs. The windows were covered with brown drapes, which glowed richly from the amber lights. Gleaming copper pans hung on the walls.

The place was quiet, the only sounds were the murmur of customers as they lunched. The waitresses, all of them blonde, wore dark-beige uniforms. They moved silently and did their serving without so much as a clink of china.

Rae-Ellen went to a booth at the far end where the drapes were closed. That would be Mary-Lou, who adored the clandestine feeling of a closed booth.

Before she reached it, a fiery head appeared from between the drapes, and Mary-Lou beckoned excitedly. Rae-Ellen slid onto her bench, and her friend carefully drew the curtains closed.

"Now!" she exclaimed. "Snug as lovers! And see!" She indicated the array of food. "I ordered. Only cheeseburgers and fries and coffee. I didn't think you'd want anything you'd have to put your mind on. This way, we can get right to whatever it is!"

Rae-Ellen nodded, took a sip of her coffee.

"Come on!" Mary-Lou urged. "What *is* it? Don't tell me that Rae-Ellen Pettigrew is so upset—" She broke off, her hazel eyes stopped dancing. "You *are* upset . . . it's really serious, isn't it?"

"The worst thing I've ever come up against in my life," Rae-Ellen said. "I've even been crying. I went through a real tear-storm before I called you."

"But why, darlin'? What brought it on?"

"Adah—"

"You never cry! What did Adah do?"

"She—" Rae-Ellen broke off. Adah had done nothing. Except love Lance Buford. It had been Papa and Delphine who'd done the mischief. She couldn't tell Mary-Lou about that. And she'd not tell Lance. No matter what happened. Even knowing that Papa would let Adah marry him.

But the rest, the part which belonged to herself, she could tell.

Carefully, to avoid any slip about Adah, she half-whispered an account of the scene she'd had with Papa yesterday morning. She related his virtual demand for a grandson, and Mary-Lou was indignant on hearing it.

"Then—I should have listened to you," Rae-Ellen said fiercely.

The dark red brows lifted. The Cupid's bow lips were closed, the hazel eyes, quiet. Waiting. At last, unable to endure the suspense, Mary-Lou breathed, "*What* should you have listened to me about? Don't keep me on pins and needles!"

"To begin with, I should never have let myself get to the age of twenty a virgin!"

"Whatever made you decide that?"

Rae-Ellen scarcely heard the question and plunged on. "If I'd learned about men the way you, and most other girls have, I wouldn't have made a f-fool of myself!" She struck away a tear, stared half-defiantly into Mary-Lou's bewildered face, and continued. "If I'd found out how men really are, and now I'm convinced that the only place you can do that is in bed, the things that happened to me yesterday would never have occurred! And this minute I'd be in control, the way you are, not all mixed-up and in a mess that I've got to get myself out of!"

"Rae-Ellen! Are you *pregnant*?"

"Of course not. At least, I don't think so."

"You've been to bed at last? You finally decided to get with it?"

"It's not like that! If you'll hush, I'll tell you the whole problem!"

"Go ahead, darlin'. I'm hushed."

Speaking low, halting at times, Rae-Ellen related her troubles. She told Mary-Lou she'd been in love with Lance Buford for years, and Mary-Lou nodded. Rae-Ellen was amazed that her love for Lance was no surprise to her friend, but made no comment. She went on, described how she'd gone to him.

"I threw myself at him," she confessed. "I begged for marriage, and I begged for sex."

"What did he do?"

"Being unprepared and being a gentleman, he turned me down."

"You told him you love him?"

"Naturally."

"Mistake number one, when you offered yourself to him, darlin'. You never offer yourself. You tempt . . . lure. Mistake number two, when you said you loved him. You get a man to bed, *after* you drive him crazy first, and then you allow *him* to talk about love!"

Crestfallen, Rae-Ellen admitted that Lance was in love with Adah.

"He just thinks so! Give him time, and he'll switch to you, darlin'. If you handle him right!"

He will turn to me, Rae-Ellen thought, spurred by Mary-Lou, oh, he just will! Now that she knew what a man-woman relationship meant, now that she knew the mechanics, even the feeling, she'd win Lance! Now that she understood not only with her mind, but with her body, what sparked love, she had a tool.

"Do you think he's been to bed with Adah?" Mary-Lou asked.

"No. She's the perfect lady."

But devious.

Mary-Lou, so excited she was ready to bounce, urged Rae-Ellen on. "The *bed* part! Tell that! Who was it?"

She told about going to Burr's cottage, about their quarrel, the rape. The double rape.

Mary-Lou's eyes were wide. "Wow! That's some man! And you, proper Rae-Ellen, actually attackin' . . . why, darlin', that's stupendous! Tell me, how was it, with him?"

"It was what you'd call wild."

"Oh, wow! That's what I thought the minute I saw him! He didn't give me the time of day!"

"I certainly don't want him!" Rae-Ellen flared.

"He'll be back for more. From the picture I get of you two, from just seein' what a hunk of man he is, I'll bet money he'll be right after you!"

"No, he won't. He thinks Adah is far superior, told me so."

"It'll do him no good! Not with your appeal!"

They were silent for a bit.

"Wow," Mary-Lou said again. "Wonders always do happen! You get the tall Texan and you want Lance . . . not that I blame you. What can I do to help?"

Haltingly, Rae-Ellen confided her wish to use what she'd learned from Burr to win Lance. "Only I don't know how," she confessed.

Mary-Lou became thoughtful.

"Just one time in bed's not enough," she said at last. "Not even two or three times. And not with just one man. You need experience. It gives a woman an aura, an appeal that no untouched girl ever has. You've got to . . ." She fingered her charm bracelet.

"Nothing like that!"

"No, you haven't got the time, either," Mary Lou agreed. "Your Papa gave you a year?"

"The year has nothing to do with it! I don't care if he disinherits me! He'd not accept Lance because of the cotton and he knows a son of ours could never go into tobacco! That doesn't matter! All I want is Lance!"

"And if he thinks he's in love with Adah, you've got to get concentrated experience! I know . . . Jim Reed!"

"What about Jim?"

He had been Mary-Lou's Old Faithful since their teens. Mary-Lou was always telling what good friends they were, what perfectly attuned lovers.

Once, Rae-Ellen had asked why, this being the case, they didn't make it legal.

"You serious?" the little redhead had laughed. "Jim will never work. He's a jet setter!"

"He's got millions. Why should he work?"

"I want a husband who has serious work, darlin'!" Mary-Lou had cried, amazed that Rae-Ellen hadn't understood. "That makes a solid marriage. The husband with work, and the wife raisin' the children!"

"You want a dedicated man. Like Fawn or Pete."

"Yes, on that order."

"Why don't you date them?"

"Because! They see only you and Adah! And I wouldn't poach!"

Rae-Ellen made a moue and shrugged.

"Lance is solid," she said. "He has the cotton."

"He's perfect. But first you've got to get him. Before Adah does. And don't think I'm bein' untrue to Adah! You're my real friend; she's my best friend's little sister!"

Rae-Ellen managed a grateful smile.

"Now," Mary-Lou continued, "about Jim. He's so good in bed he can teach you things your cowpoke didn't have time for and maybe doesn't even know."

Rae-Ellen swallowed. She liked Jim. He was personable, with brown hair and green, laughing eyes. He maintained his summer tan in winter with sunlamps and trips to sun-filled lands. And she'd known him forever.

But to plan and plot with Mary-Lou to go to bed with him to gain experience was another matter. She frowned. Yet, her heartbeat stepped up. Maybe from the one time with the Texas bum and once with Jim, and with coaching from Mary-Lou, she could learn what she had to learn in one more lesson only.

"Once with Jim won't do it!" Mary-Lou declared. "I can read your mind, just like that! I'm tellin' you! Okay. One thing at a time, all right? There's the dinner your folks are giving tomorrow night—Jim and I are invited."

Rae-Ellen recalled the dinner with a start. So much had happened, it had slipped her mind.

"I can't ask Jim to go upstairs with me," she half-teased.

"Of course not, silly! But on the way over, I'll work on him. I'll tell him you've got the hots for him—"

"Mary-Lou!"

"That's what they call it, honey! And Jim . . . I'm a little surprised he hasn't . . . maybe he has, and you've been so proper—anyhow. That's what I'll tell him. He'll take it from there. You might get by with just him; he's been with so many women, he knows all the things they like. A crash course with Jim is more valuable than to skip from one man to another!"

"But even if I did this, how could it work? If I learn these intimate things, learn them fast, how do I apply them with Lance?"

"Learn all about Jim. Watch how seductive those green eyes are when he looks at you. Notice how he puts one fingertip on your arm and, just barely touching your skin, makes tingles go all over you! He taught me how to do that to him, and I've used it on men. It never fails! But it takes practice, and that you get with Jim. He'll give you a rush, you bein' new to him and in a seductive—mind, I say you bein' in a seductive mood. You can practice leadin' a man on who's used to bein' led on and loves it! He never gets bored with that!"

"What other things are there?" Rae-Ellen asked. In spite of herself, she was becoming interested. She could see how right Mary-Lou was, and understood that she could repeat sex with Burr Travis a thousand times and never learn to seduce Lance.

"Well, there's not so very much else, darlin'."

"But Lance will see what I'm up to!" she cried. "If I begin to run my fingers along his arm—because I told him, because I threw myself at him! It won't work!"

"It's your only chance, honey. And he's a man with a man's . . . just be honest about it, with a man's desires . . . and if you take on that aura and learn nuances . . ."

"That's it," Rae-Ellen said eagerly. "Nuances. They're the only thing that'll work with Lance!" She was trembling, she was so eager to learn from Jim, so anxious to take on the aura of seduction, to learn the skills she must acquire to pull Lance from Adah to herself.

She felt a twinge of pity for Adah. This was swept away by impatience. Adah didn't deserve him because she'd take him if she could get him, in spite of her blood.

She grew sick with love for Lance. Maybe it wasn't too soon to make another move. Tomorrow night, say. If only she could manage to use the ploys of which Mary-Lou had spoken to capture his interest! Now that she knew the mechanics of sex, knew one of the things Jim did, even though he hadn't done it to her, she could use it to at least tempt Lance.

She'd tempted Travis, in a way. Her wild anger had stirred his passion, even though she hadn't meant it to. But anger would never work with Lance.

Mary-Lou was right. Lance required quiet allure, a sweet manner. Hidden seduction. All these were qualities Adah had, whether they were in-born or she'd acquired them from her wealthy, cultured southern background. If Lance married Adah and never learned of her blood but did learn that her gentleness was veneer, that underneath she was devious and scheming, what then? He'd be hurt, deeply hurt.

Rae-Ellen realized that she was looking for excuses to downgrade Adah. But the girl *was* secretive, no getting around that. She'd kept the truth of her blood all these years, had deceived Lance about it, was still deceiving him. She did nothing else wrong, Rae-Ellen had to admit that, but the fact that she'd never told even Rae-Ellen, her half-sister, the truth, indicated that she actually was devious and underhanded.

"What are you thinkin' about now?" Mary-Lou demanded.

"That I'll try your way," Rae-Ellen said. "I'll watch Jim with you tomorrow night. Then, if he asks me for a date, I'll accept. And whatever he does on the date I'll accept."

"Don't give in too fast," Mary-Lou warned. "Don't be a roundheels! Don't give in before the third date, and then make it seem like you're a bit reluctant, that he's winnin' you over your better judgment! That's what Jim'll expect."

"Understood."

The third date! It was going to take longer than she wanted. But it was worth the time if she came out of it with Lance Buford's ring on her finger!

enough that maybe Lance would take a second look at her.

Since it was fall, the women were to wear evening gowns, the men dark suits. Just last month the men had dressed in white, but now the darker look was in order.

Finally she found a white dress she'd never worn. She'd bought it last month because it appealed to her, and now, as she looked at it and fingered the sheer, soft crepe overskirt through which white satin gleamed, she thought it looked something like a bride's gown.

That settled it. She'd make herself look as bridelike as possible without being blatant. Let Adah shine like pale winter sun or glitter like rich summer sun, Rae-Ellen Pettigrew would subtly draw glances whether the thought "bride" went through any mind or not.

She tossed aside her terry cloth bathrobe, put on the white lace bra and bikini panties she'd bought when she bought the dress. She fastened on a new style, low-slung garter belt, smoothed on wafer-thin silver nylons and, for glitter, three-inch-heeled silver sandals entirely composed of narrow straps. The high heels gave her a statuesque presence.

She slid the dress on over her head. It was close-fitting in the bodice, with soft folds crisscrossing and outlining her breasts, and it nipped in at the waist, then fell in swirling sheerness and satin gleam, to her ankles. Narrow, draped straps crossed each shoulder, almost an illusion. The gown was so cleverly designed that no line was marred by zipper, button, or hook.

She brushed her hair back so that it waved and turned up at the ends. The white of the dress brought out the red streaks underlying the brown.

She used a bit of powder. Her only ornament was a pair of diamond earrings, a debut gift from Papa and Mama, each stud being a full carat of perfectly cut gemstone, catching the light and flashing. The effect of her costume pleased her. So simply was the gown designed that as she studied herself, she detected an impression of nakedness.

Nakedness and beauty. She'd never looked better. If she couldn't be a beauty like Adah, at least she could be stunning.

Just in case, because the evenings were cool, she went to her smaller closet and, from a tissue-lined box, lifted the ermine stole Papa and Mama had given her last Christmas. This she put around her shoulders to see the effect, which was perfect, but she preferred the bare look when she removed it and laid it on her bed, ready to use should some of them decide to go nightclubbing.

Should Jim Reed ask her for a late date.

She started for the hallway, ready for anything.

A tap came on the door which connected her suite with Adah's.

"Come in," she called. She knew Adah wanted reconciliation. And, even though they were rivals for Lance, she didn't want to be her sister's enemy.

"You still angry?" Adah quavered, shutting the door.

She was wearing the sequin dress. It, too, was formfitting at the bodice and beyond, covering every inch of Adah's body. She wore no jewel at all. The sequins were enough.

"I'm still aware of the situation between us, if that's what you mean," Rae-Ellen replied. "But my affection for you is still—It's changed, but it's there."

"Me, too!" breathed Adah. She stood hesitant,

and Rae-Ellen knew she wanted to embrace, but she wasn't ready for that.

"How does my dress look?" Adah asked timidly, her dimples not showing. "I've never worn anything so—"

"Daring," Rae-Ellen supplied.

She studied Adah. Her spirits fell. She was used to the other girl's quiet, glowing beauty; she hadn't known she could be dazzling.

This girl was a glittering, flashing torch; even her golden eyes flashed. Her arms glittered, for the ankle-length gown had long, tight sleeves which came to a point at the wrist. She wore rosy lipstick with a gold overcast, and her tawny hair was upswept and came into a soft roll atop her head. The sequins brought out the gold in that straight, beautiful hair as nothing had ever done.

"I suppose I should warn you," she heard herself say.

Beneath the glitter lay the shy, gentle Adah; the one that looked out through her eyes. Or was it deviousness, the habit of keeping the family secret?

"About what, Rae-Ellen, dear?"

"Burr Travis. The beauty of you in that dress."

"You're beautiful tonight, darling."

Rae-Ellen dismissed that with a gesture. "The horse trainer. He means to date you. He's—animal."

Adah looked stunned.

"Why should he want to date me? I've never—"

"Just watch out for him," Rae-Ellen said.

Even as she spoke, she wondered why she was alerting her sister to Burr Travis. She didn't care that he'd made a point of how much a lady Adah was. If he did make a play for her sister, and if Adah responded, that would give Rae-Ellen a clear field with Lance.

And she knew how she'd use it.

Now Adah rushed over and hugged her. Instinctively, she hugged back. They stood, arms still around each other.

"I love you so much," Adah murmured. "You're the most wonderful sister a girl ever had. Even if Lance—marries you—I'll still love you, darling!"

Rae-Ellen almost succumbed to the years of being sisters. Then her inborn drive surged, held back only by her tortured sense of fairness. She could not assure Adah of her own undying love. But she did keep herself from crying out that, if Adah did win Lance, Rae-Ellen could never feel affection for her again.

She might not hate her. But she couldn't love her.

Adah understood without words. She turned away forlornly. "I just hope Burr Travis . . . I don't want a retinue of suitors. I don't want to hurt anyone."

She didn't say what she'd do about Burr. Her attitude of reluctance indicated nothing definite. Maybe she was secretly pleased, even thrilled, over Burr's possible interest. She could play one man against the other, Burr against Lance, to get a proposal of marriage from Lance.

Mystery, Rae-Ellen thought impatiently. Adah always had to be wrapped in mystery.

A rap sounded at the door and Marie opened it, looking stockier than usual, as she always did when she was displeased. Her coarse, usually kind features were scowling.

"They're downstairs, waiting for you," she said crossly. "If you'd of let me help the two of you dress —you're worse than when you was little! I knew I should of, but you chased me off, told me to help your Mama, that you wanted to be alone."

Adah put her arms around the housekeeper. "We've been talking, that's why we're late," she soothed. "We're going down right now."

Rae-Ellen made a little face at Marie, then smiled. "We're big girls now," she said, but her tone was mild and she almost winked.

"Doubt if you'll ever be a big girl, Rae-Ellen Pettigrew! Impulse! That's you! Now scoot, both of you!"

The sisters exchanged smiles, then walked together down the broad staircase. Voices and laughter and the clink of glass came to them from the living room, subdued at first, subtly louder as they descended.

They'd reached the bottom step when a tall, sharp-featured young man came into the hallway, glass in hand. His eyes, blue-green in color, were intense; his features were as intense as his eyes.

"Finally!" he exclaimed, voice taut. At the moment it was also a trifle sharp. "You've kept us waiting, kept all of us waiting, but I admit it's worthwhile. This time. You're visions, the pair of you."

His eyes lingered, piercing, on Rae-Ellen.

"I heard that, Fawn Morehead!" cried Mary-Lou, popping into the hallway with Jim Reed. "I've got on a dress as red as my hair, and you never said a word!" She laughed, glancing at Jim. "Jim thinks I'm terrific, anyway!"

"You are," murmured both young men.

Fawn set his glass on a table, offered an arm to

each sister. Rae-Ellen rested her fingers lightly on the fine midnight-blue coat, and glanced up at him.

He was handsome, sharp-featured or not. Just twenty-eight, and first vice-president of Pettigrew's Tobacco Manufacturing Company, he'd be a catch for any girl. His hair was black and straight as an Indian's, combed into a shining cap that showed off the fine shape of his head. His lips, whether sober or smiling, were as intense as his expression.

Intense—that was the word for him.

She felt a wisp of regret. Actually, she admired him. He'd make a personable, even admirable husband, he really would. But she loved Lance, and you don't take a whip to your heart and tell it where to go.

The others came chatting and laughing, on their way to the dining room. Pete Battle, thirty-one, and second vice-president of Pettigrew's, in charge of planting, harvesting, drying, and aging the tobacco, walked beside Papa, talking seriously.

Pete was very blond. He looked like a beachboy, with an open, smiling face and blue eyes which seemed faded from looking into the sun. He wore a dark brown tweed suit and so did Papa.

Pete was undoubtedly talking tobacco. Otherwise, he would be smiling and joking. Now he spied Adah, excused himself from Papa and hurried across the marble floor.

"Adah, you're something from another planet!" he called in a sunny voice. "Out of my way, Fawn! I claim Adah as my dinner partner!"

Adah, always Adah. But then Pete dated Adah on a more or less regular basis, even as Rae-Ellen dated Fawn. Always in a foursome or six when Mary-

Lou and Jim drove over. Rae-Ellen believed, from things Papa had let drop, that he wouldn't be averse to a wedding between Pete and Adah.

She managed to disengage herself from Fawn and join Mary-Lou and Jim. She held out her hand, smiling, and he took it with both of his.

She met his eyes, giving him a deliberately lingering, half-teasing look. His green eyes teased back. Under cover of banter about her gown, which he declared was shocking, he pressed the tip of his forefinger into the center of her palm.

Her face burned. Mary-Lou had actually told him that she, Rae-Ellen, had the hots for him! For, long ago, Mary-Lou had informed her that the hidden gesture Jim had made meant that he wanted to take her to bed.

Her heart began to thud. She'd told herself she was ready. But to have him turn on so fast—Still, the time was short.

In the midst of this Lance arrived.

Right behind him was Burr Travis.

At first Rae-Ellen thought the hallway was spinning. Then she realized she was dizzy. She could see Lance only in a blur.

But Burr Travis, she saw full and clear. Big, wearing the very latest thing in a dark suit, looking as she'd never have believed he'd look—arrogantly presentable, his eyes took her in boldly, seeing the nakedness.

She didn't speak to him, didn't acknowledge him.

Heart knocking, flesh burning, she moved to Lance, got to him before Adah escaped Pete. She held out her hand, put what she hoped was a very gentle smile on her lips.

"Lance," she murmured, "it's so good of you to come."

"Where else would I be?" he countered, and smiled. "The Pettigrew sisters—" he looked across at Adah, who smiled at him, "—are the beauties of the world tonight."

"That's right," agreed a Texas drawl, and Burr Travis was right there, interfering with her moment with Lance. "Ain't you going to welcome me?" he demanded baldly, those damnable brown eyes steady. "After all, your own Ma invited me!"

The others saved her, all the others. They swept her, in the center of the laughing, friendly, cultured group, into the dining room. Then, since it was an informal, intimate dinner, Mama was telling everyone where to sit.

And she put the unspeakable Burr Travis right across the table from Rae-Ellen. Where, every time she looked up, she'd see that homely face, those shining eyes!

Why, she wanted to scream at Mama, why did you have to ask this man to our dinner? Why did you ruin the intimacy of our evening?

In her outrage, she even forgot Lance.

9

They were ten at the table; the senior Pettigrews, Rae-Ellen and Adah; Mary-Lou and Jim; Fawn Morehead and Pete Battle; Lance Buford and the unspeakable Texan.

Jim gazed at Rae-Ellen, and this made her uneasy. She saw admiration in Lance's eyes and in Pete's for both herself and Adah.

Mama and Papa were really working at throwing Rae-Ellen at Fawn Morehead and Adah at Pete Battle. That would be just perfect: their daughters married to the first and second vice-presidents of the company.

This aggravated Rae-Ellen, though she was used to it. Fawn and Pete were always underfoot. If they weren't working madly at their jobs, they were at

Magnolia Hall, it seemed. She wondered if it had ever occurred to her parents that if she and Adah saw the chosen candidates less frequently, they might be more interested in them.

But, inviting Burr Travis to the family table, was the outrage. To have a raw Texan, a cattle rustler sitting across from her was more than she could stand!

Now he was talking. He didn't even have the decency to keep his mouth shut. What's more, he was talking to Papa about the fox hunt, was discussing it with Fawn, even.

She stabbed a look at him. From his manner, which was assured to the point of arrogance, it was unbelievable that he'd done the things to her he'd done. That he'd tricked her, at the time, into thinking she liked them.

Well, maybe she had liked them. While they were happening. But they weren't happening now, and she saw more clearly than before that he'd raped her, brutally and roughly.

And made you like it, that far, honest mind, taunted.

It had been the shock, nothing more. She'd work him out of her system. She'd wash what he'd done out of herself with other men. With Jim Reed. She'd accomplish two things at once, rid herself of Burr Travis, and learn how to deal with Lance.

Boiling, she saw how well the young men—Fawn, Pete, Lance, Burr, and Jim—got along. No matter what they talked about, fox-hunting, hounds, hunters, race horses, cotton, and tobacco, all were interested and contributed ideas and opinions in a lively manner.

"I've a suggestion," Pete said finally. "If any of you are free tomorrow."

They fell silent, waited.

"It struck me, Travis," Pete said, "that you being from cattle country, might like a tour of Pettigrew's. We could take you to see the fields, the drying sheds, the factory, everything."

"Spendid idea!" Fawn exclaimed.

Raymond Pettigrew nodded. "Can you spare the time, Travis?"

"The groom and stableboy can look after things," Burr replied. "If that meets with your approval, sir."

Pettigrew smiled. "Smith's a dependable groom, has been for five years. And Williams has been with us almost a year. I see no reason for you not to go."

That Texas bum! Rae-Ellen thought. She pierced another look at him. Did he have ideas of his own? Did he have the gall to think he could choose between the Pettigrew sisters and march the one he picked to the altar? Talk about fortune hunters!

She stopped listening. She was so furious at his scheme that it wasn't until Lance, at the far end of the table, spoke her name, that anything registered.

"Rae-Ellen," he was saying, laughing. "Wake up! Burr and Pete and Adah and I are going. How about you?"

"I don't—" she began, then changed. "Yes," she said, "I'll go."

The outing held possibilities. Pete would be leading the tour, pointing things out, explaining them to Burr. Rae-Ellen would try to stay with Lance. The cowpoke, with his notion of wedding bells, would try to get better acquainted with Adah. Which meant that Rae-Ellen could put into practice on Lance a

128

policy of Adah-like gentleness, Mary-Lou come-on, and whatever allure she could drum up before she had a lesson from Jim.

In preparation for this, she turned to Fawn for practice, glad now that Mama had seated him next to her. Blandishments were so foreign to her driving, forthright nature, that she needed to try them on a willing victim before she tackled Lance again.

Fawn responded beautifully. She glowed.

When dinner ended and they were moving toward the living room, she saw Lance and Adah slip out the front door. Adah had her blond mink stole around her shoulders. Rae-Ellen gasped, lips closed. What were they up to?

Common sense helped her to overcome the trembling that started. Lance would never slip away from a gathering without making his excuses; if he meant to take Adah for a drive, he'd say so. They'd probably just gone outside for a breath of air.

The others began to set up card tables. She didn't want to play. When Papa approached her, ready to insist, she forestalled him.

"I want to see you," she said urgently. "In the library. It won't take but a minute. They won't even miss us."

Indeed everybody was so occupied with tables and laying out cards and score pads and pencils, that none glanced toward them. Papa nodded, and they went to the library.

Rae-Ellen closed the door.

"Papa, I want you to fire that bum!" she cried.

"What bum?"

"You know what bum! You know I don't call Fawn and Pete bums!"

"You're speaking of Burr Travis?"

"You've got to, Papa, simply got to!"

"Why? Give me one good reason."

"I hate him, hate the ground he walks on! He's rough and arrogant and cruel!"

"There's no cruelty in the man. A little arrogance is an asset. You've nothing valid against him."

She clenched her fists, dug her nails into the flesh. If only he knew! But he couldn't know, now or ever. She had to convince him, and she had no grounds.

"You see, daughter. Must we have another fight? First it was—"

"I know what it was! You don't have to remind me!"

"Now it's the Texan."

"I don't like his looks! I don't like his ways!"

"You'll get used to his ways. He's the best trainer we'll ever get. And he's a real man, which is essential to being tops in anything. We're keeping him."

Her father turned and left without another word.

Rae-Ellen closed the door hard, paced. She was not going to have the Texan around, she just was not! He'd be a constant reminder; he'd get in the way of what she had to accomplish with Lance.

Unless—but that was unlikely. He was too animal for her sister. Adah would never consider him; she'd not even play one man against the other. She was too much in love with Lance. Adah was the type, if she couldn't get the man she loved, to live and die an old maid.

She considered. Then she buzzed the kitchen. When Andrews appeared, she sent him for Fawn Morehead.

In two minutes, Fawn was there. The look on his face was so keen that she almost wished she hadn't sent for him.

"I hope I didn't take you from the card table," she said.

"Your parents and Mary-Lou and Jim are playing contract," he told her. "Pete and Travis are at a game of backgammon. Pretty big stakes. I'm not in the mood for either game, not with you free."

"Please sit," she invited, and sank into a chair.

He took the one nearest it. "What's on your mind, beautiful girl?"

"It's that horse trainer," she blurted. "I can't stand the sight of him. I want him fired, gone! And Papa won't fire him!"

"That's not like you, Rae-Ellen. I've never known you to take a dislike to anyone, to be so . . . well, ruthless isn't quite the word. What has Travis done?"

She had to bite the tip of her tongue to keep from crying out what Burr Travis had done.

"No answer? Besides, Rae-Ellen, I have no jurisdiction over what trainer your father does or does not hire."

"But you have influence with Papa! He respects your opinion. If you'd just remark to him that the Texan doesn't seem right, it'd set him to thinking."

He shook his head. "Why don't you ask Travis to leave?"

Pride wouldn't let her tell him she'd done that and got nowhere.

"No," she said.

"You and Adah together, then."

"Adah knows nothing of my feeling."

"Get her to agree with you. She always does,

whatever it is, and the two of you approach your father. He's a hard man, once he's made up his mind, but with both of you asking, you may get what you want."

"Not this time. Fawn . . . please reconsider."

"I have to beg off. Your father's respect for me and my opinion lies within the confines of Pettigrew's, what is good for the company or what is bad for the company. A horse trainer has nothing to do with tobacco."

She pushed aside her disappointment.

"I don't resent your refusal, Fawn," she said.

And she didn't. Fawn was tobacco. She could respect that.

"It might put you higher in his esteem if I told him what I asked of you," she said, and smiled. "It would show how dedicated you are."

He smiled back. "Please don't." He seemed about to say more, even to want to put his arms around her. Then, as if having second thoughts, he suggested, "Shall we join the others?"

The first thing she noticed was that Lance and Adah were still gone. The next thing that happened was Mama insisting that she and Fawn share a bridge table with Pete and the Texan.

"And play contract!" Mama ordered charmingly. "When Lance and Adah get back we'll do something else. Maybe turn on the stereo and dance."

So Lance had made his excuses. He and Adah had gone for a drive.

Gritting her teeth, Rae-Ellen sat opposite Burr. Fawn sat opposite Pete. The deal went to Burr; his hands were so big the cards seemed to be invisible. Her rage at having to play with him was overshadowed by a feeling of desolation. She was even a little sick at the stomach.

Where were Lance and Adah? What were they doing?

Why didn't they come back?

10

At this moment, while those at Magnolia Hall sat playing bridge, Adah and Lance were seated in the end booth. It was the same booth Rae-Ellen and Mary-Lou had occupied yesterday. The curtains were drawn, and they were close together, on the same bench.

The mugs of coffee before them were getting cold.

Still, neither of them had spoken.

At last Adah murmured, "What is it, Lance? You asked me if I'd come for a drive, and here we are. You haven't said a word. Are you angry with me?"

She wondered, forlornly, if Rae-Ellen had made good her threat about telling the family secret. She rejected the thought. Rae-Ellen had a temper; Rae-

134

Ellen was impulsive, but she hadn't done that, never would.

"The reason I haven't spoken," Lance replied in his gentle fashion, "is there's so much to say I don't know where to begin."

"Just begin, Lance. It's only me; it's only Adah."

"You must know how I feel about you," he said softly, eyes gray as rain. He dared not go too fast, not with shy Adah, who held her thoughts to her heart.

He waited, saw the golden eyes widen, saw what he prayed was understanding in them.

She replied in a whisper, "I hope . . . about what you feel for me. I know when I was a little girl, you loved me then. But that was a long time ago. Things are different now."

She could feel her pulse throbbing in her throat, her heart hot and fast under the sequined dress. She let her eyes speak love. And now she was the one who waited.

"Tonight, Adah, I saw Burr Travis look at you. I watched Pete Battle; he couldn't look at anything but you. Even Jim Reed. And I knew they were seeing what I saw, not a young, pretty girl, but a dazzling woman. They all wanted you. I dare not wait another week, another hour. I have to speak now, before one of them—" He paused, studied her deeply. "You know what I'm trying to say, don't you? I love you, have always loved you, until now— Am I wrong, Adah love? Wrong to hope that you love me?"

"You're not wrong, Lance." Her voice shook but this was Lance; he'd understand. It was all right that her voice was unsteady, that her hands in her lap were trembling. He'd know that this was the most important moment of her life.

"Say it, Adah love! Let me hear the words!"

"I've loved you since I was a little girl, Lance. It's been awful! First I was too young, and then—I thought I was deceiving myself, that you considered me a child, that you'd never think of me in any other way!"

"Then you'll marry me?"

He reached for her trembling hands, clasped in her lap, and held them, still clasped, in his own.

Her whole body was shaking as he drew her into his arms. He held her, put his lips on hers, and they kissed. She took his caresses thirstily, lips now firm, now shaking, growing firm again under the pressure of his.

His hand came to her breast, fingers pressing. Her heart burned; this was what she'd been created for, to rest in this man's arms, to receive his caresses, to learn with him the ways of love.

Now he was holding her so that her breasts rested against him. One arm circled her; the other was wandering, caressing her back and her legs, slowly coming nearer and nearer to that tingling spot between her thighs. Helpless, Adah snuggled closer.

As if her move had awakened him, he pushed her away. He captured both her hands.

"You didn't give me an answer, darling," he said.

"An answer?" she quavered. "What answer is there except what . . . we just did?"

"I need the words, my sweet. I need to hear you say you'll marry me. Next week. Tomorrow."

She almost cried out, oh, yes . . . yes!

And then she remembered the secret.

Oh, dear God, the blood!

It seemed to stop in her veins, then surge in painful waves. Mama and Papa had said never to tell anyone about it, that there was no risk.

But how could she marry Lance and keep the blood secret? Some other man, yes. Pete Battle, for instance. She'd double-dated him occasionally. But once, when they were alone, he'd begged her to marry him. He'd even held her as Lance had done a moment ago, and she'd felt warm, and if she'd felt even a bit of affection for him, she might have married him and kept her lips closed.

But there'd always been Lance. Always the hope that, miraculously, he would want her. She had never let herself think of the blood when she yearned for Lance. But now she had to think of it.

"You're troubled," he murmured.

He could feel it in her trembling hands, sense it with every breath she drew. He knew her moods; he knew there was mystery in her, but attributed it to her inborn, gentle shyness. Only now there was more.

Drawing her close, holding back all passion, he thought he divined her problem. She must suspect how Rae-Ellen felt about him. And she was not a girl to take that for which her sister yearned.

"If you're reluctant to marry right now," he asked, "can't we be engaged?"

Miserable, she shook her head. It wasn't because she might lose him that she hesitated to tell him about the blood. It was that knowledge of it would disappoint him, make him unhappy. Perhaps make him reluctant to have children. Mar his life.

"Secretly engaged?" he pressed.

She couldn't say yes, could neither confess nor deceive.

"Need time?" he whispered.

She nodded. She needed time to think about whether or not to tell him. Whether to hurt him with the truth or to protect, yet at the same time betray by withholding the truth.

"Semi-engaged?" he urged. "Engaged to be engaged?"

She couldn't resist. She had to agree to that much or burst into tears and confide the whole problem. So she whispered, "Yes," and he kissed her again and she kissed him, fully.

Her tears got into their kisses, and they both tasted salt.

It was while Adah and Lance were kissing that Jim Reed, as the others continued to play cards, cornered Rae-Ellen and suggested they go for a drive. Startled, reluctant for him to come on so fast, she held back.

"We can't do that, Jim," she protested. "You're Mary-Lou's date! I won't leave with you!"

"She doesn't know I'm alive," he retorted. "Look at her with Travis!"

Rae-Ellen glanced across the room. Mary-Lou was chattering and laughing, hanging on to Burr Travis' arm with both hands, dragging him to a card table. He was grinning and holding back, but permitting her to win.

He was nothing but a tomcat, Rae-Ellen thought hotly. First he raped her, then he said things which indicated he would like to chase Adah, and now he was letting Mary-Lou lead him around by the nose! She felt no resentment at Mary-Lou, who was only being her natural, flirtatious self. Well, Burr Travis was being natural, too. But in him it was inexcusable.

"You see," Jim said, and smiled at her meaningfully. "Where can we go then, to the library?"

Burr was allowing Mary-Lou to push him into a chair. Apparently he'd been ready to leave, and the redhead objected. He didn't so much as glance toward Rae-Ellen. Instead, he grinned at Mary-Lou, then settled down to the cards.

Adah and Lance still hadn't come back.

"The library will be fine!" Rae-Ellen snapped.

She scooted out of the room and down the hall so fast Jim had to hurry to keep up. "What're you so angry about?" he asked.

She flipped into the library. He closed the door. "Rae-Ellen?"

"Nothing! I'm angry about nothing!"

"You act like you've got the hots for that cowboy character," he said, watching her.

"Don't be ridiculous!" she flashed. "I hardly know the man!"

"Neither does Mary-Lou, but you can see how she's after him." He smiled, untouched by his date's behavior.

"Well, I'm not Mary-Lou! She's only having fun!"

"Hey," Jim said in a seductive tone, "what do we care about them? I had a reason to be alone with you. Give me a chance, beautiful!"

It was so fast. Too fast. But it was here and she'd face it. Her heartbeat, which had been quick from anger, fell into a slow, uneven throb. Even knowing Jim's objective, she felt uneasy.

Discussing it with Mary-Lou had been one thing. Faced with an amorous Jim was another. Well, he couldn't do anything here, in the house.

Smoothly, he rested his fingertips on her upper

arm, just a hint of touch. She felt an instant tingle down her spine. Now he trailed the fingertips along her arm, and the tingle grew. Her breathing got mixed up with her pulse. She was trying to subdue it when he spoke.

"Nude," he said very slowly. "You may as well be nude as in that gown. I've never seen such a beautiful woman, one so enticing, one who gives the most experienced man the feeling he's never met a real woman before."

"You've said that to a lot of girls!" she accused, keeping her tone light.

"I've said similar things, yes. But never exactly this. In reality, you're dressed; also in reality, you're naked. That gown was created to stir a man up."

"Jim, stop it! Do you think Papa would let me wear anything as scandalous as you say this dress is? You're exaggerating!"

He shrugged. "I only know what you do to me." With that same light touch which so affected her, he slid his arm around her. She started to push away, remembered why she'd come here with him, remained unresisting.

He lowered his head until his lips were touching, barely touching, hers. He kissed, moving his lips in that lightly touching manner across hers, back and forth, and even knowing this was an art with him, the tingling was all over her.

No crude Burr Travis here. No slam and bang. Just the delicate titillation, the inward quivering which reached, instinctively, for more.

His lips parted, and the tip of his tongue traced the outline of her lips, leaving a trail of delight. He pressed his tongue tip between her lips, and they parted for him. The tongue came against her teeth, which did not part, and then he kissed her teeth.

She was quivering in his arms.

Handling her delicately, he guided her to the sofa.

"You see?" he asked. "Why hold me off? We're matched. We're perfectly matched. Date me tomorrow night, and the night after that. Every night!"

Don't give in on the first date, Mary-Lou had warned. And here she was, just about ready to do the very thing she shouldn't!

What was wrong with her? What kind of girl was she?

"Date?"

"I . . . don't know." She shook her head.

To plot a course of experience so she could win Lance had been easy. Exciting, even. But to actually go to bed with a jet set playboy, no matter what the provocation from Burr Travis, or the reward of enticing Lance into marriage, made her pause.

Not Jim, her far thoughts said, not Jim. She told him so, honestly. "I can't date you."

"Why not?"

"I'm not . . . liberated enough."

"Mary-Lou—"

"She meant well, but it's no go, Jim."

She'd learned all she ever would from this man. She'd never have sex with him. He belonged to Mary-Lou; he'd belonged to too many other girls. She wanted someone—cleaner.

Jim shrugged. He removed his arm.

"No offense," he said. "The world is full of girls."

"We may as well join the rest," she said, feeling guilty despite his lighthearted air.

He agreed, but before they went, he described a huge birthday bash he'd attended in Paris, spoke of a wild party he'd gone to in Rome, mentioned trips to the Greek islands.

And always he described the girls.

This made her feel less guilty. Jim had his girls. He had Mary-Lou. Soon he'd be flying to London or some distant place; he'd find girls there.

But Rae-Ellen would remember what he'd taught her in a few short moments. She'd remember his fingertips along her skin, the tip of his tongue tracing the outline of her lips, his tongue opening them.

She'd remember how he'd kissed her teeth.

When the time came, she'd use these things—on Lance!

11

She didn't get much sleep that night. When she did fall into a doze, the dreams began. They were filled with men: Lance, Burr, Jim. Burr and Jim were trying to get her into bed; Lance was trying to keep her from getting into his bed. Burr had a big club in his hand. He threatened her with it. Jim kept running his fingers over her lips. Lance pushed her away every time she got near him.

Still tired, she got up before dawn. She dressed in blue slacks and shirt, stole down to the kitchen. Fixing coffee, her motions were quick and angry.

Everything was Burr Travis' fault. Well, Lance's turning her down. That *had* come before she'd laid eyes on the cowboy. But all the rest was his fault.

If she hadn't been raped, she never would have been upset enough to have had the fight with Adah.

She was in the biggest mess of her life. The only mess. Before, there'd been only the yearning for Lance and his saying he was in love with Adah.

Well, she was going to clear up the mess. Last night she'd settled Jim Reed. Today, she'd tackle Burr Travis again, get him out of her life.

She wasn't going to fight with him. She was simply going to say what she'd come to say, behave like a lady, and if he had one iota of decency he'd accept what she said like a Texas gentleman, if such creature existed.

It wasn't quite dawn when she opened the door of his cottage and walked in. She wouldn't knock; if she heard his voice first, she might lose her nerve. Or get so furious she couldn't accomplish what she'd come for.

He was in the kitchen, and he didn't know she was in the cottage until she appeared in the doorway. He was dressed in tan slacks and shirt and he was frying bacon. He looked at her, face still. If he was surprised, he didn't show it.

"Come for breakfast?" he asked. "How do you like your eggs?"

"I didn't come for breakfast."

"Oh?" His tawny eyebrows lifted. Those aggravating eyes sparkled and seemed to dance. If he thought she'd come for a repeat performance . . .

"I'm here as a lady," she informed him, keeping her tone quiet.

"Fine, fine. What can I do for you?"

"I suppose I want to appeal to your better instincts," she continued. "Seeing you at dinner last night, it occurred to me that—"

She broke off. She couldn't go on, couldn't say

the words. They'd choke her. What she wanted was to scratch him, beat him with her fists, physically chase him from Magnolia Hall.

"What occurred to you?"

"You looked—"

"Most men do look more civilized when they're dressed up. I'm glad you were pleased."

"I didn't say that! I didn't come here to say any such insipid—"

"Why did you come?"

"I came to dismiss you."

"I see. To fire me. Again."

"Precisely!"

"I'm sorry, but I refuse to be fired by you. I never, as I told you before, work for women or take orders from them. Only your father has the power to fire me."

"Which he'd do instantly if I told him—if—"

Those eyes held hers. "But you won't tell him. There's your pride."

She glared.

She felt like a bug under his thumb.

He turned the fire off under his bacon, under his bubbling coffee. He wheeled and came right at her.

She darted into the sitting room, got behind an armchair and stood trying to kill him with her eyes. "Don't you touch me, you sex-fiend!" she screamed.

"Lower your voice, or the fellows will hear you at the end of the stable. I'm not making a pass at you. As for that," he continued easily, "I'll have you when and how and if I please. Relax. There'd be no time now, anyway. Fawn and Adah will be here to go on the tobacco tour."

145

She went completely out of control. "You're fired!" she cried, but she kept her voice down. "Fired, fired, fired!"

"Shut that up. Where's your sister? Want her to hear you carry on?"

"She knows the way down here! She'll come on out when she finds me gone!"

"Looks like, being sisters and all, you'd come together," he said, eyes narrowing a bit. "You two having a fight?"

"Why should we have a fight? We're sisters, we've got everything in the world we want!"

Only they both wanted Lance. And Adah and Lance hadn't come in last night until twelve, just as the others were leaving. Rae-Ellen hadn't been able to tell, looking at them, what they'd been talking about. And Adah hadn't come to her room to discuss the evening. Instead, she'd gone to her own suite, and Rae-Ellen hadn't seen her since.

They hadn't got engaged, on that she'd bet a million dollars. Because, if they had, Adah would have told her. Whether her motivation would have been true happiness or masked triumph, she didn't know, but Adah would have told.

That was the only solid thing Rae-Ellen had to hold to at the moment. Adah and Lance were not engaged.

A quiet knock sounded at the outer door.

Burr opened it, and Adah stood there, dressed in a deep gold pants suit, hair caught back with a ribbon.

"Is Rae-Ellen here?" she asked. "I got back so late last night we neglected to make arrangements about this morning."

"Come in, come in!" Burr sang out. He was all

warmth and welcome and diamond-in-the-rough gentleman to Adah. No bellowing at her. This infuriated Rae-Ellen, who knew him for the bum he was. "Your sister's here, just arrived!"

"Thank you, Burr," Adah said softly, and came into the sitting room.

Rae-Ellen moved from behind the armchair, so it wouldn't look as though she'd been using it for protection. Adah ran to her, gave her a hug. "Morning, sister dear," she said.

She endured Adah's kiss, gave her one in return for Burr's benefit.

"It was my impression last night," Burr said, "that Buford was to pick the two of you up at the big house, then come on past here."

"He did say that," Adah agreed. "But when Rae-Ellen was gone—Marie was up when I left. She'll tell Lance to drive on down when he gets there. We're way earlier than he expected."

They ended up eating breakfast with Burr. Rae-Ellen didn't say much, just listened to the two of them, speaking only when her sister demanded a word of agreement or an opinion.

"You don't suppose," Adah asked Burr at one point, her dimples in the smile she gave him, "that we are foolish to want all our racing horses silver gray?"

"Seems fine to me," he replied noncommittally.

"I didn't know whether breeding for color could detract from breeding for stamina and speed," Adah said.

It was the first Rae-Ellen had heard of this from her sister. Had she been brooding about it, as she was prone at times to brood, or had the idea just struck her? With Adah, it was hard to tell.

Nobody, nobody at all, looking at her, so golden and dimpled and lovely, with that straight, dark-blond hair, would dream that she was octoroon. Certainly no such thought was in Burr Travis, who was gazing admiringly at Adah and assuring her that breeding for color would make no difference in the speed of their horses.

His admiration for Adah, for her gentle speech, her quiet manner, was all over him like a coat. Pour a cup of water on him, and he'd melt! His behavior toward Adah grew more gallant by the moment. It was enough to turn a person's stomach.

If Adah had the least hint, she'd be afraid to sit at the same table with him. It was, for this reason, fortunate that she thought herself in love with Lance.

Rae-Ellen set her jaw, glared.

She'd never known a man who was so thoroughly untrustworthy so far as women were concerned. Jim Reed was a playboy, but open. This one sneaked around; he stole his kicks. He hid what was really under that homely, rough-and-ready exterior.

His talk and Adah's blurred as she fumed.

Lance drove up in his station wagon just as Adah, who had insisted on cleaning up after breakfast, stood the last plate in the drainer. Rae-Ellen, not to be outdone in the domestic bit, had cleared the table and dried the silver.

Lance greeted them in his easy manner, said he'd eaten. He suggested they make the tour in his car, and they agreed. Rae-Ellen watched, and he showed no more warmth toward Adah than he did toward her. But he also mentioned nothing about where he and Adah had gone last night.

At Lance's suggestion, Burr rode in the front seat with him so Lance could point out things. The girls rode in the seat behind them, Rae-Ellen seething. Just like two old married couples, men in front, women in back!

After a twenty-minute drive, Lance, who had been following a dirt road through harvested fields, stopped the station wagon where Pete was waiting in his parked car. Pete came smiling to greet them.

He hugged the girls, laughing, but held onto Adah a bit too long. She pulled away, gently. But she didn't look toward Lance. The men shook hands all round, which irritated Rae-Ellen. You'd think they hadn't dined together a few hours ago, hadn't spend a whole evening together.

"I thought we'd start with this field," Pete said. "It's one of the many in which we grow our choice tobacco."

Rae-Ellen saw the Texan turn his gaze slowly about. It was old stuff to her, but she did the same. Actually, she wouldn't mind learning to run the company, but didn't want it strongly enough to argue with Papa and lose because she wasn't a man. As far as eye could reach here, stretched the fertile, now fallow, tobacco plantation. It really was big; its size impressed her. And it was only one Pettigrew stretch; there were scads more.

"Puts me in mind of Texas," Burr said. "Wherever you look, land, and beyond that more land."

On the horizon loomed the foothills.

"You haven't got those in Texas!" Rae-Ellen snapped.

"Nope. Not on the range, we ain't."

"These fields, and the others, are ideal for tobacco," Pete explained. "We cultivate with extra care so that the soil is in proper condition, and we have the right amount of sun and rain."

"I ain't seen growing tobacco," Burr commented. "Cotton, yes, but not tobacco."

"The leaves are wide, and grow from a thick, tough stalk," Pete told him. His open face was serious now, as it always was when he discussed tobacco. "They grow to a length of twelve to forty-two inches and a width of six to fifteen inches."

Burr whistled.

"Yes, indeed. Big leaves," Pete agreed. "The plants themselves are from two to eight feet high. Ours run about seven feet. The seeds are so tiny it's hard to believe, even when you're looking at them."

"That's right, Burr!" Adah exclaimed. "The seeds look exactly like finely ground pepper! The tiniest things you can imagine!"

Burr shook his head, impressed. Then he turned to Pete. "Surely you can't plant that fine a seed directly into the fields."

"Indeed, not," Pete agreed. "Come this way."

He walked across a space of ground, followed by the others. At a section marked by stakes, he came to a halt. "This is a seedbed," he explained. "The seeds are planted in beds like this one early in the spring. We cover them for several weeks with a big sheet of special material. That protects them from heavy rains, late frost, and hot sunlight."

"How long do the young plants stay here?" Burr asked.

He was deeply interested. This irritated Rae-Ellen. She told herself the interest was pretense. All he cared about was horses. And sex.

"Until they're about six inches high, isn't it, Pete?" asked Adah.

"Right. That's when we transplant them to the fields. As they grow, we cut the tops off so the nourishment will go to just a few leaves."

"When do the leaves mature?"

"They begin in July and August. Ours all came off early this year. Harvesting and curing are both finished."

"The fields are a beautiful sight at harvest time," Lance put in. "I'm not a tobacco man, but next to a growing field of cotton, I appreciate a healthy tobacco field."

Rae-Ellen heard this with a small shock. She'd never dreamed that Lance admired tobacco! Well, admire it as a plant or not, he certainly refused to grow it. Cotton was his love.

"The curing, Pete!" Adah urged. "Let's go to the curing barns!"

With the men smiling at her enthusiasm, they piled into the station wagon, Pete getting in front with the men. Lance, following Pete's directions, drove along a series of dirt roads until a row of long brick barns loomed ahead.

They parked at the first one and followed Pete inside. The interior was lined with row after row of empty metal racks. An ugly furnace stood in the center of the barn. Fans were set in the walls. Rae-Ellen watched Burr look around, face serious, eyes questing.

"It doesn't look like much," Pete said, "but the tobacco has to be cured, and this is where it's done. Curring is simply a special drying process by which all tobacco is readied for market. Our method is flue-curing. We put the tobacco leaves on these racks and they're dried by heated air from that oil furnace, blown by the fans. We use gradually increasing temperatures."

"Smoke and odors can't be allowed to reach the leaves," Rae-Ellen put in. She knew all this, even half-liked it. She wasn't going to let Burr Travis think she was ignorant of her own father's operations!

"That's right," Pete said. "We hold the heat at a moderate temperature for thirty to forty hours. This brings the tobacco to a bright yellow color. The heat is then raised to dry the leaves; finally it's raised to the boiling point to dry the thick veins and the stems."

"How long is this process?" Burr asked. He was either truly interested, or he was putting on a good show, Rae-Ellen couldn't tell which.

"Three to five days for the tobacco to be really dry. Then air is let into the barns and the leaves take on moisture and grow soft, pliable. Our flue-curing fixes the natural sugar content of the leaves. That improves the smoking excellence."

"And after the curing," Adah said, smiling at Burr, "comes the aging! You didn't know there was so much the poor tobacco plant has to endure, did you?"

Burr grinned, shook his head. "I'm all ears."

"I've heard this all my life, Pete!" cried Adah. "Let me tell!"

Pete grinned, shrugged. Lance was smiling. Rae-Ellen put a smile on her face, but behind the smile she was gritting her teeth. Trust Adah. Somehow, with her gentleness, her spontaneous enthusiasm, she'd snag the interest of every male!

"The tobacco is packed into huge hogsheads!" Adah related, golden eyes on Burr. "It can stay in the warehouses—Papa has warehouses in Durham —for three years without being harmed. It's *got* to be aged for at least a year. Papa ages it—how long, Pete?"

"On an average of two years. Some of it nearly three," Pete said. "Pettigrew's is never in a hurry. Quality is the word. But we get quantity, too, by buying the best leaf to be had at auction."

Despite her frustration over this outing, which wasn't working out the way she'd hoped, Rae-Ellen recognized anew Pete's love for his work. That was good, and she admired it. But his enthusiasm was keeping them all in a bunch; there was no pairing off. She hadn't had one instant in which to use any wiles on Lance.

Even when they drove to the factory, the men were again in the front seat, the girls in the back. Pete remained at the barns; he said he had to check over the furnace in barn five.

Fawn was waiting for them at the factory. He introduced his foreman, Arnold Beecher, to the Texan. He himself shook hands with Burr. As if he were the visiting head of some Far Eastern country, Rae-Ellen thought, instead of cowpoke-turned-horse-trainer!

Fawn, however, did show Rae-Ellen special attention. His manner was warm. He took her hands in his, told her how pretty she looked, insisted that she walk with him as he conducted the party through the plant. The place was humming with activity, green-uniformed employees working deftly on all sides.

Well, this was better, being with Fawn. It would show Burr Travis, and Lance Buford, too, that a man existed who knew she was alive. Her satisfaction was dashed when she saw Lance fall into step with Adah.

They traversed one factory area after another. The smell of tobacco filled Rae-Ellen. They passed more uniformed workers, intent on their jobs. They watched a continuous flow of big leaves pass by on conveyor belts.

Fawn spoke, explaining the cigarette-making process. "The leaves, as you see, are now damped," he said, stopping so they could watch. "This makes them soft and workable. Observe how the stems are now removed. Over here," he continued, guiding Rae-Ellen, the others following, "the different types of tobacco are mixed in measured proportions. That's how we attain our blend."

After they had viewed this, he led to another section, tended by busy, contented-looking men and women. "Here are the cutting machines," he said. "They chop the tobacco to the needed degree of fineness. After being flavored, the blended tobacco then goes to the cigarette machines."

These machines, which fascinated Rae-Ellen, rolled each cigarette. The party stood for some time, watching the slim white cylinders come rolling out and down the conveyor belt.

"Next, they are packed and put in cartons here," Fawn said, leading to another section. "The cartons, in turn, are packed into shipping cases that hold—"

"Let me guess!" cried Adah. "Though I think I know—they hold ten thousand cigarettes!"

"Correct," said Fawn, and smiled.

"It's all a complicated process," Burr remarked.

"I'd never stopped to consider how many steps—it's remarkable! You make cigars, too?"

"Not any more. Most cigars today are made by machine, like the cigarettes. Pettigrew's used to hand-roll. It cut the efficiency of the plant."

"You don't manufacture smoking tobacco, either?"

"We dropped that, too. The profit lies in cigarettes. We make the finest on the market. And the safest."

By this time Rae-Ellen was ready to scream. She was tired of Fawn's attentions. She'd come along on this tour to be with Lance and to prove to Burr Travis that she wasn't going to avoid *him*.

Presently Burr said he had to get back to Magnolia Hall.

"That stallion is due to be delivered any day," he said, looking right at Rae-Ellen. He moved his eyes to Fawn. "And I've used up enough valuable Pettigrew time now, too much. I need to get back to my work. If it's all right with the rest of you."

They left, Adah insisting that one day Burr must visit the Pettigrew Building. "That's where Papa has his offices," she said. "I think you'll be impressed."

"I'm sure I will be," Burr agreed, and grinned.

Rae-Ellen, unreasonably, wanted to slap the grin off his face.

12

They rode home the way they'd come, men in front, girls in back. Burr sat half-turned, his arm along the back of the seat, so he half-faced them all. This gesture of familiarity aggravated Rae-Ellen.

She heard the others talking about tobacco, from seed to cigarette, and spoke not one word. Then she became aware that they were discussing the expected stallion, Thunder Boy.

"I hope to get early delivery on him and the filly both," she heard Burr say, and began to pay attention. "If we're going to have them in shape to race in Florida, every day's training I can give them here is to their advantage."

"I'm going to work with my Samson's Lad, too," Lance said.

"Won't it be fun," Adah asked, "if we run horses against each other at Gulfstream? Your Samson's Lad against our Thunder Boy? Or our filly, Starstruck?"

Crossly, Rae-Ellen wished she could shake her sister. Why did she always have to play up to Lance? Why did she have to drag up the subject of racing? What did it matter which horse raced against another?

Only it did matter. She didn't want either of their horses in a race against Lance's Samson's Lad. She didn't want to risk beating his horse. Not that he'd take it amiss; he could accept defeat more gracefully than any man she knew. She simply wanted his horse to win. And she wanted their horses to win. But not against each other.

Lance braked at Burr's cottage.

Before they'd more than got out of the car, the short, thin figure of Terry Smith, the groom, came running from the stable.

He waved, shouted, ran faster.

His thin, tanned face was grinning from ear to ear. A lock of streaked brown hair flopped into his eyes. He looked more like a boy than an experienced groom of twenty-one.

"Thunder Boy's here!" he shouted in his thin voice. "He was delivered less than an hour after you drove off!"

"Damn!" swore Burr. "I should have been here!"

"Mr. Pettigrew took delivery, sir. Looked him over. Signed the papers. The guys that delivered him left. Mr. Pettigrew had us rub him down and feed him. He's in his stall, getting used to the stable."

Burr was long-legging it to the stable before

157

Terry got all his words out, cursing under his breath that he'd been off the place. Rae-Ellen ran beside him, Adah matching her step for step.

"Papa wanted you to see the tobacco!" Adah cried. "He was—anxious! Thunder Boy wasn't due—"

Burr just ran, outstripping them. Lance came at a run too, with Terry.

At the stable, they stopped. "The rest of you can come inside, but stand back, away from his manger," Burr ordered. "Terry."

"Yes, sir?"

"He let you handle him?"

"Me'n Ken together. He high-stepped right after he was unloaded, but soon's them delivery fellows left and we got our hands on him, we did manage to rub him down."

Ken Williams, the slightly built, teenage stableboy, came out of the front part of the stable. "He's still nervous," he reported.

In accordance with Burr's orders, the party tiptoed into the front part of the stable, going to the outer wall to be as far as possible from the stallion. He was a big fellow, a perfect shade of silver.

He threw up his great head and tossed it, whinnying sharply. He pawed. He looked at them, threw up his head and whinnied again.

Rae-Ellen held her breath. Her scalp prickled. She wondered if they'd ever be able to race him. She doubted that Burr Travis would be allowed to lay a hand on him, much less train him.

"He's so fierce!" Adah whispered.

"He's a king," Lance agreed. "A handful."

"But Burr can handle him, don't you think so, Lance?" Adah appealed, whispering still.

"I'm sure of it. Watch."

Now Burr and Terry and Ken came into the stable. They stayed well back from the manger. Thunder Boy pawed. He started to toss his head, didn't. Instead he stood like a beautiful silver statue, and looked right at the three handlers, who stood equally still.

"Back up," Burr told them quietly. "Stand against the wall with the others."

When they were in place, he approached Thunder Boy's manger, soft-footing. The stallion watched.

"Thunder . . . Thunder . . ." Burr half-spoke, half-sang. "This is Burr . . . Burr . . . Thunder . . . Thunder . . . fine Boy . . . friends . . ."

Not twitching even his skin, the stallion waited. Burr drew nearer, edged up to the manger, and still Thunder Boy didn't move. His ears were erect, his eyes big and shining. Everything about him showed that he was listening, waiting, ready.

Burr continued his singsong. Thunder Boy dipped his head, grabbed a mouthful of hay, began to chew. He was still watching.

Carefully, murmur-singing, Burr put out his hand and stroked his palm down Thunder Boy's forehead. The stallion paused in mid-chew, then, as Burr stroked again, resumed his chewing. But he was still alert.

Rae-Ellen began to quiver. She didn't like Burr Travis, hated him, but this was something to see. Papa had been told by the stallion's former owner that he was spirited and dangerous, and look at him now!

As she watched, Burr moved away from the manger, out of the stable door and away. Thunder Boy stopped chewing, turned his great head.

Silently Burr appeared at the rear of the stall. Thunder Boy let fly with both back feet, and then he reared, whinnying.

Burr, safe outside the entrance to the stall, resumed his soothing chant. Thunder Boy came down on all four feet, shook his head, snorted, stepped about restlessly. Murmuring, singsonging, Burr went into the stall, laid his palm on Thunder Boy's right hip, patted, never breaking the rhythm of his caressing words.

Miraculously, Thunder Boy quieted. He stood. Burr moved up along his silver length, patting his loins, his back, his withers, his neck, stroking between his ears. Not for a breath did he cease the soothing, murmuring singsong. Now at the front of the animal, he stroked the forehead, face, muzzle. He put his hand on the halter.

And still Thunder Boy stood.

"Cripes!" Ken Williams breathed. "The monster likes Mr. Travis! He let us rub him down, but I can tell you, we had some job doin' it!"

"Right," agreed Terry. "I was glad to get out of that stall!"

Now Burr had a grip on the halter, put his shoulder against Thunder Boy's shoulder, still murmuring.

"He's wonderful!" whispered Adah. "His touch is magic!"

She wouldn't think Burr's touch was magic if she knew what Rae-Ellen knew. Glaring at her sister, she caught Lance looking at her.

"So I don't agree!" she whispered fiercely at Lance.

He smiled. "That's your privilege. I'm inclined

to think he's great. If I buy more racers I'll ask him if there are any more of his kind in Texas!"

Furious, Rae-Ellen itched to slap Adah. If she hadn't drooled over Burr Travis, Lance would never have seen Rae-Ellen glare, and he wouldn't have spoken to her so. She wasn't going to make the impression on him she had to make if he saw nothing but the bad side of her!

Burr kept petting the stallion while Lance and the groom and the stableboy watched admiringly. Adah gazed at Burr and the stallion, fascinated, and this left Rae-Ellen weak with rage. Rage at Adah for being so feminine, rage at Burr for being the low-class bum he was.

It spoiled her pleasure in Thunder Boy.

After everyone had gone to bed that night, she paced her rooms. She couldn't get the chant Burr had made for Thunder Boy, for a stallion, out of her ears. They burned in her, those sounds, and she wondered whether, should he court Adah, he'd make a song for her. Oh, not a horse-chant, but the kind that would make putty of Adah or any girl.

Any girl except Rae-Ellen Pettigrew! He'd never be able to impress her because she had seen him with his mask off. She'd met the real, raw Burr Travis. She knew the animal.

And she knew that the heat in her body was for that animal. If she'd gone out with Jim last night, maybe now she wouldn't have this feeling. No, she thought instantly, Jim was too practiced. Any feeling he might rouse in a girl could never touch that raging fire Burr Travis had lit in her.

Lance could do it.

But Lance she couldn't have. Not yet.

And the hot desire was searing her now, this moment! At least, she thought angrily, I can identify it. I can admit I want a man.

She undressed, went into the shower and turned on the cold spray. She stood for moments, for half an hour. She soaped herself, rinsed. She soaped again, rinsed again. The hotness still tortured.

She put on her terry cloth robe to blot the water, went onto her balcony, which overlooked the swimming pool. It was full, sparkling in the moonlight.

The pool would be colder than the shower and on impulse, she slipped out of the house. She shed her robe on the tiles and dove, silent and naked, into the pool. The icy water took her breath.

She began to swim, that hot urgency driving her. She swam the length of the pool twice, three times, more. She swam until she felt blue with cold, swam until she was so tired she couldn't force her arms to another stroke.

Heavily, she pulled herself out of the water and onto the lip of the pool. Her robe lay on the far side. She was too tired to go after it, but she had to.

She pushed to her feet, walked slowly to the other side, teeth chattering. She was beginning to struggle into the robe when the great, burly figure loomed out of the moonlight.

It was Burr Travis, and he was wearing bathing shorts.

She dropped the robe. He grabbed it and slammed it around her, rudely covering her.

"Your Pa said I could swim when I wanted," he growled.

And then he was gone, striding into the night.

And she was stumbling for the house.

The burning deep within her hadn't gone at all. First sight of that animal, and it was back. She faced it squarely. She desired this male from nowhere. And, she didn't want him at all!

She wanted Lance. Lance, who, in one sweet encounter, could quench this raging desire. Lance, who could wash Burr Travis right out of her.

13

Again she lay awake. Really awake, all night. And naked. Not once did she fall into uneasy sleep and tormenting dreams. The burning she'd tried to quench with icy water kept building.

She tossed, both from the fire in her, and from rage because it existed. She tossed because of hatred for Burr Travis. He was the one who had driven this misery into her, this necessity to rid herself of the hunger.

Hunger. That was it. He had caught her in a weak movement, right after Lance denied her the lovemaking for which she begged. He'd jumped her in a torn, unguarded moment. It was as if she'd been ravenous for food, had been given some, but of the wrong sort and not enough, and now she was starving-wild for more.

She lay and yearned for caresses, Lance's caresses. His touch, his lips, his man's passion. She lay and relived the time with Burr, refusing to dwell on the storm of sensation he'd roused.

She wrestled her mind away from him. Lance. Where had he gone with Adah last night? What had they done? She turned her head from side to side. A moan escaped her. She was so stricken with yearning for Lance, and this got so mixed with her loathing for Burr, that she felt ill.

She was in the same miserable state when dawn touched the sky. She paced her rooms, feeling weak, almost trembling from the wracking emotions she'd suffered all night.

One solid fact emerged. Burr Travis had put this ravenous need into her body. There was but one way to rout it out. The method was bold, it both angered her and made her shrink. It would build his ego beyond imagination. But it would do the job. No matter how repulsed she was, she'd see it through.

A tap sounded at her hall door. It opened and Marie came in with a breakfast tray before Rae-Ellen could cover her nakedness.

The housekeeper clicked her tongue. "Shame! And the nights so cool!"

Flushing, Rae-Ellen belted a robe, tossed back her hair. "You always did jump to conclusions!" she snapped. "How do you know I wasn't just now dressing?"

Marie set the bed tray in place. "I don't see no shortie pajamas on the floor," she clipped. "Now get into that bed and eat."

"How did you know I was awake?"

"You were pacing. Told you that's bad, girl your age."

"You couldn't hear! I was barefoot!"

"Some things I can just smell, young lady," Marie said grimly. "Like you being upset lately, and that don't mean but one thing. You've got your car and your clothes and your horses. That don't leave but one thing. Man trouble."

"Ridiculous!"

"I'd say you and Adah is crossways over Mr. Lance Buford," Marie continued, settling the tray, shaking out the napkin and poking it at Rae-Ellen. "I know you're mad to the bone about something, and I don't think you'd get that mad at Mr. Buford. My guess is that horse trainer's mixed up in it somewhere."

"That's enough, Marie!"

"And when you go to saying things like that to me, I know for sure I've got hold of a piece of the facts. I've not seen the horse trainer much, but my advice about him is, take care. He's a headstrong one, that fellow. You could get hurt worse by him than you'd ever get by Mr. Buford. Or any other man."

With Marie hitting so close to the target, a thing she'd done since Rae-Ellen was a toddler, the girl made no reply. Instead, reflectively, she began to eat.

When Marie left, carrying the empty tray, warning her to behave, Rae-Ellen jumped out of bed and began to dress. Defiantly, she put on a nubby, scarlet dress with a matching scarlet bolero jacket. She used scarlet lipstick, tied her streaming hair back with a matching ribbon.

The household was beginning to stir. Papa was an early riser, and Mama always breakfasted with him downstairs. The two girls joined them or had trays in their rooms as the mood struck them.

She opened her door, looked up and down the corridor and was relieved that all doors were closed, including Adah's. She tiptoed to the staircase, down it and out, passing only Andrews, on his way to lay the table in the breakfast room.

"If they ask, tell them I've gone for a spin!" she said.

"Yes'm," he said, and flashed his teeth.

She headed her car straight for Burr's cottage. Not wanting Thunder Boy to start bucking and kicking in his stall, she made the approach smoothly and braked without a sound. Early as it was, before workout time even, she was surprised and angry to see Adah's car parked even with the kitchen door.

Because her sister was there, sweet lady Adah, so innocent she didn't even know Papa's intention to disinherit Rae-Ellen, she rapped lightly at the door instead of walking right in.

Adah and Burr were sipping coffee. There was a plate in front of Burr with scraps of bacon and egg on it, none at Adah's place. So. They hadn't eaten together. Rae-Ellen wondered how he had lured Adah here. She was certain she'd interrupted his scheme to get her sister into the bedroom.

"Might as well sit," Burr said and pulled out a chair. "Want breakfast?"

"I've had my breakfast," she said shortly, but she sat down.

He poured her a cup of black coffee and she drew it over in front of her. "Did you tell Papa where you were going?" she demanded of Adah.

"No, sister dear. I wasn't sure they were awake. I didn't see anyone."

So! Already he had Adah sneaking out to him!

"I suggested to your sister that she come down

to see Thunder Boy fed this morning," Burr said arrogantly. "Reckon I didn't make myself clear, though. My intention was for both of you to watch him."

"I suppose he's eaten?"

"Yes, he has!" Adah exclaimed. "Don't blame Burr! It was my fault! I forgot to mention it."

"Don't fret, Adah. It wasn't your fault," Rae-Ellen said.

It was Burr Travis' fault. He'd lured Adah here on the pretext of watching Thunder Boy so he could get her into his bedroom. Adah, accustomed to Lance's gentlemanly behavior, would never suspect until it was too late. What are you up to? she ached to cry at Travis. What's your scheme? To try me out, then try Adah out? Decide which of us is best in bed, then marry her?

There was a way to deal with this hombre. He had to be outwitted, outplayed. So she smiled, for the first time wishing she had dimples like her sister, and dismissed the oversight.

"Actually," she said, "I came to watch Thunder Boy's first workout."

"I ain't going to work him out until tomorrow, and then very slow and easy," Burr said. "Just a little way, for him to get the feel of our track. First thing I've got to do with all the race horses is see to it they look on the stable as home—and on the track as their playground, so to speak."

Adah laughed spontaneously. "That's a wonderful idea! I'm so happy that you see the horses as individuals!"

"Racers are high-strung, delicate creatures," Burr said to Adah, but he looked at Rae-Ellen.

As if he were double-talking, she thought indignantly. If he was comparing her to a filly, he certainly hadn't handled her the way he handled horses!

Adah laughed again, caught Rae-Ellen's eye, and she forced herself to smile again. Burr gave Adah a meaningful look and Rae-Ellen felt suddenly that maybe her sister wasn't a pure, untouched virgin. Well, she wouldn't be for long, not if she fooled around with Burr.

Adah finished her coffee and rose.

Burr stood with her. "Sure you won't have breakfast?"

"No, thank you. I'll eat with Papa and Mama. You coming, Rae-Ellen?"

"As long as I'm here," Rae-Ellen said, "I'll take a look at Thunder Boy. Maybe watch them rub him down."

Adah smiled, went through the door, which Burr held for her. She ran to her car. As Rae-Ellen came to her feet, intent on her own purpose, Adah drove off and Burr turned back into the kitchen.

She smacked her hands on her hips, stared at him venomously, hoping her eyes were so blue they'd cut that upsetting brown of his eyes.

"Caught you!" she accused. "In the act!"

"In what act?" he demanded.

"You asked her here to . . . do what you did to me! And don't deny it! I know exactly what you are, know what you're after, right down to the last Pettigrew dollar!"

He looked at her, bewildered.

She couldn't stand it. He wasn't getting away with the innocent act. She flew at him, nails out.

He caught her wrists, transferred them to one huge hand, held them in a viselike grip. She kicked his shins, but he was wearing heavy boots. She started to scream, but then remembered Ken and Terry, who were busy at the stable, and choked back the scream. It came out as a gurgle. She twisted, yanked to get free, but only hurt herself. The beast was made of iron!

"What's eating you?" he demanded.

She twisted and yanked. Her hair came loose from the scarlet ribbon and fell around her face, tumbling over her shoulders. He shook her.

"You going to talk or not?"

"You know very well what's wrong!"

He didn't know. He stood holding her and had no idea of what she'd lived through, the tortuous night just past, all because of what he'd started.

"It's what happened between us!" he exclaimed now. "But you liked it as much as I did! Though if I'd known you was a virgin—"

"You don't know whether Adah's a virgin! What are you trying to do, find out, the way you did with me?"

He shook her again, so hard this time her teeth came together. "You sure-hell are askin' for more of the same!" he gritted. "I've been a fool. Thinking maybe I'd better tighten my belt and beg your pardon."

"I wouldn't pardon you if you got on your knees! Let . . . me . . . go!"

He kept holding her. His eyes raked her from top to bottom. "You *are* asking!" he whispered, "coming here on your own early in the morning— uninvited—wearing red! And your eyes blazing like before! You might as well wave a flag!"

She went into a frenzy. He let go of her hands, and she almost fell backward. Then she dove at him, hooked her fingers into the neck of his buttoned shirt, ripped it open, and yanked it halfway out of his breeches. She arched her fingers, scratched them down his bare chest, leaving red, oozing trails which she didn't have the satisfaction of enjoying, because he grabbed the neck of her dress and tore it from her in one strong motion.

Before she could move, he scooped her under his arm and went in two—she'd swear it was only two—long strides into the bedroom. He threw her onto the bed so hard she bounced and she felt her bra snap open. He flipped it away, ripped off her bikini panties.

She lay panting, glaring, willing him to drop dead.

He pulled off her shoes and she heard them hit the wall. "I want my women naked to the toe, don't you know that yet?" he growled.

Then he got out of his clothes, boots and all, moving faster than she'd have thought possible, even for him. Her breath was a ball in her throat.

She could try to get off the bed, to run.

But this was what she'd come for. To provoke him into raping her again. To trick him into washing out the rage of burning he had implanted in her. She felt a small, triumphant smile tremble onto her lips.

He saw the smile.

It enraged him. She was using him. For some female purpose, she was goading him. Well, he didn't give a damn. She wasn't a virgin now. He wasn't damaging the goods. But this time he was going to look it over first.

See her, lying there so quiet, yet quivering. That red in her hair showed up more when it was against her skin. If he didn't have an aversion to red hair, even a tinge of red, he'd almost think it looked good.

Her skin was smooth, still tanned from summer. Her arms were shapely and tapered to slender wrists and fingers. He gazed at her breasts. They were high and a bit full and sweet as honey, with erect pink nipples, the area around them pink.

The hair between those rounded thighs was a cluster of loveliness. Even if the red did show up. Her belly was so flat it fell in instead of rounding out, and her legs were perfection. He'd remembered right.

Everything about her was perfect except her disposition. And that came from the red hair. He looked last at her face. Her eyes were stabbing, and her lips—by damn, they really were quivering!

"You want this, don't you?" he asked hoarsely.

"Get on with it!" she retorted, but the lips still quivered.

He didn't know why she wanted him. First he raped her, then she fought him like a wildcat, now she goes into this shrinking-violet-routine. But he couldn't wait; he was a flesh-and-blood man, and it was all laid out for him to take.

This time she really gave him movement for movement. She was strong; she was tireless. Even when he began to pant, the strain of holding back telling on him, she kept prodding, up and up. Once she had him clear off the bed, and he thought then, slamming her down, that he'd have to give in, but he managed to hold out.

When it finally happened, he felt like the top of his head was blowing off. He pressed, long and close, and she pressed back, moving slightly. Still coupled, he rolled to his side, bringing her with him.

"You're wonderful, know that?" he whispered, amazed.

Now. She had him! He'd done exactly what she'd wanted him to do. Her fire was quenched. The trouble was that somehow she wasn't ready to leave his arms, to get off the bed.

She hadn't caught her breath yet, for one thing. Her deep insides were still singing and sizzling; it'd take a minute for that to die down. And she was a little bit tired. His arms were restful; she didn't object to the man-smell to his skin. She might as well get some extra benefit from having freed herself.

When he sat up, she still lay there. Watched him examine her, inch by inch. That bullheaded look was gone. She wondered if he had any idea of how much more human he seemed.

"You're as beautiful as a filly," he told her.

That should have made her mad. She knew it should, but it didn't. It even pleased her. Lazily, looking at his strong body, it occurred to her that revenge was indeed sweet. Now that she'd taken revenge, she could admire his few good points.

Unexpectedly, she laughed.

He waited. "What's the joke?" he asked, finally.

"I was just thinking, you're as—well, powerful and male as Thunder Boy. Or any stallion."

He grinned.

He scooped her up, one arm under her shoulders, the other beneath her knees, and went striding across the room. She didn't know where he was taking her. It didn't matter. She'd got him out of her system; she'd have no more troubles.

He set her on her feet beneath the shower, and joined her in the stall. He turned the water on, tempered it until it held just a touch of warmth. She laughed again. Now he was washing himself off her after washing himself out of her! And he suspected nothing! In this instant, she almost liked him.

When they were both wet, he drew her out of the spray and lathered her from neck to toe. His hands were slow and gentle. The suds were white and fragrant and so thick she could scoop them off in handsful.

"Now. Do me," he ordered, and gave her the soap.

She lathered him slowly, feeling how hard his body was, trying to make the suds thicker on him. He was chuckling, and she was giggling. Oh, deep down, she despised him, but this was fun, this was really getting him out of her system.

When she would have stepped under the spray to rinse, he caught her in his arms again and carried her. This time, both covered with suds, she kept slipping, and he had to sort of toss her up and catch her again to keep from dropping her.

They fell on the bed together, him on top. He slid into her, slid out. They struggled to engage, laughing at their failures, trying again. At last it was only their bodies which slid as they moved, and this was better than before. Now they had to work for delight, but they moved and slid, slid and moved until, at the end, Rae-Ellen thought she might die of ecstasy.

"Now we rinse," Burr said, holding her soapy body in his soapy arms. "Next—"

Next?

"We rinse off, we dry, then get down to serious business."

She didn't know what he meant by that, but she went along with the rinsing and drying. She even dried his back and let him dry hers.

In the bedroom again, he spread a fresh sheet over the soapy bed. She watched. It didn't occur to her to grab her shredded clothes and run. She was being swept along by events; she'd even forgotten the underlying reason for her being there.

With surprising gentleness, like that he'd used on Thunder Boy, he eased her onto the bed. He bestrode her at her knees, but there was no weight on her.

He lowered his homely lips to her right nipple. They brushed lightly across the nipple as they parted, and then it was inside his mouth, which was moist and warm and—tender. Ever so lightly, he ran his tongue over it, then pressed his teeth, just barely pressed them. A shiver went down her spine. He released the nipple, kissed it, then moved to the other breast.

Later, he kissed down between her breasts, pushed his tongue slowly into her navel, trailed kisses down through the nest between her thighs. When he would have moved beyond, lower still, she felt herself grasp his head on either side and urge it upward.

When his face, homely lips smiling, was above hers, she pulled it down. Holding his head, she traced her tongue across his lips.

This set him off. He clutched her roughly to him. She jerked her hips to one side, stiffened. Reality slammed her. This was Texas bum Travis, and she was Rae-Ellen Pettigrew, come to rid herself of the torture he'd implanted in her.

That had been accomplished.

She was free of him, free for good.

She began to struggle.

"You redheaded witch!" he growled.

He held her immobile, came into her so hard their bodies smacked together. He thrust hard and fast, harder and faster than he had ever done. She fought him, thrust for thrust. If she could buck him out, if she could—

He really was raping her again, was undoing all that had been accomplished! She pounded her body at him. When the tide of hot, scalding sensation took her, the fierce-sweet, hated peak, she bit his ear until it bled.

Even so, the wave of sensation swept her, and she clung to him, digging her nails into his flesh. It was never-ending this time, the intense throbbing, the sharp, undulating wave, the cutting nails. When it was over, she was lost in sweetness which looked deep into the jaws of hatred.

14

She sat on the bed naked, glaring at his un-
abashed nudity. She wouldn't start to dress first,
wouldn't give him that satisfaction. He had no
shame, none at all. Those eyes were shining at her;
there wasn't a trace of stubbornness to his mouth.
She hated those eyes, that mouth. She loathed him.

He'd been washed out of her, he really had.
For a moment. But now, anew, his awful maleness
streaked her, went deeper, and she didn't know
what to do about it.

Holding her glare, he spoke.

"Would you marry a Texas bum?" he asked.

He might as well have lit the fuse to a stick of
dynamite. "I wouldn't marry you if you were the
only man in the universe!" she cried.

"I don't recollect proposin' to you. I was finding

out something. A fact. You do look on me as a Texas bum."

"Your Texas lingo proves that."

"Think of it! And I went to the University of Texas!"

"You've been to college?"

"Yep. Graduated. Degree. The works."

"Then why do you speak such a . . . a lingo?"

"Because it's comfortable, like a pair of good-fittin' boots."

"So? You were saying . . . ?"

"You look on all Texans as bums?" His mouth was bullheaded now.

"Don't be ridiculous!"

"You think only cowpokes, them that wrangle cattle and do the dirty work are bums."

"And they drift from place to place!"

"I reckon you're in a position to know that for a fact."

"You drift! You worked on a Texas ranch, then you went to—to—"

"Kentucky."

"You went to Kentucky and played at being a horse trainer, and now you're here! And you have every intention of going to Florida with us! If that's not drifting, what is?"

His whole face was bullheaded. "It's going from one job to a better one, way I see it."

"A drifter, that's what you are!" she cried. "Taking what you can get, where you can get it! With never an apology, never any . . . any responsibility or . . . or guilt!"

"You ain't such a perfect number yourself," he drawled.

She almost went for him with her nails. Then, aware of what that would lead to, animal that he was, she clenched her fists and breathed deeply.

"And what," she demanded finally, "do you find wrong with me?"

"You're hotheaded, with a temper right out of hell. You wanted a man, and when you got him, you didn't want him. Not the first time, and not today!"

"I didn't want a man!"

"You sure acted like you did. For quite a while, there. You're also spoiled. You're used to getting your own way. If you don't get it, you go into a tantrum, like with me."

"After what you did to me . . . because I'm soiled and upset—"

"You have got some emotions, then."

"Oh, shut up! Because of what you did to me—"

"You helped; you helped right smart."

"That doesn't count!"

"What does count, according to you?"

"A man, a true gentleman—"

"As I recall, we've agreed I'm a bum."

"Even that! If he had a scrap of manliness in him, he'd never—He'd never treat the boss's daughter the way you've treated me!"

"Ha. You're a snob, on top of it all."

"That's a lie! I have friends in every—"

"Jet set."

"I don't travel with them! That's one thing you can't put a finger on!"

"You might as well. You lead an empty life. Racing that car, hanging around with the Buncombe girl, who—fox-hunting."

179

"I ride, I swim, I play tennis! I design and make lots of my own clothes! I read, study history! I spend lots of time with horses!"

"Horses," he repeated flatly. "That makes two things we both like." Pointedly, he did not mention bed.

"There's nothing we both like, nothing!"

"You ought to keep your mouth shut. All you claim to do, every damn thing you fill your time with—except horses—is useless."

"At least I stay in one place! I have a . . . a plan!"

"I've got a plan too, with all my drifting."

"Pah!"

"I'm going to breed race horses. Have my own farm."

"You won't get that here!"

"I'll get experience. Save my pay. Add it to what I've got."

She stared.

A Texas cowpoke, drifting, working for other men, claiming to have money put aside! She didn't believe it, not for a moment, and she told him so.

His mouth got worse.

"Strikes me," he said, "that between us we've got the makings of your ordinary marriage. Fightin' every step of the way except when—" He motioned at the bed, and for an instant she thought he was actually going to grin.

"I'd die an old maid first! I told you that!"

"Do that. I ain't asked you to marry me, and I ain't about to. Watchin' you turn into a spinster'll be some sight, after the demonstration you gave this morning."

She was too mad to get off the bed and start

snatching up her clothes. She was furious that he took it for granted she'd never marry.

Goading, he said, "No man in his right senses would marry you. Not under any circumstances."

"There's one man! There's one who's known me all my life, who—"

"That'd be the day. Him knowin' you."

"Lance knows me, and he loves me, always has! And I'm going to marry him!" she cried wildly. "Lance or no one!"

"Then I reckon it'll be nobody, for sure," he told her easily. "Because he proposed to your sister. For some reason, she ain't made up her mind what to answer, but my guess is she don't look on him with disfavor."

"You big-mouth! To tell a thing like that, told you in confidence!"

"She didn't ask me to keep it secret."

"Common decency—"

"That's what made me tell you. If you ain't got a chance with the guy, you need to know. So you won't try any drastic—" He gestured at the rumpled bed, at the scatter of garments on the floor.

"You *louse!*" she whispered.

"Hold on. I didn't do the proposing. Buford done that on his own. You might as well swallow it down."

Frantic, she whispered, "I'll put a stop to it! I can, you know."

"I don't see how."

"I'll tell Lance the truth!"

"What truth?"

"That Adah's an octoroon! That she's my half sister, that Papa got of a quadroon housemaid!"

The bullhead lips fell apart, clapped shut.

"Lance is Old South," she continued, "born and bred! He'd never marry a girl who has a touch of the tarbrush!"

Suddenly she bit her lips to hold back tears. She had betrayed Adah, and she'd never meant to. It was all Burr's fault, like everything else! She'd never, really, tell Lance about Adah. She wouldn't hurt him that much, even though it might be to his eventual benefit.

It struck her that the cowpoke had been quiet for a very long moment. She glanced at his face; it infuriated her afresh, for now it had added a rock-like hardness to its other faults.

"I've spent considerable time," he said now, "wonderin' what it is with you. Spoiled, stubborn, cat-dirt mean, redheaded temper, all them things I saw. But now there's worse. You're underhanded."

"I'm not! I've kept this secret for years!"

"But now you'd use it. Glad I found out. At first, I figured what happened between us, you and me, was just sparks that fly between man and woman. But it's more."

"Oh, no, it isn't!"

"Might've been. I'm talking truth to you. I couldn't decide, in my own mind, which one—you or Adah—I'd go after. If I was to go after anybody. When we—that first day—"

"You egomaniac!"

"Maybe. Fact remains that I was turned on to you and turned off, both at the same time. And turned on to your sister. In a different way. You're nothing alike, but both of you have strong man-appeal. Now it looks like maybe I can decide. I might give Buford a run for his money."

"You *are* a maniac! If you think that a lady like Adah would ever—"

"She might. She just might. She's been awful sweet and friendly."

"She's like that with all men, with all people! She's gracious and warm! If you so much as laid a finger on her the way you've done with me, she'd swoon!"

"Any time I'd lay a hand on Adah," Burr said, those tight lips barely moving, "she'd have my weddin' band on her finger and my name with hers on a piece of paper."

Sitting naked on the bed still, feet tucked under her, Rae-Ellen simply glared. Words were gone. Everything was gone except the rage which streaked her, which burned to her depths and ached for soothing.

He turned away, began to put on his clothes.

She flounced across the room, gathered up her scraps of clothing. The bra and bikinis weren't really torn. To hide the condition of her dress she put it on backwards, belted it tightly, then struggled into the jacket, which hid the ripped waist. She tugged on her shoes, shook her hair out of her eyes.

Burr was pulling on his second boot when she whirled at him. She'd never seen such a homely, sober face. She wondered how he himself could bear it.

"You stay away from Adah!" she ordered.

He merely looked at her; his face didn't change.

She ran out of the cottage, got behind the wheel of the Lincoln, went speeding home. There she dashed past a gaping Andrews and fled up the stairs and into her own suite.

Locking herself in, she soaked in a scalding bath to cleanse herself of Burr. That inner ache subsided, and she dressed in a tailored beige pants suit.

She had to talk to Adah.

Lance or no Lance, she wasn't going to let Adah pass another day unwarned about Burr Travis' unspeakable intentions. She knocked at Adah's suite and went in.

Her sister wasn't there.

She paced between the two suites until Adah appeared.

"Where have you been?" she demanded. "I've waited and waited!"

"Why, down at the track, Rae-Ellen. I watched Burr take Thunder Boy out. I thought you'd be there."

In her rage and in her contrition over betraying her sister, Rae-Ellen had forgotten the training period. Trust cowpoke Travis! No matter what indignities he inflicted on a girl, or what insulting, maddening things he said to her afterward, he wouldn't forget his darned horses! That's what he should marry, a horse, a whole string of horses!

Unwilling to admit she'd forgotten, Rae-Ellen shrugged. "I wasn't in the mood," she said. "Adah, you've got to listen to me! Burr Travis isn't to be trusted, especially by you!"

The golden eyes widened. "Whyever not? He seems—"

"He's got a split personality! He shows one side of it, the bad side, to me. He makes darn sure you see only the good side!"

"But why? Why should he do a thing like that?"

Rae-Ellen found herself blurting facts, but concealing the final truth. Her account described Burr

Travis as he was—arrogant, overbearing, rude, sex-mad, not to be trusted. She went so far as to reveal he'd mauled her.

Adah listened breathlessly, olive skin pale, eyes swimming. Once she tried to embrace her sister, to comfort her, but Rae-Ellen pulled away.

"He even said you told him Lance proposed to you!"

Adah gasped. Then she said, "To be fair, I didn't ask him to keep it secret."

"But you assumed he would!"

"I . . . yes."

"And he told me, first thing!"

"But you won't tell, darling. I haven't given an answer . . . the blood . . ."

Rae-Ellen gestured impatiently. "That's not all!" She told the rest, including Burr Travis' statement that he might court Adah and take her away from Lance.

Adah fell quiet. Her lips moved, but no sound came.

"We had a fight," Rae-Ellen said. "If there'd been something I could have thrown at him, a pressing iron, a hammer!"

"I'm glad you didn't, sister dear. If you don't mind, I'd like to think. Alone."

Rae-Ellen shot her half sister a look. Then she went back into her own rooms. The more time that passed, the more evident it became that Adah was deeply secretive. Secretiveness about the blood was understandable.

But this was another matter. She'd said nothing about whether she'd accepted Lance's proposal conditionally. And she'd given no indication of what she'd do if Burr turned his crude charm on her. She hadn't even acknowledged Rae-Ellen's warning that he was a dangerous man.

Burr Travis' mere existence was problem enough. Now, he'd mixed himself into the family, and Adah, admonitions aside, chose to keep quiet about her intentions. Well, let her be quiet. At least she knew the score. Miserably, Rae-Ellen realized Adah knew she had two men on the hook. And Rae-Ellen had none.

15

The filly, Starstruck, was delivered hours behind schedule. Traffic had been heavy and the handler, a careful man who knew the value of his cargo, had taken extra time on the road.

Infuriated by Burr's order that none of the family come to the stable for the unloading, Rae-Ellen waited impatiently at the house. Adah, Papa, and Mama waited with her; Lance drove up in his farm truck, having torn himself away from his recently delivered Samson's Lad.

He was smiling as he came into the living room. He gave a nod which included all of them, but spoke to Papa.

"I appreciate it, sir, that you phoned me."

"Natural thing to do. You're as interested in our horses as you are in your own."

"Except that I have only one two-year-old, opposed to your two. Plus your upcoming twin yearlings."

"These racers all belong to the girls, remember," Raymond Pettigrew said.

"Indeed they do!" his wife laughed. "I know race horses are costly, but for two unknowns and two yearlings—!" She flung her hands out in a gesture of surrender.

"Travis said they were all bargains," Papa responded, his smile a bit grim. He shrugged, "If it makes the girls happy—"

"I'd be a good deal happier if we'd been allowed to see our own horse unloaded!" Rae-Ellen said crisply.

"If she's as high-strung as Thunder Boy," Adah put in, "I think Burr's right to get her settled. Remember how Thunder Boy was, and he's been stabled. Goodness knows what he'd have done if we'd all been there."

"But Burr's taking over!" Rae-Ellen retorted. "As if he's the boss!"

"He is the boss of those horses," Papa said, and he wasn't smiling. "He's the trainer, selected with care and brought here at some expense. His aim is ours, to race those horses in Florida and, hopefully, to win a purse or two."

"I'm afraid you're outvoted, Rae-Ellen," Lance said, his tone soft; gray eyes on her. "And I have to go with the vote, as you will, once you consider. You don't want the filly nervous."

Lance was right. He was always right. She clung to his eyes with her own, trying to read them. Was he thinking of the way she'd thrown herself at him?

Was he, oh, please, let it be so, regarding her in a new, more tender manner?

Too shaken to trust her voice, she nodded reluctant agreement. Then she just sat, listening to the others, noting that Lance included Adah in his remarks, but that most of them were addressed to Papa and Mama.

On the surface things were normal. But underneath lay the fact that Lance had proposed to Adah.

Ken, the stableboy, appeared at the front door, and Andrews admitted him. The lad was ill at ease, seemed uncertain where to turn or look, finally addressed himself to Raymond Pettigrew. Starstruck, he stammered out, was now in her stall and Mr. Travis said it'd be okay for them to come see her.

They all piled into Lance's truck, Papa and Mama in front with him, the girls and Ken in back, legs dangling over the tailgate.

At the stable, Burr met them. He behaved with extreme propriety toward the sisters, reserving his grin and his comments for the parents. To see him now, Rae-Ellen thought angrily, you'd never believe he'd done unspeakable things to her. That he might be plotting to do the same or worse to Adah under cover of a wedding ring!

Burr led to the stable, and they gathered as close to the stall as he directed. This infuriated Rae-Ellen, that he should have such authority, and then her eyes lit on Starstruck.

The filly was small, dainty, beautifully formed. She was a perfect silver all over, from the tips of her ears right down to her hoofs. She had eyes, and a spirited arch to her neck.

"Watch," murmured Burr. He went around to the stall and entered.

Starstruck stepped about daintily, fluttered her nostrils. When Burr began to stroke her face, she quieted, and when he produced lump sugar, lipped it out of his fingers.

"She's even gentler than she was in Louisville," Papa remarked.

"That handler had something to do with it," Burr responded. "He was a bit heavy-handed, and this filly likes a gentle touch."

"That's obvious," Papa agreed. "Don't you think so, my dears?" His eyes swept across his wife's face, across his daughters'.

They all nodded.

Rae-Ellen, by this time, was seething. Now he was boasting about himself! Well, what could you expect? A braggart, that's what they had in charge of their stable. She stole a look at Lance, to see if he noticed the boasting.

"If you weren't my friend," he said in a teasing manner to Raymond Pettigrew, "I'd develop some plot to get your trainer. He's as important to your winning races as the horses themselves."

Papa laughed. So did Mama.

Burr took the compliment seriously. "Thank you for the kind words," he said to Lance. "I'll live up to them."

Not, do my best to live up to them! Never that, not him. As if he were the trainer of all trainers. As if he hadn't practically just come off the ranch, where he'd dealt with only steers and an occasional cowpony!

She wondered how Papa, a man who ran a tobacco empire, who managed millions of dollars, could be so wrong about this Texan. If it had been anyone but Burr Travis, whom she knew so intimately, she would have accepted the premise that Papa saw true worth in the fellow. But this time, he'd misjudged.

She took her turn at stroking Starstruck's face. The hair felt like silk. She loved the little filly instantly and, though Starstruck belonged to both Adah and her, knew that the filly was her own special love.

As they went back to Lance's truck, Mama declared they must celebrate. "Both Thunder Boy and Starstruck are safely here," she said. "Also, Samson's Lad. They're in their new homes, and we love to have them! Tonight, we'll gather at Magnolia Hall for a simple—but I warn you, a dress-up dinner! Anybody object?"

They all expressed pleasure. Burr was silent.

"The same group as our last dinner," Mama said. "Our family; Fawn and Pete; Mary-Lou and Jim; Lance and Burr."

Rae-Ellen wondered if Mama had any idea she'd just included a roustabout in their group of intimates. She glanced at Adah; she was smiling at something Lance had said.

To make things worse, Mama spoke directly to Burr. "You will come? You can trust Terry and Ken with the horses?"

"Yes, ma'am. I'll be pleased to join you."

He didn't look toward Rae-Ellen, who was glaring. He didn't look because he didn't dare; he was fully conscious that she didn't want him within a mile of their dinner!

Back at the house, she played the piano, thundering out Wagner. That didn't even take the edge off her anger. She tried to interest herself in a new volume on Roman history, but the words seemed to blur, and she dashed angry tears away.

She wouldn't sit around and cry because Burr Travis was coming to dinner! If there were tears, it was from worry over Lance and his loving Adah, over Adah's final decision, over what she could do to keep that marriage from ruining her own hopes.

At last it was time to dress. Rae-Ellen soaked in a fragrant tub, both to fill time and to relax, her hair pinned atop her head to keep it dry.

She pulled on her sheerest nude pantyhose, giving her legs a bare look plus a sheen, and then she added nude strap sandals with high, slim heels.

The dress was of nude silk, with long, fitted sleeves, a fitted bodice which outlined her breasts, and a wide inset nipped in at the waist, from which rich folds swirled to midcalf. Every move set the skirt to stirring. She brushed out her shining hair to below shoulder length, then fastened on the sapphire pendant which matched her eyes. She used no make-up. Her skin tones tonight were perfect. Her lips, though, were too red, so she dabbed a bit of powder on to tone them down.

She took a long moment at her mirror and was satisfied. In the event she'd shocked Lance with the white dress, this outfit would show him a perfect lady.

She'd been wondering about Adah. Now, curious as to why her sister hadn't come into the suite at all, wanting to see what she'd wear, she went to Adah's door and tapped.

Adah, in yellow so pale it was almost white, was pinning her hair in a braided coronet. Her dress was short-sleeved, with flowing lines, the material gauzy with a slightly deeper yellow underlining. It was ankle-length, and with it Adah wore her topaz pendant and earrings.

"Rae-Ellen!" she exclaimed. "You look beautiful!"

"So do you, as you well know."

Adah smiled. "I hope I look well. Papa and Mama do so much for us. I'm happy we can make them proud."

"Yes," Rae-Ellen agreed. She did like to please Papa and Mama. In all but the one thing: marriage, the proper grandson.

"I asked Mama if we couldn't dance tonight," Adah said. "She thought it was a good idea."

"So do I."

Together they went downstairs and into the living room. They selected albums for the stereo, stacking as many as it would hold, making several piles to be used later. When they left, music was heard in every room, even the kitchen, and its pervasive softness enveloped the guests as they arrived.

Rae-Ellen caught Burr piercing a cold look at her legs. She set her jaw, but he looked past her eyes as though they didn't exist.

He wore the same clothes as before, but tonight for some reason, his appearance was such that if she hadn't known he was a roustabout, she wouldn't have recognized him for one.

Dinner talk was horses. Much about Thunder Boy and Starstruck and about Lance's stallion, Samson's Lad. There was talk about the hunters, about the foxes, which Lance declared were more numerous than he'd earlier thought.

Later, they danced. There were four women

and six men, which was ideal. Every woman had a partner for every dance.

. Burr was first to dance with Rae-Ellen, Adah being with Lance. Rae-Ellen ached to slap Burr when he stepped up and told her he was available, but went into his arms.

He held her properly, and she followed him as naturally as though they'd been poured from the same mold. This infuriated her. It also infuriated her that tonight he looked so homely he crossed the borderline to a certain rough handsomeness.

They didn't speak. He danced perfectly, as did she. At the end, he let her go, waited until Jim Reed claimed her, then went to Adah. Next, he danced with Mama. Last, he danced with Mary-Lou.

Then he sat talking to Papa and that left four couples for dancing. Rae-Ellen boiled. He'd insulted her by dancing with her only once, then had covered the insult by dancing with each of the others once.

She began to dance mostly with Fawn, who was looking keenly handsome. He was warm and attentive, and she found herself liking him more than usual.

Pete danced with her twice, but paid her a minimum of attention, his eye on Adah. Jim danced with her, flirtatious as always, but he kept winking at Mary-Lou.

Lance partnered her a few times, but always returned to Adah. And while they did dance, he spoke of nothing more personal than the upcoming fox hunt, so she pretended a greater interest in it than she really had. Anything to hold his attention.

Then he'd be gone again. Burr and Papa still sat and talked.

At one point, Mary-Lou cornered Rae-Ellen alone in the powder room. She lit right in.

"You better watch yourself!" she bubbled. "It's all over you, plain as plain! I can see it, and if you don't be careful, others will, too! You're hooked on that cowboy! You've been to bed with him again, haven't you? Truth, now!"

Half-angry, Rae-Ellen admitted it.

"Are you on the pill?"

"Of course not! Don't be silly!"

"I'm not silly, and you'd better get on it fast! That Texan is po-tent!" She rolled her eyes, turned her hands, palms up. "Take care, hear? That Texas stud'll have you pregnant!"

"I don't need . . . I'm not going to . . . any more!"

Mary-Lou gurgled. "Yes, you will, honey-pie! That's no hombre any girl can—just once or twice! He's habit-formin'," take my word!"

Adah opened the door at that moment. She smiled at them, closed herself into the private cubicle.

"Let's go, let's dance!" Mary-Lou sang out.

Rae-Ellen followed.

She had to admit the truth. She did ache for sex with Burr. She was feeling the pangs, which he could assuage, which belonged, really, to Lance. She ached for Lance, for his lovemaking, which would eliminate forever this crazy yen for the Texan.

She danced next with Fawn. Burr was still talking with Papa. About ranching, she caught that much.

"You're restless," Fawn commented. "Dancing isn't enough for you. Let's slip away."

Yes, she was restless. She wanted to get out of

this house, rid herself of the sight of Burr Travis. But she didn't especially want to go with Fawn.

"What would we do?" she asked, dancing on.

"Drive with the top down. Let the wind blow. It'll be chilly, but we'll get warm again. And we'll blow out all the cobwebs."

Suddenly she liked the idea. "Let me get a wrap," she murmured.

He danced her to the hallway, and she ran upstairs, got her blond mink stole, returned to Fawn, waiting in the library. They slipped out of the house unseen.

They scrambled, giggling, into Fawn's Buick. He touched a button and the top rolled back. He eased the car along the driveway, turned on to the road, put on speed. The wind lifted Rae-Ellen's hair, froze her scalp.

"Wonderful!" she cried. "Why didn't you think of it before?"

"We haven't been together enough—only on double-dates with Adah and Pete. And where did we go? To concerts and formal dinners."

"Where my parents also went!"

"Right. I haven't seen you often enough alone. Like this."

"No, I guess not!" She laughed, doubled with the humor of it. Here she was, running away with one of the very men she'd fought over with Papa! It was really funny! She was doing exactly what Papa wanted her to do! It wouldn't lead to what he wanted, of course, but if he knew she was with Fawn, he'd certainly hope he might be getting his way.

"What's so funny?" Fawn asked.

She couldn't tell him. It would be cruel to let

196

him know what Papa was determined to accomplish. It might get his hopes up, and there was no hope for him.

There was hope only for Lance.

"Not going to tell, eh?" he laughed.

"N-no!" she said, laughing so hard she hiccuped. It had turned into near hysteria, and she tried to subdue it.

"I get it now!" Fawn exclaimed, and laughed. "You've foxed them all! They don't know where we've gone, and if they've missed us, are trying to figure it out!"

That his male conceit would put this interpretation on the matter, sent her into a gale of hiccups. She thought of Burr, of how cocky he was; of Papa, with his demands; of Pete, who strutted a bit. Tears ran down her face and the wind made them cold.

"That right?" laughed Fawn.

"Right!" she gasped. "But not all that funny!" She hiccuped, loudly.

"We've got to get rid of those," he declared. "We can't run away so you can hiccup! Come over here!"

Weak with laughter and shuddering hiccups, she let him pull her against him, rode with his arm around her. He dropped speed; the arm which held her was warm and firm and assured. A blast of wind hit them, and she snuggled closer.

When she did that, his free hand came under her stole and cupped her breast. It felt so natural, so almost—right—that she made no protest.

"Sweet!" he murmured.

That was all, for the moment. He drove, the night wind swept them, her breast warmed in his hand. She closed her eyes, rested her head against the back of the seat.

Riding through the cold night, she was on fire again with the hunger Burr Travis had caused. Then she recalled that actually the fire was for Lance, that it had lain dormant in her for years, then had been set ablaze by Burr Travis. It was deep inside, a fire that had been banked and had now flared.

"Rae-Ellen . . . sweet," murmured Fawn.

"Hmm?" she asked, between hiccups.

"Why don't we go to my place?" His fingers moved on her breast, seeking the nipple through the silken fabric. "We'll fix you hot milk and we can—it's a comfortable place, sweet. You've never seen it. And I'd be honored if you'd say yes."

Well, she thought, her breast so warm in his hand, his voice persuasive, his every thought of her and only her, why not? Why not go to his apartment? Why not, if he made the advances, go the whole way with him? Sex with him would wash Burr out.

She'd find that sex with one man was no different than sex with another man. Well, that was a bit drastic.

Lance would be different, because she loved him.

16

Fawn's apartment was as sleek, polished, and suave as he was himself. The carpeting and walls were off-white, the furniture in the living room was ebony covered in black suede, built on slender lines. The kitchen area was behind a low, gleaming black wall, topped by a counter. The cabinets and fixtures were stark white.

"Like it?" he asked.

"It's—you," she said.

"I decorated it, the bedroom, too."

He opened a door and here the colors were black and scarlet. The bed was extremely wide, extremely low, covered with scarlet velvet the exact shade of the carpet. The furniture was ebony.

"Like this, too?" he asked, his arms stealing around her, drawing off the stole.

She'd never seen such bold decor. She told him so. He smiled, that intense smile. Then he began to laugh, a quick, keen laugh not like that which he'd used in the car.

"What's so funny?" she asked.

"Your hiccups. They're gone. My apartment scared them out of you."

It was true. She started to laugh, cut off lest the hiccups start again. She let him draw her into the bedroom, holding her so close their bodies touched.

He let her go long enough to hang her stole in a closet. The gesture both amused and alarmed her. He was careful with fine things; he assumed she was going to be here for some time. Though she'd made up her mind to that in the car, for him to assume it— Mentally, she shrugged. Fawn was like that.

He came to her, took her into his arms, and she let him. Her own hands went quite naturally to his shoulders.

She saw those intense lips coming at her, and closed her eyes. This was what she wanted, what she really wanted. This was the beginning of her treatment. It was ridding her of the misery Burr Travis had caused.

Fawn's lips were cool, and they kissed a long, cool, seeking kiss. His lips were like a hunter which stalks its prey, she thought fleetingly.

Now he pressed her to him, so that every line of her body followed the lines of his. She felt his manhood, and the kiss deepened. He moved against her, once, in an exploratory manner.

She moved in return. That fire Burr had built, but now she wasn't sure it was all Burr. After all, it was Fawn's body against which her own was pressing.

"I've planned for this," he whispered. "Waited. For you to be in the mood." He moved one hand so that it was inside her dress, her bra. He caressed her nipple and she felt it stiffen, felt the gnawing fire in her depths, thought of Burr, of Lance.

She lay against Fawn, offering no resistance.

"Now, at last you're pliable," Fawn whispered. "Will you permit me to do it my way, the way I've dreamed?"

She felt herself nod, thought she was like a windup toy, that Burr Travis or Lance Buford or Fawn, or even the three of them together had turned a key in her back, and she would go through certain motions until the spring ran down.

"Splendid!" he murmured. "Just stand right there, in the middle of the room. Let me do everything."

She stood, the wound-up toy, where he put her.

She felt his fingers at her back, heard the long zipper of her dress whisper open. He helped her step out of the dress, then took it to the closet and hung it on the hanger over her stole.

He returned, hooked his long fingers into the top of the pantyhose and pulled it slowly down to her ankles. He lifted her, set her on the bed, took her sandals off, and then the pantyhose the rest of the way. These he put neatly on the nearest chair, the shoes under the chair.

Coolly, deliberately, he unfastened her bra and drew it away, pulled off her bikini panties and added them to the things on the chair. She stood naked on his scarlet carpet, wondering if she was a scarlet woman.

But I can't be! she thought. He can't make me one, because Burr has already done it!

"Watch me, now," he said, his eyes going over her, lingering. Down they went, then up and down again.

It was thus that he removed his own clothing. He hung away his suit, draped his shirt on the back of a second chair, folded his underwear and laid it on the seat, stood his shoes beneath, on the scarlet carpet, the socks in them.

Naked, he looked every inch of his six feet. He was medium-boned, flesh smooth and strong and muscular, build proper for his height. His hair had never seemed blacker. There was a line of black hair down his belly, where it broadened and from which sprang his long, eager manhood.

Why, she thought, it's like his features! They were keen and sharp and intense. But suave. And this maleness resembled a knife. She was almost frightened of it.

But she'd gone this far. She was going to see it through. Her whole future hinged on what she was about to do with him.

He came to her, stood so that the tip of his maleness barely touched her above her own hidden part. It set up a tingling of her spine, a singing in her ears.

Standing thus, he stroked the sides of her hair, using both palms, slowly, very slowly. They slid down her neck in that same manner, and as the tingling grew, she found it impossible to breathe normally.

Now his hands were traveling her shoulders, slipping to her breasts. His thumbs moved her erect nipples, and the singing of her ears mixed with the tingling of her spine. In her depths the hotness grew.

His hands moved downward, lingered between

her thighs. His breath hit her face softly as he whispered, all the smoothness of his nature in the sound.

"Silk, satin. The texture of your body. Velvet!"

"Y-you like that?" she whispered. Despite the tingling and the singing, she had to learn, to find out about men.

"I adore it," he told her softly, "so velvety outside, such inner spirit! You are the perfect woman!"

"You don't know that—yet!" she breathed.

Her heart was thundering. She was daring him to the act which he had every intention of committing. Even now it wasn't too late. She could still decide against him.

But there was so little time. And she didn't want to stop. Not now. Not on the brink of learning. Not when this heightening flame could be quenched, could be banished, never to be felt again, except for Lance.

He set his hands at her waist and urged her gently backward, to the bed. She was aware of confusion, of roaring heart, of the carpet under her bare feet. And then she was lying on the bed on her back, and he was above her.

She had one glimpse of his face. Like a knife, she thought. And then he smoothly stabbed that other knife-part into her secret opening, and she felt it go far in, heard the moan of pleasure from her own lips mingle with his groan.

He went into action immediately, fast stabbing all the way in, almost all the way out, then all the way in. It was an easy rhythm to follow, and one she found pleasing. She matched it exactly, as though he were leading her in the dance, to the pulsing of music. Caught up in this, hotness building, she had only a fleeting memory of how it had been with the cowpoke, fierce and burning and blazing. She blocked out this memory and gave herself to Fawn's expertise, enjoying every fluid stab, giving it back, memorizing.

When he ceased, when his body stiffened, she pressed upward, squeezing his throbbing organ instinctively with her inner walls. Then, swiftly, there came over her the pleasure drifting up from deep within, spreading through her until she glowed.

He withdrew, but kept her in his arms. He murmured constantly, voice so low she couldn't distinguish the words, but they were terms of endearment. She listened with pleasure, with a sense of how different everything was after all, with a different man.

"Did you like that, my sweet?" he asked, speaking more distinctly.

"Yes, Fawn," she said honestly. "I did. I liked it."

"It wasn't your first time."

So he knew; he'd been able to tell.

"Almost the first," she murmured.

"The quality, how does that compare, my sweet?"

"You were perfect," she whispered. "You are my first perfection."

He held her closer, though lightly. He stroked her. "There can never be too much perfection," he whispered back, and with that utter smoothness entered her again.

This time it was even better. Her own passion rose faster and she recognized it, almost joyfully, as sheer passion. Their stabbing dance, that mating dance, was faster, hotter. At the end they clung, it seemed, forever.

The burning in her was gone. She thought of the Texas bum and felt no hatred, merely crossness at herself for having let him disturb her. Fawn had eased that burn the first time; now she was filled with contentment.

He broke in on her thoughts quietly. "In our parents' day," he said, "this joy you've granted me would have had an inevitable ending."

"What ending?" she murmured.

"Marriage. Without marriage, possible disgrace. For you."

"Women are liberated from that now," she told him idly. "They do as they please, have sex as they please."

"Only you haven't, Rae-Ellen."

"I told you, you aren't the first."

"But I'm almost the first, isn't that so?"

"That's—right."

"The second?"

"I don't choose to tell."

"Then I lay claim to second. You're too honest to lie, so when you evade I know you're telling the truth in a backward sort of way."

"I should scratch your eyes out for that," she said, and smiled.

He was right. He was so right. He knew her better than she'd dreamed. But then, she'd given him scant thought, had thrown up a barrier against him.

"Liberated woman or not, my sweet," he said. "I'm going to take advantage of the fact that you're newly liberated. I'm asking you to marry me."

Lying in his arms on his ridiculously big, low bed, filled with the juices of his love, his marriage proposal in her ears, she was abruptly confused. She was mixed up with three men—Lance, whom she loved but who wanted Adah, Burr Travis, whom she loathed, now Fawn.

The first peace she'd known in days was here, right now, in bed with him. Maybe she should marry him, remain in this state of contentment, put an end to misery and anger.

"You're very quiet, my sweet. Does it take you so long to decide? Is it, perhaps, that you haven't known me long enough?" His last words came on a keen little chuckle.

"Goodness, Fawn! I've known you practically forever!"

"But never had a thought in that lovely head about marrying me?"

"Oh, thoughts!" she retorted, and managed a laugh. "Any girl has thoughts! She looks at a man and wonders how it would be to marry him."

"And how he'd be in bed?"

"That, naturally."

"And how was it tonight, for you?"

She had to give him an honest answer. "In my experience, it was perfect, Fawn."

"Then what's holding you back?"

Papa's ultimatum, mostly, at this instant. But she couldn't tell Fawn that. Besides, it was so new. It was too soon; there were too many men involved. And it was Lance she loved. Loving him, she couldn't, when actually faced with it, marry anyone else.

"Sweet?" Fawn whispered. "Your answer?"

"I—can't answer," she confessed.

"I'll wait. If you'll see me, even on the old basis. Or date privately, get better acquainted."

"No, not that. Tonight was wonderful, but I'll not repeat it."

"Nor will I. Tonight was perfection. Our wedding night will be the ultimate perfection. All I ask is that we have pleasant times together, grow toward each other."

The request was reasonable. After the way she'd behaved with him tonight, she owed him at least friendship. It would be unfair to love and run. In addition to that, she'd learned a different sex with him, a kind she could, given opportunity, use with Lance. And, of immediate importance, Fawn had cleaned that unholy burning for Burr Travis out of her.

"Sweet one," Fawn persisted, "you will see me?"

She promised, let his lips take hers in a lingering kiss. Then she permitted him to dress her, a procedure in which he seemed to take as much delight as he had in undressing her.

She watched him dress.

When they left the apartment, no one meeting them could have suspected the manner in which they'd disported. They were a suave young gentleman and a lovely girl, meticulously dressed, not a wrinkle anywhere.

Rae-Ellen wondered how adept at such evenings Fawn actually was. There'd been his extreme care in hanging away their clothes, equal care in bringing them out to put on again.

He was experienced, that she knew. He was also discreet. There'd never been a hint about his sex life, not even from Mary-Lou, who found out everything.

Magnolia Hall was dark except for the dim lights kept burning in the hallways. Rae-Ellen kissed Fawn good-night, then slipped inside and put the lock on the door.

She tiptoed up to her rooms. The crack under Adah's door was dark. She hoped her sister was asleep. Of course they all knew by now that Rae-Ellen and Fawn had slipped away together, but she didn't want to discuss it, even its innocent aspects, of which it had few.

She examined her feelings.

She was no different. Having sex with Fawn hadn't left her soiled. She was herself again.

Without the physical uproar Burr Travis had created in her.

17

She got into bed naked, pulled the sheet to her chin. She'd never felt so relaxed, so ready for sleep. She wondered if marriage would give this lassitude, every night. If marriage to Fawn would do it.

No. Thoughts of Lance would creep in as they were doing now. Fawn could provide relaxation on occasion. But Lance was the only one who could do it over the years, because, with him, it would be founded on love.

She curled up, happily certain that she'd be able to satisfy Lance's manly appetites. Experienced Fawn had been delighted to the point he'd made love a second time, then talked of marriage. She felt now, in this cozy moment, that one session of love with Lance would make him hers.

She felt herself drift into sleep.

At the bottom of slumber, was commotion. Midway of slumber, there was the shrill whinny of horses, the distant shouts of men. Nearby, feet were running along hallways. Downstairs, a door slammed. A car motor started.

Rae-Ellen sat up as the door between her suite and Adah's popped open. "Something's wrong at the stables!" Adah cried, and switched on the overhead light.

She was in a woolly yellow robe that reached her ankles. Her hair was down.

Rae-Ellen, naked, dashed to her closet, snatched out a robe, stepped into fur-lined slippers. "It may be Starstruck! Or Thunder Boy! Or both!"

"You can't go like that!" Adah protested. "With nothing but a—"

But Rae-Ellen was already out of the room and running down the stairs, clutching her car keys. If Burr Travis had let anything happen to those racers, she'd personally decapitate him!

Outside, as she rammed the key into the ignition, the whinny of the horses was louder. One of them almost screamed; she thought that was Thunder Boy. She trod the starter, put the Lincoln at the curving driveway. Now, the pounding of blood in her ears, the purring of the motor, the night breeze rushing past, cushioned the noise from the stable.

She pulled up fast, burning rubber, jumped out of the car. Papa's Cadillac was parked just in front of her. There were voices, low and rumbling now, in the stable. No whinnying, no kicking in the stalls.

She raced to the stable, slipped inside, careful to make no sudden move. The interior was dimly lit. Papa and Mama and Terry were grouped at the end box, where Rusty was kept. Burr wasn't in sight, but she could hear his voice, that singsong soothing, hear the horses moving restlessly.

Papa had an overcoat over his pajamas. Mama wore a coat, too. They, along with the stableboy and groom, were bunched outside Rusty's stall, looking in.

Rae-Ellen tiptoed over.

"It's Rusty," Papa breathed. "Got a stone in his hoof."

Rusty, an extremely high-strung gelding, was Rae-Ellen's favorite hunter.

"Not from his bedding, I swear it, sir!" Ken whispered. It was his duty to put fresh straw in the stalls. "I go through that straw first with my hands, the way Terry—and he knows—'cause he's the groom."

He rolled his light brown eyes from face to face, pleading to be believed.

Terry swiped his sun-faded hair out of his eyes, spoke quietly in his thin voice. "I already told you, Ken. It's no fault of yours. Mr. Pettigrew knows that. And so does Mr. Travis."

Just at this time Burr stood up, fully dressed, a wet rag in his hand. He looked at the waiting group and gave an easy grin. Rae-Ellen couldn't tell whether he knew she was present or not.

"He's all right," Burr said. "I've treated the bruise, and it ain't but a very small one, with my own concoction. It always works. It'll heal fast." He handed a small pebble to Papa. "That's what made him raise all the ruckus and start up the other horses. Some horses wouldn't pay it much mind, but not this one."

"Will he be able to go on the hunt?" Papa asked.

"Likely. I'll keep up the treatment. The boys

and me are going to drag the track again, and inspect it. Rusty must've picked it up when he had his workout. It sure wasn't in the bedding. The boys go over that like you wouldn't believe."

He looked only at Papa.

He ignored Rae-Ellen, even though she was one of the owners. So she stepped right up to the stall, naked under her robe, and made herself known.

"What about the other hunters?" she demanded. "And Thunder Boy and Starstruck? Did any of them hurt themselves?"

"Not a one," Burr drawled, and he did drawl, pulling out the words as if he thought he was on the Texas range talking to some ignorant cowgirl. "They all got excited when Rusty cut up, and Thunder Boy let the end of his stall have it. But he ain't hurt. Starstruck ain't, either. Nor any hunter. They all got upset, being highbred."

"No reason why we should stay, then?" Papa asked.

"None, sir. I'll have Terry sit. He can give Rusty a treatment now and again the rest of the night. But the injury's practically nothing, just a light scratch. If he'd been worked with that stone in there, it'd be a different story, though that wouldn't happen, not with the fuss he made over just standing on it."

"Then we'll go back to the house," Papa said. "Rae-Ellen, come along."

"I came in my own car," she said.

"So. Come along fast, then. Looks like rain."

He left, Burr dismissed Ken, who departed for his quarters at the far end of the stable, then paid Rae-Ellen the first unsolicited attention he'd deigned to give her. He had that stubborn look on his mouth; his eyes went over her dark wool robe, and it was as if he saw through to her nakedness, because his mouth got worse.

"If you'll do as your father suggested," he said, "we can all get a bit more sleep."

"Not just yet, if you don't mind!" she snapped.

Then, for no reason, she wanted to cry.

"Why should I mind?"

She flipped away and through the door, so Terry couldn't hear what she had to say. Burr long-legged it after her, thinking, she knew, that he was seeing her to the car. Well, he had a surprise coming to him, him and his damnable brown eyes looking her over, him and his mulish mouth!

He stopped at the car, but she kept going for the cottage. He followed; it was all he could do. She marched in, switching on lights, went straight to the bedroom to show him she wasn't intimidated, not a bit.

"What the hell you doing in my bedroom?" he demanded, stomping in after her.

"It's not going to be your bedroom long!" she flared.

"What's your idea this time—that you're going to move in with me?"

She whirled, almost attacked him, but did not. She clenched her jaw. "You must see now that you're not fit for this job!"

"Because Rusty picked up a stone?" he asked, incredulous. "You're saying I ain't fit to be a trainer?"

"A good trainer never lets anything happen to the horses in his care!"

"If you aim to quibble," he drawled, "your pa hired me to train a pair of two-year-old racers and twin yearlings. That's all he was after. I offered to keep an eye on the hunters, and he accepted."

"Just the same! It shows you're not competent! Your own pride should make you see that! But of course you haven't any pride!"

Again, for no reason, she wanted to cry.

"What do you base that statement on?" he asked, through his teeth.

"On the fact that you're not wanted here!"

"Your pa wants me."

"But I don't! Especially after what happened to Rusty. No telling what—and I'm one of the owners! That's where pride comes in!"

"Your pride, I take it?"

"No, your pride! I'd think you'd be too proud to stay where you're not wanted!"

"As I said, your pa wants me, and your sister—"

"Half sister!"

"She's half owner. And she's satisfied. Way it looks to me, you're outvoted, two-to-one."

She glared at him, wordless with rage. Her blood was pumping through her with such force it created an inner shaking. She felt the pulse in her throat jump, drum. A shiver went over her, and she trembled, unable to hide it.

And he saw.

He took one step, yanked her robe, had it off. He turned dull red, he was so mad. He swung, pulled open his closet, brought out jeans and shirt, threw them at her so they struck her naked body.

"Put them on before you get pneumonia!" he grated. "And get that robe over them. Then go home where you belong!"

She hurled his clothes to the floor. In a frenzy that he had the gall to think she'd actually wear them, she jumped up and down on them in her fur slippers. These flew off, and her bare soles hit the tough fabric of his hated garments.

She felt herself being lifted, then she was flying through space. She landed on the bed. She sprang up, and he was there, pushing her back.

"Seeing what's happened between us in this room," he said, breath slamming her face, "and seeing that you came straight in here naked—"

"I had my robe on!"

"Same as naked. Makes a man think you want more of the same. Every time I see you, you're wantin' it."

She lay still, waiting, seething because he spoke the truth. The instant he started to take his clothes off, she'd run out of there. She'd grab her robe if she had time, but if not, she'd go naked.

A sudden burst of rain hit the windows broadside. Immediately it swathed the cottage, pounded and poured onto the roof. It thundered; lightning cracked.

"Want to go out in that?" Burr demanded.

"I have to. My car . . . Ken and Terry . . . the others . . ."

"They'll see nothing. The boys. Too far away."

"My parents . . . my sister . . ."

"They'll know you're waiting out the storm."

It was almost as if he were inviting her to stay.

"Oh, damn the storm!" she wailed.

Wailed because she was alone with him, and naked. Again. Because that deep place in her, the evil fire which he alone had lit, was smoldering.

She stared up into his eyes, those damnable eyes, seeking escape, but only entrapment lay there. His eyes, which had no right to be beautiful, increased her rage, and the rage fed that smoldering fire and made it worse. His headstrong mouth fed it. The way he flung off his clothes, and the way his maleness sprang forth, quickened it.

She bit her lips to keep from screaming at him to get out, to keep from screaming for him to hurry, to ease her before she exploded.

She moaned as he kissed her; she moaned as she kissed in return, angrily, hungrily. She moaned as he came into her, surely bigger than the other times, moaned again as he began to move.

He started from side to side, groaning on every breath. She matched him, side to side. He started a clockwise motion; she adjusted to it, going the opposite. She felt her inner self grip him; she felt that blaze flash through her and envelop them both.

He gasped, the breath hurting his belly, when that grip took hold of him. He drew another breath and held it.

Somehow he kept to his movements, switching them so as to hold out, so as to make the big moment, when it came, better than any of the other times. But that grip got him; suddenly he was erupting, and she was crying out and hanging onto him, and when he'd finished, she was sobbing, "More . . . you've got to . . . more!"

He rolled off her, but not out, holding her. The rain clattered and flowed and drummed. Thunder rolled, lightning flashed and stood. He wished the hell the ceiling light was out, but he didn't dare risk getting up to turn it off. No telling what this wild woman would do.

She rolled her head, one side to another, her breasts surging. "I—told you—more."

"I have got to have a minute off," he said. "Even

a Texas bum ain't like a light switch. Give me a little time and I'll oblige you gladly."

She mumbled something he didn't quite catch about if he'd hurry, then she could get something washed out. For keeps. It didn't make sense.

"I'm going to turn off the light," he said. "Okay?"

"It doesn't matter."

He thumped across the room, pushed down on the switch, and there was darkness. Outside, the rain continued to pour. The only light was that from the flashing storm.

Because she wanted him for some female reason, and because he was still stirred up, he began to caress her. He kissed her slowly, top to bottom and up again in the flashing dark. By the time he'd finished, he was ready, and from the way she was squirming, she was more than ready, and he entered her again.

This time, when they came to the top of the hill and saw what was on the other side, he knew he'd never find a woman anywhere that could match this one for bed. No matter what wife he later married, he'd never forget these times with this spoiled, unreasonable, bratty girl.

He was still thinking this, with her curled in his arms and asleep, when he himself fell asleep. It was the rain stopping that put an end to it.

"Wake up," he said, giving her a little shake. "Put on your robe and scoot. It'll be daylight before you know it."

She put on the robe, the slippers. She looked tired. By gum, she had a right to. He'd not been gentle with her, not a whit. She'd had what she wanted. She'd offered, and he'd taken.

She stared silently at him. Once she shook her head. Fawn had eased her; she'd thought she was free. But it was Burr who quenched her fires. Burr Travis had done that. And this time it was for keeps. She felt nothing for him, nothing at all. Not hatred, not that awful burn.

"I'm going," she told him.

He nodded. In her robe she ran through the dripping predawn to her car. At the big house she stopped it silently.

Marie was waiting in her sitting room.

"I know where you spent the night, and I've got a pretty good idea of what you've been doing," Marie said after one look.

"Marie . . . please!"

"Don't 'please' me, young lady! It's all over you! You've been with a man; you're all wrung out. I won't say more, but I do warn you against sleeping with that Texan another time. He's nothing but trouble to you. Watch yourself!"

18

The third Saturday in September dawned cold. The exclusive membership of The Fox Hunt Club assembled at Twelve Oaks before seven in the morning.

The mounts were stepping about; jigging. The hounds, tied at leash, were whining and giving low yelps. The arriving hunters shouted back and forth, each greeted in person by Lance, astride his big hunter, Black Prince.

The breaths of people and horses alike puffed white on the air. Rae-Ellen felt relaxed, almost lighthearted, for the first time in recent days. For one thing, Burr Travis wasn't there. He'd been at the stable, helping saddle up, long-legging it in his work clothes, giving a friendly good morning to all but Rae-Ellen, at whom he merely grunted.

She and Adah walked their mounts, Rae-Ellen on Lola. They greeted fellow hunters, laughing, getting excited at the prospect of the chase. It was a small club, having only twenty members, which was the way they preferred it.

The men wore red coats, referred to as "pinks," which were perfectly tailored and had a gold stripe, the club's color, at one side of the collar. They wore black riding breeches and boots, white stocks at their necks, and black top hats. Their riding crops and saddles were black.

The women wore black or navy coats with the one gold stripe, and buff or canary-yellow breeches. They wore derbies and black riding boots and carried black hunting whips. Their stocks, too, were white.

Rae-Ellen urged the bay, Lola, close to Adah's roan, Misty.

"What did Lance say," she teased, "about your yellow breeches?"

"He doesn't know I'm alive. Just watch him!"

Indeed, Lance was at a constant, slow move, surrounded and followed by riders. He was talking to club members, to Papa and Mama, the Buncombes from Raleigh, to others. He was giving directions to the huntsman he'd hired, repeating orders to the whippers-in, who had bred and trained the hounds, so they'd be kept together in the field. He looked very handsome in his red coat and his Master's hunting cap of scarlet with black visor.

"We'll raise a fox in no time!" he called out once so all could hear. And then his attention was claimed by riders, by Newley, the field-master.

Mary-Lou and Jim came loping up the driveway. Immediately, they seemed to be everywhere at once, saying hello, laughing, excited.

Adah was so happy she tingled. Rae-Ellen was friendly again, the hunt was getting ready to start, and Lance was in charge. She was so proud of him she thought she'd burst. Not only was he one of the most respected men in the Piedmont, but he loved *her,* Adah Pettigrew!

It was a wonderful, perfect day, and she didn't have to decide anything. She didn't have to ponder whether to tell Lance her dark secret. She could simply be happy, a carefree girl on the first fox hunt of the season. That she loved the Master of the Hunt only added to her joy. She was a very lucky girl to be cherished by such a man.

Rae-Ellen, too, felt increasingly good. She'd ride her best, let Lance see what a fine huntmate she'd be. Adah, though she rode well, wasn't in Rae-Ellen's class, and Lance couldn't avoid noticing.

He was too busy to hang around Adah, thank goodness. Right now he was again talking to his field-master, who would lead the mounted hunters, call the field until and even after they flushed their fox.

Now he rode over to the two girls.

"The day is perfect," he said.

"Indeed, yes!" exclaimed Rae-Ellen. "We'll be ravenous for breakfast at ten!"

"Where's Pete?" Adah asked. "Isn't he coming, Fawn?"

Fawn gestured at the drive. "Here he is now."

It was two horsemen in pinks, not one, who cantered up. One was Pete, his beachboy looks enhanced by the coat and the top hat. The second rider, his own top hat set on tawny, sun-faded hair, was Burr Travis, astride Rusty. The coat and especially the top hat made him look bigger, rougher, homelier, more rugged, than ever and to add to the confusion, handsome.

Rae-Ellen put Lola alongside Rusty.

"What are you thinking," she demanded, "to ride Rusty?"

"His hoof's okay. He's one hundred percent fit."

"Where did you get those pinks?" she demanded.

"Had them tailored. In Raleigh. Rush job. How do they fit?"

She tossed her chin, didn't answer.

They fitted perfectly. She might have expected some high-handed move. He'd not wear borrowed pinks even if he could find some that would fit him. So big, so rough-hewn, so . . . raw.

Adah and Fawn now rode up. "What made you so slow?" Adah asked gaily. "Five minutes, and I don't know what Lance would have done."

Mary-Lou and Jim cantered up in time to hear.

"He'd never wait!" Mary-Lou sang out. "That's one thing makes him the best Hunt Master in the Piedmont! The hunt goes on time, no matter who's missin'!"

"I had things to do at the stable," Burr said. "I had to dress. Pete was good enough to help me saddle up."

"Two are faster than one," grinned Pete. "Glad for your company on the ride over."

Rae-Ellen was no longer feeling gay. She heard Mary-Lou go on and on about how handsome Burr looked, that he was terrific.

Until now, since the night she spent at Burr's

222

cottage, a short time actually, Rae-Ellen had avoided any confrontation with the beast. She'd gone, with Adah and their parents, to the early workout, but kept her distance from him. In this manner, she'd prevented an upsurge of that torturing fire she had seemingly managed to quench with him. And she meant to keep it that way.

The field was waiting, mounts restive. Some horses were fretting and jigging, some were throwing their noses in the air, were being reined up. Others had their ears erect and twitching; a few had their ears slicked back.

Lance took his place at the head of the field with Newley. He gave the field-master a nod. Newley gestured to the bugler.

The clear, shrill notes cleft the frosty air.

Lance led the field, starting at a trot, Newley off to one side. Following, going into an easy lope as Lance rode faster, the hunters rode, led by the Master of the Hunt, to where they could see and hear the hounds without interfering with them.

Burr rode ahead of Rae-Ellen, off to the left of Pete. Fawn rode near Rae-Ellen. Adah loped easily, graceful in the saddle, Mary-Lou and a space to her left, Jim, out to her right. The rest of the field followed along behind, keeping pace.

The speed built. Ahead loomed a considerable section of rail fence. This was one of the jumps Lance had ordered erected. She saw his black horse sail over, clearing it by inches. Riding for the fence, she kept half an eye to see what the roustabout, on Rusty, would do about the barrier, but he, too, sailed right over. He didn't clear the top by as much as Lance had done, but Black Prince was a better jumper than Rusty.

It gave her some satisfaction, as Burr jumped, to see him list to the right. So. Cowboy or not, he wasn't perfect in the saddle! None of the others listed. Rae-Ellen, gripping Lola with her knees, whispering, "Take it, girl!" felt the mare lift and fly, then they were on the other side of the jump, galloping with the field.

Now the terrain was rough. There were stands of trees. There were thickets, fallen logs. Riding, gaze keen ahead, she waited for the hounds to give tongue.

They were baying, yelping. They had their noses to the ground, running ahead of the field. The huntsman and the whippers-in drew, or flushed a covert, searching the thicket for fox by taking the pack through it.

Suddenly, on the far side of the covert, there was a flash of red.

The hounds gave tongue.

Rae-Ellen's heart leapt. They'd flushed their fox at first try! It broke into the open, a running, red streak, moving like the wind.

The hounds, huntsman, and whippers-in settled on the line, or trail, of the fox. At their heels, Lance put Black Prince to a gallop, the field-master rode at top speed, and the members of the field did the same, using their crops when needed.

Rae-Ellen had the sensation of flying. Her heart winged faster than her mount. Exhilaration flared. Burr was riding abreast of her now, but she scarcely noticed.

The hounds ran silent, gave tongue, went silent.

The scent was good, then. The hounds were soon faster, and so was the field. They cleared a wide ditch, Rae-Ellen rising in the saddle for the jump, easing back when it was over, thundering on.

The chase quickened, became harder, more intense.

An old stone wall. They cleared that, raced after the hounds. Rae-Ellen exulted at every reaching stride of her mare, at every jump, thrilled when the hounds gave tongue constantly.

She never feared for the fox. The fox almost always got away. Actually, the field played no part in hunting the fox. A good ride over the country, the hills, ever-harder jumps, was their sport, rather than to kill. In fact, most of them were afraid the fox would be killed.

Sometimes the pack caught the fox, but not often.

Suddenly the hounds lost the scent.

The field reined up at Lance's signal. They waited, giving their mounts a breather. The huntsman helped the hounds hit off and recover the line.

This took some time, but at last they had the scent and were off again.

Now the entire field sped like the wind.

The pack was in full cry.

Ahead, an old, broad stone wall blocked the way.

Black Prince lifted, flew across, hit ground on the far side, galloped on, Lance taking the jump as though he was a part of the stallion. Now the field-master cleared the wall, and the flowing field made for it.

Lola was running like a sweetheart. Rae-Ellen tightened her knees. Lola lifted and sailed, hit square on the other side, unexpectedly reared. Fighting the reins, getting the mare in control, Rae-Ellen saw the next horse clear the wall, saw the pinks tilt to the right, saw the rider flat on the ground. The oncoming field jumped the wall, pounded ahead.

The figure on the ground leapt to its feet and waved to a rider who would have turned back. Rusty was galloping after the field, saddle hanging to the right.

The dehorsed one had to be Burr Travis!

Fawn and Adah reined up, trotted back.

"You-all go ahead," Burr said. He brushed leaves and twigs and dirt off his habit, retrieved his top hat and riding crop. "Nothing's hurt. I only got my breath knocked out for a second. I've had plenty of experience being thrown by Texas broncs."

"You don't know you're all right, it's too soon to know!" Adah protested. "Fawn, tell him!"

"She's right, Travis. You know that. We'll ride double back to Twleve Oaks. You can wait there for the breakfast, or I'll borrow a car and run you back to your cottage."

"Not to the cottage!" Adah protested. "Papa wants you to get acquainted with the hunt people at breakfast, Burr! You can't disappoint him!"

"Reckon not," Burr said slowly, "seeing he's my boss." He flicked a brown-eyed look over the two girls. "Best ride on, Miss Rae-Ellen, Miss Adah. Take them word there's no injuries."

"I'm staying!" Adah declared. "With two handsome men!"

She dimpled, but her face looked innocent, and for a second, Rae-Ellen wanted to slap her. But never mind. Maybe, riding ahead, she'd get a moment with Lance.

"You go then," Burr told Rae-Ellen.

Furious at being dismissed, too proud to refuse

and fight with him in the presence of others, wanting to be near Lance anyway, Rae-Ellen pulled on the reins. She put Lola to a quick gallop.

She rode fast, deliberately ignoring the crazy need to feel Burr over, to know, with her own fingers, that he was all right. Well, he had Adah. He had the one he wanted; let him take joy in it. Besides, he was too tough to be hurt.

She poured on speed, took the jumps, came up at the end of the field. When someone shouted a question, she shouted back there'd been no harm done, and the hunt continued.

After miles and hours, the fox disappeared.
They searched until even the hounds gave up.

They rode back, laughing, exchanging stories of the various jumps, congratulating the fox, the Hunt Master, the field-master, the huntsman, the whippers-in, each other. They assured Hal Buncombe, who would serve as Hunt Master when Lance went to Florida, that he'd make a fine Hunt Master, too.

When they got back to the house, the first thing Rae-Ellen saw was Burr Travis sitting with Adah on a porch bench. Fawn was nowhere in sight. This marred her satisfaction at riding all the way home beside Lance, laughing with him, building a closeness between them.

Papa had caught Rusty on the way back and was leading him. He dismounted, tethered both horses, came to Burr, who stood to meet him.

"Seems your saddle slipped," Papa said.

"That's right, sir. I felt it slide, right under my —under me. I can't understand it. I saddled Rusty myself, cinched it tight. I'll look it over, see if it's faulty."

227

Part III
THE WRECK

19

Fawn and Pete were having lunch at The Meeting Place, a private club outside Durham. The tables were widely spaced and by speaking quietly, privacy was insured the members, who were all businessmen. The decor was rugged and masculine—oak, copper, heavy beige curtains. Many an excellent lunch was eaten here, many a business deal closed.

Fawn and Pete, distant cousins, had disposed of their tobacco talk, but sat on, each suspecting that the other had something more on his mind.

Fawn, deeply stirred over his encounter with Rae-Ellen, felt that he must now court her seriously. First, win her love, hopefully rouse in her affection to match his own. He frowned, casting about for an opening with Pete.

"What's on your mind, fellow?" Pete asked, his

blond hair glinting from the lights. "Haven't seen you look this way since Duke University, when we were working our way through. Hell," he corrected himself, "when we were both working our asses off to climb to the top at Pettigrew's, for that matter. We're at the top now, so what's eating you?"

"We're not all the way to the top."

"Right next to the old man himself."

"And he won't sell us stock. So when he's gone? And the widow sells out?"

"Hell, if we can get Rae-Ellen and Adah to get the hots for us the way we've got it for them, no problem. Perfect marriages, for us and for them."

"*If* we can win the girls," Fawn mused.

"No reason why not. We've been dating them, stealing a kiss. They don't slap us down."

"Dates, but usually in a group," Fawn reminded. "The four of us; Mary-Lou and Jim. Even Lance Buford."

"The tar-bucket."

"Because the girls want him," Fawn said.

"Family friend!" snorted Pete. "They've both got the hots for him, too, if you ask me," he continued, his usually sunny face sober.

"Their father would never let one of them marry Buford," Fawn said. "He as much as told me he wants them to marry tobacco. And Buford's cotton. He'd never let a son of his go into tobacco, and it's all over the boss that he wants a dynasty."

"I don't know of another tobacco man in the Piedmont who has a son old enough for either girl," Pete said.

"That should be in our favor, then."

Pete grinned widely. "Say, that's right! That cuts out all tobacco competition! We've got to make the girls feel toward us the way we do toward them!"

"You spoke of the hots," Fawn said. "I'd suggest you stop laying every girl who comes your way."

"Hell, what's a guy to do? They throw themselves at me, sit up and beg for it! I'm normal. I'm healthy, and tell me when I've had a real chance with Adah!"

"Regardless, stop playing around. And don't go too fast with Adah. She's not that kind of girl."

"You can say that again!" Pete agreed, sober. "I will cut off all the others, concentrate just on her. She's far and beyond the loveliest girl I've ever known. You going to do the same with Rae-Ellen?"

"Yes. It's time. The old man's pleased with us and our work. He comes to us for ideas."

No need to let Pete know what a sexpot Rae-Ellen had turned out to be. No sense in outlining his hope to keep passion simmering in her. Passion was the keynote with Rae-Ellen. She was a bundle of fire. And he loved her for it.

When she married him, his life would be complete.

Pete grinned, marveling at the turn their discussion had taken. "If we'd had this talk when we first went to work at Pettigrew's," he said, "I wouldn't have played the field the way I have. Do you suppose Adah has heard—stories? Mary-Lou—"

"She knows Mary-Lou is a chatterbox. And it would have been out of order for us to have courted Rae-Ellen and Adah before now."

"I don't see how we can do it now. Always, the group."

"We'll proceed naturally," Fawn advised. "Continue the group dates, but press for separate ones. Then, when we all go to Florida for the racing—"

"Can we get away from work for that?"

"The old man suggested it himself. Besides, we're executives. You've Simpson to take over for you, and I've Langford. They can follow directions, contact us by phone, if need be."

Pete took on his sunny face again. "You know, Adah attracted me from the very first. That quiet, gentle kind—I've never had one of them because I didn't want complications."

"Adah has depth, too. Enough, I'd say, to overlook your premarital behavior if she finds out the stories are true. She might even be understanding enough after marriage—"

Pete solemnly held up his hand. "I'm a quarter gone on Adah now. I'll be half-gone if I put a ring on her finger, and she'll have all of me once we've gone the route. I'll never want another woman, so help me!"

Fawn laughed, shook his head.

"You don't think I'll be true to her! Even when I swear it!"

"While it's new, yes. But the years grow long, my cousin."

"You'll find out!" Pete declared. "Say, that'll make us brothers-in-law, as well as cousins!"

In good humor, hearts high, the two young men left the club, each returning to his private office and his duties.

Burr Travis, since the fox-hunting, had wrenched his mind off sexy Rae-Ellen Pettigrew, off gentle, alluring Adah. He put all his attention on his job and kept it there.

At the time Fawn and Pete were discussing the

girls, Burr was interviewing Henry Cartson, horse trainer. They had inspected the hunters, which Cartson admired, and had spent time watching Thunder Boy and Starstruck. The two racers were galloping about in the pasture. They tossed their heads, whinnied, stopped, now and again, to nibble at a patch of green, galloped on.

Burr watched them, but missed nothing about Cartson. He was carefully sizing up the man, liking him better all the while.

The trainer was short, wiry and alert. He said he was forty-two. He had a bald patch behind graying brown forelock and quick, dark eyes.

"I gather you wonder why I want a job as assistant trainer," he said.

"Well, yes. You've worked some mighty good racers. Some that have won purses."

"That I have. My racers have won at Hialeah, Aqueduct, Santa Anita, Churchill Downs, Gulfstream. You name it, I've had winners."

"And good money."

"Yes. Mighty good. And tension, plenty of that. The big owners, the ones that want big purses, want the trainer's blood, too."

Burr stared.

"That's right. They don't know it themselves, but they're so hell-bent on another Man-o-War, they work the ass off the trainer. I'm up to here with it."

"The tension, you mean."

"Exactly. I've saved money and invested. Now, hooked on racers, I still want to work with them. At a slower pace. This job is what I want. If you think I'm the man you want."

Hell, Burr thought, why am I holding back?

This man can teach me! And he sure-hell is reliable. I can leave him in charge here and go to Florida with an easy mind.

He told Cartson that. The trainer stuck out his hand, and they shook on the deal. "If I suit your owner," he said.

"He left the choice up to me," Burr replied, "and you're it. I'll show you your room. It's at the far end of the stable, adjoins the rooms of the stable-boy and groom. There are cooking facilities."

The next morning, as usual, the Pettigrew family showed up for an early workout. So did Fawn and Pete, who managed to stand at the rail with the two girls. Lance appeared too, which he seldom did, being occupied with Samson's Lad's workouts.

Burr introduced Cartson as the new assistant trainer, and he shook hands all round. He held Adah's hand a shade longer than the others. There was a twinkle in his eyes.

"You're a sunbeam in that yellow," he said.

She dimpled, smiled shyly.

"He's right, love," Pete declared. "You're the sun in the sky!"

"Only because it isn't time for sunrise!" Adah protested.

"You'll outshine the sun," Lance put in quietly.

Rae-Ellen watched Adah go scarlet at Lance's remark. He smiled, seeing no one or anything but Adah, and Rae-Ellen was livid. To show she wasn't bothered in the least, she tucked her hand through Fawn's arm, since he was standing practically against her.

His hand covered hers, pressed. "Don't think," he murmured, "that anybody can top you in beauty!

Adah may be the sun to these oafs, but to me you're the world itself!"

Her turmoil quieted. Fawn began to stroke her hand, and she permitted this. Let Papa see, let Burr Travis know that she was attractive to other men. And, yes, much as she hated to deceive him, let Lance see the same thing!

Let him be jealous, she willed, oh, let him be jealous! Through the whole workout, she clung to Fawn, talked only to him, laughed when he laughed. Surprisingly, it wasn't as bad as she'd earlier thought, when she had had the fight with Papa. Even catching him glancing approvingly at her now, didn't irritate her.

At noon, when Mary-Lou and Jim showed up for lunch, the twin silver colts were delivered. Everybody drove down to watch them be unloaded. They waited while the colts were put into their stalls, then went back to the house.

"What beauties!" Mary-Lou exulted. "How old are they? Not two-year-olds?"

"No," Rae-Ellen said, "yearlings."

"Are they real, true twins, out of the same mother?"

"Yes. They're identical. Most unusual for mares to drop twins. They're exactly alike, to the last hair."

"We've got to go out tonight and celebrate!" declared Mary-Lou. "It's not every day you get twin colts! And I want to celebrate my goin' to Florida with you for the racin' season, too!"

"Yes," Adah agreed. "All of us—Lance and Fawn and Pete and Burr!"

And, thus, to Rae-Ellen's displeasure, it was settled.

To her added displeasure, all accepted. Even Burr, who should be intent on his new assistant. Instead, he put on that suit of his, stuck his jaw out, and went right along with them.

Somehow he got himself paired off with Adah. Then Pete shouldered in, and Adah had two escorts. Mary-Lou claimed both Lance and Jim, and that left Rae-Ellen with Fawn.

They dined in a restaurant, danced to the small, good orchestra.

"We need more girls," Adah said.

"Oh, no!" Mary-Lou cried. "Better to have extra men!"

Burr, as usual, danced once with Rae-Ellen.

"Decided what to name the yearlings?" he asked.

"Timothy and Thomas," she said. "We'll call them Tim and Tom. Start calling them by their names."

"That," he said coolly, "was my general idea in asking."

The music stopped, and he took her back to the table.

She danced with Fawn. His fingers stole to beneath her breast, fondled. Any other time she would have stopped it, but now she didn't even mind. Mary-Lou was dancing with Burr, and Adah with Lance.

She reminded herself that she was now a liberated woman. She'd slept with two men. She compared them—Burr, Fawn. They were different; which was the better? She was too upset to decide.

Because right there, a few feet away, Adah and Lance were dancing slowly, languorously, body-to-body.

20

Marguerite Pettigrew announced at breakfast the next day that she meant to give a ball before they left for Florida. "October sixth, far enough ahead of our departure."

"Not much time to prepare for it," Papa commented.

"We'll manage! We haven't had a big affair in months, and we'll be away at least two months, one month to train the horses in Florida, and another month, maybe more, to race them."

"How many guests?" Papa asked.

"Oh, a hundred. All our Durham-Raleigh set. I'll start writing the invitations today, if you girls will help me."

She looked from Rae-Ellen to Adah, both of whom said they'd be glad to help. So, after a quick trip to the workout track to see their racers, the sisters devoted the rest of the morning to addressing invitations. Mama, once they were busy and said they'd do the entire chore, closeted herself in her little office to telephone caterers, florists, and one or two talent agencies for an orchestra.

When she saw Adah addressing an invitation to Burr, Rae-Ellen protested. "He's not in our Durham-Raleigh set! Tear that up!"

"He's one of our intimates now!" Adah retorted. She dampened the flap of the envelope, stamped it firmly. "Burr comes to the dance or I don't come."

"So now you've got a yen for him! As well as for Lance! How many men do you want?"

"Don't be a goose. I like Burr. He's . . . different . . . but he fits in, you know he does. Mama and Papa like him. They'd be very upset if we skipped his name on the list!"

"How about the new trainer? Are you going to invite him, too?"

"That's silly, dear. He's an older man, he's a stranger. He'd be embarrassed. Burr wouldn't."

That was the truth. Rae-Ellen wondered, crossly, if Burr was capable of being embarrassed. She decided he wasn't.

The night of the dance, Magnolia Hall was alight from top to bottom. Andrews, in butler's regalia, answered the bell, announced the guests. Marie, in black uniform, white cap and apron, showed the ladies upstairs to the bedroom set aside for their wraps and their primping.

The specially built orchestra dais was walled at the back with masses of fragrant yellow roses. The orchestra members wore white. Yellow roses were banked at the white marble fireplace, and urns, set at intervals, were filled with the roses. There were a few splashes of the palest beige roses.

The great, long room was all glowing gold, glimmering white, and touches of beige. The Pettigrew sisters were the lovely, graceful heart of the room, both in new gowns.

Adah had chosen soft, diaphanous gold, which lay in folds across the bodice and fell in full, unpressed pleats to her ankles. She was all softness and golden beauty, and moved with a matching softness.

Rae-Ellen's gown was a replica of her white evening dress. The only difference was in the color, which was a rosy nude, blending with her skin so closely that tonight she looked naked indeed.

She glanced at Adah as they mingled with the guests. She'll not draw all the attention, she thought, content. Even Lance will notice the way I look, whether he shows it or not!

The orchestra struck up. The dance floor filled, little dance cards fluttering from the wrists of the girls and women. Lance, who had filled Adah's card with his name until she made him stop, danced with her most of the time.

He danced with Rae-Ellen once. "You're too popular," he smiled. "I couldn't get near enough to claim my rightful dances."

No. Because he'd been too busy with Adah. But she'd not so much as infer it. Instead, she laughed up at him, sparkled, and was more charming, more gentle and Adah-like than she'd ever been with him.

She saw him look at her dress, saw his puzzled expression, and this excited her. At least he knew, in this instant, that she was alive! The memory would linger. And she'd add other occasions of startling gowns, of gentleness, other memories. She'd out-Adah Adah!

He spoke of how beautiful she was tonight, warned her, jokingly, against all other men present. "I'm the only one to be trusted," he said solemnly, then smiled.

She was making an impression, she really was!

To hold him, she started talking horses. He said he'd hired a man named Ruble as groom, and spoke of him at length.

And then the number ended, and she had to go to another partner.

Fawn danced with her often. Once he kissed her cheek, a butterfly kiss, and she didn't object. She hoped that Lance had seen, that Burr Travis had, too.

She noted that when Lance wasn't holding Adah in his arms, wrapped in the soft beat of music, that Burr had his big Texas arms around her. Just seeing this roused that deep, unwanted hotness in her she'd thought was quenched.

Pete Battle also noticed how Lance and Burr monopolized Adah. Oh, she danced with others, even with some of the old, married men, but she surely was with Lance and Burr most of the time.

Pete had got his name on Rae-Ellen's card three times.

He claimed his dance, grinning. "My first, I believe."

He looked so sunny and handsome that she smiled. Pete was always good fun. No matter what Mary-Lou said about him and women, she liked him.

The orchestra began a waltz, and Pete swung her into it smoothly. All over the floor, skirts were dipping and swaying to the music. The scent of roses lifted and became a part of the music.

Suddenly, Rae-Ellen was enjoying herself.

"You're gorgeous," Pete declared, and held her close.

She let him. It felt good.

He turned on his beachboy charm and though she recognized it, didn't mind. Her pulse even stepped up. She could understand his reputation. When he was like this, if she wasn't in love with Lance and in hate with Burr, she might get excited.

The waltz ended. Burr appeared. He'd put his name on her card just once, hadn't asked for more, and here he was to claim his turn. She'd rather slap him than dance with him. She was so hot in the depths, and he was fresh from Adah's arms, from dipping and swaying in that sensuous waltz with her sister. And now, just as if it didn't matter a whit, he'd put his arms around her!

The orchestra had struck up again. It was, unbelievably, another waltz. He swept her away gracefully. She followed him with ease, perfectly, as she always had on the rare occasions when they danced.

As usual, he wasn't talking. She wasn't going to let him get away with it.

"I don't understand," she said, and waited.

"Don't understand what? I wrote my name on your card for this dance."

"It wasn't to be a waltz. We never have two waltzes together."

"This time you have."

"How do you know?"

"I've got ears. Also, I arranged it."

"You *bribed*—"

"Bribed, hell. I asked your Pa if he wouldn't tell them to play a waltz. Told him the truth. That I'd never waltzed with you, and this was my only chance tonight."

"And he did it, just like that?"

"He asked your Ma. She was willing. And here we are."

They danced on. She felt what seemed like electricity flow from his body to hers. His arm tightened; she tensed, then relaxed. No scene, she reminded herself, no scene. Just get it over with.

But when the waltz ended and he turned her over to Fawn, he'd managed to really ignite that burning. She considered luring Fawn away to his apartment, maybe repeat that other evening. His expertise had calmed her. Perhaps, on a second occasion, the calm would last.

Anything, she thought, dancing with Fawn, watching Lance with Adah, Burr with Mary-Lou, is better than this. But then she threw the crazy idea out of her mind. She was liberated; she'd seen to that for herself. But there were limits to liberation.

Adah, in Lance's arms, holding a smile on her lips, praying that it looked real, wanted to do one of two things. She wanted either to melt to Lance, to link her hands behind his neck and dance closer than close, or she wanted to pull away and run to the ends of the earth.

It was silly to be dancing when she felt torn. She wanted so much to be Lance's bride, his beloved. To bear his children. They'd be only one-sixteenth black, she kept telling herself, and their children, in turn, would be only one thirty-second black.

Not two minutes ago, Lance had pressed a soft kiss on her lips as they danced, and whispered, "Tonight, my darling, can it be tonight?" And her knees had turned to butter, but somehow she'd stiffened them and never missed a beat of the music.

"I don't know," she whispered. "Truly!"

Now, in her distress, she felt she had to talk to her sister. She waited until she saw Pete ready to claim his second dance with Rae-Ellen, then lost herself from her own next partner, a junior cotton broker, and fled to Rae-Ellen and Pete.

"Pete," she said, smile beseeching, "I've just got to speak with my sister . . . girl talk! If you'll let me have her now, I'll . . . I'll ask Papa to have the orchestra play two extra numbers, and one will be yours!"

He agreed, his expression a perfect blend of regret and expectation. "Don't forget," he reminded Rae-Ellen, "I still get two more dances with you!"

Adah led through the dancing couples, weaving in and out, smiling. She ran up the stairway and into her sitting room, Rae-Ellen at her heels.

She waited only to lock the door, then whirled. Her heart was going so fast, and certainly Rae-Ellen didn't look very receptive. But she had to discuss this with her. She couldn't bring herself to mention it to Papa or Mama.

"You're the only one who can help me!" she cried. "Please, darling, don't look so . . . bewildered and half angry! I wouldn't have left the ballroom, wouldn't have dragged you away unless it was vital!"

She saw the anger fade from her sister. It was

245

replaced by concern. "All right," Rae-Ellen said, "but let's be quick. We can't disappear from our own ball, not the way our cards are jammed."

"It's Lance!" Adah wailed. "I thought he'd give me loads of time!"

"And he won't?"

"Oh, Rae-Ellen, honey, he wants to announce our engagement tonight! Here, at the ball!"

"Are you engaged?"

"No! I haven't dared accept him! What shall I do?"

"Isn't that your decision?"

"Please, darling, don't get that little sound in your voice! I know you're against our marriage, because of the secret! But I know, too, that you'll give me advice!"

"What brought this on, Lance turning fervent? It isn't like him."

"That's my trouble!"

"Something happened. You did something, said something."

"He stole a kiss on the dance floor. Then he asked if I love him like a grown woman, not a girl. I had to tell the truth. So I said I love him that way and want all of him. And that's what set him off!"

"He wanted to announce your engagement?"

"Yes! He said it's foolish for us to wait. I protested, said it'd never do. That I'd only said I love him deeply, not that I'll marry him! And he smiled and said that marriage just naturally follows love!"

"I suppose he's spoken to Papa and Mama?"

"Before he even proposed!"

"And they approved?"

"Yes, they did! What *am* I to do?"

246

"Make up your mind. You gave me to understand that if he ever asked, you'd marry him."

"Only because I lost my temper, darling!"

"And I said I'd tell the secret. For all you know, I still might."

"You wouldn't, you never would! You're the dearest, best, sweetest sister any girl ever had! That was only temper with you, too! And shock about mixing my blood with his! You were only shocked that day, and hurt, because Papa and Mama hadn't confided in you!"

"Maybe you're partly right."

"Please, darling! Tell me what you think is best!"

"Best for you. Well, have you changed from what you said the day we quarreled?"

"That I might marry him, if he asked? Rae-Ellen, I do so want to be his wife!"

"There. You've found your own answer."

"But I haven't! And you know why! One minute I think I'll be silent. The next, I know I'd be living a lie. And, if I tell him, and he marries me and then begins to worry . . . Oh, sister, please help me!"

Rae-Ellen regarded Adah. No, she hadn't the least idea that she herself was determined to win Lance.

"Ask Papa again," she said. "Ask Mama."

"You know what they said! But I'm not sure!"

Rae-Ellen clamped her lips to keep from crying out, I'd help you if I could, but I can't, because I want Lance myself, have always wanted him! And there's no taint of blood between us!

Maybe she should do that. Maybe then Adah would reject Lance and she would get him on the rebound. But pride held her silent.

If ever she married Lance, she knew now, she must be his own, his true choice. She couldn't endure a marriage in which her husband longed for another woman. She had to be all or nothing.

"The decision," she told Adah, "is on your shoulders. It's too important for me to influence one way or the other."

This was true. But it was further true that she'd win Lance away from Adah if she could. They weren't married yet. She wasn't giving up.

21

The moment the girls reentered the ballroom, they were surrounded by men. Gracious, laughing, they consulted the tiny cards and gave themselves into the arms of their partners.

Rae-Ellen danced until she was dizzy, until her partners became a blur. She rejected every date she was asked for on the grounds that every moment of every day was booked.

"What can keep you that busy?" demanded the young Durham cotton broker. "Your mother has put you and your sister to scrubbing floors?"

She laughed. Don was really fun. He said the most ordinary, most outlandish things.

"Not that kind of work, silly!" she retorted. "We spend time at the stables—"

"Yes. You've got the racers now."

"And twin yearlings! Both of us are making friends with all of them. And we pay attention to the hunters, too—they're very jealous! And we have to assemble clothes for the trip, buy some new things."

"Surely you haven't filled the evenings? You can't pet horses and buy dresses after dark."

"Evenings are taken, Don. Until after we get back from Florida. I'm sorry."

"If you say so, it's true," he said, and smiled. He swept her into an intricate step, which she followed perfectly, though her mind was only half on it.

She hadn't lied to him. Evenings were taken, in her own mind. She was going to see to it that, failing any other plans, Mama invited their intimate group to dinner. That it meant the presence of Burr Travis irritated her, but it was a necessary evil. The dinners would throw Lance and Adah together, too, but it would also bring him within reach of Rae-Ellen.

Which was her objective.

Even if he and Adah announced their engagement, which, judging by his unsmiling face, they wouldn't do tonight, she'd carry out her plan to win Lance.

The orchestra played on. Couples danced, dipped, swayed. Couples stood sipping champagne, nibbling at tidbits the caterer's men served from a long, white-draped table.

Rae-Ellen had grown warm from constant dancing. Now she was very thirsty. She and her partner joined the sippers and nibblers.

Though she rarely had even one cocktail, she

drank three glasses of champagne. It tasted good, and it quenched her thirst.

It also went right to her head, and she knew it, so was extra careful. The thick feeling in her brain persisted. She scarcely spoke to her partners, just rested her head on whichever male shoulder presented itself and drifted to the ever-softening throb of the orchestra.

Dancing thus, she became sure of one thing: Lance still looked solemn. Adah would not permit any engagement to be announced tonight, because Adah was not one to make up her mind on the spur of the moment. Also, she had a serious problem, a solemn decision facing her. She'd be very, very careful. Very slow.

In fact, she wouldn't be able to make this particular decision for days, maybe weeks. And every moment was precious to Rae-Ellen. Lance, considerate man though he was, remained male. And no male of his calibre would allow himself to be kept dangling.

Adah would cut her own throat. Not knowing its cause, Lance would tire of her indecision. Tiring of that one quality in her, he would begin to tire of others, probably the gentleness most of all. He'd come to associate gentleness with indecision until they became the same in his mind.

And all the while, there would be Rae-Ellen, gay and laughing. For Adah, in addition to indecision, would have quiet, solemn moments; Rae-Ellen would use these moments to be her most charming.

What a schemer I'm getting to be, she thought fuzzily. It's the champagne. It's supposed to confuse you. It's made my head thick, but my thoughts so sharp they cut right through! I'm a little drunk! She stifled a giggle. This wasn't a bad feeling, not bad at all.

"Hey, let me in on the joke, you naked little sphinx!" said a laughing voice.

She glanced up. So. Now it was Pete Battle with whom she was dancing. "I'm not naked," she protested, but felt her lips curl into a smile. "I've got on as many clothes as any woman here!"

He drew her closer; it felt good. Now she could feel his maleness. It seemed to bore through the white fabric of her gown and lie along her, skin to skin. He moved against her, dancing, and she returned the movement, partly because of that burning in her, and partly to see what he'd do next.

His lips came onto her hair. He drew her closer still. That maleness was growing. Deliberately, when he moved against her again, more firmly this time, she returned the movement as firmly.

She felt warmth rise to her loins.

She pushed back from him, and he eased his hold. Now they were merely dancing close, not quite touching. She glanced at his sunny hair, at his smiling face.

"Know how you're behaving, you little minx?" he asked.

"I'm full of champagne," she confessed, "but I know what I'm doing!"

"You're acting like—"

"I'm a liberated woman," she told him, not meaning to, but the words were out. So she might as well say the rest of them. "I know your reputation, Pete Battle. Nothing you do—or say—can shock me!"

He smiled broadly. "Just how liberated are you?"

"I've slept with two men, that's how!"

He whistled, low. "Never thought to see the day! Little Miss Priss! Two men!"

She happened to glance to the right. Yonder was Burr, holding Mary-Lou in his arms, dancing like he was the happiest man in the world. He and Mary-Lou were very close together. Too close. Well, she wasn't surprised. But she wasn't upset, though she'd like to inform that Texas bum that Mary-Lou wouldn't get into any bed with him because she considered him Rae-Ellen's property! See how he'd like that!

He didn't even look at her. He was laughing at something Mary-Lou said. Rae-Ellen jerked her attention back to Pete.

"You don't believe me!" she accused. "Just because you've slept with hundreds—"

"Dozens, if you want to be generous."

"—dozens, of women, you think I can't get two men! You think you're the world expert! You think I don't even know what to do when—when—"

"How could I know otherwise?"

"I dare you!" she whispered fiercely, the words coming out of the very thickest part of her brain. "I dare you to take me away from here, take me somewhere, to a . . . a motel!"

"You've had too much champagne."

"I've had some, yes, but I know what I'm doing. I want to go to a motel!"

That would show Burr, dancing close to Mary-Lou.

It would show Lance, in a way. She explained

253

that part to herself. Having sex with Pete Battle, the expert, would teach her new things with which to give Lance joy in the future.

She thought, as Pete accepted her dare, Why not? To go with him was all to her benefit. She'd not be in a crowd; she'd forget Lance and Adah for a time. She'd have sex with Pete until this burning left her loins. After him, she'd be ultraliberated.

Before the last dance, which was Pete's anyway, they slipped out of the house. He helped Rae-Ellen into his convertible, tucked her ermine stole around her when she asked him to leave the top down. He ran to his side, got behind the wheel, sent them down the driveway to the road.

He felt only slight disloyalty to Fawn, who meant to marry this girl. To him, this was simply a pleasant, unexpected chance to bed a lovely girl. Hell, probably Fawn was one of the men she'd been with. All he wanted with her was tonight, the pleasure they'd have. It was Adah he felt affection for, Adah he wanted to marry. Rae-Ellen, he thought suddenly, would keep a man on a short leash.

"How about going to my apartment?" he asked, as they sped along.

"I've been to a man's apartment, and I've been to a man's c—house. The motel is new for me. That's why I want it."

He drove with one hand. With his right arm he pulled her so close their bodies were practically plastered together. He ran his hand teasingly up and down her leg, under her gown and up into the edge of her bikinis and stroked her with just one finger until she felt a heat that had nothing to do with Burr Travis or was mixed up with him, not that it mattered. Heat was rising, rising in her loins. She thought they'd never get to the motel, though he didn't drive very far before he turned in at one.

Their room was very large, very new, very complete. It was brown and green with touches of blue. There were two double beds, two double dressers, two low tables with big chairs drawn alongside, an enormous bath and mammoth white, fluffy towels.

Pete caught her up into his arms and went dancing about the room, carrying her. She'd known he was strong, that he played racquet ball and tennis and jogged and swam, but she hadn't dreamed he could handle a girl as if she were a feather.

Midwhirl, he tossed her onto one of the beds. He began to take off his clothes, throwing them over one of the chairs.

She lay waiting for his next move. He looked over at her and laughed. It seemed that sunshine broke over his face.

"If you could see yourself!" he teased. "Acting as if you're about to be raped! Come on, liberated woman, get those clothes off! One thing about me is, when I get a beauty in my clutches—" He made a mock, threatening face. "—I haven't any patience at all! I want to be at the fun!"

She jumped off the bed, hastily undressed, and tossed her clothes onto another chair. She was giggling so at the outrageous names he kept calling his garments that she was afraid he'd beat her at their stripping race.

It was a tie.

They faced each other. They'd swum together in near-naked suits, but this was different.

He sucked in his breath. No laughter. "Stand, girl. First I look, and then—whatever strikes me." His very light blue eyes rested on the red-brown spot at her thighs, and his mouth seemed to tremble.

Sun-god, she thought, gazing boldly at him. Six feet tall, perfect build, flat belly, body golden from the sun, sunny fuzz on chest, arms, legs, all these she'd seen at the pool. But his maleness! It bloomed like some great, sun-kissed rigid flower from the bed of blond hair.

She'd never seen anything so astounding.

"Now, for the fun!" he declared, and had her in his arms. He rubbed that flowering part between her thighs, and she felt a new sort of flame, one which was happy and ready. Impatient.

"Down," Pete said. "On the carpet. Hands and knees."

Bewildered, she dropped into that position.

"Brace yourself," he warned and then, as she stiffened, pressing the heels of her hands and her bare knees into the thick carpet, he put his hands on her hips and thrust into her from behind. He began to pump, chuckling. To keep from being knocked on-to her face, she had to lunge backward.

He continued to pump, hands squeezing, and she kept leaning backward to escape falling. Her knees ground into the carpet, began to sting.

At first she felt nothing but the sensation of being filled. Then, gradually, a deep uneasiness arose, hurting, yet glorious. It was growing until, at the very instant he gave the last of three final, long thrusts, she was consumed by flame. She wished it never to end.

He fell away from her, she collapsed, and they lay on the carpet facing each other. Both were panting. He chuckled and she giggled.

"Bet you never did it that way before!" he challenged.

"Never!"

"Always on the bed," he teased. "Missionary position."

She giggled uncontrollably.

"Where'd you find out about missionary position?"

"Mary-Lou. Books."

They laughed until they were breathless. Then, without asking, he got her on her side and entered sideways, and they rode one another for a long time before they reached the peak. This was even better, Rae-Ellen thought hazily, than the first time.

They lay chuckling in each other's arms. Rae-Ellen was getting used to the feel of the carpet, even liked it, at least with Pete beside her.

"I vote for the floor," he declared. "Firmness. I'm no water bed man."

"How about one of these beds?"

"After we rest."

"Then you'll show me a new way, not missionary?"

"I'll show you a new way."

They sported with each other's bodies. He caressed her, top to bottom, and she did the same with him. Learning, learning. It was akin to what Fawn had done, but only slightly. With Pete it was pure fun and lightness.

On the bed, Pete lay on his back, his maleness at right angles to his body. He sat her down on it so that it pushed inside.

"Now. Pretend you're riding a horse, and I'll give you a hard time," he grinned.

They did that until both cried out with joy and passion. And from the absolute fun of it all.

They rested, not even touching.

Pete wasn't like Burr. Burr was fierce and almost sweet. And Burr wasn't like Fawn, who was smooth, exciting expertise. Pete was pure, madcap fun.

Lance, she thought. How will it be with him?

Now, completely educated in sex, she knew enough to bring Lance to the heights. Her only problem was to entice him into bed.

Once more before they left the room, she and Pete indulged. Giggling, they used the missionary position. And it, surprisingly, was the best of all.

Pete had calmed her utterly. He really had. As a husband, he could keep a woman content. Maybe —But no. There was Lance.

Lance, whom she loved.

22

Pete Battle slept little during what remained of that night. He should have slept like the dead. That little hot-ass Rae-Ellen—and who would have suspected—had literally drained him.

She'd set him to remembering, too.

He'd never met a girl her age so hungry for sex, so eager to try different positions. With most of them it was a quick roll, and that's it, brother. Even Mary-Lou seldom went for it twice in a row.

When he was working his way through Duke and always short of cash, it was the rich widows and the dissatisfied wives who'd gone all out, who had wanted any offbeat practice.

He'd had to draw the line more than once. Fun, plus a generous tip, was one thing. Sadism was another. No whips. No chains, no odd-shaped objects, regardless of money. And some of those cash tips would have been solid.

He worked his beachboy stints in Florida during summers. Easter, he went to Fort Lauderdale, along with the thousands of other college students. Christmas, he went to Miami Beach. By that time the big hotels were swarming with older women, lonely women, sex-starved women. All loaded. All generous.

The summer after his junior year, he decided he'd get more loot if he signed up with one of the escort services. He had to pay a percentage, sure, but the agency didn't come in for any of the tips. Thus, what had formerly been income, became velvet, and his share of the agency's charge to the client was his college stake.

That was how he met Maureen, his hottest number. The pitch was she needed an escort for dinner and dancing. She specified that he be young, good-looking, and of a fun-loving nature.

This was relayed to Pete when he was assigned. He went to the door of her suite at the Fontainebleau Hilton wearing a tux, his blond hair giving off an extra sheen from the brushing he'd subjected it to.

He tapped at her door, and she opened it. Beyond her was a beautiful sitting room. Flowers everywhere. So. She had a suite. She had luxuries; she patronized an escort service.

"I'm Pete Battle," he said.

"Ah. From the escort service."

"Yes."

She looked him over with eyes of midnight blue. He looked right back.

"And your name, madam?"

"Oh!" she exclaimed. "Sorry. I'm Maureen Riley. Divorcée."

Even then she didn't invite him in, but continued to examine him. He returned the favor.

She was an older woman, naturally. Rail-thin, in a glistening, midnight blue lace dress and opera-length, four-strand pearls, she was almost as tall as he was. The dyed auburn brows were too thin for his taste, but arched in a stunning manner.

She had expertly dyed auburn hair, worn sleek and shining like a mirror, drawn into a satiny knot at the nape of her neck. There were no bags under her eyes, but she had lines from her patrician nose to her thin, artfully rouged lips.

He only glanced at the lines, but she caught him at it. She lifted her hand, the wedding finger laden with an enormous baroque pearl and diamond ring which would have paid his tuition for a year, and touched one of the lines.

"I laugh too much," she said.

"That's good. There's not enough laughter in the world."

But her eyes didn't laugh.

She smiled then, and her face glinted with beauty she must once have possessed—before the years crept over her. Before she had the eye-lift he thought responsible for the smooth, tight look to the upper part of her face. He wondered why she hadn't gone the route, had the laugh lines softened, realized that would make it necessary for her to abandon the sleek hair style to hide scars.

"Shall we go?" he asked.

She caught up a midnight blue velvet stole, a glittering evening bag. "I'm not being inhospitable," she explained. "It's just that I made the reservation for half an hour earlier than I told the escort service. It's a special table, in a corner, private."

"That's splendid," he told her. He was a little puzzled. Maybe this was a first time for her; maybe she felt awkward about asking him in before they got acquainted.

The vast, newly decorated dining room was filled with flowers and the whisper of music from a good orchestra. Most of the white-covered tables were occupied; a number of couples were dancing. All sound was subdued, blending into the music. Waiters moved about quickly, noiselessly.

The maitre d' escorted them to their table. It stood out from the wall, which was latticed and on which fresh red hibiscus blossoms had been placed thickly enough to cover it.

They don't stop at expense, Pete thought, knowing that, by morning, the fragile blossoms would be dead. They'd have to be replaced every afternoon, not long before the diners began to arrive.

The wine steward came with his wine list, presented it to Pete. Pete glanced across the table inquiringly.

"Brandy Alexander," Maureen Riley said. "Always."

"The same here," Pete said. He always drank what his date selected. It made for a comparison of tastes, opened many a conversation.

The steward left so quietly Pete was surprised to find him gone. "No waste of time," he said, and grinned.

."They're paid to be quick. This has always been my favorite hotel, but now it's even better. They have new owners and everything's . . ." She broke off, seeking a word.

"Jazzed up," he supplied, and she smiled.

"That's it. Only, in a nice way." Her smile faded. "You're so . . . how old are you, Pete Battle?"

"Twenty-two," he lied, adding to his age.

"So young," she smiled, and when she smiled those lines really became laugh lines. "I'm forty. Old enough—"

He held up an admonishing hand, grinning. "Don't pull the mother bit! Sister, at most. You've not been a mother to anybody, not a chick like you!"

"My husband didn't want children." The lines were back. "At first, I— He was in hardware. Has a chain of outlets. You'd recognize the name. He traveled a lot, and wanted me with him. Later—" She shrugged, tried to smile, lost it.

He suddenly felt sorry for her.

She wasn't bad-looking, just on the jaded side. She was probably out for a husband, like so many of them, and couldn't get one. The single men her age were already married, or getting engaged to young chicks or balling it with the beautiful hookers who had the fix in at a few of the plush hotels.

She couldn't make it on her own, even for dinner, without resorting to an escort service. A shame she didn't have a kid or two and a bunch of grandchildren. But then she wasn't exactly that type, either.

They dawdled over dinner three hours. They danced. She was a hep dancer, though she let drop that her husband had hated to dance.

They got pretty well acquainted. He told about his North Carolina background, about Duke Uni-

263

versity. He mentioned the Pettigrew Tobacco Company, of which she'd heard, and told her he meant to get in with them if possible.

She told him about Indianapolis, the mansion she'd lived in with her husband, her social life. She'd been active in charity work, too.

"I thought we had a good life, Wilson and me," she said. "There was all that money, we were 'society,' we had many friends. Then it happened."

He waited. He didn't ask what happened. He had a pretty good idea.

She told him anyway.

"Wilson fell in love. Fifty-five years old, and he fell in love with a girl young enough to be his granddaughter. Eighteen years old . . . *eighteen!*"

"That *was* raw!" Pete exclaimed.

"He was generous. He settled two million on me. Admitted I'd been a good wife, but that this great 'love' rendered him helpless. I said all the wrong things, did all the wrong things. I said he was a silly old fool—but you don't want to hear this!"

"It helps you, Maureen. How long . . . ?"

"Two years. I left town, went to New Orleans, to San Francisco. Now here. Wilson moved his office to New York." She gave a short laugh. "Now, neither of us has to face our friends!"

"You're lucky to be solvent," he said.

She gave him a keen glance, measuring.

That was the first intimation of what was to come.

Later, in her wide hotel bed, he discovered that she was a fabulous lover. She was better than the young girls, better than the older women he'd serviced.

He also discovered that she was fifty-five if she

was a day. He could tell from her breasts, which were shapely, yet not firm enough for the more youthful age she claimed.

But he didn't mind. He liked her and became her permanent escort.

He came to like her deeply, to respect her.

September and college neared, and with it his chance of a lifetime. It came as a shock.

They'd dined at the hotel that night, then had gone nightclubbing and had drunk a few more of her favorite cocktails than usual. Pete was in a happy, relaxed mood, and so was Maureen.

Now they were back in her suite and had made love. They were sipping champagne because it was his last night. Tomorrow he was flying, at her expense, back to Durham.

She was naked except for a midnight blue lace robe. He was nude under the blue silk robe she'd bought for him. She smiled at him, slowly, the laugh lines cutting deep, and he smiled back. Thanks to her generosity, he wouldn't have to wait tables next winter and, judging by the correspondence he'd had with Pettigrew's recently, he was pretty sure they would hire him after graduation.

"Pete, my love," she said, breaking the easy silence, "I don't know whether you've noticed or not, but I haven't been as . . . lively . . . this past week as usual."

"I noticed."

"What did you think caused it?"

He was as straight with her as she was with him.

"That you hate to see the summer end. Maybe hated to see me go."

"Right. Because now I'll be lonely again."

"There are some good guys at the service," he said carefully. He didn't want to insult her. "I mean —it doesn't have to be—"

"No, and it wouldn't. I don't want another man from the escort service, Pete."

He didn't know what the hell to say. She knew he'd be back at Christmas and Easter. They'd even made plans. Christmas, they were going to fly to Freeport and gamble; Easter, they were going to fly to Nassau and gamble some more. Their association wasn't ending. Not until graduation, anyhow.

"Pete, my love. I've told you one lie, and I want to set it right, because I have more to say."

"Shoot," he said, when she paused, watching his face. He smiled, to encourage her. Hell, she reminded him of a kid about to make some big confession.

"I told you I'm forty years old. I'm fifty-six."

"I'd have guessed fifty. Makes no difference."

"I don't think you're as old as you said."

"No," he admitted. "I'm twenty-one."

"That makes me thirty-five years older than you."

"So? We get along fine. We have fun. We're friends."

"I've a proposition," she said, speaking a bit rapidly, as though she must get the words out or she'd never say them. "All summer, every night, I've paid for your company, and you've given me far more than I dreamed I'd get."

He waited. He didn't know what else to do.

"I'd like for us to get married, Pete. I've thought it out from every angle. You say there's no girl in your life?"

"Not the kind you mean."

"I have two million dollars. I'll share it with you, leave it to you in my will in exchange for your companionship, in exchange for what we've had this summer to last as long as I live."

His brain thickened. At first he thought it was the drinks, then knew it was shock. Most of the guys at the service would jump at a chance like this. The question was whether they'd see it through.

"Pete? Can you answer now? Or do you want time?"

"It's a terrific offer," he managed to say. "Any man would be a fool to turn it down."

"But you're not accepting."

"I don't mean to imply that. There's college."

"I know what it means to you. I know your interest in tobacco. I'm willing to underwrite the rest of your study, naturally. After that, we'd do whatever you wanted—settle in North Carolina so you can work, or we could travel. Take a house in Spain . . . France . . . anywhere."

He swallowed. This was too big for him. He couldn't handle it. He'd have to be on a tight rein until she was eighty, ninety, and himself, fifty! He wouldn't two-time her, not this woman. He couldn't commit himself to just her bed, her old-woman bed.

"It's the age thing, isn't it?" she asked softly.

He stared at her miserably.

"I've come to terms with it. If an older woman wishes, she has as much right to marry a man younger than herself as a man has to marry a girl young enough to be his granddaughter."

Suddenly, he understood. The thing she'd lost sight of.

"It's still your husband, isn't it? You like me, but you aren't . . . it isn't love."

She gazed at him, those midnight blue eyes wide. He saw realization rise in them, saw the tears. Slowly, she murmured that he was right.

"Now I've proved to you that I'm an old fool," she continued. "Of course it wouldn't work. Not for me, now that you've helped me to see the facts. Who knows? Wilson may get dumped. If he does, I'd like to be there so he can come back."

A look of abandonment crossed her face, was gone.

"I've decided," she said, "here and now. I'm going home. I have friends. I'll make myself a life."

He was sorry to part from her.

He never saw her again, though he spent Christmas in Miami Beach working for the escort service and Easter in Fort Lauderdale, making love in the sand with college girls.

He had one card from Maureen. It was postmarked Indianapolis.

Now, at dawn, this morning after being with Rae-Ellen, he wondered, whether, given the same circumstances, she'd turn out like Maureen. He thought not. Rae-Ellen was snappy and independent. Maureen was quiet, had much of the same gentleness in her that Adah had. He could come nearer to picturing Adah as another Maureen.

He was hit by a sudden thought. He liked that similarity. Wondered if it would carry to the bedroom.

He pondered. Rae-Ellen and Adah, different on the surface, were sisters. The same blood flowed through them. And he knew that Rae-Ellen was a sexpot.

There was only one way to find out about Adah.

He waited, impatiently, for time to pass so he could telephone her.

He wasn't keeping his courtship low profile another day. Tonight, some way, he was going to get her into bed and make her his own.

23

Adah, this same October dawn, felt tired and heavy from her own sleepless night. Her mind had gone around in the same old circle. Exhausted from tossing and trouble, she knew she couldn't imagine life without Lance as her husband. Further, having agonized for so long, she knew that she couldn't endure a life of deceit.

She'd been doing a great deal of reading, slipping into Papa's library, selecting certain books and taking them to her own rooms to read in privacy. She wasn't surprised that Papa had assembled a collection of books on genetics, and she had studied every one of them.

All the experts seemed to agree. Genetically, there was no risk of one-sixteenth Negro blood showing in her children if she married an all-white man. If the man, however, had an unknown strain of black blood, the fraction in herself and the fraction in him could combine and the children might bear Negroid characteristics.

The possibility that Lance carried a hint of the blood was nil. Married to him, they'd breed the black out. Their grandchildren would have scarcely a drop remaining. In the end, their descendants would be pure white.

She'd made her decision. She was going to tell Lance about Papa and Delphine, about their blood. Then if he was still eager, not just willing, to marry her, she'd be the happiest girl alive.

She'd know tomorrow night. He'd be here for one of Mama's little dinners. She would get him into the library and tell him. If he accepted her eagerly, they'd announce their engagement on the spot. If he felt the least shock, she'd release him completely.

Today she'd rest, not even go to the workout. She'd sleep, if she could. She'd be as normal as possible tomorrow night.

When the phone rang, and then her buzzer sounded, she was surprised. Could it be Lance? Was he going to suggest some plan for tonight? She'd accept, of course she would. And if they were alone, she'd tell him tonight.

It's probably Mary-Lou, she thought as she picked up the phone. She decided to fall in with any plan Mary-Lou might suggest. It would fill time, probably rest her more than trying to sleep.

"Good morning," she said, into the phone.

"Morning yourself, beautiful!" said a gay, sunny voice.

"Pete! Where are you?"

"In my apartment. Getting ready to go to work. Wanted to hear your voice. To talk about tonight."

"Tonight?" She thought of Mary-Lou. "What's Mary-Lou scheming now?" she asked, and laughed.

And realized this was the first time she'd so much as smiled in hours. That was one reason she liked Pete. He could always make her laugh.

"It has nothing to do with the redhead!" he declared.

"Then what?"

"Me. You. Us."

"Oh?"

"It's time we had a date to ourselves. When we go double or triple, it's super, don't get me wrong, but not as good as you and me. Alone."

"I don't know, Pete."

She didn't like the idea of dating one man tonight, then hope to become engaged to another man tomorrow night. Somehow it didn't seem aboveboard.

"Please, Adah," Pete said, voice serious. "Don't turn me down. I want a chance to know the real Adah. To have conversation the gang isn't breaking into. I never sat up and begged before. It's just for tonight."

His uncharacteristic seriousness troubled her. She didn't know what to say. She was free tonight. She was still free to date whomever she pleased. She liked Pete, was drawn by his sunny disposition, but to date him alone after the things Mary-Lou had told her, made her doubly reluctant.

Pete didn't let the silence last. He pressed, handling Adah the way he'd handled Maureen once when she'd turned moody. With utter respect. As if she were a great lady. Both of which were true. Even as he spoke, Adah and Maureen blended together a bit more.

"Don't let my talk of conversation throw you off," he said. "It can be fun-conversation, a strictly fun evening."

It seemed ridiculous to turn him down. Yet wrong to go out with him tonight, and tomorrow night—

"You haven't got yourself engaged to anyone?" He was teasing now.

"N-no."

She hated to give these ridiculous answers. They were half-truths. Cross at herself, she surrendered.

"Where do you want to go, Pete? So I'll know how to dress."

"Dancing after dinner. Wear something yellow, if you can find it."

They laughed together.

"Seriously," he said. "I'd like you to wear the gown you wore at the ball."

"Will do," she agreed.

They chatted a moment more, then hung up. She turned away, glad now that she'd agreed to go.

He wanted her company so openly it seemed almost a pleasure to grant it. One evening out of her life. Spending the hours with him, laughing because to be with Pete was to laugh, was better than worrying over Lance's upcoming reaction. About what direction her life would take from tomorrow night on.

Lance wouldn't mind if she went out with Pete. She'd tell him about it if he called.

But he didn't call and after dinner, while Mama and Papa settled down to a game of chess and Rae-

Ellen flipped restlessly from stereo to television, to a book, Adah went to her room. She bathed, perfumed, and was zipping up her dress when Rae-Ellen came in without really knocking.

Rae-Ellen stared. "Where do you think you're going?"

Nightclubbing."

"With Lance?"

"No. With Pete."

"Pete? Nobody else?"

"Just the two of us."

"I've a good notion to dress and go with you."

"I . . . no, sister dear. I'm sorry. But for some reason Pete specially wants us to be alone."

"You must have a pretty good idea what that reason is! Every time he gets a girl alone, he—no girl has ever—I know that for a fact!"

"Mary-Lou gets carried away. I don't believe Pete's half as wild as his reputation, and I'm fore-warned. Don't worry about me, darling."

Rae-Ellen threw her hands apart in a gesture of exasperation and left the room. Adah smoothed her hair and, hearing the doorbell chime, caught up her stole and went tripping down the stairs.

Pete whistled softly as he offered his arm.

Adah laughed chidingly.

"That wasn't a cheap whistle," he said. "It was one of utter, knocked-in-the-head respect. I've never seen you so beautiful!"

"I wore this at the dance."

"Your beauty has grown since then." He opened the convertible's door, helped her in. He got behind the wheel, pushed a button, and the top rose and covered them. He pushed another button and the windows slid shut.

"Now," he said, and trod the starter. "Not a breath of wind can move a hair of your head. My sole objective is to preserve perfection." He reached over, put his hand on hers, returned it to the wheel. "I'm kidding in a way, serious in a way."

"You're a goose! But a nice goose!"

"Even a sweet goose?"

"Even sweet!" she laughed.

He pulled up at the newest, finest club in the area. Crusted golden lights on the outside blinked off and on like those in a disco.

The inside of the club had the same crusted, golden glitter, the same disco play of lights. It was **subdued, soft, enveloping. Everything** was gold and lights. Walls, ceiling, carpeting, chairs, linens, the single bud in the vase on each table.

They followed the gold-uniformed captain of waiters to a table. Pete waved him aside, and held Adah's chair himself.

"Two brandy Alexanders," he told the captain.

The captain bowed and departed.

Adah glanced about, at the decor, at the tables, most of which were in use, at the marvelous, graceful play of lights. A gold-uniformed orchestra at one side of the lounge began to play soft, sparkling music, and quite a few couples moved onto the floor.

"Dance?" Pete asked.

Adah smiled. "Not yet, thank you."

Her polite response was like Maureen's had been.

He made a small gesture, indicating the decor. "You see why I wanted you to wear that dress. It was made for this place."

She smiled. "If I'd known—"

"You wouldn't have worn it. Well, it is a little much, all this gold. People will get tired of it, but

275

before they do, the owners'll make a bundle. Then they'll do it up in something else, silver, maybe, and make another bundle."

Their drinks came. Pete lifted his, waited for Adah to lift hers. "To the most beautiful golden lady in the world," he said, and meant it. He sipped.

Adah took a very small taste, looked at him in surprise. "Why, it's really good!" she exclaimed. "Better than a milkshake!" She sipped again, several times.

"You should have listened to Pete long ago," he chided. "Always drinking plain cola. Never touching a cocktail! Regular little Carry Nation!"

"I've tasted some drinks," she defended herself. "I just never like them. This is different."

"It's delicious, and you're to have another one when you've finished that!"

"I don't want to get high," she said.

"You taste any booze in that?"

"No."

"There's your answer. You don't like the taste of alcohol. I've known ladies to drink these all evening, heads clear as a bell!"

And Maureen, who was used to them, had done so.

After the first drink, they danced.

He held her as he'd held Maureen, properly, bodies almost but not quite touching. He murmured a compliment from time to time. About her gown, about the grace with which she followed his lead, about how well-matched they were on the dance floor.

He made no allusion, as he had once to Maureen, that a man and woman well-matched in the dance would also be well-matched in bed. He'd learned on that one. Maureen hadn't appreciated it, though she'd been too well-bred to say anything. He'd never used the remark again.

"Don't you agree, love," he murmured, holding her delicately, "that we're well-matched in the dance?"

"Oh, yes, you're a wonderful dancer, Pete. So easy to follow."

So far so good.

They went back to the table, had two drinks in a row. They murmured nonsense, laughed. He watched her grow more and more relaxed. She smiled most of the time now. They drank a fourth cocktail; her golden eyes looked deep and dreamy. He ordered another drink. When she was completely soft, when she agreed with everything he said, even that, yes, maybe she might be the most beautiful woman in the lounge, he made his next move.

He drove straight to his apartment.

He had her inside before she spoke, voice dreamy. "What club is this?"

"The Battle Digs. My apartment, love. It's nearly like Fawn's place. He had us over there, remember."

"But I've never been to a man's apartment alone!"

"You've been to Twelve Oaks."

"That's like home. And never alone, at night!"

Far down in her something was trying to get through, something about Twelve Oaks, but she couldn't quite grasp it. Seeing the look on her face, aware of what it meant, Pete hastened to open a bottle of champagne, to put a glass of it into her hands. He had to keep her from thinking about Buford or the whole evening would be a waste.

This was his chance, win or lose. Here and now.

"Drink it down, little love," he whispered.

In a bewildered manner, Adah sipped. Then, as the bubbles touched her nose, she laughed. She sipped again, hiccuped once, drank down all the wine. The glass fell to the carpet and she didn't notice.

He took her into his arms, lifted her chin, put his lips on hers. He kissed her. She kissed back, gently, sweetly, with purity, as if she didn't really know what she was doing. In that instant, he knew that he was going to love her. That he must have her for his own. But he kept on with his plan, its success vital.

He was amazed by her reaction. After all she'd drunk, she was still only half-out, but that was the way he wanted her. He kissed her again, fervently this time, and she returned the kiss with equal fervor.

She made only weak protests as he stripped her. She made another half-hearted protest when he deposited her on the bed. She lay there, eyes closed, while he undressed.

Her eyes were open when he bestrode her, open and wondering. Yet she made only a small gesture of pushing away.

She was a virgin. Entering her was tough, and her tendency to shrink away from him didn't help. But at last he broke through and began to move.

After a moment, she stirred. Slowly, then warmly and sweetly, she moved to his move, murmuring. And he grew within her and blazed. She was hot and moist; she was very tight around him. Her inner parts embraced, clutched, caressed in response to his movements until, at the end, he seemed to ride with her into the stratosphere, endlessly, hotly, avidly.

So it can be like this, he thought, holding her. Love like this.

"Adah love," he murmured. "You awake?"

She murmured that she was.

"Will you marry me, little love? Will you be my wife?"

"N-no!" she sobbed, suddenly weeping. "Oh, Pete, why did we let this happen?"

"It was meant to happen, my love. Why do you think I've always been in the gang? It was you. Always you."

He'd always been pulled toward her, had always meant to marry her one day, it seemed. Now that he'd had a taste of sex, and she'd put all the others out of the running, he had to have her. Career be damned, he thought. I'd almost take a job a thousand miles away if I could have her.

But plead with her though he did, she would not consent to marry him. "I'm sorry, Pete, honestly sorry! It was my fault, drinking all those . . . when I'm not used to drinking! But I don't love you."

"And that's the only reason?"

"I t-think so."

"Then I'll not give up."

In his arms she wept on and on. She knew she was still half-drunk. She knew, now, that she'd betrayed Lance, that everything was changed, that she had more than the accident of her birth to confess.

She had no idea how she could ever bring herself to tell Lance what had happened between herself and Pete. Or that she had liked it!

Her tears dwindled. It did no good to cry, changed nothing. Rae-Ellen had warned her, and she wouldn't listen. There was no way she could atone for what she had done to Lance, trusting, beloved Lance.

"What do you want, love?" Pete whispered.

He'd give her the world, he'd dance to her tune.

She sat up on the bed, naked. "Let me dress. Take me home. Stay away from me."

"Because you're afraid, afraid of love?"

"No, Pete. Because I'm ashamed. To the marrow of my bones, ashamed!"

24

Rae-Ellen fumed the entire evening Adah went out with Pete. Once, she suspected that her sister might be using Pete, comparing him with Lance. She rejected the idea instantly.

It was possible that Adah had slept with Lance; she was enough in love with him to have done so. But she'd not try one man against the other sexually. There was no point to it. Adah's hangup was whether to tell Lance about her blood.

While her sister was drinking with Pete, Rae-Ellen was glowering at the pages of a book. The words were a blur. Her thoughts weren't much clearer.

After the orgy with Pete, she'd felt at peace. She could even think of Burr Travis with no inward stir. She was sated. She'd been sated after Fawn, too, all

Burr's contamination of her vanished. She'd been cleansed, longing only for Lance.

She closed the book with a snap, turned on television, switched it off. That Burr-fever was stirring. She hated him more with every breath she drew. As her hatred rose, so did the burning.

Sleeping around hadn't got the Burr-rage out of her at all, had made it worse.

Only one man could satisfy her, and that was Lance Buford. Lance, whom Adah would certainly promise to marry. Lance, whom Rae-Ellen must have, the only man who could satisfy her, because love would blend with sex and the excitement and passion she'd known with three men would pale to nothing.

She had to make her move before they started to Florida, and her plan would take at least a bit of time. And their departure date was the twenty-fourth of October.

She was still awake when she heard Adah come in. She paused only for a tap at the connecting door, then opened it.

One glance told her Adah had been drinking. Adah's crushed manner told her that the girl had been to bed with Pete.

"Why?" Rae-Ellen cried. "Why did you do it?"

Tears ran out of the golden eyes. The gentle lips quivered. Adah began to sob.

"Oh, sister!" she wailed. "What can I do? Pete said . . . I thought— He said it was to be a fun-evening, and then I drank those . . . and then we were in his apartment and . . . !"

"And you had sex. On the carpet."

She wished she could get her hands into Pete's

sunny hair, wished she could yank it out. For him to ply Adah with liquor, Adah, who absolutely never drank, and he knew it, to lure her into his apartment and take her to bed, was rape, pure and simple.

That Adah's misadventure had increased her own chances with Lance did not, at first, come into her mind. Then suddenly the thought struck her. She wondered why it didn't please her.

It gave her an edge, because now conscientious Adah had something new over which to agonize. It would delay her decision, and any delay helped Rae-Ellen.

Sure enough, Adah had it on her mind already. "I'd decided to tell Lance about . . . Delphine and Papa," she sobbed. "But now—"

"Don't be a fool!" Rae-Ellen snapped, saying the opposite of what she should say for her own good. "You don't have to tell him about Pete! What difference does it make?"

"Honesty! And he'll know, if I'm not a v-virgin!"

"Not for sure. Remember, when we were little, and you fell on your tricycle bar and bled? Remember how upset Mama was? There's your explanation, and probably true, at that."

Adah's tears slowed. "I do remember. It hurt, and the blood scared me." She put her hand on Rae-Ellen's arm. "Oh, sister dear, do you suppose it d-did happen then and not tonight?"

Rae-Ellen pulled away.

"Could easily be," she said, angry at herself.

Why, when things started to go her way, did she have to open her mouth? But she needn't have feared. Adah was still deeply troubled and after all, she *was* her sister!

283

"Even if I married Lance and he found I wasn't a virgin, and even if the tricycle was the true reason," she said, "that doesn't change things."

"What now?"

"I still slept with Pete! It doesn't make any difference! I still went to bed with Pete, and I l-liked it! But I love Lance! And I don't see how I can tell him about Pete, and I don't see how I can k-keep it a secret any more than the blood! The same principle is involved!"

"You'll have to work it out for yourself," Rae-Ellen said, not patiently. "I've concerns of my own."

Adah's tears ceased. Her face softened. "Why didn't you tell me, darling? Let me know your troubles! Maybe, together . . ."

"You solve your problems and I'll take care of mine!" Rae-Ellen cried. She pulled away from Adah, who had laid her hands on her again, fled into her own rooms and locked the door.

When Adah's soft knocking ceased, Rae-Ellen paced again. She blacked all thought from her mind. At last she was so tired she fell across her bed and slept.

And as she slept, that burn smoldered.

She dressed in jeans, shirt, jacket when she woke. Marie brought her breakfast. After she'd eaten, she went to watch Thunder Boy and Starstruck at their workout.

She was the only member of the family to show up. She understood why Adah hadn't come. And Papa and Mama didn't watch every morning, anyway.

The stable crew—Terry and Ken, Cartson and especially Burr Travis, were much in evidence.

Terry rode Thunder Boy and Ken rode Starstruck. Both trainers had stopwatches.

Rae-Ellen held on to the fence rail nearest the stable, so as to stay as far away from bum Travis as she could, and watched. Thunder Boy had a longer stride than Starstruck, but he was bigger. Starstruck was more graceful, her delicate legs a blur as she seemed to glide, with the speed of wind, around the oval.

When it ended, and Ken and Terry led the blanketed racers to cool them, Burr came to Rae-Ellen. Her impulse was to turn her back and go for her car, but she stood her ground.

"Fifty-nine seconds for Thunder Boy," Burr announced, putting his watch into his pocket. "Sixty seconds for Starstruck."

"That's better than yesterday," she conceded. "But the Florida tracks are longer."

"Your father says the workout track on the place he's leased there is longer than this one."

"Quite a bit," she agreed stiffly. She looked around. "Where are the colts?"

"In the far pasture. Beyond the timber. We turned them out early and they went at a gallop. Heads and tails up."

"I'm going down to see them," she announced.

Maybe she could walk off some of this burn, this anger that just the sight of him roused.

"I'll walk along," he said. "I've got a matter to discuss with you. And your sister."

"Then wait until my sister is present."

"You can talk to her. It'll take discussion."

She climbed over the fence and started into the pasture, his long legs keeping pace with ease no matter how fast she went. So he wouldn't think she was trying to compete with him in anything, even walking, she dropped speed.

"Well," she said, "talk."

"It's about them names, partly. Tim and Tom. I can't—According to me, they don't fit the colts, and you ought to change them."

"Adah and I spent hours on those names! Tim and Tom are perfect twin names!"

"They ain't identical."

"They're exactly alike, to the last hair!"

"They ain't."

"I can prove that they are! Anybody with eyes—"

"I can prove to you that they ain't identical. Wait and see."

They tramped the pasture in silence. She knew she was right. He had the nerve to blare out that she was wrong. Well, let him try to prove the unprovable.

"There's not much grass left," she said, kicking at a lone tuft of green. "I hope you're feeding the horses well."

"I reckon so," he said. "But they like to run, and they find a bite of grass. Them colts are going to be racers, once they're trained."

"Naturally."

"Spring."

"What about spring?"

"That's when I aim to break them to the saddle proper."

They came upon the colts on the far side of a thick stand of timber. They'd found a sizable patch of green and were nibbling.

Rae-Ellen's breath quivered. They were silver

beauties. And exactly alike. Their coats were identical; even their tails and manes matched perfectly. Their legs were shaped the same, slender and dainty, yet with underlying strength.

"You see!" she whispered, so as not to disturb them. "Identical!"

"Come a little closer," he whispered. He took her arm to steady her in case she might step into a chuckhole. Her impulse was to jerk away, but a sudden motion would send the colts racing, and the ridiculous argument wouldn't be settled.

They drew closer. The colts jerked their heads up, ears erect, nostrils wide. Rae-Ellen and Burr froze in their tracks.

"The one in the black halter," he breathed. "Look at his right front hoof and above. See how the silver deepens into almost gunmetal, about three inches long, there."

She looked, eyes slitted, and saw what he meant. Her look flew to the other colt, to his right forefoot. The shimmering silver continued, with no darkening, to the hoof.

"Why didn't you and Papa see the difference when you were buying?" she whispered.

Even that sound sent the colts racing away, tails high. She glared at Burr. "Just tell me that!"

"The deep gray wasn't on Tim at that time. Colors do darken. I just discovered this myself. You can race them as twins, but not as identicals."

"Near enough! For publicity. Oh . . . now, you've ruined it all!"

"You can't mean that."

"I do! You're a jinx! Ever since you came, you've been bossy! About the horses—"

"That's what I was hired to be."

287

"You've assaulted me, raped me—"

"With plenty of cooperation from you."

He was right, and that was what made her so mad. He was always right. Because she was so upset over the colts, over Lance, over everything in general and him in particular, and him being right there, she flew at him, fingers arched.

He grabbed her wrists, got them in one big, horrible hand. She wouldn't give him the satisfaction of struggling. She'd stand like this till hell froze over. Unless the blazing hatred of her glare melted him down to hell's own lead.

"There ain't but one way to carry on a conversation with you!" he snorted. "And that's to fight, and then—"

With that one hand he gave a yank. It slammed her against him so hard it almost knocked her breath out. And then he slammed his mouth on hers and ground it so hard that she had to move her own lips in defense. This led, inevitably, into furious kissing. He even got his tongue into her mouth and instead of biting it, she felt her own tongue slip into his mouth and she could taste him.

Next they were on the ground, hidden in the trees. Their clothes were open, and he crashed into her the way he'd rammed his tongue into her mouth, and they were moving very fast together in the dried grass, among the crackling twigs.

At the end, she was crying.

Crying because it had been so damnably wonderful, because she'd started it by flying at him, because he could always subdue her, because he never failed to bring her to rapture.

Could always make her feel, despite rage, replete.

Like now.

Crying too, because that torturing burn for him would commence another time, she knew it would.

She forced herself to glance at him.

His mouth, which had looked—well, different—stayed that way for an instant. Not a trace of bull-headedness.

"I hate you, despise you, loathe you!" she whispered, straightening her clothes.

"I know," he said. "The feeling is mutual."

His mouth went back to normal.

25

While Rae-Ellen and Burr were in the timber,
Pete Battle drove up to Magnolia Hall. When he got
out of his convertible, he carried a huge box em-
blazoned with the name of a Durham florist.

He had a solid idea of where everyone connected with Magnolia Hall was at this hour. Marguerite Pettigrew was shopping for luggage. She'd
stopped at her husband's office, found Raymond
Pettigrew dictating to his secretary. Fawn Morehead was conducting a tour of the factory. Rae-Ellen,
according to her mother, planned to spend the morning with the twin colts.

No mention had been made of Adah. Pete,
knowing the amount of liquor the girl had drunk
last night, tinglingly aware of every nuance of the
evening he'd spent with her, was certain she would be

confined at home with a hangover and her conscience. Consequently, he was losing no time in getting back on a solid footing with her.

He pressed the doorbell.

When Andrews tapped at her door and said that Mr. Peter Battle was downstairs, Adah's instinct was to refuse to see him. Then, head pounding so it seemed ready to fly into bits, she reconsidered. Do it and get it over with, she thought, and told Andrews to show the gentleman into the morning room.

As she went down the stairs, holding her head high, careful not to jar it, she hoped Pete wouldn't be his usual, sunny, laughing self. That would be more than she could bear. It would not only pain her head, but it would be a slap in the face, considering what she'd done with him last night.

He wasn't even smiling. She took one glance at him, then looked just past him. She'd never seen him serious before, not bone-serious. He looked as though he'd suffered a death in the family.

"Adah," he said quietly, "the night I've been through! Berating myself, cursing myself!" He held out the huge box from the florist. "Please. For you."

He set the box on a table when she didn't take it, and she began to unfasten the yellow ribbon which was tied around it. It was something to do; a way to pass a moment, to avoid speech. She lifted the lid, folded back the tissue. The deep box held yellow roses, dozens of roses, from buds to full-blown blossoms. Their fragrance wound into her stomach, and she felt nauseated.

"Three dozen golden roses for a golden girl," he said. "Supplication for you not to hate me, to give me a new chance."

She forced herself to gaze at him. He looked as if he might weep. Pete. Tears.

"A new chance?" she repeated, the words jarring her head.

"A chance at—I don't ask forgiveness, love. What I did can't be forgiven. I'll never ask that, not in all our lives. What I'm begging for is a chance to just be with you, to court you the way a proper southern gentleman courts a sweet and lovely and innocent girl."

"And to—forget?"

"Forget isn't the word, love. What I want is to wipe out all of last night. Yes, even the joy, the glory! What I'm pleading for is to start fresh as good, close, dear friends who, I pray to the heavens above, will grow together into love and marriage."

"I have a hangover, Pete, a double hangover. One from the cocktails—"

"—which I urged on you."

"—and the other from what happened as a result."

"All my fault, love! Because I love you so! Can you possibly understand? How I'm so in love with you that I got carried away when you actually gave me a real date?"

She looked at him, head miserable. He appeared to be sincere. She didn't want to hurt him. What happened last night truly was equally her fault; Rae-Ellen had warned her of what would happen. And it had happened.

"I . . . think I understand, Pete," she said. "I know that with you, when it comes to girls—"

"Don't speak of girls, please! I think subconsciously I've only been trying to get your attention, to make you see that I'm alive! Adah love, I'm throwing good sense to the winds! Seeing what happened between us and how good it was—" He broke off, plunged on. "You did find it good, not repulsive?"

Face burning, she murmured agreement.

"Then, don't you see? That's one basis for love! Since last night did happen, will you marry me, marry me right away?"

"No, Pete. Definitely not."

"Why not, love? Did I . . . violate you beyond redemption?"

"It's not that."

"What, then?"

"I must love the man I marry, Pete."

"And you don't love me?"

"That's right."

"You don't hate me."

"No."

"Then I'll take my chance. I'll leave you now so you can rest. When I see you again, I'll make you laugh again."

"Thank you," she whispered. "And Pete . . ."

"Yes, love?"

"The flowers. Please. They . . . I don't feel . . ."

He pressed them into the box, crammed on the lid. He tied the ribbon.

"Another time," he said. "If you'll permit me?"

She felt so ill, she was so anxious for him to go. She wished she never had to see him again. But her breeding prevailed. "Perhaps, another time," she said.

Pete was in a cold sweat. He had to watch every move. He couldn't lose this girl, not after last night. Not knowing what a perfect bedmate she was, to say nothing of her social position and the tobacco business. He'd have to use a blend of respect, tenderness, gaiety, and sobriety with her. Yes, that was it.

And, at the end, sweep her off her feet.

Rae-Ellen, distraught, did remember to tell Adah of the slight difference in their twin colts. She'd just got back from her encounter with Burr and wanted, somehow, to vent her spleen, and chose this way.

Adah, equally distraught, head pounding, wasn't really disappointed. But when her sister angrily reported that Burr wanted to change the names of the colts, she began to cry.

"What d-difference can it make to him?" she sobbed. "Why can't we keep what we decided? Does it matter to you?"

"No," Rae-Ellen agreed unhappily, knowing the reason for her sister's tears. "Our word settles it. We'll just bill them as twins, not identicals, and as Tim and Tom."

They drifted apart, each to her own rooms, her own troubles. Rae-Ellen had never been so miserable in her life. The more she tried to get Burr out of herself, the worse the mess got. Every time she saw him, almost, she jumped into bed with him.

It had now come to the point where, if she thought about Lance, darling Lance, she remembered Burr, and all was confusion. How could she love one man so deeply and get no place with him, and hate the other so furiously, yet, with him, touch ecstasy again and again?

It was all Burr's fault.

Well, in spite of him, she was going right ahead with her life.

Consequently, on Saturday, she dressed to go on the fox hunt. Adah, so quiet she made Rae-Ellen want to scream, wasn't going. So, while Adah was battling her problems, Rae-Ellen would have a clear field with Lance.

She dressed while it was still dark and rode Rusty over to Twelve Oaks. She had more than an hour before dawn, before others would arrive.

Lance himself answered the door. He greeted her, but his glance went beyond, into darkness. "You're alone?"

"That I am, kind sir! My parents aren't awake yet, and Adah is busy and isn't riding today! So I came now, hoping to substitute by being here twice, once for breakfast with you, and once for the hunt! If having me doesn't inconvenience you, kind sir?"

He chuckled. "When did all the fine lady behavior start?" he teased. "Of course I'll not be inconvenienced . . . how could I be?"

There! He was playing up to her! Step number one.

"As of today," she said, dropping the exaggerated manner. "It's time I actually became a lady. A true lady."

"You're a lady born, Rae-Ellen. It's in your bones."

"But I've always acted the hoyden."

He chuckled again. "Charmingly."

"Do you honestly think that, Lance? Even when I—?"

She couldn't put into words the way she'd pleaded that he make love to her. He knew what was in her mind, however, for he smiled soberly.

"Certainly I think it, little girl."

"You're not just being a gentleman?"

295

"A gentleman never lies," he reminded her. "He may soften the truth, but it's there. You have been a hoyden at times, but a lady just the same. And that's not softened."

"Thank you, Lance dear," she said. "I need— unsoftened truth."

In that moment she knew she could even tell him about what she'd done with other men. And why. And he'd understand and still consider her a lady.

And if she should win Lance, she would tell him. The conviction took her that he'd say that she was a modern, liberated girl, that what she'd done before she became his wife was no concern of his. What came next was the important thing.

With sinking heart, she knew he'd say the same to Adah.

"If being a great lady makes that bright face so sad," he said now, "I suggest you leave in a dash of the hoyden."

The half-serious, half-teasing note quickened her pulse. He did notice her moods! He did care how she felt! Step number two.

He took her arm, urged her toward the breakfast room. "Hattie's going to clap her heels when she sees you," he said gaily.

"And why?" she laughed, suddenly carefree.

"She's making blueberry muffins."

Laughing, they took their places at the table.

While the fox hunt was in progress, Burr spent the morning and most of the afternoon demonstrating his training methods to Cartson. Thus occupied, he did a fair job of keeping his mind off that hellcat. He'd never had a female get under his skin the way she'd got under his. One look at her and he wanted to bed her, subdue her. Which was crazy, and which he was going to stop.

Late in the afternoon, Raymond Pettigrew, Fawn Morehead, and Pete Battle rode up to the stable on their way back from the fox hunt. They examined and admired all four of the racers. At Burr's invitation, they piled into his kitchen for a glass of cold beer. No women were in the party, and for this Burr was grateful. He was in no mood to face Rae-Ellen. They chatted pleasantly about the upcoming races in Florida until it was time to go.

Rae-Ellen, pleasantly tired from the hunt, went to bed at eleven. The day had been a success as far as she was concerned, for she'd been at Lance's side a great deal, and he'd treated her wonderfully. Also, he'd sat with her at the hunt breakfast.

She lay in bed, reliving the day. By midnight she was restless. By one o'clock she was dressed in jeans, shirt, sweater, and slipped outside. The night was crisp—it was the second week in October—and she walked fast to keep from getting cold.

At first, she merely walked. Then she headed for Burr's cottage, just to glower at it. Maybe, in the clear, cold dark her mind would sharpen and she'd think of a surefire way to get rid of him.

It was as she rounded the last curve of driveway to the stable area, that she saw the fiery tongue of flame against the black sky. It seemed to be shooting out the window of Burr's kitchen. She walked faster. The tongue of flame grew.

She began to run, screaming.

26

As she raced for the burning cottage, dark figures poured to it. By the time she arrived, Ken and Terry and Cartson had a hose on the blaze, and it was dying. She burst into the kitchen, screaming for Burr, and there he was, naked under the overhead light, streaked with black, holding a dripping towel over a spot on the wall.

Smoke was oozing from it, and Burr was coughing. Now, Rae-Ellen, drawing breath to scream at him about being naked, got a lungful of smoke and began to cough, too. Angrily, she dashed into the bedroom, flipped on a light, grabbed a robe, ran back to the kitchen and threw it into Burr's face.

He let it drop, still pressing his rag to the wall.

The other men spilled in, shouting, then they began to cough and throw open windows.

"Fire's out!" Cartson yelled.

Burr lifted his rag, looked at the wall. He dropped the rag, caught up his robe and put it on, still coughing.

Air was flowing through the room now, clearing it. They could breathe again.

"Thanks, fellows," Burr said, "for pitching right in. If we'd taken time to call the fire department from Durham, the whole cottage might have burned."

That, Rae-Ellen thought crossly, was the most sensible thing she'd ever heard him say. The kitchen didn't look bad, either. One window curtain had burned, and there was that place on the wall. Water to be mopped up, too.

Burr and Cartson examined the outer wall, trying to find out how the fire had started. There was a wire pulled loose on the outside light above the door.

"It may have caused a short in the wall near the switch," Cartson speculated. "Where it burned, where you smothered the fire, and another short in that sink light." He leaned over the fluorescent bulb above the sink. It dangled at one end.

"Why didn't all the lights go out?" mused Burr. "And how did that wire work loose?"

"It'll take an electrician to figure that out," Cartson replied.

By the time Rae-Ellen and Papa went to the cottage later, the stable crew was tending the horses and Burr was inside, scraping down the burned portion of wall.

"All this needs is scraping and paint," he said. "The windowsill, too."

"And a new curtain!" Rae-Ellen said, cross because he'd barely nodded at her.

"I reckon I can buy curtains," he said.

"No need. I've more of that red-checked material that matches the other one. I'll make it and hang it."

"That's mighty kind of you, Miss Rae-Ellen," Burr said, but in a drawl.

It was a wonder Papa missed it, but apparently he did because now he said, "You seem to be handy at a number of things, Travis," and motioned at the wall. "I'll have an electrician in this morning. I can have a painter, too."

"No call, sir. I learned to do chores on the ranch I worked."

"I thought," Rae-Ellen put in, to show him she wasn't to be ignored because the big boss, Papa, was present, "that you grew up on a ranch!"

"That I did. Worked on a couple others, too."

Papa grinned. "And got interested in horses."

"Yep," Burr agreed, with a sidewise grin. He picked up his scraper and set to work again. "Got interested through the broncs, right on the spread."

"If I hadn't been born to tobacco," Papa said now, surprising Rae-Ellen to her toenails. "I'd have ranched out west. I've always been intrigued by those vast spreads and thousands of head of cattle."

"If you were raised on a ranch," Rae-Ellen said, determined they weren't to ignore her, "why did you work on other ranches?"

"I did that a couple of summer vacations while I was at the University of Texas. Spent a vacation in Kentucky as a sort of roustabout at a little track there. Really got hung up on racers then. Knew for sure I didn't want to spend my life raising critters to be slaughtered and eaten. I'd rather raise horses to race, and then turn out to pasture."

His longwinded reply exasperated Rae-Ellen. He was showing off to the boss; he was also informing her, obliquely, that he was far above what she'd been considering him.

She was relieved when Papa left.

She stayed in the kitchen and watched Burr scrape. He really was getting down to the bare, clean wood, and it looked as if there was no weakened spot. Much as she hated to admit it, he was probably right. A new coat of paint would set things right.

"How'd you happen to show up at the fire?" he asked.

"I was taking a walk," she said, aching to inform him it was none of his business, but not wanting to start anything which could, so easily, get out of control.

"It was your screaming alerted the boys in the far end of the stable," he said stiffly. "Thank you for that."

"You're welcome," she said, just as stiffly.

She was being snippy, but she couldn't help it. He brought out the worst in her, he really did. Because the mere look of him infuriated her, because he kept hanging around Adah when she came to the stable, because Adah had Lance in the palm of her hand, because . . . oh, *because!*

"It's too bad," he said now, "that you didn't hire a married horse trainer."

"What do you mean by that?"

"Only the curtain. The kitchen curtain."

"I told you I'll make it! I don't want ready-made curtains at these windows!"

"I didn't realize you like to sew," he drawled.

"Well, I do!"

"Like I said. It'd be different if I was married. If I had a wife, she'd make the curtain."

Beside herself with exasperation at him for making such a ridiculous point of a simple curtain, she clenched her fists, but so he couldn't see them. Making no effort, however, to keep irritation out of her tone, she demanded, "Well, why aren't you married? You seem to have it on your mind."

"For one thing, hardly any girl wants a cowpoke."

"At least you realize that much! I have news for you. Girls don't want amateur horse trainers, either."

He didn't have to turn to know how she looked. Those hell-hot blue eyes would be blazing, the red showing in that hair, the spoiled-rotten mouth thinking up what to say next. He longed to drop his sandpaper, turn and grab her into his arms and carry her to the bedroom and throw her onto the bed.

Where she belonged. The only place she ever calmed down, and then only at the pulsing, throbbing end. That was the one time she wasn't fierce as a wildcat, the only time she turned sweet. Hell, maybe it was worth it. When she did turn sweet, it was like honey. But the fighting, the hot words, the wrestling it took to get there!

Nope. Not again. Not with the crew just down at the stable, in and out with the horses, sure to hear if she started to scream. He kept rubbing with the sandpaper, stroking with his bare palm, then the sandpaper again.

He'd already gone too far with this one, way too far. She was a real beauty, and she had the spirit a man wants, but when she was mad she was something else. And, unfortunately, she got mad a lot.

Rae-Ellen watched him rub that wall with his bare fingers. A shiver went down her spine. She knew how they felt on that smooth wall; she'd felt them on her skin. The wall should be thankful it had no feelings, that he could stand there and rub it all day long, and it'd never know the difference.

It'd never glow and burn to his touch, which was more devastating than the real fire had been. Watching his big, stubborn back, seeing him sandpaper and rub that wall which didn't need it, which didn't have a brain or a nerve or any appreciation of what was being done to it, she longed for him to turn and grab her.

Even as she longed, she recognized fact. Burr Travis was in her way. He was the fly in her ointment. This Texas bum—No, she thought. Face it. He was no bum. He'd chosen his life and was following it in his own stubborn way.

She moved to get a better view of his hated face and the movement snagged his attention and he half turned. She caught him looking at her hungrily, with that merciless desire.

"There! I saw that!" she accused.

"Saw what?"

"The way you looked at me!"

"So?"

"Don't think you can get away with it! Not this

time, never again! I've seen you look at Adah the same way!"

"With appreciation. Respect."

"But you do look!"

"I ain't denying it."

"Why, that's what I want to know! What do you want, a harem?"

"Hell, no. I believe in making sure, is all."

"Making sure about what?"

"About everything. Horses . . . women."

"Pah!"

"There's a similarity. Some horses are high-strung and half-mean, like Thunder Boy. Others are spirited, but gentle, too, like Starstruck."

"You're comparing me to Thunder Boy!"

He shrugged, eyes all over her.

"And you're comparing Adah to Starstruck!"

Again he shrugged.

"You've got the world's most colossal nerve!"

"My interest is horses. It's natural I'd think of them in relation to women."

"Which horse, if you were a stallion, would you mate with? Thunder Boy or Starstruck?"

"That's hard to decide." Those brown eyes were saying one thing, that Texas tongue another.

"What about . . . virgins?"

"Ain't all that important. It's better to know your woman ahead of time. Make the right choice, so it'll stick."

"Have you dared . . . with Adah . . . ?" she scream-whispered.

His answer was to whirl to her, sweep her into his arms, stride for the bedroom. "You stubborn, sweet little fool!" he muttered. "Don't you scream, don't dare let your voice reach the stable . . . don't you dare!"

He set her on her feet beside the bed, but kept his arms around her. He brought his mouth onto hers and kissed, and there was a stinging sweetness to the kiss, along with a fierceness that set her whole spine tingling. Her arms went around him, held him close.

He didn't wait to undress her. He merely stripped her jeans to her ankles, worked at his own jeans, pressed her backward. She seemed to dive onto her back, arms eagerly stretched up to receive him.

He started moving instantly, and she moved with him, fast and faster. Now they seemed to be in a fierce, sweet race to see who would get there first. It was a tie, their bodies clinging at the same instant, moans low, filling the room.

He noticed that she was trembling in his arms. Then he realized that he was trembling, too. That got his dander up. So he'd shaken her, that was all it amounted to. He'd moved her with sex. But he would not—could not—trust her, not this hellion.

"Burr," Rae-Ellen heard herself speak.

"I'm listening."

"Have you ever—been in love?" Now, why had she asked him that? Burr Travis, the Texas cowpoke who thought of nothing but horses, who was incapable of any tenderness!

"Back in Texas. Felt like love. *You'd* call them quick lays, I reckon."

He'd be drawn and quartered before he'd let her get the notion he'd ever bedded a filly as many times as he'd bedded her. He wanted her to believe that he'd got tired of them after once.

"I don't say things like 'quick lays'!" she cried.

305

"You may not say it, but you think it."

She'd been right about one thing. He admitted it himself. That he was incapable of love.

"Why'd you ask me that damn-fool question?" he demanded.

"What question?"

She knew, sure-hell she knew, but wanted to trick him into saying the word. She'd never heard "love" pass his lips, and she had a devilish curiosity, and thought if she could get him to say it, she'd win some kind of victory over him.

"I don't know what you're talking about," he told her. "Ain't got the least notion."

"I asked if you've ever been in love, and you—"

"I said, no."

"You did not! You said— You're an egotist!"

"Like fun I am. I just know my own mind."

"Oh, but you are!" She sat up on the bed, yanked first at one side of her jeans, then the other, got herself covered and zipped. "You really are!"

"Now what are you driving at?" he said through his teeth, adjusting his own jeans.

"You and your talk! Comparing horses to women! Your transparent classing of me with Thunder Boy and Adah with Starstruck!"

He looked bullheaded all over, even the way he held his shoulders. Now they were both sitting cross-legged on the bed, glaring at each other. He'd eased her inner burning, but now she was furious with him in spite of it.

"Do you deny it?" she insisted.

"I ain't denying or admitting."

"So! You are comparing me to Adah! Deciding, in your own mind, which you'll 'honor'! In other words, you're trying to make up your mind between me and my sister!"

"I wouldn't say that," he told her soberly. "But I can say this much. If I take a woman—any woman, at any time—it'll be on my own terms, not hers or her Daddy's or my Pa's."

27

She got away from him and back to the house without bursting into tears. What kind of girl was she? What had Burr turned her into? Why couldn't they be alone together without jumping into bed? It was as if they were trying to devour each other.

In her own rooms, Rae-Ellen locked both doors. This was another thing, she'd never spent so much time in her rooms as she had since Burr Travis came.

He was a plague, that was it. Like the bubonic. He was a disease she'd caught, which she couldn't shake off. Her only palliative was sex, but even that didn't last. The disease continued, eating at her. This wasn't liberation; it was enslavement.

She brooded for two days, even refused dates with Fawn. She was going to trust no man but Lance. She saw him when she and a brooding Adah rode over to see Samson's Lad. She managed to behave gently. He responded as gallantly to her as he did to Adah. He said nothing of his engagement to Adah, who, Rae-Ellen knew, wasn't ready to make the announcement.

If only, she berated herself, I'd had sense enough to tame down two years ago, I might be celebrating my first wedding anniversary now, not trying to get Lance to change his mind.

Burr, during this period, noticed that the two girls stayed as far from him as possible. Their parents stood at the rail at the midpoint of the track; the sisters parked themselves at the far end.

His rancor centered on Rae-Ellen. Before he set his stopwatch, he'd glower at her. Look at her there, flaunting herself, flaunting her sister, staying just out of reach. It was just as well. In fact, nothing could suit him better.

Both of them were dangerous, Rae-Ellen with her compelling sex appeal, Adah with her quiet, insidious attraction. Now if you could pour them together, you might come out with an acceptable blend —a girl who had both spirit and femininity. Let Rae-Ellen steam, let her sulk, she wasn't going to get the upper hand, no matter what she was plotting.

For plotting she was. That he knew to his bones.

Mid-October came, and with it another fox hunt. Again, Burr declined to ride, saying he needed to work the racers. Both Rae-Ellen and Adah rode; both were quiet.

The sisters spent time with Lance. Rae-Ellen was careful to present a mild manner; in fact, she was beginning to enjoy this rôle. It was refreshing to hold her tongue, to avoid the quick reply, to blend so with Adah that there was no contrast between them.

She knew that Lance had noticed. At the hunt breakfast he sat with her, Adah having been captured by an unsmiling, importunate Pete. He even persuaded Adah to ride back to Magnolia Hall with him. Rae-Ellen, surprised, said as much to her sister.

"I'd think you would have had enough of Pete Battle!" she whispered. "After the way—and you ate with him! What are you, a glutton for punishment?"

"I'm riding with him for privacy," Adah whispered back. "I must make him understand there's no hope."

"You mean . . . marriage?"

"Yes."

"I can't imagine him, of all people—But, yes! He's ambitious, and you are the boss's daughter."

"Oh, Rae-Ellen, don't think the worst of him!"

"He's a man, isn't he? You're a beautiful girl. Why wouldn't he decide to go for you? It's all to his advantage."

Adah looked unhappy. "If that's true, it's all the more important he should know there's no hope." She frowned, looked ready to cry. "He's so persistent! I only hope this ride will convince him."

Watching her sister canter down the driveway with Pete, the word "persistent" rang in Rae-Ellen's ears.

On impulse, she knew her next move. Persistence, but sudden and intensive. Lance was in a warm mood toward her. There wouldn't be a better time than now. She had to gamble, to risk all on one bold move.

While Lance was seeing off the last hunters, she told the groom to leave Rusty tethered. "I'll get him myself when I'm ready," she said.

She waited in the library. Lance didn't know she was there, so she sang out to him when she heard the front door.

"It's Rae-Ellen," she called.

He appeared in the doorway. "I wondered where you'd got to," he said.

Her pulse took an upbeat. He'd noticed! Then the pulse beat dropped. Of course he'd notice. He was, after all, the perfect host.

She'd meant to assume an expression of despair, but there was no need. Despondence took her; she felt it in the droop of her shoulders, in the sadness that made her face heavy.

He noticed. He noticed right away.

"Why Rae-Ellen, dear, what is it?"

"It's nothing, nothing at all."

"Are you injured? From one of the jumps?"

She shook her head, blinked to banish tears—real tears.

The manner in which her plan was becoming real frightened her. She wanted to fling herself into his arms and sob out the confession that she'd plotted to trick him.

But she couldn't do that now. Because it wasn't a trick any longer. It was an act of desperation. Her entire future—and his!—rested on it.

"What is it, then?" His voice was gentler than she'd ever heard it. "Something's wrong . . . tell me."

"H-Hattie's still in the kitchen."

"I'll send her to her cabin. Clear the house."

"That's all she needs. Just let her find out there's something you don't want her to—"

"I know. She'd manage. We'll outwit her."

"H-how?" She knew, oh, she knew.

"Our mounts are still saddled. Let's go for a ride through the woods. We can have privacy that way."

She managed a smile, the pulse in her throat beating wildly. Blessed, darling Lance. It was as if he were reading her mind. Oh, it was so much better to have this real! With things going so naturally as a result of her cultivated gentleness, she'd never give in to impulse again.

"I'd thought of that," she said. "But I didn't know if you'd—"

"Certainly I would. You're troubled, aren't you?"

She nodded.

"You need a friend?"

"I need a close, dear friend."

"And you have one. Come. To the horses. I'll tell Hattie we're riding to check some of the jumps, which we can do, as there were two I didn't like. At any rate, we'll not exactly lie. Hattie can smell out a fib faster than a hound can scent a fox."

They walked silently to their horses, mounted.

"You know the clearing beyond that old wall?" he asked. "Where Travis had his tumble?"

The very name, Travis, caused shivers to run down her spine.

Lance broke into her resentment. "You know the place I mean?"

"Yes, Lance. It's a delightful spot."

It was also the very place she'd selected when she planned this.

"We'll sit by the stream, let the horses graze, talk as much as you like," he assured her. Then he put his stallion to a trot, and she urged Rusty into the same gait.

312

Lance got there first, dismounted, waited for her.

This was actually a small, outdoor room, its walls of magnolia and live oak, its ceiling the cool blue sky, its floor an early mixture of leaves, twigs, grass. Nestled within its thickly timbered walls, it was also silent, except for the gurgle of the little stream which cut through at one side.

Lance noticed Rae-Ellen's seat as she rode into the small wilderness chamber, and his loins stirred. Even with her lovely face so solemn, he'd never seen her more beautiful, the sunny auburn streaks in her hair so striking, her eyes so intensely blue.

She was a bit like Sukey, the widow with whom he'd consorted so many years, but poor Sukey could never be considered even pretty. Yet, with her open, smiling face, her soft and generous curves, her honest liking for him and what they'd shared together—in this moment, Rae-Ellen made him think of Sukey. He'd broken off with her when he proposed to Adah. She'd been understanding about it, and they hadn't seen each other again.

He helped Rae-Ellen dismount. Her body was even more lithe than he'd thought. Or, maybe, deprived of Sukey, he had a keener eye for women. The man who married Rae-Ellen would be damned lucky.

He put the horses to graze. Then, taking Rae-Ellen's hand, he drew her to the bank of the stream, and they sat, fingers entwined.

The tears were right behind her eyes. She must not let them flow, must not turn him off, not when he was being so wonderful.

"Don't hold back," he murmured, drawing her into his arms. "Cry. Then tell me about it."

Her sobs burst like a storm. She laid her face

313

against his chest and let the storm rage. All the terrible things Burr Travis had done to her; going to bed with Fawn and liking it; going to bed with Pete and liking it; all these gushed out in her tears and she felt Lance's shirt grow wet under her cheek.

At last she was finished.

He produced a handkerchief, and she used it.

"Now," he said, "talk."

"M-men don't like a crying woman," she hiccuped. "They feel no attraction to them."

"You're attractive to me," he said.

And she was. There was still the warmth in his loins. Not for Sukey. Certainly not for Rae-Ellen. Just male hunger deprived of woman.

She sat back from him, mopped her eyes, blew her nose. She crumpled the handkerchief, stuffed it into her pocket. She'd return it later, washed and ironed.

Her voice quivered when she spoke. She told him the whole thing. She told every bit of it, from the first time Burr Travis raped her to the last. She told how she'd used Fawn and Pete. She told how everything had failed to wash that awful, inner fever out.

He listened carefully. His face was gentler, kinder, more concerned than she'd dreamed it could be. He was the only perfect man in the world. She told him so.

"How can I help you, Rae-Ellen, my very dear?"

He was sickened by the torment she'd suffered, was still suffering. His loins grew warmer. He resisted the desire to draw her into his arms again.

"You know I love you," she said simply.

"Yes, dearest girl. I know."

"That I want to marry you."

"Yes," he said, eyes gray as rain, mouth tender, loins hotter.

"And you—there's Adah." She leaned toward him. "You can help me. If once, just once, you'll make love to me. Now—here. The one time will drive out all that other, all that evil. And I'll have a memory to cherish."

"It wouldn't change my plans, Rae-Ellen, dear."

"I'll take that chance."

She moved fast then, tugging off her riding boots and socks. She threw her riding breeches one direction, jacket and stock another, her shirt and underwear dropped at her feet. She sent her derby sailing. There she was, standing proudly, before him.

"Hurry, darling," she urged. "We can't stop now!"

Lance groaned, swore inwardly because she was so appealing, irresistible. Even while he was trying to explain that this would never do, that he was going to marry Adah or no one, he felt himself tearing off his riding habit.

He stood naked before her, the afternoon sun striking through a sliver in the trees. He was perfectly built, with very blond hair on his smoothly muscled body. He was magnificent.

Rae-Ellen came against him, and the resilience of her perfect breasts, the brush of the auburn-streaked hair between her thighs, set him atremble.

In spite of himself, he bore her down and took her. It was like homecoming, like Sukey, but beyond Sukey. He felt himself spill into her, hot and throbbing and blending with her and the earth and the secret, tree-walled room. He heard the gurgle of the stream, bore deeper and moved, felt her strong upthrusts, answered them, and burst within her again.

She gripped him ferociously, hands on his shoulders, her depths around his maleness, which she'd barely glimpsed, big and velvet-hard and reaching, before he'd driven into her. Her passion rose. When he spilled, she spilled; when he gushed, she gushed. Together they glowed.

It was all warm, throbbing, spontaneous. No wild sweep of passion, no suave expertise. No sunny, boyish fun. No rugged, panting, bated breath. Only never-ending rapture.

They lay together, not touching.

The stream sang.

Rae-Ellen was relaxed.

Lance had washed out all the burning, all the confusion put in her by Burr, all the turmoil of which Fawn and Pete had failed to rid her.

She had Lance now. After this heaven, after he'd murmured, as he did once, "Darling!" as they fused, he was hers.

Now he broke into her glow.

"This," he said, "means that I'm obliged to marry you."

"Obliged? How . . . 'obliged'?"

"I sullied the daughter of a lifelong friend."

"You did no such thing! You know how many men—I wasn't a virgin!"

"That I realize. The obligation remains."

"If you love me, how can there be obligation?"

"I love Adah, Rae-Ellen, dear."

"Even after we . . . even then?"

"I'm sorry."

"But you called me darling!"

"At such a time a man gets . . . carried away."

"You can learn to love me! We proved it!"

"I'm truly sorry. I can't fulfill my obligation."

"Why not?"

"Adah has, at last, accepted me."

"When?" Rae-Ellen gasped, sitting erect and naked.

He sat up, too. "After the second jump this morning. She said she couldn't tell me any other way, couldn't face me."

"How did you have time . . . at a jump?"

"It was when the dogs lost the scent. We had a moment alone."

"Then she . . . ?"

"She told me about her mother. It makes no difference."

Then undoubtedly Adah hadn't told him about Pete Battle.

There was still hope. Knowing Adah, there was yet a hurdle for her to take before she announced the engagement.

Lance was dressing now, rapidly. Mentally, he berated himself for what he'd done. Desire was no excuse. That Adah had withheld even her kisses of late, didn't alter things. Even Rae-Ellen's pleading, her alluring presence, not even that. He had betrayed both girls.

Reluctantly, Rae-Ellen began to put on her clothes.

"You know," she told him, "that I'd not want to marry you without love."

But she would. Now she would. She'd marry him under any conditions.

"Understood. This hurts deeply, Rae-Ellen. I had no right to— After this—" He gestured at the spot where they had lain in delight—"if you didn't have a sister—"

"But I do have one."

317

"Rae-Ellen. It could have been different. You're deeply appealing, and under different conditions I'd have chosen you. But I love Adah as a man loves the woman he marries, only Adah. What you and I had was near perfection, but if I could undo it, I would."

She snatched up her derby, slammed it onto her head, and ran to Rusty. She adjusted the bit with trembling fingers, mounted, set the gelding to a gallop, away from Lance.

He watched her go, a sadness in his soul.

28

Burr Travis, of all people, stepped forward to take Rusty's rein when she reached home. His face looked like ugly rock; his fingers brushed hers.

His very touch made that burning flare.

It wasn't out, not at all, even after Lance! She jerked her hand away, and went at a run for the house, ignoring his shouted offer to drive her up in the truck.

She'd not sit in the same car with him. Not with her body clamoring for his. Impossible, but it was. That's what he did to her. Lance had cured her, he really had. Then one look at Burr, one accidental touch, and the whole thing was undone.

He was indeed a one-man plague. There was only one way, she decided furiously, to get the disease out of her system. That was to have sex with him constantly. To have him until she was streaked with it, sated, worn out. Free.

He'd infected her. She'd get her cure from him. It made sense.

Adah had been waiting for what seemed hours for Rae-Ellen to get home. She didn't know whether her sister was down at the stables, or whether Lance had detained her to impart their news. No, not that. He'd leave that to her.

When she heard Rae-Ellen slamming around in her suite, she tapped on the door, then went in. Rae-Ellen was in the bedroom, furiously yanking off her riding habit and flinging it away.

"What happened?" Adah asked. "What kept you so long?"

"None of your business!" snapped Rae-Ellen. Then, seeing the bewildered, hurt look on her sister's face, she relented. "I'm just in a foul mood. What I've been doing has no effect on you. Let me get over it my own way."

"I'm sorry, darling. It simply isn't right!"

"What isn't right?"

"For me to have such h-happy news, and you to be so upset! I've such good news, sister dear! I finally decided to tell Lance about the blood. Today, I did tell him, and it didn't matter a bit! And we're engaged!"

The last words came out on a rush of delight and Adah threw her arms around Rae-Ellen and hugged her. "Are you surprised?"

Rae-Ellen half-heartedly returned the embrace, then stood free. "Yes, I am surprised that you actually told him," she said.

"I'd almost argued myself into thinking I'd be

protecting him if I married him and didn't tell about my mother and our father. That it would be wrong for me to burden him with my problems. I did see it was wrong for me to keep talking to you, putting my worries on your shoulders. And I beg your forgiveness for that, my darling, patient sister! It was realizing how strong you are that gave me the strength. Because of you, I finally saw it couldn't be but one way. That it would be wicked for me to hold such a secret from my husband. So, right after one of the jumps, when the dogs lost the scent, I blurted out the truth, and it makes no difference to him, and now everything's wonderful! And I have you to thank for it, darling!"

"Did you tell him everything?"

"Not the whole story, not in detail. That'll come when we have time and privacy."

"I don't mean that. Did you tell him about Pete?"

Adah felt herself blanch.

She went weak. The room seemed to whirl. But she couldn't faint, couldn't put that extra burden on her sister. Somehow, she steadied herself, though she believed she was still pale.

Rae-Ellen verified this. "No need to go white as death!" she snapped. "I would have thought—"

"Me, too!" whispered Adah. "But when I actually got up the courage to speak about the blood and he didn't *care*, I was so carried away with happiness that I *forgot!*"

"Maybe it doesn't matter. Maybe it's not important."

Adah's heart winced. "Oh, but it is! Lance thinks I'm clean! He thinks—"

"How do you know what he thinks?"

"From things he says. That I'm different. That

I'm not . . . liberated." She managed to get the last word out in a whisper only.

"If he'll sit still for mixed blood," Rae-Ellen said, "he'll overlook one slip, and one only, with a guy like Pete."

"Then you think I should tell him?" Adah asked fearfully.

"That's for you to decide."

Despite her turmoil, Adah became thoughtful. This helped to quiet her racing pulse. She had, again, on the heels of a vital decision, to consider and make another.

Which of her secrets was the more serious, the mixed blood or letting Pete get her drunk and take her to bed? Lance had brushed aside the first, which was an accident of life over which she'd had no control. But no one forced her to drink; Pete didn't maul her and force her to bed. She'd even co-operated to a shameful degree.

This new decision now loomed as the more serious.

"There's no need to tell him," Rae-Ellen said. "As long as you're not . . . did Pete take any precautions?"

Miserable, Adah shook her head, held her breath, watched her sister frown. "Then you won't know, won't have the least idea for a month."

"No," Adah whispered, dazed. "And Lance wants to announce the engagement right away."

"There's just one safe way," Rae-Ellen said firmly, filled with a mixture of pity and scorn for this troubled girl. "And that's to marry as fast as you can get married."

"But then, if I'm . . . I'd never know whose baby it was!"

"That's the point. Lnace wouldn't know either, never know there was the chance it wasn't his own. Don't you see how simple it is?"

"Simple, yes! But wicked, deceitful!" Adah moaned. "You're talking off the top of your head, Rae-Ellen! You're not like that, not at all! If you were in love with Lance, you'd tell him if you'd slept with a dozen men! You'd take your chances!"

"You can take yours."

"I'm so afraid I'll lose him! If I wait a month before we announce the engagement, maybe, please God, I'll find out Pete didn't ... that I'm not ... !"

"Then there'll be no point in telling Lance, ever."

"But the problem of honesty isn't solved," Adah protested. "I still have to decide which is more important, that Lance know about Pete and have the privilege of forgiving or not, or that he never know and we lose complete honesty. In my eyes, this is more serious than my blood."

"Nonsense. It meant nothing to Pete. It should mean less to you. No more, I'll say no more! I know that conscience of yours, heavens above. I know it! Go ahead, weigh and measure and make up your mind."

Adah ran to her and they embraced, the younger girl pliant and trembling, Rae-Ellen rigid with her own conflicts. As soon as Adah trailed away, Rae-Ellen went into her bathroom, turned on the faucets so water rushed and tumbled and turned back upon itself in the tub. When it was filled, she climbed in and began to scrub away the dusting of dried leaves and soil that had got on her skin while Lance made love to her.

And the whole time she burned.

Not for Lance, but from the plague which had

invaded her to torment and torture and make her
life a feverish hell.

She got through the rest of the afternoon. She
tramped the grounds, avoiding the cottage. She
never wanted to lay eyes on Burr Travis, never
wanted to hear that deep, maddening, assured voice
again.

Now you're acting like Adah, she thought angrily. Only instead of trying to make up your mind,
you're avoiding the thing you've decided on—to
wallow in bed with that cowpoke until you get over
him!

Thinking thus, she began to run. Straight for him.

She didn't know what time it was, but the stable
crew's rooms were dark. They retired early because
they were up at four-thirty with the horses, getting
Thunder Boy and Starstruck ready for dawn workout. Burr, she'd noticed, kept his light burning later
than theirs, probably with his nose in a book on
horses. It was like him. Make a big show, and at
the same time really prepare himself to be a trainer.

She punched his back doorbell. There was no
quick response, so she punched again, harder. This
time a light sprang on, the door opened and she
was looking up into his hated face, which assumed a
look of surprise.

Well, maybe he was surprised. Maybe she had
that much power.

"Something wrong?" he asked.

He didn't open the screen door, didn't invite
her in.

"Does something have to be wrong for me to ring
your bell?" she demanded.

"Nope."

"I want to come in." She made her tone frigid.

He held the door open and stood aside as she stepped in. For want of any other ploy, she went to the sink window and adjusted the red-checked curtain she'd made. Then she went to the other window and arranged that curtain. When that was done, she faced him.

He was watching her out of that homely face.

Those damnable eyes! She concentrated on the mouth, willed it to look balky, not just surprised.

"You come here to admire your sewing?" he asked.

"I came, damn you," she said in a fierce whisper, "to go to bed with you!"

Now he really looked surprised. Then his mouth got as bullheaded as ever she'd want it to be. She set her own mouth. Glared. Waited.

Damn her red-streaked hair, damn her hellcat tongue, damn her boldness! She was under his skin like a cattle tick, boring deeper, keeping him so busy fighting with her, going out of his head and quelling that flame of hers, that he hadn't been able to get around to any serious consideration of Adah, who was the wife type. She was the kind he required and was, devil take all, going to have.

"You seem to think," he grated finally, tired of the way those electric blue eyes were ripping him to shreds, "that all you've got to do is walk in here, and I'll jump into bed with you!"

"That's the way it's been! Every chance you get!"

"It don't give you no rights."

"It gives me all sorts of rights! We've got a . . . a relationship! You started it! I don't want it, but you've kept it going, and now you can't stop until I say so!"

It would never do, no matter how mad she was, to let him suspect the true reason. He was just dirt-mean enough that he'd let her burn, make no effort to drown the rage of fever he himself had put into her.

"We ain't got the kind of relationship that keeps a man and woman together," he informed her. "There ain't no feeling—"

"Oh, yes, there is! I hate you . . . loathe you!"

"That don't mean a thing."

"Take me into that bedroom! Undress me! Do what you've done before! Find out if it's got meaning! I dare you!"

That was what got him. Her standing there so spunky and mean and hating, daring him to do the very thing he was afire to do. He wouldn't give her the satisfaction of carrying her to the bedroom; instead, he strode in there and she had to follow on her own two feet.

He didn't undress her, either. He undressed himself. She yanked herself bare to the skin. And when she stood waiting for him to push her onto the bed, he wouldn't do that either. She endured that situation for a few seconds only, then flung herself onto her back on the bed and waited for him to come to her. He did.

They flamed and fused. They rested, then fused again. No talk. Just the fusing, the silence afterward, the ticking of the old wooden clock on the kitchen wall.

After a long time he croaked out a few words. "You're under my skin, and I'm under yours. There ain't but one way for either of us to get loose."

For some reason, Rae-Ellen began to cry, and

326

angrily at first. Then when she began to sob, Burr had to hold her in his arms. Gradually, her sobs quieted, but he kept holding her.

While he was doing that, he experienced tender thoughts of her. He pictured her holding a baby, a Texas baby, to her breast and letting it suckle.

That was sure crazy. Adah, now . . . yes, her. She was no modern girl. She belonged to the historic Old South, to history itself, to perfection. Groaning, he entered Rae-Ellen again.

After she got back to her room, Rae-Ellen found out for sure that she wasn't pregnant.

For some reason, she felt let down.

29

Marguerite and the servants, helped by Rae-Ellen and Adah, plunged into getting Magnolia Hall ready to close while they were in Florida. Jim left Mary-Lou behind and flew off to Switzerland for a party. Burr and Lance trained their racers. Raymond Pettigrew flew down to Florida for a final inspection of the estate, complete with stables and track, which he had earlier leased.

Adah and Lance had not yet announced their engagement. Rae-Ellen went to a concert with Fawn, to a dance, and he courted her in the most gentlemanly way. She found herself beginning to respect him. Pete didn't ask for a date; this, she assumed, sprang from his feeling that Fawn had priority. She avoided Burr, who was busy with the horses. He asked for no date, nor did she expect him to.

Adah had dinner out with Lance, and once even dated Pete. She reported that he was on his good behavior, and she'd been careful not to lead him on, but had striven to get their association back on the old friendly, laughing basis.

Every time Rae-Ellen did see Burr, they quarreled. Even one day when she found him in Rusty's stall, treating a scrape on the gelding's shoulder, they began to fight.

"What do you want now?" he demanded when she stuck her head in. He kept rubbing salve on Rusty.

"You can't even be polite!" she accused. "You've never, not once, spoken to me decently!"

"I ain't heard you exactly talk like you think I'm even human," he countered.

His attention was still on Rusty.

"You've never given me a word of liking, or admiration, or even hinted at such a thing as love! You've never—"

"Love ain't a subject we've had reason to discuss. Though this is the second time, as I recall, that you've dragged the word into our conversation."

"No, it certainly hasn't been discussed! All you've done is rape me—"

"How about the other night when you rang my doorbell? When you dared me."

"The first time, that was rape!"

"With your assistance."

"If you'd been a gentleman—"

"Only I wasn't."

"Every—single—time," she whispered, spacing her words, "you've been an animal!"

"You ain't been what I'd call a purring kitten yourself."

"You—you've *rutted!*"

"What a word for a lady to use! Well. It that's how it seemed to you, there's been reason."

"What reason?"

"At the start, as I recall, you came at me with your claws out. Mad enough to kill me. Or you've made me so danged mad—happens I've got a temper, too—I couldn't spit, and there wasn't but the one way to quiet you down. So I done it."

"Be glad you could! Or you'd not be alive!"

"I'll be glad when it's over, that's when I'll be glad."

"When what's over?"

"This war between us. If bed'll settle it, I'll go for that. It might even— But no. Not with you."

"What were you going to say?" she demanded.

"Won't help to tell you. But when you do quieten, especially in a bed, a man might get the notion you had a drop of sweetness in you. Somewhere."

"Thanks, thanks a lot!" she hissed, aching to pull his sun-faded hair out by the roots, to drag him into the cottage. To conquer him. Again. There was a difference in him at those times.

"See," he drawled, "I pay you a compliment, and you don't recognize it, but spit like a wildcat. I can't see why I put up with you at all, except maybe besides being under my skin like a cattle tick—

"—or maybe it's because you're a challenge, and I never backed down from a challenge."

He watched her, expecting her to go wild. Instead, she looked as if she might cry. Then, she got simply mad, and looked familiar again.

Next, she strayed back to that love-talk and accused him of being unable to love anything but a horse. He told her right out to shut up . . . she was so mad she did!

"It's you that ain't capable of love," he told her then. "I'd bet every horse in the stable that you've sent packing anyone who's dared to mention it. The thing you've got to face is what every woman has to come to grips with."

"And what is that?"

"A woman has got to give up the crazy dreams of childhood and face the realities of life," he said coldly.

Rae-Ellen knew instantly that he was right. Lance had been her dream. She'd had him, she'd received his passion, and it had faded as quickly as that of Fawn and Pete.

Burr Travis was her stark reality. Of which she was going to rid herself.

They made up a caravan for the trip to Florida, the senior Pettigrews, along with Marie, Adah and Rae-Ellen, their racers; and Lance with his racer; Burr Travis and Terry Smith, the groom; Ruble, Lance's groom; and two truck drivers. The horses had a trailer each, drawn by a powerful truck.

Burr was designated to drive lead, pulling Starstruck. He climbed into the cab of the truck and Rae-Ellen followed, bouncing into the seat beside him.

"I aimed to drive with Terry," he objected. "For horse-talk."

"Did Papa order you to have Terry?"

"Nope."

"And you're not one to take orders from a woman." She settled herself. "Want to make an issue of it with Papa?"

"It ain't worth the trouble," he drawled, slower than usual. "Not when all you want is to pick a fight."

"All I want is to ride with you," she replied, looking innocent. "I mean to keep an eye on the driving, since you're leading the caravan."

He said no more, just told Terry to hop into the second truck. His mouth was like concrete. He fastened his seat belt. She fastened hers.

Third in the caravan, behind Thunder Boy's trailer, was Lance's truck, pulling Samson's Lad. Ruble, his groom, rode with the driver. Ruble had been hired on Burr's recommendation. This made Rae-Ellen very cross. That Lance should ask Burr Travis' advice on anything was unthinkable.

Behind the last truck, and fourth in line, were Papa, Mama, and Marie in their sleek black car, Papa at the wheel. Fifth, were Fawn Morehead and Pete Battle in Fawn's car. At the very end, Lance and Adah were alone in Lance's car.

The caravan pulled onto the highway at dawn. Rae-Ellen noticed Burr's eyes were everywhere. The least he can do is be alert to traffic, she thought resentfully.

They rolled along, keeping within the speed limit. The cab windows were open, and the early morning air nipped at Rae-Ellen's face. She was just as glad that Bullhead Travis wouldn't look at her; he'd get an unholy kick out of seeing her frostbitten. In fact, that was probably why he had the windows open!

She began to roll her window up.

"Leave it down," he said, eyes on the road.

"It's cold!"

"Sun'll be rising directly. You'll warm up."

She kept her fingers on the handle, but she didn't raise the window another notch. "I suppose you have some Texas reason for wanting that wind to sweep through."

"I sure have. It wakes a driver up, keeps him awake. Use your coat collar. I'm here to pull that filly to where we're headed, not to make anybody snug."

She lowered the window, turning the handle in a jerky motion. He was the most exasperating man alive, especially when he was right.

They rode in silence. The sun came up, streaking through the cab windows and into her eyes. She put on her dark glasses, Burr put his on, too. The traffic was increasing, but he kept their outfit where it belonged, following the highway as if he were glued into the proper groove. Rae-Ellen looked into the rearview mirror on her side and saw that the whole caravan was following as though he had them on a string.

So, he thought grimly. At least she doesn't chatter. She's got that much sense.

They went through towns; they passed farmhouses, barns, country stores. They slowed for school buses. They drove on and on.

She gazed at the scenery. They rolled past strands of moss-hung live oak, stretches of mimosa, which would be laden with pink in early summer, and groves of magnolia, which would also be beautiful with their white, sweet-smelling blossoms next summer.

But this was now. This was October, and she was trapped in the cab of this truck with the sphinx. Let him sit there and drive like a stone man!

The thought of Lance and Adah, way back, kept

returning to torture her. No telling what they were talking about. If she hadn't done so already, Adah would relate the story of Papa and Delphine. Whether Adah would go further and confess what happened with Pete, Rae-Ellen couldn't guess. After the agonizing about the mixed blood and finally confiding, did Adah, gentle Adah, have the brashness to confess about Pete?

Strength, the tires rolling beneath Rae-Ellen seemed to sing. Strength, the hill-ringed stretch of road they were traveling, seemed to whisper. Not brashness . . . strength. Adah had the strength.

She also had an overdose of compassion. She would be thinking more of the pain she would bring Lance than of the fear of losing him. Adah could cope—but would she?

She risked another glance at Burr. He didn't look bullheaded. He was intent on driving. She tried, but could find nothing wrong with that. She began to feel safe, comfortable. The burning in her had died down. If just being this close to him held the burn under control, maybe she'd not have to go to bed with him again. Maybe the last time had washed his plague out of her.

At rest stops, he checked the horses, the trucks, the trailers. He had the horses watered and fed, patted them, soothed. Lance helped, as did the grooms. The drivers looked into their motors. The whole crew inspected the trailer couplings.

At the late lunch stop, Burr and the crew stayed outside, first tending horses and trucks, then grabbing bites of hamburger and guzzling colas. The rest of the party went into the roadhouse and lunched quickly. Burr didn't want to lose time; he

334

was determined to reach the stables where he had reservations for their horses, before dark.

They had crossed the state line and were in Florida. Once in awhile, as they drove south after lunch, he actually pointed out horses in fields to Rae-Ellen. They agreed that, from this distance, the horses didn't look to be blue-blooded.

"Burr! Watch out," Rae-Ellen screamed suddenly.

One moment the lead truck was cruising along at fifty; the next moment the left side of the cab toppled, hitting concrete. The left front wheel rolled crazily past the line of metal light posts in the median strip.

Rae-Ellen was thrown toward Burr, jerked back by her seat belt. He fought the wheel, face like granite.

There was a shrill, never-ending scream from behind. The truck crashed into the next light pole, which bent from the impact. The trailer jackknifed. The frantic scream inside the trailer was abruptly cut off.

Tires shrieked as the other trucks jammed on brakes, as all drivers in the caravan and the cars behind them, stopped as fast as they could, barely averting a chain collision.

Before the shrieking of brakes died, the lead truck exploded into flame. As the people who spilled onto the highway ran forward, the cab was ablaze.

Part IV
FLORIDA

30

There was a brilliant flash inside the cab. It seemed a vast furnace had opened, red and hell-hot. It rose upward, growing as it reached everywhere into the oncoming twilight. Beyond the roar were tinny-sounding screams and thin voices.

Rae-Ellen felt a pain knife through her side and then it was gone, leaving her whole body feeling as if it had been wrenched in pain, wrung out, and flung aside.

The deep whoosh of the explosion—it had to be an explosion—still lay in her ears. It was then, only then, that she had any understanding of what had happened.

Something had gone wrong with the truck. It had rammed into an immovable object and burst into flame. And she and Burr were belted into their seats!

That stabbing pain pierced with every gasping breath, made it impossible for her to move. But she *had* to move, had to unfasten Burr's seat belt, had to get him out of this blazing trap before the extra gas tank exploded.

She lunged toward him, reaching. Pain impaled her, and she gritted her teeth and pushed forward, her own belt holding her back.

He was sprawled against the back of the seat.

Hands on the buckle of his belt, working at it, screaming at him, letting the anguish in her side go where it wanted, do what it would, time seemed to escape.

"Burr!" she screamed, and torment grabbed her breath. "Burr . . . wake up! Burr . . . we've got to get out of here!"

The others, those in the caravan, people driving the road. They'd come, they'd help, they'd try. But there wasn't time. She had to get him out now, this instant.

She couldn't open his seat belt. "Burr!" she screamed again, gripped his shoulder and shook it, jaw set against the spear of pain in her side. But he lay inert, head back against the seat, mouth slightly open.

Dimly, in the torture, the snap and snarl of fire, the terror for Burr, she tried to unbuckle her own seat belt. She fumbled, tried again. Her fingers had no bone. She tried anew. She had to get the belt off before she could help Burr, but every time her finger slipped bonelessly away, only to try again.

All the while she was screaming his name, "Burr . . . wake up . . . Burr!"

He heard a fearful, hot screaming. It wouldn't let up, screamed on and on, and the more it screamed, the hotter, the shriller it was. There was a rage of pain in his head, in his right shoulder, the one that something kept gripping and shaking. Or was it the other shoulder?

In his confusion he knew, somehow, that he was sprawled, that he hadn't moved at all. Rae-Ellen, that's who it was. Rae-Ellen shrieking, burning him, getting in his way. As usual, she was clawing at him; he could never do anything because of her!

There was a crackling. Flame. Fire. The floorboards were hot; he could feel it through the soles of his boots. Any minute the fire would eat through, be at his feet, grab his clothes and consume them.

Her feet, too. Her clothes.

With him stirring, Rae-Ellen abandoned her own belt, tried for his again, couldn't even touch it now because his hands were in the way.

"Unbuckle it!" she shrieked.

He knocked her hands aside so hard they stung. She strained toward him, her belt holding her, ready to make some final, miraculous lunge which would let her free him.

"Buckle's jammed!" he roared, and her heart lunged.

He was conscious! He knew what was happening, knew enough to help!

"Pocketknife . . . right hip!" he shouted. "Get it!"

Hand numb from where he'd slapped it away, she rammed it into the pocket, found the knife, yanked it out. She tried to open the blade, and he grabbed it and then she felt the quick slash through

341

her seat belt and she was free. He cut his own belt through with one motion.

She got a look outside. There were people; there was noise, voices. There were police. Sirens were screaming, winding down to nothing.

She had to get Burr into an ambulance. The floorboards were so hot they'd break any instant. She grabbed his shoulder and began to pull. He pushed her away.

People were coming at them. Lance was there. As she saw him, the flames bit through, into the cab. They were worse on Burr's side, the down-side.

Lance leapt into the cab, clapped a sweater over Rae-Ellen's head, and tugged to pull her out. Desperate, her only thought to save Burr, she resisted; she pulled back from Lance, twisted, tried to scream that Burr must be got out first, but the sweater muffled her. But still she fought.

Hands came onto her left side. There was a mighty punch on her eye, which sent her into Lance's arms. He dragged her out of the cab, onto the ground, away from Burr.

She fought the sweater off her head. The first thing she saw was Burr, at the edge of the seat. Flames were leaping at his ankles. She dived headlong to get hold of him.

Just as she sprang up the step and into the cab, Burr's fist took her on the jaw. She fell backward, into Lance's arms. Jaw numb, head singing from that blow and the one to her eye, she yanked free of Lance and jumped into the cab again, hands out to grab Burr.

Suddenly, instead of her dragging him out of the cab, he was pushing her and Lance was pulling.

Between the singing in her head and the ever-growing fire, the lack of time, she struggled with them both.

It was like that, caught between the two men, struggling and fighting them, that they at last ejected her from the burning cab. She darted back to Burr, and again he hit her on the jaw, and she went backward in a staggering run, coming up against Lance, who held her.

"It's all right!" he shouted. "Calm down . . . you're in shock! Burr had to do it! It was the only way he could get out before—"

There was a great, velvet whomp that drowned out his voice. The spare tank spouted flame, the leaping fire grabbing it. Now the trailer, Starstruck inside, burst into flame and the crew of men who had been trying to jack up the trailer so they could get its door open and the filly out, were forced to fall back.

Rae-Ellen, aware that she was supported by both Lance and Burr, stared, stricken, at the flaming trailer.

"They've got to save Starstruck!" she cried. "She can't be . . . she simply cannot be . . . !"

"She ain't feeling the fire," Burr said.

"How do you know?" she screamed at him. "She's a living creature! She feels pain as much as you! She—"

"What he's trying to say, Rae-Ellen," Lance put in gently, "is that— Don't you see? If she were conscious, she'd be—there's no sound from her."

"She'd have kicked the sides out of that trailer before now," Burr added.

Rae-Ellen sucked in her breath. It was like stabbing herself, but she didn't care. How could they be so heartless, these two men she'd thought were so sensitive?

Even as these muddled thoughts tormented her, she saw the great sprays of water playing over the trailer. She noticed the police and ambulance next to the fire truck. They struck the top, all along the sides, down the ends. Still there was no sound from Starstruck. One fireman, when the blaze died some, wrenched and wrestled open the door in the side of the van, hoisted himself inside, and the crowd waited.

It took only seconds. Flashlight in hand, he leaped out. "Broken neck!" he shouted. "Never felt a thing!"

Rae-Ellen sagged between Lance and Burr. Then she pulled away from them, but they seemed to think she couldn't stand on her own feet. She ignored them both as tears streamed down her face. Starstruck, her favorite, the filly she loved, was dead!

Papa and Mama were there. They'd been there all the time, she realized now, and Adah and the others, only she hadn't noticed them. Her head was still hurting from the slugging Burr had given it, and her jaw was still numb.

She turned, groggily, to tell him what she thought of him. And her eyes came, first thing, to his brown, beautiful eyes, and she remembered how near he'd been to death not three minutes ago.

Next she saw the huge lump which had already sprung out on his forehead. It looked purple even this soon. And she could tell, the stiff way he held his right shoulder, that it was injured. His neck was bleeding—she hadn't known about the broken glass before—and when he shifted his weight, she could tell he was bruised all over. Also, his left foot was burned because his boot gaped at the toe, the sole charred.

Ambulance attendants came through the crowd, which parted for them. They moved fast; that meant that all the events and impressions had taken place in five minutes or so.

She looked at Burr. He was white under his tan. Panic took her. If he was this banged up on the outside, no telling what internal injuries he had! She felt herself go lightheaded. Starstruck dead—please, God, of a broken neck—Burr internally injured, maybe with third-degree burns, even worse. She swayed, felt arms hold her, steadied herself, pulled free.

It was Burr who caught her. Burr, who should be in the hospital right now, not standing around at the scene of the accident.

Papa was speaking, raising his voice, and she realized that he'd been speaking for some time. Now he was firm and angry and his mood got through all the excitement, shock and confusion.

"Driver . . . you . . . here!" Papa yelled. "Bring that cot! For my daughter!"

The attendants set the cot down, moved to put her on it.

"Don't be ridiculous!" she cried—tried to cry, because it came out more as a quaver. "I'm perfectly all right!"

She twisted clumsily off the cot and stood. Burr came at her again and this time, instead of struggling, she attacked. She grabbed each of his arms in her hands and pushed him down to the cot as hard as she could. He resisted and was about to get the best of her.

So she tried talking.

"I'll go to the hospital! I'll go to shut your big mouth! But I'm not riding on that cot! You're riding on it, and I'm riding in the seat beside you!"

He was so dumbfounded that when she gave the next shove he sat down on the cot, hard. She rammed her hands against his shoulders and with that look still on him, he forgot to stiffen himself and first thing he knew he was laying flat on the cot, the attendants sliding it into the ambulance, and sure enough she was scrambling in, and by the time the motor purred, she was in the seat beside the cot.

Papa got into the ambulance before it moved. "At least ride in the other ambulance, Rae-Ellen," he reasoned. "So your mother can ride with you. She's very worried."

"It's not fair, Papa, to put it that way! You can see for yourself that I'm perfectly all right! And you can see with your own eyes that Burr needs someone with him, someone who knows him well enough to tell whether he's getting worse! Get out and let us go, will you, Papa?"

White with shock, Raymond Pettigrew dropped speechlessly to the ground. The attendant closed the doors, then got in beside the driver.

Rae-Ellen immediately worked her way to the foot of the cot, began to tug at Burr's burned boot. When he groaned, she hesitated, then pulled harder.

"What the hell you doing?" he swore, and sat up.

"You lie down, lie down this minute!"

"Leave my foot alone and maybe I will!"

"I'm going to look at it, give first aid! I know it's burned!"

"Sure it's burned! But what the hell do you

think you're going to give first aid with? You lay off that foot or, so help me, no matter what shape you're in, I'll turn you over my knee and spank the daylights out of you!"

She settled back into the seat. He lay back down.

They rode in furious silence. Her eye hurt and her jaws and ribs ached. She was numb over Starstruck, numb that Burr might be seriously injured. Much as she hated him—yes, hated! she didn't want him dead.

She got so dizzy that she nearly toppled off the seat, but she managed to steady herself before he noticed. She kept steady by refusing to think at all.

31

They were taken to a large, bright, modern emergency room. Rae-Ellen was admitted to one cubicle, Burr to one adjoining.

She lay on the narrow table, repelled, yet comforted, by the glaring white walls, the silent-footed attendants in white. The Cuban doctor who examined her was very young and had a charming accent.

"You hurt here, no?" he asked, probing gently at her side.

She nodded through clenched teeth.

His fingers probed very lightly. If she breathed carefully the pain wasn't too bad.

"You are most lucky señorita," he said after a time. "You could have many broken ribs. But you have not even the one. You have the bruise, which I will tape because the ribs, they are sore, and you will be of more comfort."

"What about him?" she asked, indicating Burr's cubicle. "Has he internal injuries?"

"He has another doctor. I do not know his condition, señorita."

She lay impatiently while he taped ribs, while he put a dressing on her eye, while he explained. She could expect to be sore for about a week. Aside from a few minor bruises, she had only the aching side and an upcoming black eye and a lump on the jaw.

The moment she saw Burr, she lit into him. This was two seconds after the curtain between them had been opened and the doctors had gone.

"Your foot's bandaged!" she accused.

"It got burned a little, remember."

"What degree burn?"

"What do you mean, what degree?"

"There's third-degree, maybe fourth . . . tenth! I don't know how high! What is yours?"

"Not bad. The doctor said I can walk on it now and wear an outsize sneaker in a week. Go about my business."

"What else is wrong? Tell me, this minute!"

"My shoulder got a bruise, my neck a superficial cut, and you can see this." He pointed at the lump on his forehead.

Now he was mad. Bullheaded mad. It was on his mouth.

"Where did you get hurt?" he demanded, that mad way. "It's the ones like you, running around wild at the scene of an accident, who topple over from the internal injuries you talk about! How many of them did you get?"

"None! None at all! Just a bruise and this black eye and my jaw. And you know where I got the eye and the jaw!"

"I didn't aim for the eye!" he retorted.

"What did you aim for, then?"

"Any place to stop you, to get you out of the truck."

He could see that she was ready to fly into a real snit, when her doctor reappeared.

"The family of the señorita," he said, "I have talk to them and they wait to go."

The entire party, shaken and concerned, met in the motel suite which Raymond Pettigrew had taken for himself and Marguerite and Marie. He'd reserved a suite for the three girls; and one for Fawn and Lance and Pete. He'd arranged for Terry and Ruble and the drivers to stay in rooms near the stable.

"I reserved a separate room for you, Travis," he said. "Thought you might like quiet and privacy."

"I appreciate that, sir," Burr said. "I'll have to see how Thunder Boy is before I'll know whether I can use it. I may need to spend the night with him, probably will."

"That's the way with me," Lance said. "Ruble and I got Samson's Lad eating, but he's on edge."

"Where did you find a stable?" Burr asked.

"The police. They knew about Griggs Livery. Horse owners use it enroute between Florida and the northern tracks. I hadn't heard of it, but it's fine."

"What about Starstruck?" Rae-Ellen asked, a catch in her voice. "You all sit here and talk about Thunder Boy and Samson's Lad and whether they have a comfortable stable, while Starstruck . . ." Tears in her throat choked off her words.

Mary-Lou was at her side instantly, arms around her. "There, darlin'! Starstruck's being taken care of! And I'm the one who thought of it, aren't I, Lance?"

He almost smiled, and Rae-Ellen, knowing him, was convinced he'd had the thought before Mary-Lou ever advanced it.

"Adah and I went with Lance and the grooms and the truckers to the stable," Mary-Lou continued. "And Mister Griggs has a burial ground for horses right back of the stables. It's a field . . ."

"A lovely pasture," Lance put in quietly.

"Six other horses are buried there, all race horses, and then he's got other horses runnin' in the pasture. It's all right, you see, darlin', because they keep the grass down. And Starstruck's being buried there right now, and you can pick out a marker for her tomorrow."

Rae-Ellen's first impulse was to go to the pasture where, even now, they were putting Starstruck into her grave. Her next impulse was to remember the beautiful little filly as she had been in life, dainty and intelligent and loving and fast on the track.

"You pick a marker, Papa," she said. "Something simple, with just the dates and her name on it. Starstruck."

Tears stung the backs of her eyes.

"How did the racers act?" Burr asked Lance. "When they were taken out of the vans at the stable?"

"Jittery. Scared. Thunder Boy was frantic. Terry used that soft-talk on him that you use, and he quieted."

"I'm surprised."

"So am I. But I doubt we should hit the road tomorrow."

351

"Out of the question," agreed Burr. "They need at least twenty-four hours to calm down."

"If not more," Raymond Pettigrew said thoughtfully. "As high-strung as these racers are, I'm in favor of treating them like babies."

"That's right, sir," Burr said. "That settles it. I stay in the stable with Thunder Boy tonight."

"But your foot!" Rae-Ellen protested. "A burn can become infected!"

"Not the way I'm bandaged. And I'll pin a thick towel on top of that."

Lance said he was going to spend the night with Samson's Lad.

"The question is," Fawn said, speaking for the first time, "when we do take to the road, which way do we go, north or south?"

"Yes," Pete said. "What about the race horses? Would it be better to take them home, to their own stables?"

"That would get them back to normal," Fawn said.

Rae-Ellen was stunned. Going home hadn't entered her mind. Still, if it was for the good of the horses, if it would hurt their future to push on, she wanted no part of it.

"It's worth considering," Lance said. "Even loading them into vans after what they've been through is traumatic."

"You mean," Papa speculated, "that less harm will be done if they find themselves in their home stables next time they're unloaded."

"Perhaps," Lance replied. "Burr, what's your thinking?"

Burr was frowning. "I don't know. We've got

352

to be careful. If we go right home, it can work like it does with humans. Like getting behind the wheel and driving after you've had an accident. It you make yourself drive, you overcome fear. If you shy away from it, you may never drive again."

"That's sensible," agreed Lance. "I vote we go on."

"And enter them in the races?" asked Fawn.

"Certainly," Papa spoke up. "Give them time to get acquainted with the new stable and workout track. Time to feel at home, the way every racer must do when he's moved from one racecourse to another."

"Right, sir," Burr agreed.

"How do we go about it, Travis?" Lance asked.

In a way Rae-Ellen was proud that Lance would turn to Burr for advice, yet it irritated her. Lance, she'd bet, knew as much about horses as Burr. Still, his experience had been with hunters, not with racers. That was why he turned to the supposed horse trainer.

"After they feel comfortable in the new stable," Burr explained, "we ease into workouts. Not saddle at first, but lead them on to the track for a time."

"Let them get the feel of new soil," added Lance.

"Right. Walk them further each time. Then put a blanket on and lead them clear around the track, with Terry and Ruble each riding a lead horse."

"You've got other horses?" Mary-Lou asked.

"I leased training horses," Papa said.

"When they settle down to being led," Burr continued, "we'll have the boys ride them around the track with you, Buford, on one training horse and myself on another, beside them."

Rae-Ellen was still raked by conflicting emotions. Who was Burr trying to impress? Sleeping with Thunder Boy when he himself needed, with all his injuries, to be in a bed.

They went through the motions of voting. It was decided to go on to Florida.

The country estate which Raymond Pettigrew had leased for the season was located in Davie. It was sprawling, with low white stables, a low, two-storied white house with a white roof. Australian pines lined some driveways, tall palm trees lined others. Citrus trees, in groves, showed ripening oranges.

Rae-Ellen fell in love with the grounds on sight. Every time they visited Florida, it seemed that they entered a fairyland of pastel-tinted houses with white roofs under a sunny sky.

Her pleasure was dashed when Mama said that the entire party, except for the grooms, who would stay near the horses, were to be lodged in the main house. She dropped this bomb when she and Papa and the girls were alone in the master suite, admiring it.

"What do you mean?" Rae-Ellen cried.

"There's so much room. I see no reason to open and maintain all the stable quarters."

"Even Burr Travis? Even that—horse trainer? You mean to keep him in the house?"

"Naturally, dear."

"But why? Why can't he stay at the stables, the way he does at home?"

"He has a cottage there, dear. The quarters here, your father says, are one-room efficiencies. With sketchy cooking facilities."

"He's even going to eat with us?"

"Naturally, dear."

Rae-Ellen glimpsed a quiet flash in Adah's golden eyes, or thought she did. She looked closer, but it was gone.

"Sister dear," Adah said, "Burr is presentable. He has as much right to stay in the house as Fawn and Pete, and you don't object to them."

"And Lance? Don't forget Lance!"

"He's always been with us."

"Men!" exploded Rae-Ellen, so pent up over Burr's sleeping under their very roof she couldn't contain herself. "Men . . . men . . . men! Adah, you're collecting a harem of men!"

"Now, look here," Papa **interrupted in his most** hardboiled manner. "Your mother is mistress of this house, just as she is of Magnolia Hall. What she says goes. If she wants to keep even the grooms in the house, she's free to do so."

Rae-Ellen didn't back down. "It's bad enough to have that Texan to meals and parties back home! I've kept still about that! But this is different, it's taking him to live with us, and he just isn't what I'm used to having around!"

"That I agree to," Papa said. "He's one to throw himself into his work even harder than Fawn and Pete."

"So! They're all working fools! I couldn't care less!"

"But you'll tolerate it," Papa said firmly. "Travis learned to work on a cattle ranch, learned the hard way. He's more man than I've met in years. His Texas edge may differ from southern manners, but I challenge you to find a southerner who's more of a man!"

That stopped her short. Even if she knew he certainly had no manners, having him nearby could be helpful if . . . her fiery ache returned . . .

She made no further protest.

32

The three girls spent most of their time in the pool as the week dragged past. Rae-Ellen's black eye faded and her side healed quickly. Burr and Lance had decreed that only they and the grooms should be near the horses.

The four of them slept in the stable so they could speak soothingly to the horses. Thus, far from being annoyed by Burr's presence, Rae-Ellen didn't even see him. One of the efficiencies had been opened for the grooms and Burr ate with them, as did Lance.

By the end of the week Thunder Boy had quieted until he was content with just Terry. Samson's Lad, too, was calm with only Ruble.

Thus Lance and Burr moved into the main house. Obeying Marguerite's command that in Florida they dress casually, the men wore pale slacks and short-sleeved shirts, open at the neck.

Mary-Lou sparkled so at dinner that Pete began to tease.

"You glitter!" he accused.

"I don't! I've got on a *pale* pink dress, and not even my birthday diamond on my finger!"

"That red hair glitters all the time. But there's more, isn't there, Fawn?" Pete persisted.

"She's happy. When she's happy, she glitters."

"It's about time!" she declared. "I'm so happy that Thunder Boy and Samson's Lad—" She broke off, hazel eyes anxious. "They are fine, they have got over being scared, and'll be able to race?" She looked from Burr to Lance.

Lance smiled, Burr grinned, assured her this was true.

"Then you're out of prison . . . we're all out of prison!"

"What do you mean, dear?" asked Mama, concerned. "We haven't meant for you to stay right on the place."

"But we wanted to . . . the way we looked! Didn't we, darlin's?"

Rae-Ellen and Adah agreed.

Fawn and Pete upheld them, saying they'd invited them to drive several times. "And got turned down," Pete laughed. "Now, maybe things will change!"

"Yes!" Mary-Lou squealed. She looked at Burr, at Lance. "You can both go out now, can't you?"

They agreed.

Burr's assurance irritated Rae-Ellen. Everything about him irritated her more than usual tonight. He looked different in casual dress. She felt cross that he was wearing off-white slacks and shirt, and that he had comb-tracks in his hair. He wore white sneakers, too, when he should be wearing only that gauze bandage.

"This calls for a celebration!" Mary-Lou declared. "I say we go nightclubbing and don't come back till all hours!"

"Splendid," Papa smiled. "But it's strictly for the young. Marguerite and I will enjoy being alone for a while, knowing you're all having a good time."

The girls rushed upstairs to freshen their make-up. Rae-Ellen had a large, airy room. It was separated by huge, adjoining baths from a still larger chamber, which Adah and Mary-Lou shared. Across the hall, identical rooms were occupied by Lance in the single, and Fawn and Pete in the double. At the back, Burr's smaller room and bath faced the doors of the senior Pettigrew's suite.

Rae-Ellen thought of how near Burr's room was to her own. He had only to walk a few steps. Her face blazed, and she dusted on a film of powder to tone it down. He wouldn't have the nerve, not right in the house!

Lance met Adah as she came off the last step of the stairway and asked her to be his date. She smiled, dimples showing. He took her hand and placed it on his arm.

Rae-Ellen missed none of this. How long, she wondered, is Adah going to play the charade? How long to thresh out her problem with Pete?

Mary-Lou, giggling, piped up. "Dibs on Pete and Burr! It was my idea, so I'm the one who gets two dates!"

"You'll need two," Burr said, grinning, as she latched on to his arm with one hand and on to Pete's with the other, "considering this foot of mine. It ain't up to tripping the light fantastic!"

Fawn quietly took Rae-Ellen's arm. "I win first prize by default," he murmured.

She shot a glance at Burr, who was laughing at some ridiculous thing Mary-Lou had said, but then she smiled at Fawn warmly. She was glad he was her date, really glad. At least he was predictable.

Fawn was elected to take them to a spot of his choice.

The place was luxurious, softly lit, and in the best of taste. The decor was as subdued as the lighting; the music of the small orchestra blended into the whole.

The wine steward came to their table, which was round and large enough to seat them without crowding. Mary-Lou ordered a Bloody Mary, the men ordered scotch, and Rae-Ellen and Adah, still keenly aware of recent consequences, ordered sparkling water.

Mary-Lou teased about this, then demanded that Pete dance with her. The others got up to dance, and Burr stretched out his left leg to ease the pressure on his foot.

He gazed over the dance floor, watching the members of his party. Mary-Lou was stepping gaily to the music, her small, shapely self plastered against Pete, who had no objection, for he was grinning and talking, his cheek against her hair.

Rae-Ellen was chatting with Fawn as they moved to the music, going in for fancy steps. She kept leaning back, eyes on his face. Fawn smiled, seemed to murmur, and sometimes one of his eyebrows lifted.

Burr scowled all he wanted to. He had the gut-feeling that she was putting on a show for him. He reckoned she knew very well that he was looking, which was why she danced like a spirited filly, one that could use a touch of the whip to calm her down.

His loins stirred.

Now he watched Adah and Lance. They were dancing gracefully, bodies not touching. There was something about them, as they danced, a tenderness, that convinced him they were in love. He gazed at Adah, at her beauty, at how that inborn gentleness, softened by the hidden strain of blood, reached out from her like an aura. He wondered why he didn't feel disturbed.

His loins remained quiet.

After another round of drinks, Mary-Lou became restless. "Let's move on!" she exclaimed over her third drink. "Pete told me about another place! Let's go there!"

"We can't, you nut!" Pete objected. "It's a common roadhouse!"

"So? I've never been to one! Or to a striptease place! Let's go to both!" Mary-Lou cried gaily.

"No striptease," Lance said sternly.

"No," agreed Pete. "The Band Wagon'd be bad enough, but I'm against it. We can find a livelier place than this. We don't have to go to the hangout of The Black Jackets."

"What're they?" Mary-Lou asked, excitedly.

"A motorcycle club," Pete said. "From California."

"Yes," Fawn put in. "I heard about them at the service station. It's a small gang, the fellow said, and traveling without women. They're suspected of a jewel robbery last week, but nobody's been able to pin it on them."

"Oh, let's go there!" Mary-Lou begged charmingly. "Rae-Ellen, Adah, you're game, aren't you? I just want to go and see . . . we don't have to stay! Then we can go on, maybe to a disco! Please . . . oh, pretty please!"

Eventually, they drove to The Band Wagon. It was a redwood structure, built in the shape of a western wagon. It was garishly lit and music blared over the sea of cars parked around it.

Inside, one end was filled by the clanging band, the sliver of dance floor was full of wild, uninhibited dancers, and all the booths and most of the tables were jammed.

Mary-Lou, ecstatic, put her lips against Rae-Ellen's ear and shrieked. "You have to scream, or nobody'll hear you!"

Burr and Lance looked grim. Fawn appeared to be as taken aback as Rae-Ellen. Adah was openly appalled. But Mary-Lou and Pete pressed on, and they all managed to crowd around a small, empty table. One of the overhead fixtures, a wagon wheel set with naked bulbs, hurled its glare over them.

Rae-Ellen saw The Black Jackets first. There were six of them and, in spite of the warm night, they wore long-sleeved black silk shirts, wide black ties, black breeches and boots. Their leather jackets were draped over the backs of their chairs, and black helmets and black-rimmed goggles showed from under the jackets.

They were drinking beer. They were in their twenties, hard-faced, and had a wild and vicious air. They were yelling back and forth at one another, loud and uncouth.

Rae-Ellen stared at them, mesmerized. The others in her party hadn't seen the hoodlums, and she wasn't about to point them out.

The loudest one, who acted as leader, caught Rae-Ellen staring. He grinned, an up-at-the-corner, knowing grin which showed fanglike teeth. He winked, swung his small eyes at his companions, shouted.

They all stared at Rae-Ellen, who couldn't pull her eyes free, couldn't breathe.

Three of them, led by fang-tooth, kicked back their chairs and came toward Rae-Ellen's table. "Watch out!" she warned, eyes still on The Black Jackets, but her words were lost in the din.

It wasn't until the three stood over the table that the others knew they were in the roadhouse. All the men in Rae-Ellen's party stood, Burr, too, on his sore foot.

"We're The Black Jackets!" roared the leader. "I'm Hammer Wilson! This—" He socked the shoulder of one of his gang "—is Dock Winkler, and this one's Pos Kalick. We left our ladies in California, and need us some ladies to dance with! You can introduce 'em or not, just so we dance!"

Burr and Lance started to protest.

Mary-Lou, excited, pushed them aside. She whirled to Pos, went into his arms, and they began to dance. She laughed and flirted, and he grabbed her against himself, grinning wickedly down into her face.

Adah, with a reassuring motion to Lance, went into Dock's arms. Even with him, a hoodlum, she danced as a lady and, though he held her too close, he didn't jam her against himself.

"What's keepin' you, Baby?" Hammer shouted at Rae-Ellen.

"Thank you," she screamed, "but I don't care to dance!"

"I'm leader of The Black Jackets!"

"That's good, that's fine, now bug off!"

"No femme tells Hammer to bug off!" He laid hold of her arm, yanked her up.

She saw all four of the men at her table go tense, fists ready.

"You bug off, too!" she shrieked. "I can handle myself!"

She jerked free of Hammer, and he let her. He turned on his heel. His roar thundered above all else. "Yo! Brothers! Trouble!"

In a flash, Rae-Ellen and the men of her party were surrounded by the six Black Jackets. Mary-Lou and Adah, abandoned on the dance floor, drew in at the edge.

"Got a lady that dancin's too tame for!" bellowed Hammer. "Any ideas?"

"Ride on the handlebars!" howled Pos. "First they ride with half of us, then they ride with t'other half! Then they'll dance!"

"Different dance!" Hammer chortled.

"We'll do no such thing!" screamed Rae-Ellen. "Take your hands off me!"

Hammer had her by both arms. She kicked for his crotch, missed. Then their whole section of the room erupted.

Simultaneously Burr and Lance threw themselves on the hoodlums. Fawn was only a breath behind, with Pete following. Rae-Ellen swung with her fists, she kicked. She bit. Somebody, one of The Black Jackets, or one of her own party, gave her nearly healed eye a blow. Even Adah was in the fray, getting in any blow she could, and Mary-Lou was wielding a candlestick on heads.

Burr, sore foot and all, got Hammer down on the floor among the legs of chairs and tables and pummeled him. The rest continued to fight, throwing punches, swinging chairs, hitting more than one innocent party.

Every woman in the place was screaming. Burr was rolling on the floor, Hammer on top of him. Rae-Ellen threw herself bodily onto Hammer, her fingers in his hair and pulled until he was forced to let go of Burr.

It was while Burr was diving for Hammer again that the proprietor and his bouncer clawed through to the fracas.

"I've got a rod!" the burly proprietor blared. His words carried over all the noise. Silence took the heretofore raucous place.

The Black Jackets stood in a bunch.

"Put it away," Hammer said. "We don't want that kind of trouble. No hard feelin's . . . just high spirits. Be back tomorrow night."

"Folks," the proprietor said, gesturing to the guests, some of whom were exhilarated, some frightened, "let's get on with the fun!"

The Black Jackets were collecting their gear.

Lance and Burr, who was limping, herded the girls toward the door. Rae-Ellen glanced back and was surprised to see Fawn speaking to the proprietor, then to Hammer for a moment. All were serious; none seemed angry.

"What was that about?" Burr asked when Fawn joined them.

"I just made certain the proprietor won't report this, and that those hoodlums won't make more trouble," Fawn said. "We don't want bad publicity for Pettigrew's, no matter how far from home we are. But it's all set. Over and done with."

33

In the confusion of leaving, Rae-Ellen found herself paired off with Burr. She didn't know whether it was accidental or if he wanted, somehow, to blame her for what had happened.

The others were piling into cars and roaring off. Burr shoved her into a car, which happened to be Papa's, borrowed for the evening. She had a set of keys for it.

She scooted across the seat and was behind the wheel by the time he'd hobbled around to the driver's side. "What the hell are you up to now?" he growled.

"I'm going to drive. You can't with your foot."

"My foot be damned. Move over!"

"Use your head, Travis. I'm not riding with you

at the wheel and that foot on the clutch! I'm right, you're wrong and you know it!"

He hesitated. Then, without so much as a hell or a damn, he hobbled back and got into the front seat with her. "Head straight home," he ordered.

That was what she'd meant to do, but now, because he'd ordered her, she changed her mind.

"I don't feel like going home!" she retorted, and set the car moving. "I feel like riding, letting the wind blow through to clear my head!"

"You've no business driving fuzzy-headed. Stop the car."

She pressed on the gas, shot toward the highway.

Lance and Adah were just ahead; in front of them was Fawn's car. Somehow Mary-Lou and Pete had got into it instead of this one. The keys must have been left in it. Both cars turned south. Rae-Ellen turned north and sped up.

Burr didn't miss a thing.

"They're going home!" he said angrily. "Even Mary-Lou's got sense enough for that!"

"Maybe they're bruised," she retorted. "Maybe they need first aid."

"I suppose you came out of that without a mark!"

"Somebody got me in the eye, the same eye you blacked. I hope you're satisfied!"

"Then go home and treat it. Else you'll have a real shiner."

"It's my eye!" she cried, both mollified and angry that he was concerned about her. Tears started, and she firmed her jaw. "I'll do as I please!"

"Sure. Same way you started the fight."

She gasped. True, the thought had crossed her mind that he was contrary enough to blame her for the fight, but now he actually was. Anger burned the tears away, adding a touch of rage to her voice.

"Exactly how do you figure that, Travis?"

"Your tarnation stubbornness. You wouldn't dance."

"What kind of man are you? To let the women in your party be—"

"Look. There are times you use brain, not muscle. Mary-Lou and Adah had the right idea. One dance, and we'd have left, friendly like. Instead, we're lucky the whole lot of us ain't at the police station."

"You'd just sit there and let us dance with those—"

"You were all quick enough to go there. We shouldn't have taken you, granted. But when you pick low company, you lay yourself open to what happens."

"I didn't start it! That Hammer—"

"Sure. He made advances. But you put yourself where he could make them."

She stomped on the gas pedal. The speedometer went to sixty.

"Slow down," he said. "We're in no condition to be hauled in for speeding, not the way we look."

"It's dark. You don't know how we look."

"I got an eyeful of you back yonder. I don't reckon my appearance is any better."

Rae-Ellen drove for miles in silence. Every time she decided to turn for home, he ordered her to do it, and then she went in the opposite direction. They fought some more about The Band Wagon, accused each other until they couldn't think of a new thing. Then they rode in silence.

She drove all through Hollywood, along the

beach road, drove to Dania, and all the way to Fort Lauderdale and back. Finally, because her eye was throbbing and her head felt like it was ready to fall off, she pointed the car home.

The Texas character didn't say a word. He just sat there with his foot out in front of him and let her do all the work.

It was three A.M. and the house was dark when they got home. Exhausted, she switched off the motor, then rested her head against the wheel.

But Burr Travis could move. Trust him! He popped open the door on his side, hobbled around and yanked her door open. He put his big hands under her arms, dragged her out, and stood her on the ground.

Her knees buckled, and he caught her. He got behind her, one iron-strong hand gripping each upper arm, and propelled her to the house, unlocked the front door, then half-lifted, half-carried her up the stairs and into her room, flipping on the light.

He sat her on the bed, where she remained, drooping. She was so tired and sore and beaten it was hard to breathe. She was so angry, and suddenly burning with that awful Burr-flame, she bit her tongue to keep from demanding that he do something about it. Anyway, it would destroy her. She was too exhausted.

She became aware that he was bruised, had a knot on his jaw, and his hair was on end. He looked as if he might be getting a black eye himself. She wondered if his foot had been hurt again.

She was about to demand that he take off his sneaker and let her see, when she realized that those brown eyes were all over her, that they looked sweet-hot enough to melt stone.

"Your eye *is* turning black!" he exclaimed quietly. He reached out for one arm, then the other, examined them. "And you're bruised! I didn't do this bringing you into the house. Those bastards gave you a working over!"

"My w-whole body is sore," she heard herself quaver.

That was all it took. Cat-footing, he hauled her into the bathroom, sat her on the closed commode. Then he cracked open the far door to make sure that the doors between the bathrooms and the far bedroom were shut.

After that, he turned on the water in the tub full force. Rae-Ellen sat where he'd put her, listening to the water splash, too sore to protest. She didn't care what he meant to do. She was in his hands. He couldn't do worse to her than he'd done already.

She was surprised by how gently he peeled off all of her clothes. He whispered a curse when he saw a bruise on her hip, and one on her belly. He examined her eye, said maybe it wouldn't turn any worse.

While the mammoth tub filled, he stripped off his own clothes. He didn't have the sign of a bandage on his foot, the crazy fool. It looked red and angry, but there was no blister.

When the tub was full and steaming, he turned the water off, scooped her up and lowered her gently into the tub. The warm water felt like heaven; the instant it covered her, she felt a gentle, seeping comfort and sighed.

Rae-Ellen wasn't really surprised when Burr got into the tub with her. She heard him draw in his breath when his foot sank into the water, but not again.

"The water," she whispered, speaking for the first time. "Doesn't it hurt your foot?"

"Some," he whispered back. "No matter. Heat draws out heat. It'll be better for a good soak."

"And you'll put a bandage on it afterward?"

"Reckon I'll have to. I aim to rub on some ointment."

He was so big in the tub with her. Large though it was, they were a tight fit. He put his arm around her, and that was better. Then he drew her throbbing head down to his wet shoulder and that was better yet.

Cradled thus, her eyes roamed through the clear water, to see his strong legs stretched out there. She stole a look further up his legs to see he was half ready for her. But with his burned foot, and all those bruises, he'd not be in any mood to take her to bed. Nor was she in the mood, not really, so aching and miserable.

She sighed, moved in the water, moved in his arms, stifled a moan. He held her, lightly, careful not to press, let the water buoy her up. How could she be so bone-sore, yet faintly burning for him?

He let some water gurgle out, closed the stopper, ran in more hot water. They soaked, not speaking, except to whisper of an ache, a bruise, his foot, her eye. They stayed in the tub a long while, an hour, maybe more.

He helped her out, stood her on the fluffy rug and dried her with several velvety-clipped towels. By the time he'd finished them both, the floor was covered with damp towels. "I'll hang them up later," he whispered.

He eased her, naked, onto her clean sheets.

"Be right back," he whispered.

She sensed him go, return. He had a white jar. Bidding her to lie still, though she hadn't moved since he left, he smoothed ointment on her bruised hip and belly, using fingertips only, no pressure. A blessed, soothing coolness came to her as he continued his slow, gentle treatment.

This is the way he put the ointment on Rusty that time, she thought. No wonder the horses liked him, trusted him, when he used this touch, this gentleness.

He smoothed ointment at the edge of her eye, warning her to keep her hands away from it. "Best stuff I've ever used," he said. "It's as good as what I put on the horses."

Then, she, learning that this was the ointment for his foot, insisted on treating it herself, and he let her. She was very careful to exert no pressure whatsoever. He refused, after all, to have a bandage.

"The air'll do it good," he said. "When I put on my socks and sneakers, I'll use some gauze."

When his foot was finished and she'd put ointment on his various abrasions, he told her to stretch out naked on the bed. "No nightgown on those places," he said. "Ointment and air and rest."

She lay on her back, the soreness quieted. He went into the bathroom, came back with an ice cold cloth, which he put on her eye. "Ice pack would be better," he said, "but we can make out with the ice water faucet."

She insisted that he get a cloth for his own eye, and he did. He sat beside her bed in a chair, naked. Then he got up, put on a couple of soft lights, turned out the overhead fixture, sat down again.

It began to feel very homelike, the two of them,

naked, spread with ointment, holding ice packs to their eyes. He closed his other eye, and she closed hers. Now and then she felt him take away her cloth, put an icy one in its place.

Once he said he was going to stay until dawn.

Sometime that faint burning in her ceased.

She even slept, knowing he was there.

34

Of course the senior Pettigrews had to be told the whole story. Not one of the young people at the breakfast table had escaped the mélée unscathed.

Burr's eye was black; Rae-Ellen's eye was worse than it had been. Lance had a split lip. Fawn had a big bruise on his cheek. Pete had a swollen jaw. Mary-Lou displayed scratches down one side of her neck, and even Adah had a puffed lip.

Papa and Mama regarded the various faces, inquired whether anyone needed to see a doctor, were assured that such was not the case, and listened to Lance, nominated by the others, give an account of what had happened.

"Blame me!" Mary-Lou cried when he'd finished. "I was the one who insisted we go to that place! And I was the first one to dance with them! I was so silly! Please," she appealed, "don't blame anybody but me!"

"Nonsense," said Mama. "You were all in it."

Fawn spoke seriously to Papa. "I mended our fences, sir. I had a word with the proprietor, and also spoke to the leader of the gang. They don't want to mix with the police, either."

"Then that should be an end to it," Papa said.

"From now on," Lance said, "we vote where we go for an evening."

"Do that," Papa said sternly. "What happened last night was unnecessary, and there's to be no more."

Soon they were all smiling and chatting. There was, however, an air of sobriety beneath it.

Burr and Lance got ready to leave for the stable.

"In a couple of days," Burr said, "if any of you want to come watch, it'll be okay. The horses will be ready for an audience. They'll need one to prepare for the crowds when they race."

Everyone drifted away from the table. The three girls, Fawn and Pete, spent the morning at the pool. The water felt good to their various abrasions. They began to tease one another about how terrible they looked and decided they'd stay on the grounds until they were presentable.

That evening they discussed jockeys, decided which to hire to ride Thunder Boy and Samson's Lad. Then, as on the evenings to follow, they danced in the living room. Burr was in charge of the stereo, so he could stay off his foot.

"You use it too much during the day," Papa warned. "Give it a rest at night."

"I'm not one to dance anyhow, sir," Burr said.

Rae-Ellen heard this and was irritated. He was a

good dancer, one of the best. If he hadn't done a lot of dancing, how had he learned?

She danced with Fawn a great deal, some with Pete, some with Lance, none with Papa. They had kept a silent truce since their fight back in Durham, speaking only of inconsequential things.

Adah danced with all the men, even Papa, but mostly with Lance. Mary-Lou danced equally with every man, gaily demanding that they partner her.

Rae-Ellen saw that when she herself danced with Fawn, Papa looked pleased. She began to watch him. He showed less pleasure when Adah danced with Pete, and looked downright sickening when Adah danced with Burr the one time he took to the floor.

This riled her so much that a few numbers later, when he'd had time to rest his foot, she marched over to him at the stereo. "Give me this dance," she said.

He looked at her in surprise. "Why?"

"It won't kill you. You danced with Adah."

"She said I looked lonesome. I said I was. So I asked her for one dance."

"Maybe you look lonesome to me, too."

"I doubt it."

He didn't, either. He looked mean. Last night was gone, as if it had never been.

He put a new stack of records on the player. Then he turned to her and held out his arms. She went into them stiffly, barely touching his sleeve, holding herself away from him.

"I ain't going in for any fancy steps," he warned.

"That's the last thing I expect!" she retorted.

He glided into an easy, flowing step and she matched it, no longer stiff, but pliant and eager.

Their movements fitted exactly; they were in perfect time to the music, to each other.

She glimpsed Papa's face as he danced by with Mama. He looked like a cat who'd got into the cream. What was it with him, anyway? A while ago, he'd looked pleased when Adah danced with Burr, and now he seemed about ready to melt into sheer pleasure.

Was it—could it—be possible that he'd want this Texan for a son-in-law? Her eye began to hurt, her head to throb. It couldn't be. Burr cared for nothing but horses; Papa wanted only sons-in-law who were tobacco fiends.

She yanked her mind back to dancing. There seemed to be something wrong. Burr wasn't gliding the way he'd done at first; or maybe she'd only imagined it then. How could he glide, wearing sneakers?

She kept following him, senses alert. There really was the slightest drag to his step.

"Your foot," she accused. "It hurts."

"So?"

"We go into the garden, we sit down."

"Whatever you say," he replied, and they headed for the door.

He didn't exactly limp, but there was a lag to his step. After he'd sat up with her all night, no matter how mean he'd turned now, she'd put him in pain. She didn't know which of them she was maddest at, Burr or herself.

They went almost as far as the pool, which was brightly lighted in case any of them wanted a night swim. They sat on a bench back from the pool, mostly in shadow.

"You have no business traipsing around on that

foot!" she exploded. "No business dancing with Adah!"

"I enjoyed dancing with Adah." His tone was even.

"And not with me, I suppose?"

"I didn't say that. You did."

"You put words into my mouth!"

Suddenly he seized her, kissed her violently, grinding his lips against hers. She even felt his teeth on her teeth as she fiercely kissed him back.

Before she knew it, he had her breast free of her blouse and was making a trail of kisses around it. She jerked away, that deep burning back, and knowing he'd take her right there in the garden if she didn't stop him.

She thrust her breast out of sight, blurting the first thing she could think of. "Leave me alone! You're not the only man in the world! You're not even the only one I ever . . . There have been others!"

He drew back. His face, in the shadowy light, was dumbfounded. Then he found his voice. "Maybe I'm not the only one," he said hoarsely, "but I was sure-hell the first!"

"There've been others . . . three of them!"

His dumbfoundment turned to rage. "You ain't lying!"

She shook her head, almost sorry she'd told him.

"You've got nothing on me," he said angrily. "You ain't the only woman!"

"I know that! You told me about them! That's the kind of h-heel you are! You've had dozens of women! Haven't you . . . *haven't* you?"

He didn't answer.

379.

"I don't give a happy damn!" she said, burning in spite of his wickedness. "Since that first time, I'm not bound by rules! I'm free, understand? I do what I please with whom I please!"

He stood up, yanked her to her feet. "Then we'd best," he said coldly, "go back inside. To your field of operation." He began to walk toward the house, hand clamped around her wrist, pulling her along.

She felt like a small girl being dragged away to be punished. She'd thought, when he got so mad, when he began to manhandle her again, that he wanted her sexually. Now all he wanted was to be rid of her.

She had to run to keep him from jerking her off her feet. And with every step she was madder and felt more deprived and cheated.

During a lull in the dancing, when everybody sat down to sip the lemonade Marie brought in, Papa and Burr paired off. There was a third chair and Rae-Ellen sat down in it, determined to hear what they talked about, since Papa had such a ridiculously fine opinion of Burr. Also, she was going to show that high-handed Texan she wasn't bested, that she could be where he was if she chose.

"You were saying, earlier," Papa began, "that you studied the history of horse racing while you were in college."

"Yes. On the side, so to speak. I was hooked on racers before I went to the university. I took advantage of their libraries . . . they've got seven or more big ones . . . to learn about horses. I didn't know the first thing about their origin."

"That's my condition now," laughed Papa. "I don't even know when racing started!"

"About the time horses were tamed, sir. I found

380

that early races were generally matches between two horses."

"I don't suppose they had jockeys."

"The owners rode them, mostly."

"What countries did this take place in?"

"Wherever there were horses. The English did a lot of racing. The result is that we know of three famous sires from olden days—Darley Arabian, Byerly Turk, and Godolphin Barb. Then there was one named Herod. It is stated that every thoroughbred racer in the world today can actually be traced to three horses—Matchem, Herod, or Eclipse."

"Including ours," murmured Papa.

"Right, sir. Then, back in the eleven hundreds, Englishmen found that those Arabian and Moroccan horses could run extra fast. So rich men began to import them into England."

"Which led to race tracks."

"Yes. The first one was built about 1170."

"Remarkable."

"Then steeplechasing was started by racing hunting horses across-country. The riders used easy markers, like church steeples, for guides."

"I do know," Papa said, proudly it seemed to Rae-Ellen, who seethed that he'd lower himself to the extent of being proud to hold up his end of the conversation with Travis, "that thoroughbred horse racing became popular in this country after the Civil War. My own father said that by the turn of the century it had developed into the exciting sport it now is."

Suddenly Rae-Ellen realized that she'd been listening avidly as well as resentfully to Travis' knowledge of racing. She wondered how she could feel proud of him, but angry at the same time.

"With your knowledge, the experience you've had, and what you're getting now," Papa said, "you'll want to leave us for better things."

"What better things, sir?"

"Your own stables, would be my guess."

"That costs more than I earn. It'll take time."

"And you'd not look for . . . er . . . a rich wife?"

Burr laughed, honestly laughed! He didn't even glance at Rae-Ellen, but she knew that he was aware of her. That he'd refused her and she hadn't even been offered. All her pride in his knowledge of horses fled; she sat woodenly on, listening to them go into a serious discussion of the breeding and fattening of cattle. She felt empty, discarded, forlorn. All her bruises ached.

As he talked with his employer, Burr was thinking about Rae-Ellen. He was aware of her beauty, her spirit, her temper, her fleeting sweetness, her scalding passion. There'd never been one like her before; there'd not be another like her again.

"Beefalo," he said to Raymond Pettigrew from the top of his mind, reviewing and considering all the things about Rae-Ellen, "that's a new crossbreed my Pa's trying on the home ranch. Half beef cattle, half buffalo. Makes good eating, and is hardier than pure beef cattle, easier and cheaper to raise."

"Sounds good," said the older man.

"It is good," agreed Burr. It was in that moment he determined to have Rae-Ellen, but on his own terms. No matter how mean she got, no matter what she did or didn't do, she was his. And he'd let her know when he got damned good and ready.

In deep night, with the Florida breeze cooling her nude body, Rae-Ellen slept profoundly. She began to dream.

In the dream, Burr slipped into her room, into her bed. He entered her hungry, waiting body and was making love to her in such a silent, sweetly fierce manner she thought she could not bear it. And then she knew it was no dream. She was awake, and it was happening, and her body, her treacherous, greedy body, responded to his, matching the sweetness, trying to exceed the fierceness.

She was wet with perspiration when, without having spoken a word, he long-legged across the room and out of her door, closing it noiselessly. She reached out to where he had been, just there, right beside her, longing for the feel of him.

And then, content and fed by him, she snuggled into that deserted spot and into sleep again.

35

At workout, Burr came right to where Rae-Ellen stood alone at the rail. He'd left Papa and the others about halfway around the track.

"You knew who I was last night?" he asked bluntly.

Her pulse thudded. "N-naturally."

"Didn't get me mixed up with your other three?"

He asked this so gently that, though she knew she should be angry, she found herself, instead, anxious that he believe her. "Of course not," she said.

"How come?"

"I—I'd know you anywhere," she heard herself reply and, stunned at the knowledge, was further astonished at the truth of it.

"Even in the—well, say the jungle?"

"Even there. I'd know."

"And from among those other three?"

"That, too," she admitted, and now she was getting angry. Who did he think he was, grilling her?

"Now simmer down. I'm getting to the point."

"Don't take all day!"

"Point is, if I had money, scads of money, and if I had family and could match you—"

"How could you, ever, match me?"

"In bed, for one place."

"Pah!"

"Back up, here. Say I could match you, dollar for dollar, blood-kin for blood-kin, would you marry me? If I asked you, that is."

"I—" She faltered, mind and tongue gone numb. Finally came her own voice saying a thing which could not be true, which she could not believe. "M-maybe."

She realized instantly that she'd forgotten Lance. How could she forget him? Her entire being went numb.

"How about love in this marriage if-and-if? Where the hell is love?"

"Nowhere!" she hissed, crushed that she'd forgotten Lance regardless of how upset this horse trainer had got her.

He began to talk, and despite her state, she heard what he said.

"You," he began, "don't know what love is."

I know, she yearned to retort, I've loved Lance forever! Gentleness and strength and constancy, that's what love is! Lance is what love is!

"I'm going to tell you what the love you're always yammering about is," Burr pronounced, "and you can set yourself down and think it over. It's putting your man first in all things; it's showing him respect. It's being decent to him no matter how he acts, accepting his faults because they are his. It's blending yourself into him so deep you think you're as much him as you are yourself!"

"I never heard of such a high-handed—!"

"Trouble with you is you've set yourself up on some kind of pedestal because you're a Pettigrew. Because you went to Sweet Briar College, because you fox-hunt and go to balls and jet over the world whenever the notion hits you!"

"You . . . *beast!*"

"Know what you're doing, on that pedestal, with your liberation and your three men? You're looking for whatever the hell you think is the perfect man, and he don't exist."

"He does exist!"

"He don't. Nobody's perfect, not even you!"

Furious, she raised her voice. "How dare you? All this sudden talk about love! What's bothering you? Are you in love with me, is that it . . . in love, and jealous of the other men?"

"The state of my affections ain't the topic," he said high-handedly.

So. He wouldn't answer a simple question. And she knew exactly why.

"You're in love with Adah, that's what's wrong with you!"

"If I'm in love with her, why am I with you?"

"To torment me! To keep me so mixed up I don't know what I'm doing!"

"Because I'm in love with Adah."

"Yes!"

"I'm in love with a girl and spend my time in bed with her sister! How do you explain that?"

"You're a sex-fiend! A barbarian! Ever since you

386

came here, you've done nothing but make my life miserable! In fact, you've ruined my life!"

And he had. If it hadn't been for him, keeping her in a state, she might have won Lance in that wilderness room. If her subconscious mind hadn't been divided and torn.

"Tell me how I've ruined your life."

"You started by raping me!"

"Are you going to harp on that again?"

"Who has a better right?"

"It wasn't a one hundred percent rape."

"You harp on that, too!"

"Facts are facts."

"And I was a vir—"

"I apologize. Again."

"You can't apologize that away!"

"No, I can't."

"Well!" she gasped. "Look who's wrong for once!"

"Not at all."

"But you kept it up! You made me . . ."

"I made you do what?"

"Want . . . bed!" she spat.

There was frank surprise all over him. "Then why have you been so tarnation mean?"

"Because it's wrong, all wrong!"

"You never fought me off. Like you could have."

"I had my reasons."

She'd never admit that he was a plague in her. Never! Not even if she died right here on the spot!

"And that put you to bed with three other men?"

"No! Yes . . . in a way!"

His hateful eyes narrowed. He got a sullen look. He nodded, as if he knew facts she didn't know.

"Now I've got a thing to say," he told her. "I

387

came to your place in Durham, came to Florida, to be a horse trainer. To build myself into a horse breeder, have my own farm. Just that. Nothin' else. Minute you laid eyes on me, you acted like you hated the ground I walk on."

"I did, I do!"

"So. You baited me into raping you."

"That's a lie!"

"You baited with actions, words. I thought it was just sex you wanted. Which I could supply."

"Over and over!" she whispered.

"Until you got yourself under my skin like a cattle tick. Which you know. My aim is to get you out. I ain't going to have no female, Pettigrew or no other, mess up the life I've laid out for myself."

"Horses come first!"

"They always have. I ain't found the woman yet, not that I'm looking, that'd meet all the tests to put herself ahead of any horse."

"You did it again! Compared me to a horse!"

"I don't recall that I mentioned you. I was speaking in general terms. Laying it on the line. If you think I've ruined your life, you've done your full share messin' mine up. Only I ain't going to stand still for it."

"And how do you propose to straighten out the mess I'm supposed to have made?"

"I've got my plan."

"What is it?"

"That's my affair."

"Mine, too. It involves me."

"Them other three men didn't involve me."

She felt her heart wince, actually wince. She'd been so certain that any plan of his would involve her. But he was playing this to his own rules. Maybe he'd use other girls the way she'd used other men.

She stuck her jaw out, turned on her heel and ran to her car. She couldn't bear to be in his presence another moment.

How could he be so harsh, so set on some secret, cruel course after last night? After the sweetness and the tenderness?

36

The day grew hot and humid. Papa said, as they sat in the living room waiting for dinner, that it was too hot for November.

"It feels like hurricane weather," he added, wiping his face with his handkerchief. "We almost need the air conditioning."

"A hurricane in November?" squealed Mary-Lou. "Ooh, I'd like to see one! But isn't November too late?"

"They've extended the official season to December," Lance remarked. "It begins June first. I've never heard of one in November, but anything's possible."

"Yes," Fawn agreed. "Something about hot and cold air currents."

Papa suddenly snapped his fingers. "That's it!" he exclaimed. "That's what put the word hurricane into my mouth!"

They all turned to him questioningly.

"The news last night at bedtime," he explained. "After you'd gone to sleep, Marguerite. The weatherman said something about a slight tropical depression a thousand miles south, southeast of Miami. Said it's too late—"

He broke off, switched on television, glancing at his watch. "Five minutes to six! We're just in time!"

". . . the tropical depression," the weatherman was saying, "has built into a tropical storm, winds being in excess of thirty-nine miles an hour. There is no occasion for alarm . . . I repeat, no occasion for alarm at this point. The tropical storm is a thousand miles from Miami, is standing over water . . ."

"Oh, shoot!" Mary-Lou wailed.

". . . keep tuned to our advisories," the weatherman said, finishing his report. "Our planes will fly through the storm, and we will keep you advised of any change. Current local temperatures are . . ."

Papa snapped off the set as Andrews appeared in the doorway to announce dinner. They moved into the dining room, chattering about the possibility of the storm growing to hurricane size.

At the table, Mary-Lou couldn't let go of the subject. She was excited again, and convinced there would be a hurricane. November or not.

"They name them, don't they?" she asked.

"Alphabetically, alternating between men's and women's names," Papa told her.

"What would be the name of this one?"

"My dear, that I don't know. I'm not certain

which letter of the alphabet would be used, even. There have been several hurricanes this year. I believe the last one may have been in July or August and was called Donald . . . something like that."

"Then this one would begin with an E and be a girl's name!"

Rae-Ellen didn't care whether a hurricane came or not. Maybe it would do Travis some good, she thought, blow some of the meanness out of him. Then she remembered the horses and hoped there would be no storm. After the wreck on the trip down and the time it had taken to get the horses calm, the last thing they needed was a wind that blew a hundred miles an hour, maybe even ripped the stable from over their heads.

Adah and Lance went for a drive after dinner.

Lance had entered Samson's Lad in the fourth race at Gulfstream Park the next Saturday. Rae-Ellen and Adah had entered Thunder Boy in the sixth race the same day. Today was Monday, and beginning tomorrow, Lance and Burr would use the Gulfstream oval for workouts.

Rae-Ellen meant to keep close watch on Burr, though at a distance, to find out what his plan about her was. About their situation, which, like the insensitive male he was, he considered his alone.

If he had other women in mind, he was hampered at every turn, and this gave her much satisfaction. To begin with, he was a stranger and knew no women in Florida. On top of that, he had to work hard, and on a sore foot, to get Thunder Boy ready for the race.

If he thought he could find a spare hour to entice Adah, Lance was present both at the stable and in the house. Aside from blatantly cornering Adah and extorting a date, which he could never do because she was secretly engaged to Lance, he had only Mary-Lou to whom to turn.

And Mary-Lou considered Burr Rae-Ellen's property. She knew nothing of Rae-Ellen's encounters with Fawn and Pete. She was with Pete a lot, and Pete let her flirt, but had no dates with her. This meant that his seduction of Adah had, for him, turned into as near the real thing as he could manage emotionally. She felt a little sorry for Pete. And felt, too, a tinge of sympathy for Fawn, who was still courting herself in a most gentlemanly manner.

On Tuesday evening, when they heard the weather report, storm conditions had worsened.

"Tropical storm Esmerelda, which originated as a tropical depression two days ago," the weather-caster said, "has increased in size and intensity, bearing winds of fifty miles an hour with gusts to sixty. It is moving at twelve miles per hour in a north, northwest direction. Esmerelda is being closely watched and presents no immediate threat to the Florida coast, being seven hundred miles away. All interests, however, are advised to be on the alert and to make storm preparations. Tune in for further advisories on this very late, fierce little storm. Local temperatures . . ."

"What do we do, sir?" Mary-Lou asked as Papa switched off the set. "To be on the alert? Does that mean that Esmerelda is going to hit the Miami-Davie area?"

"Not at all. It may veer, go north and blow itself out over the Atlantic. We're being alerted to check our storm shutters and have storage ready for lawn and pool furniture, things like that. Garages for cars. And boat owners need to find protected harbors. Just to be ready, avoid being caught."

"But it can build into a hurricane, can't it?" Mary-Lou pressed.

"It's possible," Lance said, "but not probable, the season being so late. They have a lot more warnings here than they ever have full-blown hurricanes."

"We've already checked the stable, sir," Burr said. "All that's needed is to close the shutters and hang a couple of lanterns in case the electricity goes off. Let the horses see their quarters are normal. And stay out there with them, of course."

Wednesday, tropical storm Esmerelda stood still over the water, whirled like a dervish, whipping its skirts of wind, wrapping them around herself, flinging them back the other way. It worked into such a frenzy that the winds built to eighty miles an hour, and she gained the status of a full hurricane.

But she was still four hundred miles from land, her chances to turn, to go east or north or east, northeast, were as great as to proceed toward Florica, so life went on as usual. The humidity was high; all suffered from the heat. All were constantly aware of the nearness of Hurricane Esmerelda, of her unpredictability, but none were frightened. No one in the area left to escape her possible onslaught.

Thursday, Esmerelda moved ten creeping miles toward Florida, her winds increasing to eighty-five miles per hour. Friday, she upped her travel speed to twelve miles per hour, spread herself wider, built her winds to ninety-five miles with gusts to one hundred twenty, held a straight course for Miami.

Mary-Lou was beside herself.

"What does a hurricane look like?" she demanded. "Why don't they tell?"

Mama laughed softly. "They do tell; we just didn't hear the right broadcast, dear. And I suppose they think everybody—they're so used to hurricanes here—knows."

"I need to be explained to, ma'am!"

"Very well," Mama smiled. "The hurricane is like a giant doughnut—the announcer said she's a hundred miles across now. She's whirling and coming forward at the same time. She has winds blowing one direction in her front half, and the opposite direction in her rear half. She's dead calm in the center, not even rain at times. They call that the eye. That's when it's really dangerous to those who are careless. Because the period during which the eye is passing over is so calm, people think the storm has ended and go out in it, and then the back half hits and—"

"Wham!" cried Mary-Lou. "Bang!"

"Big hurricanes, sometimes no bigger than Esmerelda, carry tornadoes," Mama continued.

"The announcer just said Esmerelda's got some little ones! She must be the biggest ever!"

"They can be a hundred fifty miles across," Papa said. "What I'm concerned about now is the races tomorrow. On top of that, we've had those few showers. They're from Esmerelda."

"Burr and Lance should be home from Gulfstream soon," Adah said. "We'll know then whether the track will run or batten down."

"They'll run if it's safe," Papa opined. "Thousands of people are set to go. Not many will stay home if the track opens, even if it does rain. And the track officials don't want to lose tens of thousands of dollars."

They were in the living room and had kept the television on, with the sound off, and now the weatherman's image appeared on the screen and Papa turned the sound up. Esmerelda was again standing still over water, building her winds, broadening herself. When she began to move again, viewers were advised, the chances were as great that she'd move north or northeast as they were she'd come toward Miami.

"Boating interests are warned to be on the alert," the announcer said. "All interests are urged to batten down if this big and now dangerous hurricane resumes her north, northwest course."

Burr and Lance walked in as the newscast ended.

"We talked to the officials," Lance told them. "Esmerelda is standing still, I guess you know that. She's two hundred miles away, and if she stays where she is or takes another direction, the track will run tomorrow. If she starts in this direction late enough and slowly enough, it will still run, because she'll not hit until the early Sunday morning hours. So it looks as if we'll race."

During Friday night, Esmerelda moved, ponderously veering north at the rate of five miles per hour, her winds now one hundred fifty miles an hour. Everybody in the Pettigrew household, except Mary-Lou, was relieved. She was slightly downcast and pretended to pout.

It showered a bit, stopped. The sun bore down. The earth steamed. It was extremely hot, the air heavy and humid.

Saturday noon, Esmerelda was standing still

two hundred miles from land, whirling her giant skirts, building strength, seeming to plot, within her windy brain, what next she could do to worry mankind.

37

The races were an elegant affair, so the women in the Pettigrew party donned their new outfits, chosen carefully for the occasion. Rae-Ellen and Adah wore their racing colors, gold and sky blue. Their calf-length skirts of sheer gold crepe were identical, as were the short-sleeved jackets and blouses. They wore broad-brimmed pale yellow hats and big dark glasses and carried elegant straw handbags.

Marguerite and Mary-Lou wore white and scarlet respectively, and Raymond, Fawn, and Pete were striking in custom slacks and blending coats. Raymond even wore a straw boater, though the other men were bareheaded, sporting dark glasses. Lance and Burr, who would be at the stables and paddock, were more simply clad as they entered a back gate to the stables.

Rae-Ellen gazed out over the acres of parked cars—blue, green, yellow—every color shimmering in the November sun. The air was hot, heavy, humid, threatening rain despite the sun.

It always surprised Rae-Ellen, the thousands of cars at Gulfstream, the unending throngs of people threading to the gates which would admit them to grandstand and clubhouse. She was so busy trying to avoid brushing against cars in her new outfit, that only occasionally did she notice the hot and sweating faces of the hundreds of other race fans.

"Ooh, isn't this fun!" squealed Mary-Lou. "Pete, I'm goin' to bet and bet! Trifectas, perfectas, everything!"

A thrill took Rae-Ellen, and she felt like squealing herself. Her very own horse was going to run today! Maybe he would win! She was going to bet on only two horses—Samson's Lad in the fourth race, and Thunder Boy in the seventh.

She wondered if all these hordes of people—they were now making their way through groups clustered between the clubhouse and the paddock—were as excited as she was. They had to be, she thought, or they'd never come out in such heat, with a hurricane, still unmoving, in the offing.

They arrived, at last, at the paddock. This was the section, flanked by the long line of stables, where the horses were brought to be saddled. Here the jockeys were weighed in, along with saddle and other gear, plus lead weights, if needed, to bring their weight up to that which each horse in a particular race was required to carry.

They milled about in the crowd. The owners were gathered to see their own entries; dedicated racing fans were trying to get a closer look at the horses. And scads of others were crowding the area, people who just loved horses, and also those who were curious to see how a race horse looked close up. There was a continuous babble of laughter and calling back and forth.

Owners greeted the Pettigrews. They chatted, congratulated the sisters on entering the racing fraternity, drifted on. Acquaintances came along, paused, chatted, strolled on.

The horses for the first race were led the long distance from stable to paddock, a lead-man at each halter, a rider mounted on a training horse, alongside. The racers were skittish, prancing sideways, and Rae-Ellen wondered if they had some way of sensing the nearness of Hurricane Esmerelda. Some racers were always jumpy at this point before a race, but some actually plodded, while others merely stepped high.

The jockeys were weighed in, the horses saddled, the jockeys boosted up. They lined out, filed down the spectator-jammed rails of the passageway to the track.

Rae-Ellen and the others went into the air-conditioned clubhouse. There, at Mama's suggestion, they found seats and ordered lemonade. They watched the first race from there, the Pettigrew ladies and Fawn making no bets, Raymond betting two dollars to win. Mary-Lou and Pete watched from the Pettigrew box, bet on every race, and lost. Mary-Lou was so excited, she couldn't sit still, and Pete claimed she wouldn't sit down even when he got her into the box.

They all returned to the paddock to see the horses saddled for the fourth race. Lance served as lead-man for Samson's Lad.

They watched this race from the box. There were nine horses in the race, all of them nervous. Some jigged and even reared as they reached the oval, but eventually all were in the starting gate.

The gates sprang open and the horses broke. Samson's Lad, carrying green and white and the number three, ridden by Chip Duval, one of the best jockeys, broke first. He took the lead and held it, but only for a short time.

A swift, sleek black horse, Devil, passed him, then a roan, then a bay. At the end of the race, Samson's Lad was fifth.

"Oh, Lance honey, I'm so sorry!" wailed Mary-Lou. "I bet ten dollars on him! Those other horses cheated, they just did!"

Lance smiled. "They outran him. He could do worse than fifth, his first race. He has the speed and the strength. Before this meet ends, he'll run in the money."

They returned, weaving through the hot, sweating fans, to the clubhouse. Lance went to the stable to be with Samson's Lad, to oversee his rubdown. To pet him too, Rae-Ellen thought. That's a lucky horse. Lance will treat him as well as if he'd won the race!

They went to the paddock to watch the horses come up for the seventh race. Thunder Boy, wearing gold and blue and the number seven, danced a jig, every step of the way. Burr led him, head close to the stallion, obviously murmuring to him.

Of all the nervous horses today, Thunder Boy was the worst. Rae-Ellen hated to think how wild he'd be with anyone but Burr. Give Travis credit; he could manage Thunder Boy.

Finally, all the two-year-olds to run the seventh, which was a stake race, were saddled, all ten jockeys up. Billy Jack, a new Seminole jockey who was sheer talent, was on Thunder Boy, and that talent was apparent. He was lying down on the stallion's neck, and it was plain that he was sweet-talking him, because Thunder Boy quieted some.

They got the horses into the starting gate. It opened, and the horses broke. Thunder Boy reared in his box and broke last, then laid his head on the wind and began to run.

He was boxed in by three horses who'd got the rail. Billy Jack touched, barely touched, him with the whip, and the high-strung silver stallion veered right, making for the outside. He was running eighth in the field, running more distance than any other horse, because he was on the outside.

The three lead horses now had it almost neck to neck.

Gradually, from eighth place, Thunder Boy edged up to seventh. He held. Then, pounding faster, he gained a half-length, another. Now he was sixth.

He found a hole and dashed through it and was fifth; his beautiful silver legs seeming never to move, to be in permanent flying position. He was a beautiful silver streak as he continued to gain, Billy Jack standing in the stirrups.

Spectators sprang to their feet, screamed, waved programs, leaned forward, jumped up and down. The horses streaked on.

Thunder Boy held his position. Inexorably, he pulled forward, past the fifth horse, and now he was fourth. He gained on the horse in third position, passed him, and streamed on, ever faster.

The crowd went wild. The finish line was just ahead. Thunder Boy and Roanoke ran neck to neck, and again Thunder Boy began that pull ahead. They crashed past the finish line, three horses—a black, a silver streak, a bay.

The photo finish read that Thunder Boy had come in second. Rae-Ellen and Adah and Mary-Lou were laughing and crying, all at the same time. Even Mama wiped tears out of her smile.

"I won forty dollars!" screamed Mary-Lou. "I bet across the board, so I get show and place! He won, that beauty won!" She hugged Rae-Ellen, Adah, Mama, all the men of their party who were present.

"Incidentally, girls," Papa said, "he's won you second money. He's started to pay his way."

"That darlin'!" cried Mary-Lou. "If he hadn't broken late he'd have won the big purse!"

"He will next time," Rae-Ellen said confidently. She was beaming.

By the time they got home and listened to the weather advisory, Esmerelda, now a mammoth and dangerous storm with tornadoes studding her wings, had started to move again, south, southeast, on a direct line for the Miami-Davie area. They all waited nervously for Burr and Lance to come in from the stable.

While they were discussing the advisory, Fawn asked Rae-Ellen to go with him into the Florida room, a windowed chamber through which spilled sun and air when the weather was normal.

Happy over Thunder Boy's victory, she went with Fawn. He'd been more likeable in the weeks past, and she didn't want to hurt his feelings by re-fusing him a word in private.

He asked her to sit with him on the white couch, and she did. He asked if he could hold her hand and, inwardly unwilling, she consented.

"You know why I want to speak to you," he said quietly.

She caught her breath, let it go, nodded.

"I'm in love with you. I regret one certain night more than you can ever know. I'm asking you, with all the seriousness in my nature, and I am a serious man, to be my wife."

Silence. It beat in her ears.

"You hesitate. Is it that you're not in love with me?"

She tried to evade. "I haven't spent much time thinking about love," she said. And then, under the fold of her skirt, she crossed her fingers.

"Will you marry me, Rae-Ellen?"

"I . . . I'm sorry, Fawn."

"Is it—another man?"

"N-no." She kept her fingers crossed. Actually, it wasn't a real lie, not now. She'd loved Lance for-ever, and then Travis had barged in, and between the two of them she didn't know whether she was capable of real love. She couldn't even decide which of them it was, Lance or Burr, who troubled her most.

Fawn was disappointed but not deterred. He told her so.

"We're right for each other," he said. "You'll come to realize it."

"Would you marry me without love?" she asked.

"Indeed, I would. A solid marriage, the kind your parents have, is built."

"They had love on both sides."

"They also had the other qualities. Between us, intellectually and physically, you and I have the foundation for such a marriage. Affection will grow from that and, later, a mature love."

She recognized his truth, but couldn't bring herself to consider what he wanted. Perhaps it was due to the mixed-up state she was in, but she simply could not, now or ever, take Fawn Morehead for a husband.

Though outwardly calm, Fawn was seething. There was no way to make her understand how important she was to him. He loved her, solidly and sensibly, the only way he could love. She was also the gateway to his financial ambition, his life's work. She was so laced into his plans that he *had* to win her!

He would eventually convince her. He'd prove so well how right they were together that she couldn't say no. This moment he yearned for her sexually, but gave no sign, knowing that it would only estrange her.

"I appreciate your listening to me," he said.

"It's the least I could do. I'm really sorry."

And she was. It would be heaven to luxuriate in such a marriage as he described. With no man yearning for another woman; no man ready to fight if she drew a wrong breath. But she couldn't do it. She had to get this other straightened out.

Fawn stood, "I'm going out in my car," he said.

"You can't! That's Esmerelda now! And she's coming at us fifteen miles an hour!"

"I'll be prompt. Leave my car in a garage, take a taxi back."

Her impulse was to protest further. But then she realized he might misinterpret her concern, and she was silent as he left.

38

Rain gusted.

It kept getting heavier, and drove into the windows, onto the floor. The men lowered the shutters and fastened them; the women turned on the lights and set candles, some lit, in every room for the time when the electricity might fail. They laid out extra batteries for the small radio. The big, luxurious house had become a metal-sided box against which rain threw itself steadily.

It was eight P.M. Esmerelda was one hundred sixty miles across, her winds one hundred ten miles an hour, gusting to one hundred twenty, and she was still coming this way, traveling eighteen miles every hour.

Everyone was in the house except Fawn, who hadn't yet returned. Lance and Burr had left the horses in the care of the grooms for a time, the stable already battened down.

Working fast, they filled all the bathtubs, filled big cooking pots and pitchers at the sink for household use, were relieved that they had water in the swimming pool for the horses to drink if the water supply was cut off.

They gathered in the living room. Mary-Lou moved excitedly hither and yon, listening to the storm, bemoaning the fact that she wasn't allowed to go outside and see what was happening. Papa and Mama stayed by the television set, as did Burr, who was soon going to the stable to ride out the storm.

Rae-Ellen and Pete tried to play chess, lost interest, joined the others.

Advisories were frequent. Esmerelda was still hurtling on a course for Miami, a mammoth, whirling, still-growing ring of fury. Her tornadoes were flattening mobile homes, cottages, and small stores. When her full fury reached a given spot she romped and twisted and stabbed as she went, raced madly on, leaving behind death and destruction.

"I hope Fawn is safe," Mama said.

"It's still fairly mild here," Papa assured her. "He's got delayed at the garage. There'll be a lot of people wanting to get their cars into shelter. I regret our garage was full."

Lance and Adah were sitting together, murmuring.

"I'm ready to go back to the stable," Burr said now, to Lance. "How about you?"

"I need to stay with Adah," Lance said quietly. "If it's all right with you, Burr, about the stable."

He stood, Adah with him. "There's a reason. Samson's Lad is fairly calm, and trusts Ruble as much as he does me. You and Terry will be there too. If it's not asking too much."

"No. It ain't," Burr said, puzzled.

Lance put his arm around Adah. "This is an odd moment to make our announcement," he said, "but Adah has been holding off. Now Esmerelda has moved her to consent because she's afraid to be parted from me during the storm."

He paused, glanced around the group of wondering faces.

"Adah and I are engaged to be married," he said. "She has requested—"

"I've begged, darling . . . pleaded," Adah put in softly.

"She wants either to go to the stable with me, which is out of the question, or for me to stay in the house."

Rae-Ellen found herself not breathing. This shouldn't be a shock, but it was. She'd never dreamed she'd be so crushed at the moment of their actual announcement, that she'd be shaking inwardly.

She stared at Burr, who was telling Lance, sure, he understood. No imposition, none at all. He was expressionless, impassive, but dammit, she couldn't get him out of her awareness even after this blow.

Papa was smiling, shaking Lance by the hand, putting his arms around Adah, kissing her. Mama gently pushed Papa aside and took Adah into her arms and held her; Mama was beautiful when she smiled this way, slowly and with true delight.

Mary-Lou wriggled herself between Mama and Papa and hugged and kissed the engaged couple, chattering without pause. Adah was crying and smiling, but now Lance was smiling seriously, his mind, Rae-Ellen knew, on the stable.

Pete looked absolutely blank. Eventually he managed a smile, began to horse around, as he called it, and claimed a kiss from Adah. Watching him kiss her sister lightly, Rae-Ellen, knowing that he wanted Adah as much as he was capable of wanting any girl, felt sorry for him.

Mary-Lou pushed Burr at Adah. "Don't you dare," she teased, "go to the stable without kissin' the bride! Go on, now . . . kiss her!"

Burr stepped to Adah, kissed her quickly on the lips, stepped back. Despite the briefness of the kiss, Rae-Ellen went livid. Oh, how she wished she could get inside that cowboy mind! She'd find out how he felt—hurt because he wanted Adah for himself? or not even caring? Was he totally devoid of feeling except for horses? She felt no sympathy for him, as she had for Pete. Instead, she was furious; he had no business kissing Adah, none whatsoever!

Adah came to Rae-Ellen, embraced her, kissed her on cold lips. Almost, she returned the kiss, but then she couldn't. She wasn't going to be a complete Judas.

Burr went into the hallway, returned wearing raincoat and hat, carrying a flashlight.

"Food!" cried Mama in dismay. "Wait, I'll fix—"

"Terry and Ruble brought in sandwiches and water, ma'am," Burr said.

"Oh, Burr . . . everybody!" Adah lamented. "I'm causing—"

"Nothing at all," Burr told her. "It's only a question of three of us keeping an eye on the horses. They won't do more than kick some."

But there were four horses to look after. Not just Thunder Boy and Samson's Lad, but the two training horses, as well.

Rae-Ellen knew, then, that she couldn't bear to stay in the house. She'd be far more at ease in the stable. Besides, Burr shouldn't walk alone to the stable through the storm, risk stepping on some debris or into a rain-filled hole and maybe injure his foot.

With Rae-Ellen, now, as always, to think was to speak.

"I'm going to the stable!" she said.

"No, you're not," Papa told her sternly. "I'll not have you worry your mother!"

"It ain't the place for women," Burr said, speaking almost simultaneously with Papa. "You stay here. The horses are a responsibility I can manage. A hysterical woman's another matter."

She almost flew at him, but just in time, she realized that if she did go for him, she'd be proving what he'd just said to be true. She managed to condense her anger into a glare.

No more was said, and he left. They heard the howl of wind as he opened the front door, heard it lessen after Andrews closed the door.

Rae-Ellen suddenly felt hemmed in. The lights went out, and everybody scurried about lighting additional candles. Now she really felt caged, everything seeming to be metal and flickering candlelight.

Fawn arrived, drenched. He stood in the hallway drying hair and face with the towels Marie brought and described the Hollywood waterfront.

He hadn't been able to resist sight-seeing in the storm.

"It was foolish," he admitted, "but I wanted to see a bit of it, firsthand. Rollers were coming in at the ocean, each one on the heels of the next, and waves were jumping higher than some of the older buildings along the beach front. They looked like they were trying to climb those big condominiums out there. The police are evacuating the beach now, have been for some time. I got jammed in a line of cars getting across the bridge, then had to wait at the garage, had another wait for a taxi."

"If you'd called, I'd have picked you up," Pete said.

"And have two of us wet? I'll just get on some dry clothes." He turned for the stairway.

Pete stopped him long enough to tell him of the newly engaged couple. Fawn, like Pete, looked blank at first. Then he congratulated Lance and kissed Adah before he proceeded upstairs.

Angrily, on the verge of slipping away to the stable regardless of orders, Rae-Ellen went to her own room. Better that than to hang around the lovebirds. She was going to the stable anyway, but paused to envision the scene.

She'd pound on the stable door.

Burr would shoot the inside bar and open a crack.

"It's me, Rae-Ellen," she'd have to say. "I'm here, whether you like it or not!"

"Watch the horses!" he'd yell at the grooms, and then he'd grab her arms from behind and push her through the wind and the slanting, pelting rain, back to the house. He'd wrangle her through the front door—her struggling wouldn't mean a thing, not with him so strong and so mad—and he'd let them all know what she'd done, and they'd be appalled.

And she'd be right back where she was now, caged, lights off, water apt to be cut off at any moment. And Burr would still have to get back to the stable with that foot, and he'd fight to get there, no matter how violent Esmerelda had become. He'd fight on and on to get to the stable.

To get to death. For he could be killed, the damned, bullheaded ape! She sat on the edge of her bed, quivering with anger, with being locked away with the others while Lance and Adah kissed and cooed. While Burr had the responsibility of those high-strung horses, horses which, in their terror, could turn into killers!

39

Burr laid his body to the rain-drenched wind and pushed toward the stable. His feet seemed to be cemented to the puddled ground. He ducked his head into the wind and it yanked away his rainhat. His hair was drenched instantly; rain struck his face broadside, struck his body, and ran down him from head to foot.

He'd turned on his flashlight, and he used it as best he could. The wind was bending trees and hurling rain over them and all else he could see.

As he pushed against the wall of rain, the tall palm trees yonder bent, smacked their tops on the ground, jerked erect. Now they whipped forward. A big one, just to his left, went violently flat. The wind yanked the rain aside for an instant, and he saw that its roots had been ripped from the earth.

Rain covered everything again.

Esmerelda was hurling things—tiles, boards, branches. Wind slammed swath after swath of water over him, and still he pushed against it, stepping in water to his ankles. It began to seem that he'd been slog-pushing through blowing wetness for hours, with the full force of the storm yet to come. He peered into the skirts of black rain as well as he could, saw nothing.

When the wind tore away the rain, he glimpsed, by his wavering light, grass plastered to the ground, bushes flat, Australian pines fallen, their shallow roots rearing from the sandy, flowing earth. A palmetto frond wrapped around his head, and he tore it off; a piece of board flew past, grazing his cheek.

Thunder crackled and exploded. Lightning stabbed, hissed, blossomed. Flying debris passed him constantly. Hell, he thought once, when he had an instant of thought, why couldn't I have the wind at my back? I could have ridden the storm to the stable!

Right then the wind slapped him flat. His head was in sodden grass; grass got into his ear. He managed to retrieve his flashlight, then pushed furiously to his feet, forced by the wind to stand doubled before he could even halfway straighten up. The wind held him back worse now. He had to take two steps to gain one, and at intervals had to stop and fight just to hold his place.

He should have come earlier, should have known Rae-Ellen wouldn't be scared, that there was no need to keep an eye on her. Look how she'd wanted to come with him now, too danged stubborn to trust him, the trainer, to take care of her horse! Between the endless, attacking Esmerelda and Rae-

Ellen's stubbornness, he worked himself up until he was fighting mad. Mad at the elements, and at the girl.

Esmerelda let go for an instant, and he smacked face-on into the stable, hurting his nose. He swore, shone his light, and there was the door just a step away. He got over there, mentally damning Esmerelda, wrestled the door open and stepped inside, then shut the door and dropped the inside wooden bar to hold it.

The stable was pitch-black except for his flashlight. It was silent except for the storm and the restless moving of the horses. He called quietly to each of them by name, and they were still.

"Terry!" he called, voice low.

There was no answer.

"Ruble!" he called, a bit louder.

Again no answer.

He was trying to understand this, to figure why no lantern was lit and where the grooms were, when Thunder Boy whinnied. "Now, Thunder . . . now, Boy," he called softly, "good Thunder . . . good Boy . . . quiet, Thunder . . . quiet Boy!"

He shone his flashlight beam along an upright, found the metal matchbox, struck a match and lit one of the lanterns. It glowed, sending soft rays out toward the stalls, showing the outline of the horses. They all moved and snorted. Thunder Boy whinnied again, and Burr soft-talked him some more.

He turned off his flashlight, threw his streaming coat over a bench, stuffed the flashlight into his hip pocket. He didn't call out to the grooms again lest he rile up the horses.

Something was wrong here, something more than the hurricane, something in the very air of the stable. The horses sensed it. Their quiet was unnatural, as if they were waiting.

Deliberately, he went to the horses, one after another, patted them, soft-talked. He spent more time with Thunder Boy than with the others, because he was the most high-strung, the ringleader if any trouble started. They were all nervous, flicking their tails, stepping about, tossing their heads, but his calmness, his petting, had its effect and they subsided.

It was just when he was ready to light another lantern and go search for the grooms, find out if they were in the granary, or back in the end room to eat, that it happened.

The granary door burst open and a whole crowd of black-clad figures erupted and jumped him. He dropped the lantern, hands balling into fists, and he took two of them at once—one in the eye, the other in the mouth.

At the same time he rocked from a blow to the head, and one in the belly. He doubled from the belly blow, but went for a pair of knees on a line with his eyes, hooked both arms under, and yanked.

They rolled on the floor, slugging and gouging. Burr got a kick on the back of his head, another in the side. The one he had on the floor got his thumbs onto Burr's windpipe and rammed. Burr gave a mighty twisting roll, freeing his neck but collecting kicks from all the feet, taking blows which knocked him back as fast as he made a move to stagger up.

Thunder Boy was screaming. Samson's Lad was screaming. All the horses were rearing and slashing, kicking boards loose in the backs of their stalls, whinnying and throwing themselves at the mangers, at the sides of the stalls.

Burr managed, finally, to struggle to his feet, wet hair in his eyes, fists ready, one going for a jaw, a groin, anything. Now, slugging, he dimly saw his attackers. As they converged on him, impervious to his smashing blows, even as they knocked him senseless, he recognized them as The Black Jackets.

The six of them, black figures in the dimly lit stable, lifted the unconscious man from the floor. Laughing, cursing at the rearing, screaming horses, they edged with their burden, to the stall which held the flailing silver horse.

Unused to horses, afraid of them, yet stimulated by danger, The Black Jackets carried the limp, heavy man to the rear entrance of the stall. With the clamor of the frantic horses in their ears, they laughed.

Working fast, dancing aside, keeping out of reach of the slashing hoofs of the dangerous silver stallion, they stood the unconscious man on his feet against the edge of the stall, just inside its entrance. Faster, darting, avoiding the clicking, vicious teeth of the stallion, whose uproar was music to- them, they strapped their victim into an upright position. When they had finished, he was semi-erect, but drooping.

Chortling, cursing, exulting, they left the stall and went to where they'd hidden their gear. Screaming back at the shrieking, neighing horses, they put on their black jackets, their black goggles, and they left the stable, shutting the door and dropping the bar.

Then they ran, the wind at their backs, for the spot where they'd left their motorcycles. It was the most exciting night they'd ever had, but as they shouted this to one another, Esmerelda snatched every word and tore it to shreds before it reached any ear.

And when they were on their motorcycles, roaring to safety, Esmerelda also took the thunder of their motors and swallowed that.

40

Rae-Ellen paced her rooms, Adah's. Rain kept driving against roof and shutters. The rooms were dusky with candlelight, airless. It was hard to breathe. Esmerelda roared, threw herself upon the house, banged and yanked at the shutters, tore at the rounded tiles on the roof, hurled sheet after sheet of rain.

Rae-Ellen went back downstairs. She wished she'd gone after Burr, had sneaked out behind him and followed. By the time he'd discovered her and would have hauled her back, she could have fought, nail and claw, until, in view of the rapid growth of Esmerelda's ferocity, he would have been forced to let her stay. Even if they fought the whole time.

It still wasn't too late.

She hurried into the living room. Everybody was there, huddled over the little battery radio, trying to get further word of Esmerelda.

"I'm going to the stable!" Rae-Ellen flung at them.

"Nothing of the kind!" flared Papa.

"Don't be crazy, darlin'!" gasped Mary-Lou. "Just listen to it!"

Rae-Ellen turned to Lance. "Won't you come with me? Burr shouldn't be out there alone."

"He's not alone, sister," Adah said. "Terry and Ruble are with him."

"Three men can handle four horses," Papa decreed.

"Rae-Ellen has a point, sir," Lance said. "Adah . . . darling . . . I've been very uncomfortable not looking after my share in the stable. During the eye of the storm, which is now due, and predicted to last thirty minutes, I'm going down to the stable and see how things are. I'll have time to get there and back."

"Then I'm going along!" she declared. "If it's safe for you, it's safe for me!"

"Nonsense!" Papa ejaculated.

"I'll go with them, sir," Fawn offered. "During the eye, and if we hurry, it should be safe enough."

"And if the back end hits sooner than expected?"

"We'll stay in the stable, sir," Lance assured him. "But the whole trip won't take more than twenty minutes."

"I'll go too," Pete said eagerly. "That'll make three men to take care of two girls."

"I'd prefer that you stay here," Papa said. "To be with Marguerite and Mary-Lou in addition to myself."

They waited.

Esmerelda howled, grabbed the roof and tried to shake the whole house; her wet, windy hands slipped off and she stormed on. Again she tried to grip the house, again failed. Gradually, she seemed to lose power.

Eventually, she dropped her winds and wept, rain pouring out of her, drumming and splashing so loudly, those inside could distinguish the sound.

Rae-Ellen was struggling into rain gear even as the announcer's voice came from the radio. "The eye of the mammoth hurricane, Esmerelda, is now passing over the Davie area, heading at eighteen miles per hour for Miami. All residents are warned that the storm has not ended. This is the eye, the calm in the center. The winds will resume in thirty minutes or less, blowing from the opposite direction, will be faster and carry more tornadoes than those in the front half. Stay inside . . . do not go out at this time."

A scowling Raymond Pettigrew opened the door for them.

Lance and Adah, booted and wearing rain togs, carrying a flashlight, went first. Rae-Ellen and Fawn followed on their heels.

There was no wind now, but they were almost blinded by the thickness of the falling rain. This let up suddenly, and there was only mist. They slogged, from the first step, through ankle-deep water, boot toes developing a tendency to hook into strands of grass, almost throwing them.

The dancing flashlight beams showed uprooted

trees, shone briefly on chunks of board and branches. They had to weave the comparatively short distance to the stable, the mist against their faces, the darting flashlights ever glinting on debris. They stumbled frequently. Once Rae-Ellen fell to her knees after coming up against what seemed to be a brick with the toe of her boot, and Fawn lifted her and they pushed on.

Another spurt of rain fell, streamed off their hats, past their shoulders, off the bottoms of their coats. They were walking rain-people, Rae-Ellen thought, moving slowly through this treacherous world. But Lance was within reach. They'd find out, any moment, how Burr was faring. The rain went to mist again; the mist disappeared and there was nothing.

They reached the stable.

The door was barred from outside. Lance shone his light on it.

"Look at that!" Rae-Ellen exclaimed, a stitch in her heart. "How can they bar the door from the outside? Why would they?"

No one answered.

She caught her breath, held it.

Lance dragged the heavy bar with one hand, lifted it, let it drop free. It made a loud, wet sound. He opened the door.

The first thing that hit Rae-Ellen was the warm stable smell, a mixture of hay, grain, horses. At the same time, she saw how dim the light was, just one lantern burning. She heard the noises of the horses, the rearing, the low whinnies, the crack of iron shoe against wood, and beyond, as if from a great distance, the murmur of a voice.

They shut the door, barred it.

Thunder Boy began to plunge, his high-pitched scream unmistakable.

"It's all right, Thunder," Rae-Ellen called softly, trying to attain Burr's soothing tone, "it's all right, Boy. It's just us . . . friends . . . that's my Thunder . . . that's my Boy . . ."

Samson's Lad began to neigh and rear, and even as she kept on trying to soothe Thunder Boy, edging toward his manger, Rae-Ellen could hear Lance trying to quiet his horse. Fawn moved toward the other stalls, talking low and fast to the training horses, which joined the turmoil of the racers.

It was when Thunder Boy brought his front hoofs down from above his head and they hit the straw on the floor, that Rae-Ellen glimpsed the figure at the rear.

It was indistinguishable, but the voice which murmured from it, saying Thunder Boy's name over and over, was Burr's voice.

She froze, afraid to speak, to move. The least thing could set Thunder Boy off so he'd slash Burr to death. She waited, listening to Burr, to the muted sound of rain, to Lance and Fawn, working with the horses.

Why did Burr stay there? Why didn't he move toward Thunder Boy's head, or get out of the stall? Why did he remain motionless, seeming to . . . droop?

She unhooked the lantern and held it so she could see better. The light glistened on the silver of Thunder Boy's side, on his never-quiet hoofs. It shone, at last, on Burr, and he was bound, strapped, to the side of the stall.

She moved quickly but cautiously to Lance,

whispered Burr's plight. Fawn and Adah joined them. Lance motioned Rae-Ellen to light the way, told Adah to remain at the front of the stable.

At the entrance to Thunder Boy's stall, they halted.

"Burr," Rae-Ellen whispered, "are you hurt?"

"Slashed," he whispered back. Then, "That you, Buford?"

"And Fawn," Lance replied softly. "We'll get you out."

"Knife," Burr instructed. "Right-hand pocket, next to the door."

Bless him, Rae-Ellen thought. Him and his knife.

She moved the lantern so they could see Burr. His face was bleeding. He was strapped to the upright posts of the stall, and the straps looked strong.

Thunder Boy reared, slashed down, kicked with his hind feet, bucked, almost raked Burr, and screamed.

Burr resumed his sing-song, and Thunder Boy grew less fierce.

Lance got the knife, slashed the straps, and Burr sagged into his arms. Lance dragged him out of the stall, shut the gate. Thunder Boy stood straight up, whinnying as if he'd been robbed of prey.

Fawn had the lantern now. Lance kept supporting Burr. Rae-Ellen and Adah drew in close.

Burr pulled free, stood, muttered something about circulation. Rae-Ellen grabbed his arm, her intention being to get him to lie down on hay, horse-blanket, anything, so they could see how badly he was hurt.

Hampered though he was by Rae-Ellen, Burr stood free. He stepped to the manger and took up his sing-song.

Rain began to drum on the roof.

The other horses seemed to listen to Burr, too. Then, as Lance took up the same ploy with Samson's Lad, all four horses quieted and did nothing more than step nervously about.

"What happened?" Lance asked at the first opportunity. "Who tied you up, Travis? Where are Terry and Ruble?"

"I don't know where they are," Burr replied. "I came into the stable, found them gone, was starting to look for them when all six of those Black Jackets jumped me."

"Black Jackets!" cried the others.

"Why would they do that?" asked Adah.

"Revenge," Fawn said grimly. "For what happened at their hangout."

"But you said they'd quieted down!"

"Apparently not."

"They . . . Burr, they tied you in that stall to be killed!" Rae-Ellen cried. "Why you? Why not some other one of us?"

"They took the first one they could get," Lance opined. "It happened to be Burr."

"No," Burr said grimly. "It was Terry and Ruble first."

They hastened, then, to search for the missing grooms.

It was Adah who found them. She opened the granary door, shone a flashlight, and they were lying, bound and gagged, tied together, bedded on a pile of oats. The men untied them quickly.

"We was slugged!" Terry gasped.

"We was feedin' the horses," Ruble added, "our backs to the stable while we was in here, the outside stable door not barred so's you could get in, Mr. Travis."

"First we knew," Terry continued, "they was on our backs. We tried to fight, but there was like ten of them—"

"Six," Fawn interjected, "with the strength of a dozen. You didn't stand a chance."

The lantern showed they had lumps on their foreheads and an upcoming black eye apiece. In fact, Ruble was going to have two shiners, Rae-Ellen thought. They were cut, too.

"Horses all right?" Terry asked. "They didn't make off with the horses?"

"No. They ain't horse thieves," Burr growled.

"They're devils," Rae-Ellen said. "They made a deathtrap out of the stable, barring the door from the outside! They've got to be put in jail this time!"

"That ain't exactly wise," Burr said.

His face was bleeding worse. She tried to wipe the blood away with her handkerchief, but he pulled out his own and held it over the slash. "Thunder Boy got me there, with his hoof," he admitted.

"You're right about police, Travis," Fawn said. "The creeps have had their revenge. If we bring the law into this, it'll give Pettigrew's a great deal of bad publicity, drag the girls' names through the papers and over the air, and accomplish nothing."

"It would put those outlaws behind bars," Lance said, "where they belong."

"There's sense to that," Burr agreed.

"I couldn't identify them to suit a court of law," Burr said thoughtfully. "I never did see their faces. I just knew who they were, is all."

427

"I didn't see their faces, neither," said Terry.

Burr looked questioningly at Ruble, who shook his head.

"They'll probably be on their way back to California as soon as the hurricane ends," Fawn speculated.

They agreed that Raymond Pettigrew, when he heard the facts, would decide that to try to press charges under the circumstances would be futile.

"We need to keep our eye out for them," Fawn said. "After we leave Florida, even if they stay on a bit, all trouble from them will be at an end."

They now recounted to Terry and Ruble what had taken place in the roadhouse. The two grooms agreed that both that episode and this one tonight, should be kept private, except from the boss.

"Papa will be very angry," Rae-Ellen predicted. "But he'll agree to what you've decided just as he did about that fight in the roadhouse. He's a fighter, but there aren't enough solid facts here for him to use."

Now, working fast, they gave all the horses oats and fresh hay and water. The animals, though restive, did begin to eat. There was peace and quiet within the stable.

Outside, Esmerelda was again on the rampage.

"We'll have to ride out the rest of the storm here," Lance said. "It's better for the horses, and I doubt if we could get back to the house before the full force hits us again."

41

They'd no sooner got settled than Esmerelda went crazy.

Burr stayed outside Thunder Boy's manger, Lance outside Samson's Lad's manger, and one groom with each training horse. Fawn and the two girls sat on bales of hay and kept the grooms' little battery radio turned low.

Burr's cheek was no longer bleeding, but he had a gash which Rae-Ellen was sure needed stitches. She fretted, knowing that he belonged in a hospital, not in a stable with all sorts of horse germs getting into that cut.

There was a pounding on the door.

"Someone's out there!" Fawn yelled. Esmerelda's howling wind and crashing thunder was now so great they had to shout. And didn't want to, lest the shouts put the horses wild again.

It took three men to fight the door open enough to admit the one outside. Wind slammed into the stable, sent straw flying.

It was Pete, exhilarated and laughing, clad in streaming rain togs, who stumbled in. He threw his strength, along with that of the other three, to pulling the door shut—Esmerelda, blowing from the opposite direction now pushing them back, the door with them. At last they got it shut, dropped the bar, stood panting and staring at one another.

"Mr. Pettigrew sent me," Pete said. "He's upset that the girls are here. **I'm to pitch in and help. I've** got his car to take anybody to the hospital if they get hurt."

He noticed the slash on Burr's cheek, the state of the grooms' faces. Terry also had a badly split lip, which was bleeding.

"What happened?" Pete demanded. "A free-for-all?"

They told him about The Black Jackets.

He agreed that it should be kept private. He went the rounds, inspecting injuries. "You guys need to go to the hospital for shots and stitches."

"Not while Esmerelda's blowing," Lance objected.

"That's not the way the boss is talking. He's upset. Says hospital right away for anybody that's hurt. Acts like he's taken personal offense at the storm. He was really definite about it."

"Burr, you need to go!" Rae-Ellen cried, torn between the danger of his venturing into the storm and that of instant lockjaw.

"Like hell I'll go!" he snorted.

"Then you other guys—Terry, Ruble," Pete argued. "If it's okay with Burr and Lance. Stable's a bad place to get cuts and you've both got them."

"If you get a tetanus shot within twenty-four hours," Lance said, "it's safe. Safer than driving to the hospital."

"But not as exciting!" Pete laughed. "Man, it's really something to force a car through with that Esmerelda throwing everything in the book! In any case, Adah," he added, "your father wants me to bring you and Rae-Ellen back to the house."

"We've decided to ride the storm out here," Lance said.

"Boss wants his girls in the house. Seems he thinks he's got the right to dictate to both of them, even Adah, until she's actually married."

"I'm not going!" Rae-Ellen declared. "Papa can have any kind of fit he wants!"

"Ain't no call for you to stay," said Burr.

She glared at him. Winced at that slash on his cheek.

"If you want to go to the house with Adah, Buford," Burr said, "I can keep Samson's Lad under control. All the horses, for that matter. No sense worrying either Mr. Pettigrew or your fiancée."

Lance frowned, nodded. "Thanks, Burr. We'll go."

Rae-Ellen gasped. She was appalled that Lance's affection for Adah was that great. Yet she felt sympathy for him. He was torn between the welfare of Samson's Lad and Adah's peace of mind.

It ended with six of them going in Papa's car. Adah and Lance would get out at the house. Terry and Ruble would be taken to the emergency room. Fawn, after much persuasion from Pete, went along to keep him company on the way home should the grooms be held for treatment. This was possible, since they were both more seriously injured than they had at first believed.

This left Burr and Rae-Ellen alone with the horses.

She settled herself in a corner next to the granary, determined not to have a fight with him. Not even about his cheek.

She marveled that Papa had reversed himself about going into the storm. She still held the little radio, and now the announcer said the winds weren't quite so severe.

After an eon of howling storm, restlessness of horses, yet with comparative peace in the stable, Burr limped over to Rae-Ellen. She hadn't noticed that he was limping so. If Thunder Boy had stepped on his sore foot, the injury would be worse than the one on the cheek.

Her scalp prickled. She wished now she'd thrown a tantrum, done anything, but had somehow forced him to go to the hospital. Lance could have stayed with the horses.

"How come you sit in the corner?" Burr asked. "Afraid of Esmerelda, or afraid of me?"

She knew instantly, like a blow, that she was afraid of him. Afraid that she might not be able to get him out of her system as fast as she wanted.

With no idea of what his reaction would be, she stood up in that corner and, facing him, eyes meeting those unbearable brown eyes, she began to undress. She took off her skirt and blouse, stood in bikinis and bra and boots. She took off the bikini and bra and left on the boots.

"Right here," she said. "With the horses. In the hurricane."

He had everything off so fast, except his boots, that it seemed she hadn't drawn two breaths. He scooped her up and carried her into the granary and dropped her onto the slippery, sliding oats.

He came into her fast, with a now-practiced motion, and she received him. Esmerelda set their tempo. She beat and drummed, thumped and rolled and streamed. She moaned over the roof; she cried out in her romping fury. It got so Rae-Ellen didn't know, or care, whether it was Esmerelda she heard or Burr or herself.

After it was over, she'd proved what she'd set out to prove. What she felt for Burr Travis was passion, sheer, unalloyed passion.

They dressed in silence. There was nothing to say. They'd spent themselves as Esmerelda was doing now. They did sit together, with the radio. And while they listened to it, Esmerelda whirled away, veering east and to the north over the Atlantic, there to spend her fury and die.

It took ten days, more, for crews to clear away all traces of Esmerelda. The very next morning, at Rae-Ellen's insistence, Burr had a tetanus shot. The grooms had returned after the storm, sewed up and bandaged.

Fallen trees were cut up and hauled off; broken limbs and uprooted bushes received the same treatment. New shrubs were planted where the old ones had been. Shutters were taken off windows. Broken glass was cleared away, new glass installed. Flattened mobile homes were disposed of or, if possible, repaired. Electricity was restored. Telephone poles were replaced and phones were again in working order.

Gulfstream Park held races the day after the hurricane. The oval had been cleared, dragged, and redragged until it was like new. Debris had been cleaned from the grandstands. Benches and tables and chairs had been removed from storage in the shuttered clubhouse and set on the emerald green grass.

The vast parking lots swelled with their seas of cars. The crowds were back, racing forms in hand, betting tickets stowed in pocket or purse.

The Pettigrew party attended the races that day and on all the remaining days. They raced Thunder Boy, and Lance raced Samson's Lad. Both horses came in the money consistently, and there was much happiness in the household.

Rae-Ellen, who rarely saw Burr during the day, not wanting to disturb his constant training of Thunder Boy, realized, vaguely, that she was changing. In her efforts to be honestly gentle, in Adah's manner, when she remembered, she was actually coming to feel a bit gentle.

Hungering for Burr, she slipped wordlessly into his room nearly every night. He received her silently, with open arms. Her burning flared, flamed, eased, and she left, still silent. Night after night, using the rhythm method of birth control because this was to be temporary only, she went to him. Yes, this was the only way she could deal with it. Keep it under control until it wore itself out.

One night, back in her own bed, fed and warmed by rapture, a faint, warning question crossed her mind. Could it be, she wondered, that she might fall in love with Burr?

And then, remembering their antagonism, their bitter, impassioned quarrels, the mad, wild tumult of their entire association, she knew how ridiculous that thought was.

And slept, dreaming of peace, blessed peace.

Part V
KIDNAPPED

42

Mama began to discuss Christmas one evening after dinner when all were assembled. "The first thing," she said, "is to decide whether to stay in Florida for the entire racing season or to take the horses home for a good rest before Churchill Downs. That way we can have Christmas in Durham."

There was a brief silence. Papa broke it. "I'd like to get the thinking of our horsemen on the matter. It appears to me that it rests largely on what's best for the horses."

"What do you think, Lance?" Adah asked.

"Both horses are racing so well," he replied, "that it seems a shame to take them away from it. Still, to give them a real rest before summer racing —What's your idea, Travis?"

Burr scowled so thoughtfully Rae-Ellen decided

she'd never seen him look so homely. Or, give him credit, so sensibly serious.

"I hate to cut in on their winning streak," he said, "but they're young, and according to me shouldn't be run without letup. If we take them back to Durham, after a couple more races here, the rest can do them no harm. We can work out, keep them in fettle."

"You have me convinced," said Lance. "I suggest we be content with what they've done here, take them home, and concentrate on Churchill Downs."

For some idiotic reason, though she didn't want Thunder Boy pulled off the track in the midst of a winning streak, Rae-Ellen was swept by a flash of pride in Burr. It was quickly gone. Naturally, he knew a few sensible things, had brains enough to utter them. He had to have some know-how, had to allow a certain amount of that tremendous ego to surface now and again, or he couldn't serve as horse trainer. But there was no sense in giving him too much credit, either. Sure, he'd trained Thunder Boy, but the stallion had to have inborn guts and ability or he wouldn't be winning. Thunder Boy was the star here, not Burr Travis.

It was agreed to go to Durham.

Mary-Lou, who had been unusually quiet, now made up for it. "You know that overseas call I had from Jim?" she asked.

"Yes, dear," Mama said, smiling. "You've been restless ever since. Ready to tell us?"

"What'd he call about?" teased Pete. "To propose?"

Mary-Lou made a playful fist. "Of course not, silly! But he did have an interestin' plan, and I've been tryin' to decide if I'd be a complete ingrate if I took him up!"

Mama laughed. "Out with it, dear!"

Mary-Lou giggled, then plunged into her news. "He phoned to relay me an invitation to a very important European weddin'! In London! It's a very distant cousin of the Queen, years younger, and a real beauty! Nobody's ever heard of her on this side of the ocean, except for some bitty mention in the paper! She's marryin' a very rich older man, handsome, too, has somethin' to do with Parliament! And the Queen herself is plannin' to be there!"

"Mary-Lou!" Adah exclaimed. "How did you ever keep this to yourself for hours?"

"I didn't want to break my word about spendin' the racin' season in Florida. I had to think, decide whether to even mention it! Jim's waitin' for my answer!"

"But of course you're to go!" Mama exclaimed. "How many American girls get such an opportunity? And you'll meet the Queen!"

"I did meet her when I was presented at Court, ma'am. Remember? But that was three years ago, when I was eighteen! And I would like to maintain my royal contacts. It's such fun! And other connections, even other crowned heads'll be there."

"You can't miss all that," Rae-Ellen put in, excited for her friend. "There'll be parties, too, and you don't want to miss those, either!"

"Jim said twenty-three parties are already scheduled! And side trips to Italy and France and Greece! Every minute between now and March fifteenth is crammed! I'll simply have to push dressmakers like mad over there!"

Adah and Rae-Ellen hugged the excited little redhead.

"We'll help you pack," Rae-Ellen promised. "We'll have you on the London plane tomorrow!"

They remained in Florida for a week after Mary-Lou winged off to London. Thunder Boy and Samson's Lad had been entered in two more races, and Lance and Burr opted not to scratch them, but let them run.

Thunder Boy placed in his first race, came in winner of the second. Samson's Lad showed in his first race and won a purse in the second. Everyone was happy and excited and had solid hopes for Churchill Downs.

Still, almost nightly, Rae-Ellen went to Burr's bed, or he came to her room and they met in silent, delightful sex. Aside from a murmur about position or movement, they didn't speak.

During the day, she stayed far from him, so the only time they exchanged comments was at meals, with the others present and conversation flowing. Here, where their silence would have been marked, they got by with asking for the salt or smiling in stiff agreement to something said to the table at large.

It was amazing how well she and Burr got along when they skipped all conversation. They shared silent sex, which was totally satisfying. Sometimes, she thought they might effect a complete truce. Yet she knew that was impossible.

If they began to talk again she knew they'd be into a quarrel first thing because she hadn't changed her basic opinion of him. He was still rough and raw; his grammar, even at the table, was still atrocious; and he seemed to grow homelier every day. Not that she wanted him to be an Adonis, but he didn't have to look more like a mud fence every day, for heaven's sake.

Granted, he was a good horse trainer. Good for Thunder Boy, anyhow, and admittedly he had a way with the twin colts. Also, everybody seemed to like Burr Travis.

So she had to admit that everybody except her liked the Texan, though she couldn't exactly see why. Aside, that is, from his know-how with horses. She smiled as she thought if they knew how—well, wonderful—he could be in bed, it would be more understandable that they liked him. They were deceived by his manner toward them, which was the opposite of his manner toward her.

When they talked at meals and during the evenings, she was constantly riled to hear him converse so easily and comfortably. You'd think he'd known her family and friends for years!

She caught him shooting a glance at her now and again. When this happened, a flare of that old-time burning rose, but she quelled it. It would be different in a few hours—in bed.

Burr made no effort to resist spearing a look at the stubborn filly once in awhile, nor to ignore how the red in her hair shone in lamplight. He had her number. He had his course of action, and he'd see to it that it worked. Still, she was a walking question mark, able to mix him up and get him off the track.

These days, she acted like butter wouldn't melt in her mouth. She behaved like . . . like Adah. But she wasn't like Adah, would never be.

Let him try to talk sense to her and that hell-hot temper would flare. Only way to quell her, to make her feminine, was in bed. Only way to keep her like that was what he'd decided on and was now waiting for.

So Burr bided his time. He reveled in the silent sex with Rae-Ellen, which was so incredible he'd never have believed it possible—with any woman.

Mama decided to give a farewell dance. "Just ourselves," she explained, "and the Simpsons and their daughters, Analiese and Rhoda, and Rhoda's date; the Waterfords and Suzy and her date, and the Claremonts and Rissie and her fiancé. Ten couples in all . . . four older ones, the rest of you youngsters."

They all laughed and fell in with her plan.

Much to her surprise, Rae-Ellen, wearing her white, naked-look dress and diamond earrings, danced rather frequently and in utter silence with Burr, the night of the dance. His foot was healed, the music was stereo, and they all took turns stacking records. Every couple was on the floor every dance.

Rae-Ellen let herself enjoy dancing with Burr. He'd literally swing her away to the beat of the music. All wordless, in perfect accord.

She noted how lovingly Adah and Lance moved, their steps coordinated, never missing a beat. But their dancing, exquisite as it was, didn't touch the perfection of herself and Burr. They moved, in each other's arms, the way they moved in bed, bodies attuned, never deviating, one from the other. Aside from the ecstasy of sex with him, Rae-Ellen had never experienced anything which could touch the pleasure of dancing with him.

As in a dream, she knew that he could make

her angrier than any human being. But above that dream, blotting it out as she floated in his arms, was the joy in bed last night, tonight . . . She wouldn't let herself think further, for that would suggest an ending to rapture, an end to the calmness with which she was filling herself.

This had to continue until she was free of him.

It was like tearing away part of herself when she had to dance with Fawn or Pete, even with Lance. Then she had a long period of dancing with the older men, even Papa. She and Papa didn't talk, either. As with Burr, she got along better with Papa, these days, when they didn't talk and no mention of husband or grandson or ultimatum might be made.

Lance and Adah wandered into the grounds to be alone. They walked the paths, murmuring, the December night softly warm. They stopped, at intervals, for a tender embrace.

He drew her down on a bench in shadow, keeping an arm around her. "Our wedding," he whispered. "Will you marry me this Christmas, my darling?"

Guilt about Pete flashed through her. With it came a decision not to tell Lance. Not just yet.

"That's so soon," she countered. "Mama will want a big wedding, a huge reception. You know Mama and parties!"

"New Year's, then?"

She laughed, a gurgle in her throat. He kissed her, lingeringly, and their tongues touched like soft fiery tendrils.

"You darling," Adah whispered. "Maybe in April. Things will be green, flowers in bloom, and we can have the wedding in the gardens at Magnolia Hall."

But first, oh first, what happened with Pete, yet to be told. Not now, her heart beat, not tonight!

He protested the wait, but she remained sweetly stubborn. "We can have our honeymoon," she argued, "and be back to take Samson's Lad and Thunder Boy to Churchill Downs!"

By then, she would have told him about Pete. And he would have forgiven her, of course he would.

It was then, from deepest shadow, came the metallic cough. Something whizzed past Lance's head, clipping off a lock of hair, part of which fell onto his cheek and away. There was the sound of running feet.

Lance sprang up, Adah with him.

"What was that, darling?"

"A shot," he said, dazed.

"Somebody tried to shoot you! Let's go, Lance, we've got to get help!"

"Whoever it was ran away." He turned her toward the house. "I want you inside."

As they rounded a curve in the path, they encountered Burr and Rae-Ellen hurrying toward them.

Adah told what had happened.

"We heard the shot, dancing by the door," Burr said. "Which way did he go?"

Lance pointed.

"You girls head for the house!" Burr ordered. "Say nothing. We'll take a look around."

The men left, running quietly.

"They're not armed!" Rae-Ellen exclaimed angrily.

"Oh, they'll be killed!" Adah wailed.

"No, they won't. Burr won't allow it."

"They want us to go into the house. Come on, Rae-Ellen."

"I'm staying right here!"

"But Lance wants—!"

"Move a step. Now, we're hidden by these bushes. We're in complete shadow."

They waited what seemed to be hours, though Rae-Ellen supposed it was fifteen minutes. Arms around each other, the sisters didn't so much as whisper.

The men returned, and the girls stepped out to meet them. Burr glared at Rae-Ellen and started to speak angrily, but Lance stopped him.

"No harm done, Travis. They were concerned."

"He's gone, then," Rae-Ellen said.

"Him or them."

"Who was it, do you think?"

"The Black Jackets, is our guess," Burr said. "They ain't the kind to give up so easy, after all. They still want to get even."

"Why would they shoot at Lance?" Adah asked. "It was you they were after during the hurricane."

"They don't care which one of us they get," Burr said. "Just so it's one of us. I think this is really the last we'll hear from them."

"How can you say that?" Rae-Ellen demanded.

"They know we're alerted now. We're leaving in the morning and my guess is they are, too. For California."

"Why tomorrow?"

"They've worn out their welcome in these parts," Burr said. "Ruble told me there was another robbery last night, and suspicion points to a motorcycle gang. Whether they did it or not, they ain't

447

going to hang around and risk getting into trouble."

"I think you're right," Lance concurred. "Suppose we keep quiet about that shot, the four of us."

They all agreed.

43

Settled again in Durham without further mishap, the elder Pettigrews, their daughters, Lance and Burr were at the breakfast table. The men had been invited to breakfast after the workout, which Lance had driven over to watch, and had been talking horses nearly the whole time.

Then Burr switched the conversation into a different channel. He spoke in his deepest, most maddeningly assured tone. His features got correspondingly bigger and more rough looking, and Rae-Ellen could hardly bear to see them.

"I've got an invitation," he said, using also his most irritating drawl. "It includes all present and Morehead and Battle."

"Let us hear it, by all means," Raymond Pettigrew urged.

"It has to do with my Pa's ranch, sir. I wrote him how interested you are in ranching, and he's come up with an invite for the whole party that went to Florida to spend a few days of Christmas at his place."

There was an instant of surprised silence.

Then Papa spoke. "I don't know about the rest, but I will accept here and now."

"But so many of us!" Mama exclaimed. "To go in on your mother at Christmas!" Still, her eyes were shining with excitement.

"My ma died when I was just a button, ma'am. Pa's never married again."

"Oh. I'm sorry!"

"It's all right, ma'am. I don't remember her. It's been just Pa and me and Rosita, our housekeeper and the bossiest woman ever lived, and the hands. We made out okay."

"It's splendid of your father," Lance said. "I accept with pleasure, contingent upon the rest of you."

"We must accept!" Adah said happily. "We've never seen a ranch! And it'll give Papa a chance to see one in operation. To say nothing of knowing a real, live rancher! I accept, and thank you, Burr, and your father!"

"I'll accept for Fawn and Pete," Papa said. "Their plan is to spend the holiday with us. All they need is a word to the effect that they can be spared from Pettigrew's for a few more days."

Rae-Ellen wondered whether any of them noticed that she hadn't accepted. Apparently not. Now they were busy talking about land and cattle.

She looked at Burr, and his face really was bigger and rawer than usual. It was worse than it had been at the start of breakfast. It was sickening; she

450

felt it in her stomach. And none of them noticed, just jabbered on. This trip was the silliest, craziest, most revolting idea in the world. She regarded her coffee, black and steaming in the cup, and it didn't smell right.

Papa was saying, "We can stay at a motel. Not pile in on your father."

"The Star-Bar's right sizable, sir," Burr told him.

Raymond went speechless. He'd had no idea that Burr came from that vast spread, the Star-Bar, so big it was known nationally. He'd assumed that the ranch was of moderate size, and now he was stunned.

"I'm surprised," he said at last, "that you'd leave such a big ranch for other work."

"That's what Pa said. Only in a different tone of voice and with some hells and damns." He glanced at Mama. "Sorry, ma'am."

She smiled.

"We had our fallin' out over beefalo and horses," Burr continued. "Pa's not in the same trouble with his beef that lots of ranchers are in these days, but he wanted to set up his beefalo in a big way, and I wanted to make it race horses. So, the Star-Bar being his spread, I took off. Not exactly mad, either one of us, understand. Now I've begun to prove myself and Pa's doing fine with his beefalo, and we've been mending our fences, some of 'em, anyhow. We've sent letters, had a phone call. Now this. He wants to get acquainted with the folks I'm working for."

"I'll arrange a flight for all of us," Papa said.

"That ain't needed, sir. Pa'll provide transportation. He'd be right put out to be deprived of it."

"Then it's settled," declared Papa.

451

Rae-Ellen stared miserably into her coffee. It smelled worse now. She glanced at that face, and her stomach heaved. Trembling inwardly with rage that no one, not even Mama, had asked her if she wanted to go on this wild trip, she began to choke down her eggs and grits and ham. They smelled terrible, tasted worse, balled in her stomach. Burr Travis, her family, the food, all were revolting.

She caught him watching her. Well, let him spy! Later, she'd refuse to budge; she'd not go on the trip. Her main concern, at the moment, was to get this food down. The grits felt like coarse salt on her tongue. She gulped coffee to get them down, caught Burr spearing another glance at her, wished she could claw his eyes out.

He, on the other hand, was feeling satisfaction. She hadn't said she'd go, but she hadn't said she wouldn't go, either. Look how she seemed to be holding her breath to get that coffee down. Things were working out according to his plan, he was sure of it.

He couldn't resist needling her, just a bit. "You ain't said yes to the invite," he murmured very low. "How come?"

"I don't see why you want to take us to some pinhead ranch, that's why!" she whispered fiercely.

"To show you Texas. Show you where your horse trainer comes from."

"I have no interest in how a cowhand lives," she said, taking advantage of the spirited conversation Papa and Lance had started about beefalo.

Burr leaned closer. "Only how he performs in bed?"

She started to claw, but he caught her hand so the others couldn't see, held it firmly beneath the

452

table. "Want to make it a honeymoon?" he whispered.

She replied fiercely, "I wouldn't marry you—"

"I didn't use the word marry. I'm referring to living together. Honest and open."

She tried to yank her hand loose, but he gave it a twist, held it tighter.

"Never!" she hissed.

"But you'd marry me?" he goaded.

"Never!"

"Nor I you."

"Then it's ended, over!"

"It ain't over. I get what I want."

She glared. He absolutely nauseated her. She was aware that breakfast had ended, that they were leaving the table, which suited her just fine. She was in an uproar, emotional, mental, physical. Her breakfast churned in her stomach.

She ran for her suite, straight for the bathroom. Hanging over the commode, she rid herself of everything she had eaten, then stayed there, retching.

She'd never been so sick.

And it was Burr Travis' fault, for upsetting her.

Suddenly she knew he was lounging in the doorway of the bathroom. She gave him a bitter look, then retched again.

"You threw up your breakfast," he said. Accusingly.

"Obviously!"

"That's what I've been waiting for."

She glowered, retched.

"Know why you threw it up?"

"I looked at you, that's why! I can't even look at you any more without throwing up!"

"You done it because you're pregnant."

"I'm not! I—"

But she was, she knew with absolute certainty that she was! She'd taken only the rhythm precaution, had been so sure that it could never happen to her, never to Rae-Ellen Pettigrew!

"You're pregnant," he repeated, "with my kid."

"You can't prove that! I told you there were other men!"

"I've kept track. We're close to Christmas. Since the middle of October, you and I—I know for sure. It's my kid. No gettin' around it."

He was right about that, too. She hadn't been with any other man since the time with Lance, in early October. And the very next day she'd known she wasn't pregnant.

Furious, she turned away from the commode.

"So it's your baby!" she hissed. "So what?"

"So we live together, free and open, like I said. I ain't being trapped into marriage. But nobody but me is going to raise my kid, either."

She flew at him, more fiercely than ever, even in the beginning. He swooped her up and carried her to the bed and dumped her and she lay there, too weak to stir.

He locked the doors. He stripped her, and then he stripped himself. By this time her weakness had faded and when he began to rape her, she fought him. But passion rose in her, and he subdued her and she clung to him, moaning, angry tears covering her cheeks. Moving within his embrace, lifted on the wings of passion, she knew, angrily, that she loved this cowboy in a crazy, wild, impossible way.

What she'd felt for Lance was a pale shadow. This would torture her forever!

When passion was spent and they lay in each other's naked arms, she determined never to admit love for such a brute. She waited, but he didn't mention love, which strengthened her resolve and made her furious at the same time.

"We live together," he repeated. "With our kid. Agreed?"

"Yes. Damn it!"

"And not just because of the kid?"

"No!" she spat. "Not because of the baby at all! I'll not have the baby used! If I choose, I'll not live with you, and I'll keep my baby—"

"Nobody keeps my kid but me."

"—and you can do nothing about it, nothing!"

"Oh, I'd fight you for the kid. Fathers have some rights these days. It ain't all the mother's way."

That was the clincher. That was what made her set on living with him. Her baby wasn't going to spend its life as a bone of contention. Her baby was going to have peace of mind from the moment it opened its eyes on a big, strange world.

She told Burr all this. Heatedly.

"Fine," he said. "Glad to hear it. Thing is, you've changed."

"I haven't changed a bit!"

"You've got my kid in you. That's a change. Like I knew it would be."

So! That was the plan he'd hinted at!

"You got me pregnant on purpose!" she cried.

"Yep. Took longer than I wanted, but I can't complain. We've got the kid on his way and you've changed, and will change more."

But she hadn't really changed.

She'd been crazy-wild, insane in love with this Texan from the start. That was what she'd been fighting, that unrecognized love. She hadn't changed. The only difference was that now she knew.

44

After they'd dressed, he unlocked the doors. When he cracked open the hall door, the sound of the piano drifted up and beyond that, faint as a whisper, Mama's voice speaking to Adah and the servants.

"Clear coast," Burr murmured. "I'll be at the stables. Keep mum. I'll announce our plans when the time comes."

This riled her afresh, but she only nodded, tight-lipped. It was, actually, his responsibility. He'd started the mess. Let him run it now and, eventually, clean it up. Just so the baby didn't suffer.

The main trouble was that he wouldn't marry her. A baby has a right to married parents.

She got to thinking about the baby. She didn't love it, not yet. But she felt excited that it was inside her, coiled within her body, warm and nested there. She began to feel possessive; the baby was in her body, not in Burr's. She was the mother, the one to dictate terms. She also felt upset that Burr had deliberately impregnated her.

All so he could force her to live with him.

It didn't make sense.

Maybe she wasn't really pregnant! Though she'd had no recent evidence, there were times when a woman skipped, especially when she was nervous and upset. And heaven knew Burr Travis had kept her in that state from the first day she saw him!

Consequently, she made a trip to town. Here she consulted Doctor Cline, their family doctor, a man in his sixties.

He examined her, his manner serious. At the end, when she was dressed and back in his consultation room, she thought there might be tears in his eyes. Lines cut his face as he gazed at her.

"Then I am pregnant?" she asked softly.

"A full seven weeks, child. Rae-Ellen—"

She gestured, made a smile. "It isn't quite the way it looks," she said. "The baby's father is most anxious to take care of him."

Relief erased the lines in the old doctor's face. "Then it's not to worry?" he asked.

"It's not to worry," she agreed. "I'll want you to take care of us. I don't want a specialist."

He smiled, patted her shoulder, kissed her cheek. She left the office, glowing with love for the old doctor, with the beginning of love for her baby, now that she knew for certain that he existed.

Her heart was beating high. She was carrying a precious treasure, her little baby, hers and Burr's!

As she drove home, her anger at Burr's actions

subsided. She even felt a bit flattered that he'd gone to so much trouble to get her to live with him. Tough as he was, he had to really want her. She convinced herself that he was trapped in the same crazy, fighting, upside-down love for her that she was caught in for him. They were like flies in a spider's web. They were, no getting around it, stuck with each other.

The usual group dined at the Pettigrew table that night. Rae-Ellen had only a moment in which to whisper to Burr that she'd been to the doctor. He nodded, looking jut-jawed.

Fawn and Pete gladly accepted the Christmas invitation. After dinner, they gathered in the living room for strong, black espresso served in tiny cups. Food and drink had given Rae-Ellen no more trouble and the doctor had prescribed a pill for morning sickness, so she expected to feel normal from now on.

Burr said, as they sipped coffee, "Mr. Pettigrew, sir . . . Mrs. Pettigrew, ma'am . . . this will be a shock to you, but it's got to be told. Rae-Ellen and I are going to live together."

Every face in the room turned to Rae-Ellen, appalled. They all waited for some word from her, so she gave it.

"That's the way it is," she said clearly.

"You mean to marry, of course," Papa said, very cold.

"No marriage," Rae-Ellen said. "This is 1979. Things have changed, and they're going to change more in the eighties."

"I don't care about that!" snapped Papa. "No daughter of mine is going to—to—"

"Shack up, sir," supplied Burr soberly.

"—to shack up with a man! Not instead of marriage—!"

"You'd count me the right man for marriage, sir?"

"For marriage, yes."

"I'll be as right this way, sir," Burr said, his face stubborn.

She wanted to scream at him, sitting there with that coffee cup looking like a thimble in his big hands, measuring how Papa would feel about this, how he would feel about that, telling the world that he wouldn't marry her.

"Rae-Ellen!" Mama gasped. "Please don't do this to us!"

"She ain't exactly doing anything to you, ma'am," Burr said, coolly respectful. Rae-Ellen thought she saw a flicker of warmth in his eyes, but couldn't be sure. "We'll take off. We won't hang around Durham and disgrace you."

"Rae-Ellen . . . sister!" Adah pleaded.

Rae-Ellen met her golden eyes, shook her head, and Adah began to weep. Lance put his arm around Adah, took up where she'd left off.

"Do you know your mind, Rae-Ellen?" he asked, and there was concern in his tone. "Know it truly?"

She nodded, remembering their time in the wilderness room. It meant nothing now. Only Burr mattered. Burr and their baby, of which, by mutual understanding, they would not speak.

Fawn looked pale under his Florida tan. Rae-Ellen felt guilty about him. He'd courted her so properly, contained his feelings, had striven to please her. And she had turned to the arms of the one man in the world who treated her roughly.

Pete seemed to be having trouble keeping a half-grin off his lips. "Little Rae-Ellen," he chided. "Whoever would have thought it? Mischief, I'd believe, but to shack up?"

"We'll see what your father has to say about this," Papa exclaimed, glaring at Burr.

"He'll say what you're saying, sir."

"Then the two of us—"

"Can't change a thing, sir. No more than Pa could change me from horses. Rae-Ellen and I want to live together, and that's what we're going to do."

"Love," interjected Mama. "What about love?"

"That's for time to show," Burr told her, coolly gentle.

Adah came to Rae-Ellen, pleaded with her to come to the sun room, where they could have privacy.

"It won't change anything," Rae-Ellen said, getting to her feet.

In the sun room, Adah spoke fast, tears streaming. "This will ruin everything between Lance and me," she sobbed. "Can't you see that? Please, please don't do it!"

"You want me to give up my man so you can keep yours?"

"Not that, just marry him, sister! It won't hurt to wear a wedding ring!"

"I don't agree that this will harm you with Lance."

"It's too much to ask, darling! I told him about the blood, and he brushed it aside. Then I finally told him about Pete and he was hurt, but he understood and said he'd be a fool to let that come between us. But this—for my own sister to live with a man she's not married to, openly—!"

"Would you have us hide?"

"All the world would see and gossip! I'd have to release Lance! I could not subject him to such shame!"

"Have faith in Lance, Adah. Be sensible, trust him. He loves you with the kind of love few ever know. He won't accept release, no matter how much you talk. Wait and see. He'll be right on that plane to Texas with the rest of us!"

They rejoined the others. Lance met Adah at the door, led her to a sofa and sat with his arms around her.

Papa had stopped exploding, and Mama was quiet. Papa continued to protest and argue, but in all honesty was forced, when pressed by Rae-Ellen, to admit that she had at least settled on a real man.

"We'll hope," Mama said at last, "that you will be married. We'll work for that, Rae-Ellen. But we won't be enemies over it, because we love you."

When the guests had left and the house had quieted for the night, Rae-Ellen crept to Burr's room, his bed, his arms. After they had made love with fierceness and sweetness, she nestled in his arms.

"I'm proud to bear this child," she said quietly. "*Your* child."

"I'm real proud myself, that I had the sense to pick you to be his ma."

"But you still don't . . . demand . . . marriage."

"Hell, no. It's the woman, the pregnant woman, who usually does that."

"I wouldn't marry you for anything on earth!" she cried, low, so as not to be heard outside the room. "But I'd think a man would insist, that he'd think of his baby's future!"

"He'll be my kid. That's enough! He'll be a Travis!"

"Oh, no he won't! He'll be a Pettigrew!"

"Pettigrew, hell!"

"The baby takes its mother's name in these cases," she said, voice poisonously sweet.

"We'll see. We'll just see about that," he murmured. He kissed her savagely and they were both immediately aroused. When he took her again, it was with a new fierceness and sweetness. Oh, the sweetness!

Rae-Ellen felt ready to swoon, to laugh, to cry! That this man, this raw cowhand, should show any sort of sweetness was truly one of the seven wonders of the world!

45

To the surprise of all but Rae-Ellen, a Learjet landed to pick up the Pettigrew party at the airport for the trip to Texas. Burr merely shrugged.

"This is your father's plane?" Raymond Pettigrew asked stiffly. Every time he spoke to Burr now it was with formal courtesy.

"That's right, sir," Burr said. "Pa kept wanting a Learjet with a pilot and copilot, and what Pa wants, he gets. Most times."

Rae-Ellen suggested that maybe his Pa would want a big jet one of these days. That this plane wouldn't be enough.

"He's got a couple of hedge-hoppers," Burr said. "They ain't big enough to move this whole party, though. Plus all them Christmas packages and the luggage."

"Ostentatious," Rae-Ellen muttered.

Burr heard her remark.

"Not really," he drawled. "This is how we travel in Texas."

"I suppose this is the way you hitched a ride to Durham!"

"That's right. Only I was at the controls."

Suddenly, though she'd taken her pill, she felt queasy. She could feel the blood drain out of her face, and with it, strength. Burr noticed and she saw his mouth turn bullheaded, but in a way she couldn't identify. He helped her carefully up the steps and into the plane.

The interior was rich purple, all seats upholstered in velvet plush. The cabin was paneled in white with touches of gilt and edgings of gilt.

Rae-Ellen swallowed fiercely. Burr's arm tightened around her and she felt better.

Lance remarked on the luxury of the interior as they found seats and began to fasten belts. The others expressed their surprise, but only Pete spoke the word purple.

"It's Pa's favorite color," Burr said offhandedly. "He had the whole plane done over to suit him."

The seats were as comfortable as beds, Rae-Ellen found. Burr sat beside her, their seat double with a movable armrest. He kept his arm around her, drew her against him so that, between the comfort of the seat and the warmth and solidity of his body, she felt like a kitten snuggled for a nap.

Every seat was taken. There were eight in the party. Through the glass in the cockpit door she saw the pilots.

In no time, it seemed, the plane was going down the runway, was lifting, was airborne. Its nose pointed toward the horizon; it hummed, the hum grew into a song, and Rae-Ellen slept, secure in Burr's arms.

Raymond Pettigrew watched them stonily. Not only was he disturbed about this alliance his headstrong daughter was set on, but he was puzzled. The Learjet, the purple decor flaunting richness, tasteless to the point of beauty, Burr's admission that the Star-Bar was sizable, his own knowledge that it was nationally famous, the name Star-Bar connected with the name Travis, ate at him. It was all in his mind somewhere; he'd be about to get hold of it, and then it would slip away. And he wasn't going to ask Burr a damn thing. He'd figure it out, or find it out, on his own.

They put down on the Star-Bar landing field. It was a big field under a summer-hot sun, covered with tarmac, a big hangar at one end. Two small planes, one purple and the other red, stood outside the hangar, and there were mechanics working on them and a couple of extra men tending the hangar itself. There were three vehicles parked—one van and two pickups.

Off from them a bit stood a purple limousine.

Rae-Ellen's stomach tried to spin, righted itself.

A tall, broad man in western garb made of the finest material, came long-legging toward them. The instant Raymond Pettigrew caught sight of that powerful figure, the whole picture sprang into focus.

This was Victor Travis, probably the richest man in the United States. Not only did he own Star-Bar Ranch, but oil wells by the score, and nobody knew how many conglomerates he controlled.

Rae-Ellen stared at Burr's father. He was every bit as tall as Burr, who was six feet one; his tawny hair, when he swept off his ten-gallon hat, was tawny indeed but grizzled—and she knew that Burr's would grizzle the same way—and his eyes were exactly like Burr's except, that on him, they didn't make her mad.

He was Burr duplicated, or Burr was his Pa made again. They could be twins, yet were almost a quarter of a century apart in age.

"Howdy!" he boomed. "They phoned me from the plane that you was fixin' to land! Howdy, and welcome!" He slammed an arm across Burr's shoulders. "Landin' field look the same to you, boy?"

Burr said yes, eyes making a sweep of the field.

Rae-Ellen felt breathless. It was odd to hear anyone call Burr "boy." More surprising yet, instead of going rigid, Burr slammed his own arm around his Pa and they stood like that, father and son. Incredible twins.

After introductions, with Pa Travis booming, Burr seemed to boom also, they all crowded into the limousine which, like the Learjet, was upholstered in purple and gilt. They rolled off the tarmac and onto a graded dirt road.

"All roads on the Star-Bar are dirt," Pa Travis told them. "Only natural way to live. I hate blacktop or concrete, but had to give in as far as the landin' field goes."

"This road gives a smooth ride," Papa said.

"It's part the road, part the car," Burr put in.

His Pa was driving, Adah and Mama in the seat with him, Papa and Rea-Ellen and Fawn in the back seat, Lance and Pete on the jump seats, Burr crouched on the floor behind them. Rae-Ellen's shoe kept nudging accidentally into his foot, and she liked that and wondered if he liked it, too.

She watched out the windows. The road went straight and long, taking them past growths of scrub cedar and mesquite, past yucca and lush winter grass as far as she could see. The vastness overwhelmed her. Far off, on all sides, she could see herds of cattle like moving dots, and wondered how many acres the Star-Bar contained.

The road made a turn to the right, and the car turned with it. Now there were some big, low barnlike sheds, next a double row of bunkhouses and one corral after another. There were a few horses in the corrals, and in one a great bull which didn't look like any bull she'd ever seen, swung his ponderous head to stare at them.

"That's El Toro, my beefalo bull," Pa Travis called back from the wheel. "Half beef, half buffalo. Reckon Burr's told you about the breed."

"He's mentioned it," Papa said. "I'm interested to see what you've done with it so far."

"I'll show you-all around," Pa Travis promised. "Here's the ranch house."

Rae-Ellen watched as the car glided toward the house. It was huge, sprawling, one-storied, and built of redwood and native stone. There was a gallery which ran all the way around the outside, an old-fashioned stone wall at one end with a big iron bell rigged above it.

Pa Travis caught Rae-Ellen gazing at the bell. "Use that when it's chow time for them that's to eat with us, or for any emergency. It can damn well —beggin' your pardon ladies—be heard over half the spread when the wind's right."

Inside, the rooms were vast, wood-paneled and raftered, with big stone fireplaces. Carpeting was purple. The furniture was redwood and soft black leather. A Christmas tree of native cedar was up, almost touching the ceiling in the living room, but had not yet been decorated.

A short, square woman of nearly fifty bustled in, black eyes snapping, her hair, which was black with bands of gray, braided and worn like a crown. She was dressed in Mexican blouse and full, purple-flowered Mexican skirt.

"¡Buenos días!" she cried, arms spread in welcome. She hugged Burr angrily and snapped her eyes at him. "¡Muchacho muy malo to go from casa!" she scolded. Then, of Victor Travis she demanded, "Señor Pa, why you no say me to these people?" She socked her hands onto her ample hips and snapped her eyes at Burr's Pa.

He grinned. Burr grinned.

"Folks, this is Rosita," Pa said. "She's our housekeeper, runs three young Mexican girls ragged, and a couple half-growed Mexican buttons, keepin' this place to suit her. I'll introduce you all, but warn you, don't let her boss you, that's her mission in life, aside from the house, or I should say they're so wound together you can't get one loose from the other."

Rosita acknowledged the introductions, a solemn smile halving her brown face. "What Señor Pa does not say . . . he forgets as he grows old . . ." She snapped her eyes at Pa Travis, who was only two years her senior. "It is that I, Rosita Moralez, am madre to Señor Burr since he wet his diaper. I have raised him!"

She stood proudly, accepting their praise, but only to a point. "¡No more . . . no más!" she decreed. "Bedrooms."

They followed her obediently.

Rae-Ellen and Adah shared a purple-carpeted room. There were no curtains, only wooden jalousies, as in the other rooms, but the bedspreads were orchid, as were the upholstered chairs.

Unpacking, Adah again pleaded with Rae-Ellen to marry Burr.

"Nothing doing," she said shortly.

"But it isn't right to live in sin, darling!"

"Piffle! It's not sin any more, it's honesty! And it hasn't made any difference to Lance, has it?"

"No. He's so wonderful!"

Rae-Ellen embraced her. "There! You see! I'm happy for you Adah, truly happy!"

And she was, yet she was a trace wistful. That Burr, even with a baby coming, wouldn't— But if he were different, he wouldn't be Burr, she wouldn't have this wild, unbelievable love. She'd have nothing.

Doing it his way, she had Burr and their baby.

After lunch, gathered in the living room, the two fathers talked of business. Pa Travis knew a great deal about the tobacco company.

"It's a family business," Papa said. "It came down from my grandfather."

"I know. The Pettigrew power in the South is accepted fact. And the wealth."

Papa laughed. "Speaking of wealth, I happen to know you're ahead of me there. You have at least a million acres on the Star-Bar."

Pa Travis grinned. "Closer to two million, amigo."

"And there's Star-Bar oil. Your wells cover Texas."

"And part of Oklahoma and Louisiana," chuckled Pa Travis. "Think this bullheaded son of mine will take over? No. It's race horses with him. I've got to wait for a grandson!"

Papa went very quiet.

"Money ain't all that important," Burr said. "I reckon we know the wealth represented in this room is fantastic, but I've got something that'll beat it out in nothing flat."

"Let's hear it," urged Pa Travis.

"It's time you knew that Rae-Ellen is my . . . well, fiancée. In a way."

Pa Travis stared, raked his look over Rae-Ellen, grinned. He clumped across the room and kissed her on the lips, smacking loudly. Then he clumped back to his chair, talking.

"We'll have the weddin' day after tomorrow," he planned. "Christmas Day. Get a special license." He veered from his chair, paced. "I'll deed you over that whole south spread, half-million acres, and build stables, cottages for the help you'll need, and any kind of house Rae-Ellen wants. For a weddin' gift, I'll buy you a start of the finest race horse flesh that lives. Why didn't I see it before? The Star-Bar will be as famous for race horses as for beefalo and oil!"

Rae-Ellen watched Burr.

He had that bullheaded look.

So she stood up to Pa Travis. "It can't be that way, sir. Thank you, but no."

He spun on his boot heel, stared at her, his own strong, bullheaded mouth agape. "You loco, girl? To turn down a weddin' gift such as that, to say nothin' of what your own Pa'll give you?"

"There's not going to be a wedding, sir. Or a

marriage. Burr and I are just going to live together. Wherever he wants to live. It makes no difference to me. Any place he can get a job."

"He has a job now," Papa said grimly.

"Hells bells and damnation!" bellowed Pa Travis. "There'll be no shack-up here or anywhere! Not with my boy!"

"I ain't a boy!" Burr bellowed back.

They turned on each other, meeting in the middle of the floor. They looked like two great, maddened bulls ready to fight to the death.

Papa sprang up, got between them. "That'll solve nothing," he said. "I've been trying to adjust to their idea, but it's no good! They have to be brought to their senses!"

"Mule-headed, the boy's mule-headed!" roared Pa Travis. "He ought to breed mules, it'd come more natural!"

"Between us," Papa said angrily, "we've power and money enough to put a stop to this insanity!"

"You're damned right we got it! We can see to it that Burr don't never get any job and if he does get one, we can have him fired! Let them get hungry enough, and they'll marry so fast you can't see 'em for the dust!"

"No!" yelled Papa. "I'll throw Rae-Ellen into a convent! That'll keep them apart!"

"Those days are gone, Papa," Rae-Ellen retorted, herself having to shout to be heard above their continued yelling. "You can't put me into a convent! I'm too old for one thing, and I'd burn it down to get out, for another!"

She was aware of the stricken looks on Mama and Adah, of the shock on Lance. Fawn and Pete, not being of the family, held their peace.

"Knock their heads together, that's what we ought to do!" shouted Pa Travis. "Split 'em open!"

"Violence isn't the answer!" Papa shouted.

"¡Dios!" Pa Travis whispered, but the whisper was so loud it seemed he was shouting. "What if they have a baby?"

"My grandson!" yelled Papa. "For my tobacco! He has to be legitimate!"

"Your grandson, hell!" bawled Pa Travis. "My grandson, for the Star-Bar! Hell's bells, I'll take him whether he's legitimate or not!"

By bedtime only one thing had been resolved.

Rae-Ellen and Burr maintained a solid front. They refused to be married. They were going to live together.

46

Rosita, who had heard everything, cornered Burr and Rae-Ellen in the kitchen next morning. She put her hands on her hips as she talked; she waved her hands as she talked; she screamed in Spanish and snapped her eyes. She gave them orders to marry tomorrow.

When they refused, she swore in Spanish, frightening the young Mexican maids so that they dropped dishes and spilled milk and cornmeal. And then she berated them.

Finally she expelled Rae-Ellen and Burr from the kitchen, ordering them to get the other young folks and trim the Christmas tree. "¡Do something bueno!" she cried. "¡To you Rosita speaks no more until you are of the marriage!"

They fled.

Adah and Lance were beginning on the tree.

"Where's Pa and the others?" Burr asked.

"They left after breakfast to see the ranch," Lance said. "Both your fathers are quiet, but very angry."

"So is Rosita," Burr grinned. "She threw us out of the kitchen without a bite to eat."

"Our parents are stalemated," Adah said. A tiny smile flickered at her lips. "They simply can't handle you."

"Reckon not," grunted Burr. "We're grown."

The four of them worked on the tree, chatting in a stilted manner. Adah slipped into the kitchen and came back with a big breakfast tray.

"Rosita fixed it," she smiled, "with much banging and Spanish. Which, I suppose, it is as well I don't understand."

They went outside now and then, wandered around the grounds. Before noon, while the sight-seeing party was still absent, Rae-Ellen found that the sun, which an hour ago had been brassy hot and made her sweat, had vanished. Now she felt wind blow in and smelled it, and now leaves were swirling along the ground, the sky was gray overhead and an ugly, bruised blue in the north.

"Take a good look at that," Burr told them.

"It's certainly cloudy," Lance remarked.

"It's the start of a norther."

"What is a norther?" Adah asked.

"It's a killer storm that whistles down out of a hot, blazing sky . . . that's the blue norther . . . and it drops the thermometer forty degrees in forty minutes, past believing, it's so cold." He studied the bruised sky. "Looks like we're in for it."

"What will it do?" asked Rae-Ellen.

"It's got icy winds that it pushes through towns and over plains, beats the herds that bunch together and shiver, like frozen whips. And the shacks some of the Mexicans live in, the wind just spears through and into the hides of the Mexicans."

"Does it snow, actually snow in Texas?" marveled Adah.

"Sometimes."

The wind gusted, cold and piercing, and on it rode hard, prickling drops of hail. They stung Rae-Ellen's cheeks. The wind gusted again, and Burr took them back into the house.

He went around lighting the ready-laid logs in the fireplaces, Rae-Ellen trailing. In the dining room they came face to face with Rosita, who was also lighting fires. She threw up her chin, sniffed, flounced out.

"We're still in disgrace," Burr said, and grinned. "She'll come 'round. All of them will."

Rae-Ellen said nothing, having her doubts and not wanting to get into an argument. She shuddered inwardly at what would be said if any of them found out about the baby. Rosita was the dangerous one. Rosita could probably just study her and know she was pregnant. She'd heard of women who could do that. Rae-Ellen determined to stay out of Rosita's way.

The sightseeing party was literally blown into the house on a blast of rain. Pa Travis slammed the door and started taking off his wet coat in the stone-floored foyer, as did the others.

"Texas is showin' off for you," he boomed. "She's throwin' us a wet norther. That means you best stay inside, unless you want to freeze. It's down to

forty now. And it was eighty while we was drivin'
over the spread."

Rosita appeared and helped Marguerite into a
sweater. She urged her to a chair beside the fire,
then returned to the foyer to pass out sweaters to
the men.

"Surely the norther can't be worse than a bad
hurricane," Papa said.

"Reckon so, in it's way," Pa Travis said. "A
norther, be it blue—that's with snow—or wet—that's
with rain—is bad news. My herds are better protected than most. You saw them shacks and hayricks
scattered around."

"It seemed fantastic, when you pointed them
out," Mama said, "that the cattle would need the
protection. It was so hot then. The sun was melting,
and there wasn't even a breeze."

"Northers are sudden and fierce. I feel easy
enough about my cattle. They'll go to what shelter
there is. This norther'll likely blow all night and all
day tomorrow and most of the next night. Probably
get down to twenty, even lower."

Rosita moved to stand in front of Pa Travis,
hands on hips. "The tree. *No tengo* holly. *No tengo*
mistletoe."

"So you ain't got holly or mistletoe. Do without.
No sense trompin' through the norther."

Rosita's hands dug into her waistline. "We want
the wedding, no, Señor?" she demanded, eyes snapping.

"Damn right we do!"

"For this wedding, Señor, everything is needed.
With the mistletoe comes the kiss, and with the
kiss . . ." She took her hands off her hips, threw them
apart dramatically.

477

"I'll go after them this afternoon," volunteered Pete. "Rosita is right. They're needed."

Burr shot a mocking glance at Pete, turned back to the tree. He was standing on a ladder, and Rae-Ellen was selecting ornaments from a box and handing them up to him. On the other side of the tree, Lance and Adah were similarly occupied.

"I'll go with Pete," Fawn said. "We were out in Hurricane Esmerelda. We can brave a norther. We'll stay as long as it takes."

Thus, after lunch, Pete and Fawn, wrapped against the icy rain, wearing boots, set forth in a ranch Buick to buy holly and mistletoe. Pa Travis advised them to go to Travis Forks, the best town between Fort Worth and Abilene for shopping.

They finished the tree quickly, Burr putting a big, lopsided tinfoil star at the top.

"Where did that come from?" Rae-Ellen asked.

"Burr made it when he was just a button," snorted Pa Travis from the fireplace, where he, Raymond and Marguerite were sitting. "Had more sense in them days than he's got now, that's for sure."

Rae-Ellen gazed up at that little-boy star tenderly. Next year their own little baby must have that star. Surely Pa Travis wouldn't say no to a little baby who didn't even know it was Christmas.

In late afternoon Fawn and Pete returned with the holly and mistletoe. Their rain togs were wet and their boots muddy. These they surrendered to a fast-talking Rosita, as well as the holly and mistletoe, which she placed about, fastening mistletoe in the archway between living room and dining room so it would be impossible to pass from one to the other and avoid it.

Consequently, there was much kissing despite the underlying stiffness. Pa Travis kissed Mama and Rosita and Rae-Ellen. Papa kissed them, as did Burr. Lance and Fawn and Pete kissed them, laughing. Adah was kissed frequently. This made supper more pleasant than it might otherwise have been. Afterward, Pa Travis turned off the lights, leaving only the tree lights, which winked on and off. They made conversation, telling of other Christmases.

Rae-Ellen spoke when she must, listened to rain slamming the house, shivered when Pa Travis darted outside and back again, announcing that the thermometer now stood at eighteen. By the tree lights she watched rain cover the windows, stream away, cover them again.

Burr kissed her every time she passed under the mistletoe, she reflected, but that was as far as their lovemaking could go while they were at the ranch. They couldn't steal to meet each other, not with Rae-Ellen sharing a room with Adah, and Burr sharing his room with Lance, and certainly not with Rosita ever-present. They couldn't disregard that Pa Travis was on the watch, fiercely mad. And so was Papa, now that the idea of a grandson had entered the picture.

When the others settled down, lights on again, to play backgammon, Mama opting to settle under a lamp with some needlework, Burr drew Rae-Ellen into the kitchen.

Miraculously, there was no Rosita.

Rae-Ellen's quick glance around made Burr grin. "She's gone to her rooms, down the dogtrot. She's got two rooms. Wish we had 'em."

His taking it for granted that she was all that

479

anxious to jump into bed with him, irritated her. "Can't you do without for one night?" she demanded.

"Three nights, maybe four. I don't know how long you can hold out, now that there's been a pattern established."

"You certainly are egotistical!" she snapped.

"That's a new one. What's *it* based on?"

"Good, solid fact, that's what! When you asked me, that time, if I'd marry you if you were rich and had family, and I said yes, then you gave me the news that *you* wouldn't marry *me*, because you had your head set to be wanted for yourself, no matter what kind of person you were! I never heard of such egotism!"

"And now," he said, bullmouthed, "I'd not marry you if you begged, because of what you said that time. That you would—if I was rich."

"And why not? Just exactly why not?"

"Because you put yourself on record as holding money to be the most important thing. And after money, the kind of family a man springs out of."

"Those things are important, you know that!"

"If I didn't, you sure have taught them to me. I say it's the man that counts, not them other things!"

"Oh . . . ! I didn't mean money so much! I meant family! It's important whether a man comes from decent people or a bunch of . . . of . . ."

"Bums. Go on. Say it."

"You said it, I didn't!"

"So money ain't important to you?"

"If it were, I wouldn't live on what you make as a horse trainer! Now, try to get out of that with your Texas tongue!"

480

"Reckon you got something there. Should set your mind at rest."

"In just what way?" she demanded, suspicious. There was no telling what he would say—or do—next.

"I only meant now you know that my son, when he's born, can hold up his head with the best."

"It may be a daughter!"

"It'll be a son."

"Babies don't come with guarantees as to sex!"

"The firstborn of every Travis generation is a boy."

"The Pettigrews run to girls! My father was the only boy in his family!"

"Ranch blood's stronger than farm blood."

She glared, momentarily speechless.

"I suppose you've already got him named!"

"Sure. Victor Travis. For my Pa."

"His name, if he's a boy, will be Raymond Pettigrew!"

"He's already a Travis. It's settled."

"I don't have to live with you, think that over!"

"You've said you would. A Pettigrew can't go back on his word."

"It isn't as if I'd promised to love, honor, and obey!"

"You draggin' the word love into this situation now?" he asked, and his eyes had a stubbornness and at the same time an eagerness in them she couldn't go on meeting. She looked away, firmed her jaw, muttered, "The word love hasn't been the question in the past. I don't see where it applies now."

"It don't. We're going to live. together. Love is what gets dragged into the marriage ceremony. And it don't mean much. That's where we're smart."

"What difference does it make?" she heard herself say. "We don't have to consider money. We're both so rich, or our fathers are, that it's indecent! Also, our families match! We can marry or not, as we please!"

"That's the beauty of our decision," he said, doggedly sticking to having everything his own way, not going to the trouble to ask if she might change her mind. "We can live together, free and bold. We'll raise our kid, and we won't push at him like our Pa pushed at us. He can plan his own life, like we're doing ours."

"I hate you!" she whispered suddenly. "I hate the ground you walk on! It's all off! I'll never live with you, never!"

She went running from the kitchen and he didn't even come after her.

She raced to her room, struggled into a coat. She couldn't stay inside the same house with him another minute! Him and his damn beautiful decision!

47

Rae-Ellen slipped past the living room without being seen. Burr wasn't in there. Everyone playing backgammon was intent on the game; Mama was dozing in her chair.

She eased open the coat closet, fished out a pair of boots, a dry slicker and hat, then noiselessly opened the outer door and stole through, into the gallery.

The cold struck right through her coat. Her fingers iced as she tugged the boots on. The rain flung itself across the gallery, its frigid spray wetting her hands. After the boots were on, she fumbled into the slicker and fastened it. The sleeves were too long, and she folded them back, the wet wind making her fingers into sticks, numbing her face. She thought the temperature must have gone below eighteen, that surely it had dipped to zero.

She flipped her hair to the top of her head, yanked the rainhat over it, and she was ready. Cold as she already was, the norther had not yet cooled her rage at Burr. But walking in the freezing rain was bound to clear her mind, to enable her to think.

She'd head for the bunkhouses, see if she could find one that was unoccupied. She needed a refuge to plan. She had to work out some way to get a job, support herself, have her baby, support it —and provide more than mere survival. She'd give her baby a decent life, and she'd do it alone!

She went down the gallery steps, trying not to clump in the boots. Then, turned sidewise to the slanting rain, she slogged in the direction of the bunkhouses. If she didn't find one empty, she'd go into a stable.

Head down, she trudged. Here was a stand of cedar, and she edged along it, thinking to win shelter, but rain ran off the trees and down the collar of both her slicker and coat, wetting her dress.

Out of the darkness, hands grabbed her, pulling her backward. She slid, and almost landed in the mud. Before she could even try to set her heels, she was yanked to her feet, and a gunny sack came down over her head.

She tried to struggle, but slipped and fell into a pair of hard, ungiving arms. She tried again, but the arms clenched and someone else, the one who had put the sack over her head, bound it on. The rope or strap he used came across her mouth, pressing the rough sacking onto her tongue, gagging her.

She tried to scream, couldn't, berated herself for not screaming earlier. But there hadn't been time. And now they silently bound her arms to her sides.

She heard their feet squish the mud. She heard their heavy breathing, but they didn't speak. She twisted with the wild idea of running, even blindfolded and with arms tied, but they lifted her. Rain flowed over her head, as they silently carried her. She tasted the residue of dry oats. She listened to their walking, to the rain, waited for voices, but there was nothing.

They stopped. A car door opened, and she was tossed inside. She hit a wooden floor, hurting her hip, and she knew she must be in a van. There was no rain in here—it was outside, pelting and swathing the vehicle. The door closed quietly.

She lay still, listening hard. She could hear nothing but the rain on the van.

Slowly, the van started to move. It made no turn, but went straight ahead, so they must have been ready and waiting. And Rae-Ellen, like a fool, had walked right into their clutches—whoever they were and whatever they wanted.

How could they have known she'd quarrel with Burr and run out into the storm to get away from him? Why would they grab her, throw her into this van, take her away? Burr, the thought flashed. To bring me to my senses? But, no. He'd been inside when she left. He hadn't been outside, lying in wait.

Kidnappers! Of course. The thought slammed into her.

All the money represented at the Star-Bar. It didn't mean she was the chosen victim. Kidnappers, in this case, would grab the first Travis or Pettigrew or even one of the guests, they could get their hands on. Just so they got a hostage. Just so they could collect ransom.

Thinking thus, Rae-Ellen began to get angry.

She tried to work her arms, but the binding was so tight it cut. She kept trying, but all she accomplished was to roll from one side of the van to the other, coming up hard against wood.

She tried to work the gag out, but the rope was so tight she couldn't move her tongue. In fact, it was almost impossible to breathe. The wet sacking pushed against her nostrils when she inhaled, clung, so that she had to breathe out hard, through her mouth.

On they went, forever on.

Once the van skidded, then went on. The rain was louder now, heavier. Time dragged. She wondered if the time actually was so long, whether it was her state of shock that made it seem endless.

There was a jolt. The van turned, and jolted again before it rolled on. She wondered, in alarm, if the jolting would harm her baby.

Alarm flared into terror.

Now she simply had to get out of this. For the baby. For his life. Sometime the kidnappers would have to stop. Sometime they'd have to get her out of the van, untie her.

When they did, she'd be ready.

The instant that sack came off her head, the split second her arms were no longer bound, she'd become a fighting fury. She'd kill them both.

She'd get her baby out of this, get him back to

safety, back to Burr. Oh, if only she hadn't fought with Burr, no matter how aggravating he was, this would never have happened! She'd let her temper fly one time too many.

Burr, her mind screamed, Burr . . . Burr!

The van stopped.

She stiffened, listened. Two doors opened, closed. Quietly. Footsteps sounded wetly.

They were coming, ah, they were coming!

She waited, poised within her shackles.

The van door opened. Cold rain swept through. Hands grabbed her, dragged her out, stood her on sodden grass. She thought to run, thought better of it, and waited, senses tingling.

One of them held her from behind, fingers digging in. The other one loosened the binding that held the sack and gagged her. He snatched it off and threw it into the van.

She screamed, but the sound was choked, filled with oat dust. She coughed. She screamed again, and even as she did, saw, unbelieving, who the man before her was, in the headlights.

Before she could scream the third time, he struck her in the mouth. She tasted blood.

"*Fawn!*" she croaked.

His hand was up for another blow. "Don't try it again," he threatened. "Or you'll get more of the same. We're too far away; they can't hear you. But somebody else might."

"Yes," agreed another voice, and Pete Battle stepped into the light. All the beachboy handsomeness, all the smiling friendliness, was gone. And Fawn—there was no more of the considerate suitor in him, only deliberate, cold evil.

487

"Are you out of your minds?" she cried. "Why are you doing this?"

"It's very simple," Fawn said. "We tried. I courted you, asked you again to marry me, but you preferred to live in sin with Travis."

"And I courted Adah," Pete said. "And she's going to marry Buford."

"But those things happen!"

"Not to us, they don't," Fawn said. "Since we've failed to tap the Pettigrew fortune through marriage, we'll now collect ransom. Two million dollars."

"You'll be caught! You'll—"

"No. We've laid our plans cleverly. You made it easy for us. We thought we'd have to devise a ruse to get you outside. Instead, you walked right into our arms."

Rae-Ellen stared at them in numb, speechless horror. Betrayers, they were betrayers! She had trusted them as family friends for years. She had lain in the arms of both men. Each had made love to her, had expressed affection, admiration, respect. Now they had turned villainous, evil, implacable. Her brain whirled. Not this!

It was impossible, but it was happening. Dimly, she recognized that it was her own fault, that she should never have slept with them, never have roused their hopes, their ambitions. She realized, like a knife slashing her heart, that she'd never see Burr again.

Unless she fought them, outwitted them, reasoned with them—anything! She seized on the most obvious fact.

"You can't collect that ransom!" she cried. "My father doesn't have two million in cash!"

"But old man Travis can get it," Fawn said coldly. "You're the girl he wants his son to marry. He'll pay. And Pete and I will be set for life. Now do everything we tell you and you won't get hurt."

48

They forced her, struggling, across matted, slippery grass. One of them gripped her with both hands. The other held her arm with one hand and sprayed the rays of a powerful flashlight with the other. She opened her mouth to let out a long, loud scream, but the one who held the flashlight cracked her across the mouth with it. She felt the spurt of blood, tasted salt.

"Try that again," snarled a voice which she barely recognized as Pete's, "and you'll get it across the eyes, too. We told you—you can't be heard."

She could be heard if Burr had followed, if he was searching for her. If he'd given the alarm and the others were out searching too. They could hear, if they were in the vicinity.

She drew a quick, deep breath, screamed.

The flashlight struck her across the eyes and up onto her forehead. Her whole face went numb, and she could scarely see.

"Better gag her again," Pete said. "Be on the safe side."

"We're safe," Fawn replied. "I want her tongue loose. Want her to talk, to plead and grovel."

They propelled her over slick grass, past trees, into a stand of cedar and pine. She tried to hold back, to set her heels, but they slipped and the strength of the men moved her with comparative ease deep into timber.

Freezing rain fell here, too, through branch and leaf and needle, running off her slicker and into her boot tops, Her feet were wet, and her hair was plastered to her head, water running off it over her face and down the collars of both coats, wetting the clothes beneath.

She was still twisting and fighting when they came to a stop. Fawn turned her roughly so that she faced a spot on which Pete shone the light, moving it so that the whole length and width and depth was revealed. There was some water in the bottom; the rain danced on the water, making dots and dimples.

She sucked in her breath. This was a grave! She was standing, captive, on the lip of a ready-dug grave! Dirt mounded its length on the far side, waiting dirt.

Breath gone, unable now to scream, she watched in fascination as Pete played the light back and forth. At one corner of the grave leaned an iron pipe about two inches around, and she wondered, dully, about it.

"Now," Fawn boasted, "you see how clever we

have been. When we went for mistletoe, we located this spot and dug the grave. We'd secretly got shovels from the toolhouse and put them in the trunk of the Buick. After we dug this, we stood in the rain until it washed the mud off our slickers, off the shovels, then put them back into the trunk and went on to town. When we got back, we put the shovels away, dried them with rags, spread the rags to dry the way we found them, and came back inside, with the mistletoe and holly."

"You *villains!*" breathed Rae-Ellen.

Pete laughed, but there was none of the old-time sunniness to him. He moved the light back and forth again. "Your grave, Madam," he said in an evil, teasing way. "Few people get to see their own graves!"

"Do you actually believe," she cried, voice thin and near-breaking, "that Papa and Mr. Travis will give you two million dollars?"

"To get you back. Certainly."

"Alive, maybe . . . dead, never!"

They laughed, a horrible, mirthless laugh.

"I admit," Fawn said, "that those old boys are too wily to hand out two million without assurance they'll get you back alive."

"So! You see!"

"Ah, but we've provided for that," Fawn said. "Draw the light the length of her grave, Pete. Slowly."

The beam moved, showing the water in the bottom, the dirt sides, the soil blackened by rain.

"See that pipe at the corner?" Fawn continued. "See how big it is, how generous? It will reach above the top of the grave after it's filled. You'll be alive. If you're clever—and lucky—you can breathe through the pipe. If you lose your head, that will be your responsibility, not ours."

"You're mad!"

"It can be done, has been done."

"But that girl was buried in a box! She—"

"Had a better chance, true," Fawn admitted. "This is the best we can do. It's a matter of time, understand."

"Papa still can't pay fast enough."

"Old man Travis will. He'll do anything for that lout of a Burr."

"I don't see how! I—"

"If a phone call promises—note I say promises —to direct him to you *after* the ransom is paid, he'll pay."

"There won't be time! All that money to be got in cash!"

"Unmarked bills."

"And the banks closed for Christmas!"

"Any bank will open up for Travis."

"But it still takes time to count! And with just the pipe—"

"The phone call will stress time."

"They'll find out who you are! You'll never get away with it!"

They laughed, an evil, cold laugh.

She gave a sudden, twisting lunge. Pete dropped the flashlight when he grabbed her and it lay lighting the grave dimly, and the wet grass which rimmed it, and even the waiting mound of earth.

Bound with rope, she fought, screaming. Their hands gripped her and she twisted and kicked. Kicked and slipped, and they had to lift her to her feet. Fawn gave her a blow on the face as she screamed again. Still she fought, frantically, for her life and her child's. Burr!

Eventually they stood in a tight clump, Fawn holding her, Pete stooping to retrieve the flashlight. Rae-Ellen began to talk again, desperately trying to sway them, to convince them to let her go.

"Let me walk back to the house," she begged. "I'll keep quiet, I'll not tell! I give you my word, on the Bible!"

They laughed again.

"You'll not escape!" she cried. "The moment you're missed, they'll know who did it!"

"We have no need to run," Fawn said, biting out the words. "This grave is cleverly hidden. We'll collect the ransom from one of those milk cans you see standing at the crossroads to be picked up by dairies. The place we've settled on is out in the open—no sheriff's posse, no ranch hand, can spy without our seeing him, in which case we'd simply drive on. We have the use of the Buick, and we'll be out searching. Like the others. So, we collect the ransom."

"You have no place to hide it!"

"In our room. Who will suspect us?"

"You can't hide two million! Not in a milk can!"

"We've spare suitcases we brought Christmas presents in. We'll use those."

"And take them back to Durham," Pete added. "In the Learjet!"

"You'll not get away with it!" Rae-Ellen cried. But she wasn't so certain. She wasn't certain at all.

"Yes, we will," Fawn said. "We'll stay on in

our positions at the company, avoid any hint of change. We'll live within our salaries as long as we choose. With you dead in this grave."

"And if it's found?"

"So? It won't point to us."

"We've wasted enough time," Pete said. "Let's untie her so she can hold the pipe."

Fawn laughed that awful laugh. "That's right! Go through the motions of giving her a chance!"

She stood until they'd loosened the rope. Then, before Fawn, who held the rope, could put it aside, she broke into a stumbling run.

They jerked her back so hard her neck made a snapping sound and her teeth came together on her tongue. This time she not only tasted salt, but swallowed it. She lifted her numb arms and tried to fight.

They wrestled her into the grave; she was screaming. They slapped her brutally, and she fought until she had no control of her arms, no breath remaining to scream.

They stood in the grave, all three of them, weaving back and forth in the bit of water there. They bore her down, cracking her across the knees, when she brought them up, thrust the pipe into her flailing left hand.

Instantly, she tried to slam it on the head nearest her. He swore, and she thought it was Pete, and he took the blow, not on the head, but on the shoulder. His fist crunched into her head, beside her eyes, and she saw sparkles of red, blue, green. Of a sudden, nothing about her—hands, feet, knees—would move.

She felt one of them ramming the pipe into her

hand again. Instinctively she gripped it, held to it, sensing, in her dazed and battered state, that it was her lifeline.

She was aware of motion, knew they were climbing out. She was lying on her back in icy water, holding the pipe. These things she knew.

She was aware of sound—could it be shovel biting into damp, mounded earth—and she felt something strike, thudding, onto her slicker at the waist, felt particles of dirt fly onto her face. They were filling the grave, she realized in a far-off, benumbed way. She tried to move, to get out of this deadly hole, but she couldn't move. She could only lie inert, clutching the pipe.

"Think she needs another blow?" she heard Pete ask.

"She's nearly out now," Fawn said. "The idea is to bury her alive, to know we didn't actually murder her, because we're letting her use that pipe and tell her Pa, when we call, that she'll be turned loose after we collect the ransom."

"I don't know about that," Pete quibbled.

"You're not turning chicken?"

"Not me! Shovel faster! Let's get this part done!"

She got a lungful of air. "Burr!" she shrieked, but even to her own ears, the sound was a whisper only. "Burr . . . Burr is coming . . . Burr will . . ." She whispered on.

Shovelful after shovelful came onto her. The soil grew heavy, pressed her into the water, pushed her against the ground beneath the water. She smelled dirt, wet, rainy dirt.

And then a shovelful hit her square in the face.

She turned her head, eyes closing in reflex, felt dirt slide wetly, much of it remaining on her face.

She gripped the pipe, got it over her mouth, opened wide, taking both pipe and dirt. It stretched her mouth, hurting, but when she sucked in, air blessed air, flowed into her.

Dirt landed on her head, some jumping to her face. She tried again to spring out of the grave, again found she couldn't move. Now, in addition to the numbness, there was the growing weight of grave-fill. More of it came onto her shoulders and head.

She kept her eyes shut, but accidentally tried to breathe through her nose, clogged it, sucked greedily at her pipe. The weight on her grew ever heavier. Sounds were muted now. She could no longer hear dirt hit dirt.

There came a pounding vibration. They must be leveling the top, pounding it flat with the backs of their shovels. Then, being the scheming devils they were, they'd disguise the grave with brush, make it look like any wild spot.

She gripped her link with life, the pipe through which she sucked air. She shrieked, within herself, that Burr was really coming, that he would get to her in time.

There was only silence now. But is there sound, when you're buried? Dimly, as from miles away, she heard the van start up, recede.

Desperately, she tightened her mouth around the pipe and sucked in air, sucked in life.

49

Abandoned, sucking in air, holding it in her lungs, letting it out slowly, sucking again, she fought the daze and the numbness. She had to get out of this grave, had to get her baby out, protect his precious, unborn life, win his right to be born, to grow to manhood.

To be like his father. Like Burr.

She'd read, once, of a murder case in which a hunter spied a hand extending out of the ground when he was stalking a deer. He'd dug with his bare hands and rescued a woman who had been buried alive.

She would get a hand out. Her chance was now, before the dirt packed down. When she got her hand free, then she'd tear at the dirt, dig herself out of her own grave. Already the soil was heavy on her, bearing her down, grinding her against the bottom.

She pushed her benumbed mind, forced it to reason. All she had to work with was the pipe for air, her right hand for digging upward, and her stubbornness to keep her at it.

She took a deep, deep breath, held it. If only she could open her eyes! But what good would that do? Even if they didn't fill with dirt, she'd be able to see nothing in the utter blackness.

She moved the fingers of her right hand, edging them up. The soil was loose. She made a tiny bit of headway. It was then panic almost took her. The hand the hunter had seen atop the ground, now she remembered! That woman had been left in a shallow grave. If this one was six feet deep, even if she worked her hand up so that it stretched straight from the shoulder, she'd never reach the top!

Doggedly, because it was all she could do, she kept working her fingers, digging upward. They moved, oh, thank God, they moved! She held her breath, working, aching to use both hands, not daring, for there was the pipe to hold.

Bit by bit she let out her air. She worked her hand and it crept upward, not an inch at a time, but an almost imperceptible amount. She sucked her lungs full of air again, dug her fingers upward, the muscles from shoulder to fingertips as near like iron as she could make them, separating the particles of soil.

Surely she was making progress, oh, please God, she was!

There was no time for prayer, but her whole being was a prayer.

If she got her hand near the top, she could try

punching with her fist. That might break through the last layer and, with even a small opening, she would tear and scoop, claw the earth away as she would a heavy, smothering blanket, get an opening through which to breathe, have two hands with which to dig free.

Even if the grave was six feet under, she'd do it. She'd make that hole. She'd get out, shriek so the sound would carry and help would come. And if it didn't come, she'd get out of the grave, get into blessed, freezing rain and go running back to the ranch house.

The pipe moved, and she had to turn her head a bit more to get air. This motion pulled her right hand downward. She lost the possible inch or two which she had gained.

The dirt was heavier now. She wondered if its weight would break her bones.

This time, she sucked at the pipe three times, trying to fill her blood with oxygen. The air she pulled in was heavy with wetness, sweet with life.

She resumed the upward digging. Slowly she worked, methodically, holding her breath, letting it out by degrees. Slowly she probed, felt dirt slide down her wrist and up her arm. Her heart jumped. For the dirt to slide, meant she'd made some progress!

Interminably, she breathed, held breath, probed. She wondered if she really heard rain drumming above her. And if she could hear rain, did that mean she was less than six feet under? She thought back, to how deep the grave had looked, how far up it had reached on Fawn and Pete, and feared that she did have six feet with which to cope.

On she worked, sucked air, held it, let it out in

puffs now. Oh, why hadn't she married Burr when maybe she could have? She loved him so. Wild and crazy or not, that didn't matter. She loved him and that was the way she loved him, wild and crazy, and it had been perfect and she'd not had the sense to know, until now, that it was perfect.

She loved him because he was big and rugged, loved him because he was homely. He was a real man, sprung from the roots of Texas. He was an earth-man, streaked and saturated with the goodness and glory of the land. He was fine and wonderful, and she was going to get herself and their baby back to him and tell him so! Her love entered the prayer which her body had become, and was a part of it.

On she probed, breathed, rested, probed.

50

The backgammon players were hard at their games. Fawn and Pete came into the room carrying a tray which held coffee pot and accouterments. Pete carried another tray laden with a cake, plates, forks and cake knife.

"Hey, there!" Pa Travis boomed. "Wondered about you two! Thought you'd got tired of playing."

The two young men set their trays on tables.

"We thought refreshments would be welcome," Fawn smiled, "so we ventured into Rosita's kitchen. We didn't get caught."

Pa laughed. "Rosita don't let nobody meddle in her kitchen. She'll talk a lot of Spanish come mornin' about her cake, but she'll be proud we got into it."

Marguerite glanced about. "Where is Rae-Ellen?" she asked Burr. "I thought you were together.

Then, when she didn't come back with you, I decided she'd gone to her room."

"That's what I figure, ma'am."

"Adah." Mama said, frowning a bit. "Why don't you go see? She might be ill—"

"She ain't sick, ma'am," Burr said. "She's mad."

"Mad?" repeated Mama.

"At me. Fightin' mad. She took off. I don't reckon she wants to be around me."

"I'll go, just the same," Adah said. "Maybe I can talk her into coming for coffee."

She slipped away.

"What'd you fight about?" Pa Travis demanded of Burr.

"That don't concern you, Pa," Burr growled.

Pa grunted, mad himself.

What the hell had he and Rae-Ellen fought about, come right down to it, Burr thought. Nothing. They'd fought because they'd established a pattern of fighting in the beginning, and now it was a habit. Maybe it was even some cockeyed way they had of making love. He decided that when she came into the room for coffee, he'd act decent, not apologize, nothing drastic, but let her see he was ready to let bygones be bygones.

It was then that Adah came running into the room. Adah, the perfect lady, running.

"She isn't there!" Adah cried, voice unsteady.

"Hold on, now," said Pa Travis, taking charge. "This is a big house. And we've got a wet norther blowing. She's somewhere's in the house, bound to be."

"I'll take a look," Burr announced, uncertain whether to be sore or not. Here he'd been ready to get back on a solid basis, and she pulled a disappearing act. It wasn't like her, though, to hide deliberately, try to scare him. That wasn't her style. There was nothing sneaky about her. Whatever she had on her mind, she came right out with it.

He strode from room to room, eyebrows on his nose. The others were searching, too. She wasn't in any of the rooms and he knew, even as he went through the motions, that she wasn't going to be in them, either.

He didn't think she'd gone into the norther, not in the dark. She'd been mad, but she had basic sense. That was one reason it was so easy to fight with her. Her mind was quick, and always lit on its feet.

Rosita. She might have gone to Rosita's rooms. No logical reason why, except they were both scrappers, and maybe kindred spirits, and she'd figure that was as far from him as she could get.

She wasn't in Rosita's rooms.

They searched again, calling, looked into every cubbyhole. And then they searched still again, a Spanish-screaming Rosita positive that they hadn't been thorough, that, just follow her, she knew every inch of this casa.

At the end, they met in the living room, mystified and alarmed.

It was Burr who thought of the bunkhouses. "She was sore at me, that's for sure," he speculated. "She ain't in the house. She's grabbed her wraps and made for somewhere else, and the bunkhouses is my guess. There's one that ain't in use."

"We'll look there next, and if she ain't there, we'll look at all the bunkhouses, all the outbuildings," Pa said, all but falling over Rosita, who was heading for the foyer closet.

The men got into their gear fast—Pa Travis, Burr, Raymond Pettigrew, Lance and Fawn and Pete. When Marguerite reached for a coat, Rosita wouldn't let her have it.

"No, Señora . . . stay here!" she ordered, black eyes snapping. "I will keep the coffee hot for when they bring the señorita back into the house, and you, her madre, will be waiting to comfort her and to scold her for making the so great upset with her temper!"

"Yes, Marguerite," Raymond agreed. "Your place is here."

The outer door opened and the party hurried through. The blast of cold rain reached across the foyer and into the living room. The flames in the fireplace flattened, sputtered, stood erect, blazed.

Marguerite turned forlornly to Rosita, who was lifting the coffee tray. "Isn't there something I can do?" she asked. "I feel so lost . . . useless."

"The madre is never useless," declared Rosita, her eyes leaving off their snapping and filling with sympathy. "The madre waits with the open arms, and with the scolding tongue. As now. When she runs into the storm and makes the big fright in every corazón, every heart."

The black eyes met the powder blue in understanding and liking. Marguerite murmured, "You speak wisely, Rosita. My daughter is impulsive. She does behave in an unexpected manner at times. But this—when she's a guest and with such a severe storm—she'd know we'd worry, and she'd never deliberately cause that."

After Rosita was gone, claiming she knew how to keep coffee both hot and fresh, Marguerite moved about the vast living room. She stopped at a window

505

now and again, cupping her hands, trying to peer into the rainy blackness.

She sat down, picked up her needlework, laid it aside. She wandered the room again, looking at the games in progress on the backgammon boards, hardly seeing them.

No matter how sensibly she considered this, she was terrified. Something was wrong, terribly wrong.

She was biting her lips, fighting tears, when the telephone rang.

She was on the gallery in slicker and boots, holding a flashlight, less than five minutes after she hung up the phone. Rain stood at a black slant; wind held it against the world, pushed it over Marguerite.

Before she'd gone a dozen steps toward the bunkhouses, the returning party slogged out of darkness and surrounded her. Raymond began to chide her, and so did Pa Travis, but she shouted, and they quieted.

"There was a phone call!" she shouted above the storm. "She's been kidnapped—Rae-Ellen's been kidnapped!"

They got into the foyer, slammed the door, stood there, water running off them. Marguerite glimpsed Rosita standing off to one side, lips apart.

Words tumbling out, Marguerite told what the kidnapper had said. She relayed the amount of ransom, the denomination of the bills, where it was to be left and how and when. She repeated that the law was not to be called in or Rae-Ellen would die.

There was a sharp silence. The fire snapped. Rain drove against the windows.

"Was it a man or a woman?" Burr asked, his voice almost unrecognizable, it was so rough.

"A man, I think. It sounded . . . disguised. As if he was talking through paper."

"Probably was," Pa Travis snorted.

"He said there'll be no more calls. Either he gets the money tomorrow night, Christmas night, or Rae-Ellen . . ." Her voice went into a sob and now, at last, the tears came.

"He ain't going to have it his own way!" roared Burr. "I'm callin' in the law, I'm gettin' up a posse of ranch hands! We'll cover every inch of Texas if need be! Rae-Ellen ain't going to be in that bastard's hands a minute longer than it takes me to stop it! Pa—"

"I'll wake up every banker in the county!" yelled Pa Travis. "Si Miller and Ray Lewellen and Harry Clements and Verne Bremer, to commence with!"

As he yelled, he went for the phone.

Almost immediately he was shouting at Si Miller, speaking fast, telling what he needed and why. "Get all your tellers in as of now and set 'em to countin'! What's that? To hell with your time locks! Dynamite 'em, get 'em open! Bring every hundred you can, and bring it pronto! Use that phone, and call every banker in the section—you take this county and I'll get others to take the adjoinin' counties! Hurry your butt, and hurry their butts!"

He slammed up the phone, dialed again. "I'll get that money into that milk can!" he yelled. "We've got more'n twenty-four hours, and we'll do it!"

"I'll call my bankers!" shouted Raymond.

"Can't get that money here in time!" yelled Burr.

507

"Let him do what he wants!" roared Pa, phone to ear. "It's his kid!"

Burr stood beside his Pa, waiting to grab the phone. "The sheriff!" he bellowed. "Sheriff first!"

"After I get the money! Then we get the sheriff and the biggest posse ever!"

"Please, oh, please!" Marguerite pleaded, weeping. "No sheriff . . . no posse!"

Adah was weeping too. "The kidnappers will kill her!"

"Not if we act swift and hard!" said Pa Travis.

Adah turned to appeal to her father, but he only kissed her and said, "He's right, Adah. We've got to act fast."

"The sheriff knows how to keep his men out of sight," Lance put in. "I'm in favor of both the ransom and the two posses."

Marguerite, however, continued to weep and plead. Raymond put his arms around her, but wouldn't give in. "To have the law is best, darling," he said. "Even Burr sees that, and he's as deeply involved as any of us."

"More involved!" Burr snapped. Then, more gently, "You see, ma'am, it's because the ransom's so big we've got to have the law."

"But why?" sobbed Marguerite.

"The kidnapper can't afford to let the victim live to later identify him. So he uses tricks. He says if we leave the money in the milk can, if there ain't lawmen in sight, he'll let her go. But he don't mean to, not at all. So we, in turn, have got to trick him, have our men so well hid, even with the pickup point out in the open. We'll have our walkie-talkies and stay out of sight, then close in on him, catch him before he can get even as far as Abilene."

"But if he means to take the ransom and run, if he has no intention of letting Rae-Ellen live—" Her voice broke and she put her face into her hands.

"That's the chance we have to take, ma'am," Burr said. "Pa, give me the phone."

"But if it's that way," Marguerite asked, face white, "why assemble the ransom?"

"We need all the cards in our hands we can get, ma'am," Pa Travis replied. "We've got to play every angle."

Within thirty minutes, every ranch hand on the Star-Bar was either on wheels or mounted, fully armed. Other ranchers and their men were on the way; some were already arriving.

Words crackled from the sheriff's car to the purple limousine that forty men were driving at top speed for the Star-Bar, all in unmarked cars. They would assemble outside the ranch house and from there the sheriff would deploy his posse, ranchers, and ranch hands, and Burr and the other men of the household.

Inside an hour, all had arrived and were spreading out over the Star-Bar and surrounding countryside. One of the Mexican boys was ringing the great bell, its brassy tone going through the night, riding the storm, clanging out there was trouble.

Burr insisted on going alone in one of the trucks. "I'll work best that way, Sheriff," he said. "I know every acre of the home spread, and all our spreads out from it."

He was first to leave, driving slowly, watching the wet dirt road closely. It was already tracked from the vehicles which had driven in. What he aimed to do was find a side road where there was just one set of tracks.

He was beside himself. He didn't know how a kidnapper's mind would work, whether he'd spirit Rae-Ellen off the ranch, or find some place, some cave, where he could tie and gag her, collect his ransom, and just leave her there. Scared spitless, he had to use his brain logically.

She'd been on the Star-Bar when she was kidnapped. The kidnapper might figure they'd jump to the conclusion that he would take her away. Instead, to trick them, he might hide her right on the ranch.

His mind swung back and forth between these possibilities. He decided to deal with first things first. He'd drive all the roads leading off the ranch, keep a lookout for tracks leading off, especially onto a side road. Very soon, with the posse cars on the move there'd be plenty of tracks.

The big bell stopped ringing, and he knew it wouldn't sound again until the search ended.

Fawn and Pete, meanwhile, pretending to search as a team, driving the van in which they had transported Rae-Ellen to her grave, followed Burr, lights dimmed, and at a distance behind him. They were tense, but not panic-stricken, since thus far things had gone well for them. It angered them that the law had been called in, but they believed they'd easily collect the ransom despite this.

"It'll be dark when we pick up the money," Fawn said. "Transferring the bills from the milk can to the suitcases will be tricky, but safe. None of them'll dare show themselves. We can see miles in every direction."

"But it'll be dark!" Pete exclaimed, the thought striking him. "We can't see for miles in the dark!"

"We can spot any car that comes near. I'll pack the money into the cases, and you'll stand watch. If a car does come, our alibi is flawless. We're searching, just like they are. Our worst problem is getting the cases into the house, but there'll be some moment when we can do that. Loading them onto the plane will be nothing. They're just our luggage."

"I wish it were over," Pete said. "You sure that walkie-talkie they gave us is working right?"

"Switch it on. See for yourself."

The device began to crackle. The sheriff's voice came over, ordering car number thirteen to drive north, to search all buildings, to investigate side roads leading off the north road.

Burr listened to the sheriff give that direction. He drove slowly, thinking sometimes that another car was behind him, searching. He decided that wasn't likely.

He peered through black rain. All tracks so far had been made by cars that had driven in to join the search. He kept watch, blaming himself.

Rae-Ellen was the only girl in the world worth having. She was spirit and pride and courage incarnate. She was the original woman, passionate and tender, fierce and sweet, bone of his bone.

He ground his teeth. Pain sprang into his jaw. His plan to get her pregnant and force her to demand marriage had backfired. She'd never blackmail him with a kid, not his woman! He'd find her, had to find her. Had to tell her various things. How he'd loved her the way a forest fire loves the tree it consumes, never getting enough. He had to make her understand that from now on he would control the fire. But first he had to get back his woman and his kid.

He drove the home spread, watching all branching roads, getting out of the truck to study tracks. They were all fresh. For the first time he was glad Pa would have only dirt roads. Wet like this, they could hold sign that he could read.

Driving from the first section of spread to the next, he crossed the landing field. A sheriff's car was there. All three planes were there. The hangar men were on watch with the sheriff's men. The pilots were standing by, planes ready to lift at a moment's notice, should the storm let up.

"No plane has landed or taken off," a deputy assured Burr. "The man who sleeps in the hangar said so, and common sense—" He gestured into the driving, blowing rain.

Burr drove on. He now had a gut-conviction that Rae-Ellen and his kid were on the ranch. Some place. And he was going to find them, come hell.

He drove. The norther blew, swathed itself around the blackness of night. He was on the edge of the south spread now, and there was a set of tracks in front of him. They couldn't have been made by an arriving car, the location was wrong.

He got out and studied them by flashlight. The tread looked like those new tires on the van. The tracks themselves didn't look brand new because they were filled with water, puddled here and there. Even with it raining so hard, it'd take a little time for them to puddle and run over this much. Until now, the tracks he'd examined close up had been merely wet and not puddled this deeply.

He drove on at a creep, watching. Right in

front there, the tracks made a skid mark, then straightened. He got out again and studied the skid. It was deeply puddled, too.

He drove on, just inching. Then he saw a hump of dirt that ran some six feet along the side of the road, as if a grader hadn't quite finished his job. There was a single, curving set of tracks over that hump.

The hairs on the back of his neck stood up.

51

Rain puddled that track across the heaped dirt. The car that made it must have jolted, because the track was deep.

Burr took a moment to light his powerful lantern. He shoved his flashlight into one slicker pocket, his revolver into the other. Carrying the lantern, he crossed the heap of dirt, making sure to leave no footprint.

He squatted, studied the long grass on the other side. It was flattened, but more than rain had been at work here. There was some mud, and this grass had been pressed down by a vehicle. The grass out to the side was flat, but not jammed to the ground. It was beaten by rain and rain alone.

In a crouch, he moved along the track through

the grass. It wound into timber, deep into timber, and there it looped back. He followed the loop until it straightened into the same crushed grass, and that he followed to the road again. The driver had gone over the dirt in the same place, had looped into the tracks on the road, even to the skid marks. No telling where he'd ended up. At the ranch house, say, or across the spread and away on one of the many roads.

Standing in thickening rain, he waved his lantern and shouted. There was no reply. He waited only a second, then turned back for the timber, to follow that grass track again.

Fawn and Pete, parked in a stand of timber where they'd been since Travis had begun to poke around, heard the shout.

"He's found that hump," Pete said. "I warned you about that, but you—"

"Quiet! I didn't see it! It doesn't matter. The grave isn't near where we parked the van, and even if it were, he'd never find it. Not in this dark, not the way we've disguised the place, and with this rain helping!"

"Then why sit here? Somebody could come along and wonder."

"We're searching. Perfect alibi. We've got to wait, like it or not. Because if he should find the grave—" Fawn turned on the dashlight, held his revolver under it, broke the weapon open and made sure there were five cartridges. He did the same with Pete's revolver.

"You do think he'll find the grave!" exclaimed Pete.

515

"Not at all. What I think is we wait while he stomps around and gives up. He'll come out and go looking somewhere else."

"Then we can move from here?"

"The minute he drives on."

"What if he comes back this way?"

"We're 'searching.' Chances are he won't. Don't forget those other two side roads. We can double back, ride all over the place, pick up the ransom, 'search,' meet with the others when they give up, sad as anybody."

Burr had now reached the spot in the timber where the track looped and a vehicle had stood. The hairs on his neck were like bristles. Had the kidnapper parked here with Rae-Ellen to tighten her bonds, to torture her . . . to kill her?

But there was only timber. There was no place to hide a body.

His mind jumped the gap instantly.

A fist seemed to crash into where his heart had been. It punched the way a fist would, and it hurt. Don't be a fool, he told himself. Don't fall apart because some car stopped. It don't mean he dug a grave, don't even mean it was the kidnapper.

He junked that thinking. It couldn't stand up against his gut-feeling; his gut-sureness that Rae-Ellen had been brought to—and left in—this timber. Maybe she'd been knocked unconscious, gagged and tied up somewhere.

No matter what his guts said, he wasn't going to have her dead and buried. He was going to find her and hold her in his arms, alive and breathing.

He began to search. Bent over, the freezing rain clattering on his slicker, he moved, shining his lantern everywhere—on undisturbed, rain-beaten grass; on trees, where no figure was tied, under which no figure lay crumpled. On he moved, sometimes in a bent-kneed crouch, shining his light, foot by foot, going ahead a piece, then sideways, laying out rough squares, covering every inch of each square.

He had to watch his feet, where he set them, because there was loose brush. He shone his lantern under and around every bush. Nothing.

He went further to the left, covered sodden squares of growth. The trees thickened, slowed him more than he wanted to be slowed, but he held himself back, examining the night, the trees, the bushes, the ground.

Ahead, the beam wavered over a collection of brush. It had drifted down from the trees so that it made a patch of brush for sure, thicker than he'd seen yet.

That fist in him started again. In his belly this time. He didn't give a damn whether it hurt or not. His gut-feeling was back, stronger.

He went for that brush. No matter how useless, or what time it consumed, he had to make sure. He stood at one end of it, noted that it looked to be almost rectangular, and shone his light the length of it, walking slowly. The grass and pieces of bush and even a couple of smallish branches set his back hair stiff again.

He studied how rain had flattened it all, how it was still flattening. He dropped to his knees, set the lantern down, felt along one side of the patch, and came on dirt, loose wet dirt.

The fist in his belly pounded. He tore brush and long pieces of loose grass and brush away, slinging them aside, and he saw bare dirt. And then, as he stripped away a clump of brush, he saw a pipe sticking up out of the ground.

He ripped away all the brush. Underneath was bare, packed earth the length and width of a grave. He dug his fingers into the middle and found looseness.

His heart was punching everywhere, even in his heels. His breath tore in and out, but only when it must, not through any volition of his. He dug with fingernails and hands, dug like a madman. There wasn't time to go back to the truck for a shovel. He had to open the earth now, this moment, had to find out what lay within, had to find out what—or who—it was.

Rain shrouded him. He scooped dirt, the sides of his hands together, shoveled dirt, dug more. Ass, he thought, dumb ass! And abandoned digging in the center of the grave, if grave it was, and began at the top, beside that pipe.

Dirt flew. It bounced and hit him in the face, and he tasted dirt. It got in his eyes and he batted it out. He breathed dirt. Dug faster, but in a rhythm now, and with more speed.

Digging, forever digging, his hand came on fingers, and the fingers moved. His belly leaped, his whole collection of guts. He dug toward what was the top of the grave in relation to that hand, for it sure-hell was a grave, and, the dirt being loosened, he had the face uncovered in less time than he'd have thought, only the face was turned away from him and seemed to have the end of the iron pipe in its mouth.

He lowered himself into the upper, opened part, which was about three feet deep, straddled the shoulders of the figure. Rain poured on both of them.

"Rae-Ellen!" he croaked. "Are you alive?"

But those fingers had moved. By God, she was alive, had been trying to dig her way out of her own grave!

He wrenched at the pipe which she was holding to her mouth, fingers clamped on it. Even as he got it away and was turning her, he realized that she'd been sucking air through the pipe.

She grabbed for it, tried to get it back into her mouth. Even if the lantern hadn't been throwing a dimness so that he could make out her face, he'd have known from her fighting, even in the grave, who it was.

"It's me!" he yelled. "It's Burr! Quit fighting!"

Miraculously, she did.

He got his hands under her arms and lifted, bracing his feet against the sides. He'd dug only roughly a third of the distance to the center, but the dirt was loosened from his initial digging, so he should be able to manage.

"Help me!" he yelled. "I'm going to pull! But you've got to help!"

Muscles straining, he pulled. She put her arms up and back, around his neck, and pulled, and he sensed that she was pushing with her feet.

When she could stand, he had to hold her for steadiness. Then, fastening her hands to the sides of the grave, and telling her to hang on, he scrambled to the top and lifted her out.

He held her in his arms. She was trembling, her face was covered with dirt and he brushed it off, tipped her face to the rain so she could eventually open her eyes. She got a little steadier on her feet. The frigid rain poured onto her dirt-filled hair and turned the dirt to mud, and he stroked her hair. They clung, muddy and wet, tasting dirt, aware of the terrible cold, the drowning wetness, but content, with no volition to move.

"We've got to get back to the house," he said at last. "I've got a truck . . . it ain't far. Think you can walk?"

"There's no need for her to take one step," said a voice from beyond the lantern. "She's not going anyplace."

52

Even as she recognized the voice as that of Fawn, Rae-Ellen felt Burr start for his gun. Fawn saw, from out there.

"Don't try it!" he snapped. "I've got you covered! So has Pete!"

Rae-Ellen felt Burr go stiff, alert. He was going to jump them, oh, he was, and if he did— "No," she murmured. "Please, no!"

"Now," said Fawn, stepping into the lantern light, Pete with him, "act with care. Let go the girl. Take your revolver out of your pocket, throw it at my feet."

Cautiously, Burr did as ordered. Slowly, he put his arm back around Rae-Ellen.

Fawn laughed. "That's it, hold on to her! Stand at the edge of your grave, the grave you're going to

521

share! We have shovels, and this time we'll dig six feet." He picked up Burr's revolver, thrust it into the pocket of his slicker.

"You're teched," Burr said from his teeth. "You ain't right in the head, either one of you! You're crazy!"

"Like foxes!" Pete cut in, using his new, sunless voice.

"Call us what you like," Fawn said. He was holding his revolver on them with a steady hand. "Don't the experts say we're all a little mad?"

"Only, you're not?" goaded Burr.

This frightened Rae-Ellen, though she understood he was playing for time, leading Fawn and Pete to talk, to boast, ready to jump them. Jump two guns aimed straight at them! She shuddered. Her bones ached and she felt bruised from the recent weight of the grave.

"My truck," Burr demanded. "How will you explain its absence, and my absence?"

"You'll be a mystery. We'll leave your truck where it is. More mystery."

Pete laughed.

"You, Travis," Fawn said, "have only yourself to thank for your death. You had to come here. Rae-Ellen has only her own stubbornness to thank for hers. At any time, Rae-Ellen, during our campaign, Pete's and mine, to win you and Adah, you could have ended the series of moves we made which have culminated in this moment at this spot. Simply by marrying us."

"You had a plan of action?" Burr asked carefully. "I fail to recognize it."

"It was too clever for such as you, Travis."

"Seein' that you've got us cornered, why don't

you give us a rundown?" Burr asked, voice hard, body tense. "So we can appreciate the things you done that we was too dumb to see."

"Or to figure out," Fawn said with satisfaction. He jerked his head. "Pete, the first idea was yours. You tell."

"That stone Rusty got in his foot," Pete said. "I put it there to make it look as if you were no good with horses. We had recognized the Travis name, knew the Travis money and power, and wanted to get you fired before you set up as competition for one of the girls."

"The two of you cold-bloodedly planned to marry them?"

"Right. We'd had our plans before you ever came," Pete agreed. "When that stone business didn't affect your status, I loosened your saddle the day we went fox-hunting. For the same reason."

"When they didn't laugh you off Magnolia Hall for that," Fawn put in, "I engineered the next event. The fire. I did it in the night. To add to the string of accidents you were involved in. To discredit you so that Pettigrew would dismiss you."

The wind howled, flung its rain into the partly open grave. The mud underfoot deepened.

Rae-Ellen was freezing, but it didn't matter, nothing mattered but this awful charade.

"Next was the truck wheel," Pete boasted. "My idea, my work. We hoped that would get you out of the picture. The way I loosened those lugs, I never thought that wheel would stay on, thought it would come off after a couple of turns, and you'd be fired because such an accident could result in death. And we planned no death. At that time."

"At Magnolia Hall," Fawn said, directly to Rae-

523

Ellen, "when you asked me to get your father to fire Travis, I had to refuse because of the Travis power, the Travis money, knowledge of which might then have come out and got me in the bad graces of your father.

"I had my most brilliant idea," he continued, "at that roadhouse. With The Black Jackets. After the fight, I made an appointment to see their leader. We made a deal for the gang to waste you, Travis, so I'd have a clear path with Rae-Ellen, who gave signs of being too much aware of you. They had some way they wouldn't divulge to rub you out, but then the hurricane came. I met them when I said I was at the beach, and we planned to have them get you in the stable. But as usual you came out of it. Still in my way."

"And Buford in my way," Pete interjected. "Announcing his engagement to Adah! So, at the dance, I shot at him." He glanced at the revolver in his hand. It was as steady as the one Fawn held. "Too far off. I ran, not knowing whether I'd hit him, but making sure no one got a look at me. I knew it'd be blamed on The Black Jackets."

"Now, do you understand, cowman?" Fawn asked contemptuously. "Do you comprehend that we were forced to kidnap Rae-Ellen? She's the first-born, probably best loved. It's the only way to get Pettigrew money, since we've been blocked from marrying the heiresses."

He swung a look at Rae-Ellen. "It's more your fault than Travis's. Yours and Adah's. We even made a last-ditch try to accomplish our goal in a decent manner."

"That being?" Burr asked, taunting.

"We came to Texas to make a last appeal to the

girls," Fawn clipped. "But they were so busy they wouldn't even let us draw them aside, and then you and Rae-Ellen had announced your plan to live together, too. So we were forced to settle on kidnapping and ransom to make up for our disappointment."

"The ransom call," Burr said, taut. "How did you manage that?"

"I phoned from the stable while the rest of you were searching the bunkhouses. Nothing to it."

"And this—what you're going to do now—How'll you cover that?"

"Elementary," boasted Fawn. "We tie and gag you both. Roll you into the grave when it's deep enough. Fill it. Later, we're members of a disappointed search party."

Burr didn't wait.

Even as Fawn's gun dipped a trifle, he flung himself at the other man's ankles, crashing him to the mud, the revolver flying into the night.

53

As Burr brought Fawn down, Pete swiveled, aimed. Fawn was on top; Pete held his fire. With a shrill cry, Rae-Ellen dived at him, but she was too far away. She missed his gun hand, even his wrist, fell. As she landed, she felt as if her bones were breaking.

Gun on the fighting men, Pete kicked her. "On your feet!"

Slipping, every bone hurting, hands and feet stiff with cold, she managed to stand. She swayed, trying for steadiness.

She couldn't faint, couldn't even fall again. She had to help Burr!

"Move!" Pete ordered. "On the other side of them!"

Sliding, half-falling, she inched past the struggling men, knowing that Pete had the revolver on all of them. When she reached the spot Pete indicated, she turned.

Fawn and Burr were at her feet, rolling on the streaming earth, first one on top, then the other.

Rae-Ellen, her body one great, frozen pain, fighting the tendency to sway, watched for any chance. They rolled so fast, changed position so often, that Pete couldn't fire without risking Fawn's life, and she couldn't get a second in which to jump onto Fawn.

Burr fought like some dangerous, maddened bear. Fawn twisted and slithered like a panther. Rae-Ellen, steadier now, watched keenly, and her chance did come. Fawn was on top momentarily, and while he was, she flung herself onto his back.

The gun fired, but no one seemed to be hit, for now the three of them were struggling on the grass. Rae-Ellen got her arms around one of Fawn's legs and held on and, despite the rolling and twisting, managed to keep her body so it shielded Burr.

One idea beat in her mind. Pete wouldn't risk killing Fawn. He might kill her, but the bullet could pass through her body and into Fawn. Surely he was smart enough to know that!

She and Burr rolled into the grave, Burr on top.

"*Shoot!*" Fawn screamed. "*Shoot!*"

The shot cracked and Fawn shrieked, "Fool!" He clawed at his slicker pocket for Burr's gun.

Now Burr and Rae-Ellen were up, and he was throwing himself at Pete. She saw him wrench the gun away from Pete. Simultaneously, she lunged at Fawn, grabbing his hand away from his slicker pocket.

Before Burr could fire, Fawn took him from the front, clamping both hands around his neck, pressing mightily, shouting, "Get the gun . . . get the gun!"

Pete lunged for Burr's gun hand. Like lightning, Burr whipped the hand behind his back, Pete roared, went for Burr's eyes, got his thumbs on them.

The three of them staggered about, Fawn choking Burr, Pete gouging his eyes, Burr fighting to keep his stance, trying to maneuver the revolver to the front. Rae-Ellen plunged to them, tripping on wet grass, worked her way around behind Burr, reached for the gun.

She'd hold them off, kill them! As her fingers came onto the barrel of the revolver, ice cold and slippery, Burr yanked it around in front. There was a cracking sound as he pulled the trigger, another as he shot again.

Both Fawn and Pete fell away, landing on the ground.

Rain beat steadily down over their motionless forms.

Gun ready, Burr stooped over Fawn and, alert to any move from Pete, examined Fawn. "He's dead," he muttered in an almost disbelieving tone. "Got him in the heart."

Pete stirred. Burr spun, covering him. Pete worked slowly into a sitting position, lips pulled back from his teeth. "Got me—in the arm," he snarled. "You'll not—I'll—" He clawed grass, searching for a weapon.

"Won't do you no good," Burr warned. "Don't make me shoot you again, hurt you worse."

"Or—murder me?" Pete raged weakly. "Like

528

Fawn? You've really—fixed yourself now. You're a killer—"

Unexpectedly, he collapsed.

Burr knelt beside him, opened his slicker and the coat beneath. "It's only the arm," he told Rae-Ellen. "He's fainted. He'll give us no more trouble. Brace yourself. I'm going to give the signal that you've been found."

She managed to stay on her feet, not crumple to the ground and sit there in the pouring rain, as her sore and aching body prompted her to do. Amazed, she saw Burr reload, then lift the revolver above his head and shoot into the air until it was empty.

Off in the distance a bell began to toll. Dazed, she realized that this, too, was a signal that she'd been found.

The living room was crammed with people— Papa and Mama and Adah, Pa Travis and Rosita and Lance, a big man wearing a sheriff's star on his coat, other men referred to as deputies, ranch hands with revolvers in holsters.

Rae-Ellen, refusing to leave Burr's arms, even to clean up and put on dry clothes, sat with one bath towel around her shoulders, another wrapping her head. She wouldn't let anyone wipe away the streaks of mud remaining on her face. She didn't want to be touched, wanted just to lean, safe and trembling, against Burr, who was as disheveled and wet as she was.

All these people had been searching for her as she lay buried, she realized that. She was grateful. But she preferred that they keep their distance right now, even Mama and Papa.

Adah and Lance were sitting nearby, and that was fine. She could hear every word they said, recognize their tones of deep and utter love. She snuggled closer to Burr, content that Adah could do the same with Lance.

"Darling," she heard Lance say to Adah," all the troubles are ended. You're to forget, really forget, not only what has happened tonight, but in years long gone as well. We'll marry as soon as we get home. If you'll do me the honor."

"Oh, yes, Lance!" Adah cried softly. "I'll marry you the instant you say!"

Others in the room heard. They smiled fondly both on Adah and Lance and on Rae-Ellen and Burr. Rae-Ellen felt a wave of happiness for her sister, but she was still too shaken to smile, so she rested in Burr's arms, knowing she could trust him, always.

He held her a bit more firmly. "See?" he whispered in what, even a month ago, she would have considered arrogance. "You telling me about Adah's blood was ridiculous. You didn't have the sense to know that you just imagined you was in love with Buford."

"Burr," the sheriff cut in now, "you ain't to be held for shooting that varmint. You done it in self-defense and to save that young lady you're holding. And you ain't being charged with woundin' that other varmint, for the same reasons. He'll be charged with kidnappin' and attempted murder. He's the one in trouble."

"Will he . . . Pete . . . be executed?" Rae-Ellen asked Burr softly, a tremor in her voice.

"I don't know," he replied. "He'll get whatever's comin' to him."

"I can hardly grasp what those two did," Papa

said. "They were such splendid executives, showed such potential."

"Maybe Pete will be sorry," Rae-Ellen murmured. "Maybe he can get off with a light sentence, or none at all. It's hard to accept that—he was always so carefree and happy."

"Don't go soft on that killer," Burr said firmly. "He helped put you in that grave for over two hours. Get him out of your mind. What happens, happens. We've got more pressin' matters, things to clear up, once and for all."

His tone commanded that she wait, and she did.

"Rae-Ellen Pettigrew," he said so clearly all could hear, "you **love me and it ain't because you're** carryin' my kid."

"A baby?" cried Mama, and "¿Un bambino?" squealed Rosita, at the same time. Adah gasped, smiled. Both Papa and Pa Travis stepped forward.

Burr held his hand for silence, and silence fell. The fire-snapping quiet was enwrapped by the sounds of the storm.

"You love me," Burr repeated. "And I ain't wrong. You'd best get used to the fact."

She started to flare, then snuggled against him, both of them so wet and dirty, his face so wonderful, so filthy, so ugly. So perfect.

"You've been wrong in the past," she murmured.

"We both done wrong. We loved each other and didn't have the sense to tell each other so. Or the sense to get married with a kid—a boy—on the way. But we've got sense now. Am I wrong this time?"

She shook her head, meeting his beautiful brown eyes. She swallowed; her heart shook. They were on common ground, neither giving way to the other, but in mutual agreement.

Pa Travis could contain himself no longer. "We can still have the weddin' on Christmas Day!" he whooped.

"That's right," Burr agreed, and looked at Rae-Ellen.

She gave a quivering sigh, smiled shakily.

"And wherever you live or whatever you do, that'll suit us, won't it, Raymond?" Pa Travis asked.

There were tears in Papa's eyes. Smiling, he inclined his head and put his arms around Mama, who was sobbing happily.

"We'll take part of the south spread, Pa," Burr announced. "No more. I ain't going to get so loaded with land I have to run a herd of beefalo to keep the grass down. What Rae-Ellen and I have is goin' to be a race horse breeding setup!"

He looked at Rae-Ellen, scowled. "What's eatin' on you now?" he demanded. "Here we got everything straightened out, and you—"

"It's Doctor Cline, back in Durham. Our family doctor. He's the one I went to about the baby, and he was to take care of us and deliver—"

"Hell's bells!" exclaimed Burr, sounding exactly like Pa Travis. "We'll live in the cottage at Magnolia Hall and I'll train them three horses until after the kid gets here! It'll take time for our breeding farm to be built, anyhow. If you'll oversee it, Pa."

"Sure thing! And I'll teach my grandson a lot as he grows!"

Papa began to scowl. Mama patted his face, soothingly.

Burr noticed. "We'll come up with grandsons aplenty for both of you," he said. "Enough for the tobacco company and the Star-Bar, both. But only—" he warned, as the two grandfathers began to smile, "if they want it. They ain't to be driven into any life they don't pick. Only if they want it, remember."

"They're bound to want it," Mama said softly, but clearly enough for all to hear. "Just to show their independence, to be the opposite of their bull-headed parents!"

Everybody laughed, including the lawmen and the ranch hands. But Rae-Ellen, even as Burr's mud-tinged lips came onto hers for all to see, and she tasted the mud, knew there was more than a grain of truth in what Mama said.

BARBARA CARTLAND

Her romantic novels are loved by millions. The refreshing purity of the characters, the beautifully romantic settings, the continuing theme of unfaltering love – these are the ingredients that make Barbara Cartland's recipe for love stories so appealing. And they're all there in her enthralling masterpieces THE THIEF OF LOVE and SWEET ENCHANTRESS.

THE THIEF OF LOVE

When petite, shy Alloa Derange happens upon an intruder trying to steal a priceless family heirloom, her quiet life is put into a turmoil. Alloa knows it is her duty to expose the stranger for the thief he is, but her heart tells her something completely different . . .

ROMANCE   0 7221 2274 8   75p

SWEET ENCHANTRESS

A serene voyage aboard a yacht adrift on a balmy ocean suddenly turns into a nightmare for Zania Manford – what is the yacht's real destination? Why do all the passengers seem frightened? And who is the sinister, yet charming, Chuck Turner?

ROMANCE   0 7221 2276 4   75p

And don't miss Barbara Cartland's other romantic bestsellers
THE PRICE IS LOVE
A KISS OF SILK

TREAT YOURSELF TO A LITTLE ROMANCE

A selection of bestsellers from SPHERE

FICTION
KEEPER OF THE CHILDREN

	William H. Hallahan	£1.00	☐
SPECIAL EFFECTS	Harriet Frank	£1.25	☐
BETHANY'S SIN	Robert R. McCammon	£1.40	☐
NOW, GOD BE THANKED	John Masters	£1.95	☐
SUMMER'S END	Danielle Steel	£1.50	☐

FILM AND TV TIE-INS
THE EMPIRE STRIKES BACK	Donald F. Glut	£1.00	☐
ONCE UPON A GALAXY:			
A Journal of the Making of			
The Empire Strikes Back	Alan Arnold	£1.25	☐
MIDNIGHT EXPRESS	Billy Hayes	£1.00	☐

NON-FICTION
THE BREAST BOOK	Anthony Harris	£1.50	☐
MANDY Mandy Rice-Davies with Shirley Flack		£1.25	☐
NAZI GOLD Ian K. Sayer & H. L. Seaman with			
	Frederick Nolan	£1.50	☐
A NURSE'S WAR	Brenda McBryde	£1.25	☐
TIMEWARPS	John Gribbin	£1.25	☐
TRUE BRITT	Britt Ekland	£1.50	☐

All Sphere books are available at your local bookshop or newsagent, or can be ordered direct from the publisher. Just tick the titles you want and fill in the form below.

Name _____

Address _____

_____

Write to Sphere Books, Cash Sales Department, P.O. Box 11, Falmouth, Cornwall TR10 9EN
Please enclose cheque or postal order to the value of the cover price plus:
UK: 25p for the first book plus 12p per copy for each additional book ordered to a maximum charge of £1.05.
OVERSEAS: 40p for the first book and 12p for each additional book.
BFPO & EIRE: 25p for the first book plus 10p per copy for the next 8 books, thereafter 5p per book.

Sphere Books reserve the right to show new retail prices on covers which may differ from those previously advertised in the text or elsewhere, and to increase postal rates in accordance with the PO.